Acclaim for Richard Yates

"[Yates] is an expert." —*Time*

"Every phrase reflects to the highest degree integrity and stylistic mastery. . . . A genuine artist." —*The New Republic*

"What's exhilarating about Yates is not his grasp of The Truth, but the purity of his vision and the perfection of his craft." —*Newsday*

"Yates's own distinctive virtues as a writer—his plain-spoken prose, his feel for contemporary alienation, his ability to make the reader both empathize with his characters and understand the depth of their self-deception—created a potent legacy, providing a bridge from the naturalism of Dreiser to the latter day realism practiced by writers like Raymond Carver." —Michiko Kakutani, *The New York Times*

"Richard Yates is a writer of commanding gifts. His prose is urbane yet sensitive, with passion and irony held deftly in balance. And he provides unexpected pleasures in a flood of freshly minted phrases and in the thrust of sudden insight, precise notation of feeling, and mordant unsentimental perceptions." —*Saturday Review*

"To me and to many other writers of my generation, the work of Richard Yates came as a liberating force. . . . He was one of the most important writers of the second half of the century." —Robert Stone

Richard Yates

A Special Providence

Richard Yates was born in 1926. The author of several acclaimed works of fiction, including *Revolutionary Road*, *Eleven Kinds of Loneliness*, *Disturbing the Peace*, and *The Easter Parade*, he was lauded during his lifetime as the foremost novelist of the postwar "age of anxiety." He died in 1992.

Books by Richard Yates

A Special Providence

Richard Yates

Vintage Contemporaries
Vintage Books
A Division of Random House, Inc.
New York

FIRST VINTAGE CONTEMPORARIES EDITION, MARCH 2009

Two excerpts from *A Special Providence* first appeared
in the *Saturday Evening Post*.

The Library of Congress has catalogued the Knopf edition as follows:
Yates, Richard, 1926–1992.
A special providence/Richard Yates.
New York, Knopf, 1969.
p. cm.
PZ4.Y335 Sp PS3575.A83
813'.54
74088750

Vintage ISBN: 978-0-307-45595-6

www.vintagebooks.com

Printed in the United States of America
10 9 8 7 6 5 4 3 2 1

To Martha

We are lived by powers we pretend to understand.
                              − W. H. Auden

A Special Providence

Prologue: 1944

On Saturdays, when inspection was over and passes were issued in the Orderly Rooms, there was a stampede of escape down every company street in Camp Pickett, Virginia. You could go to Lynchburg or Richmond or Washington, D.C., and if you were willing to travel for nine hours – five on the bus and four on the train – you could get to New York.

Private Robert J. Prentice made the long trip alone one windy afternoon in the fall of 1944. He was a rifle trainee, eighteen years old, and this seemed an important thing to do because it might well be the last pass he would get before going overseas.

In the echoing swarm of Penn Station that night, feeling lost and cramped and lightheaded, he shouldered his way through acres of embracing couples: men whose uniforms looked somehow more authoritative than his own, girls whose ardor was a terrible reproach to his own callowness. Once he found himself walking straight toward a girl who stood facing him in the crowd, a slender, delicate girl with long brown hair, and as he came closer her uplifted face took on the most beautiful look of welcome he had ever seen. She didn't move, but her eyes filled with tears and her lips parted in a way that stopped his heart – God, to be looked at that way by a girl, just once! – so

1

that he felt as stunned as a jilted lover when a Marine corporal came jostling past him and took her in his arms.

Prentice didn't want to stare, but he couldn't take his eyes off their greeting: their long kiss, the girl nestling to weep in the Marine's shoulder as her hands gripped his back, the Marine lifting her off her feet to swing her around in an exultant whirl, the two of them laughing and talking and then moving away, scarcely able to walk because of their need to clasp and hold each other.

He was weak with envy as he turned toward the subway, and he tried to make up for it by squaring his wrinkled overseas cap down into one eyebrow and hoping that the tension in his face and the hurry in his walk might suggest, to other observers, that he was bound for a welcome as romantic as the Marine's.

But the subway only swallowed him into the dirty, intricate bowels of a city he would never understand. He was as hesitant as a tourist about getting on the right train; he peered with fascinated distaste at the pallid nighttime faces that hung and swayed around him in the car, and when he came up into the windswept darkness of Columbus Circle he had to walk a few steps one way and a few steps another, craning his head, before he got his bearings.

He had spent most of his life in New York, or near it, but no section or street of it had ever felt like his neighborhood: he had never lived in one house for more than a year. The address now shown on his service record as his home was a walkup apartment in the West Fifties, on a dark block beyond Eighth Avenue, and as he made his way there he tried to conjure a sense of homecoming among the blown newspapers and the flickering bar signs. He pressed the bell marked "Prentice" and heard the joyous answering bleat of the buzzer that let him in; then he was loping upstairs through smells of vegetables and garbage and perfume, and then he was staggering in the clutch of his mother's hug.

"Oh, Bobby," she said. The top of her frizzled gray head scarcely came up to his breast-pocket flaps and she was as frail as a sparrow, but the force of her love was so great that he had to brace himself in a kind of boxer's stance to absorb it. "You look wonderful," she said. "Oh, let me look at you." And he allowed himself, uneasily, to be held and inspected at arm's length. "My soldier," she said. "My big, wonderful soldier."

And then came the questions: Had he eaten anything? Was he terribly tired? Was he glad to be home?

"Oh, I've been so happy today, just knowing you were coming. Old Herman said to me this morning – you know, the ugly little *foreman* I've told you about? At my horrible *job*? I was singing this morning, or kind of humming under my breath, and he said 'What've *you* got to sing about?' And oh-ho, I looked him right in the eye – this dreadful, smelly little man, you know, in his awful old undershirt, with all these awful factory noises going on – and I said, 'I've got plenty to sing about.' I said, 'My *son* is coming home tonight on *leave.*'" And she moved away across the room, fragile and awkward in her runover heels and her black rayon dress with its side vent held together by a safety pin, laughing at the memory of her exchange with the foreman. "'My *son*,'" she said again, "'is coming home tonight on *leave.*'"

"Well," he said, "It isn't really a 'leave,' you know; it's just a pass."

"A pass; I know. *Oh*, it's so good to see you. Tell you what. How about a hot cup of coffee, and you sit down and rest. Then I'll get ready and we'll go out for dinner. How would that be?"

While she bustled in and out of her bedroom, still talking, he sipped at the bitter, warmed-over coffee she'd brought him and strolled around the carpet. The unkempt coziness of the place, full of cigarette ash and sagging, rickety furniture under weak lamps, was very strange after the scrubbed symmetry of the barracks. So was the privacy of it, and the fact that it held, on one wall, a narrow full-length mirror in which he was surprised to find his own naked-looking face above the brass-buttoned torso of olive drab. He pulled himself dramatically to attention, and then, after glancing away to make sure she was safely in the bedroom, he went through a series of drill turns, whispering the commands to himself. Right face; left face; about face; hand salute; parade rest. In the parade-rest position he discovered that she'd left a smear of lipstick on his uniform.

"There," she said. "Now I'm ready. Do I look all right? Do I look nice enough to go out on a date with a handsome soldier?"

"Fine," he told her. "You look fine." And she did look better, despite a sprinkling of face powder down her bodice. She had managed to close the vent in her dress more securely, and she'd carefully fixed her hair.

When they left the apartment he noticed how she crouched and squinted to make her way downstairs – her eyes were getting worse – and out on the street, where she clung to his arm for walking, she seemed very old and slow. At the first intersection she hunched and hurried in fright, gripping his arm tighter, until they were safely on the opposite curb. She had never understood automobiles and always tended to exaggerate their menace: she seemed to feel that any or all of the waiting, throbbing cars might bolt forward against the light with murder in their hearts.

They went to the Childs on Columbus Circle. "Isn't it funny?" she said. "I always used to think Childs restaurants were dreadful, but this really is the only decent place around here – all the others are so horribly expensive – and I think it's kind of nice, don't you?"

They each had a Manhattan to start with, because she insisted it was to be a real celebration; and then, after studying the menu to make sure they could afford it if they held the cost of the dinner down to chicken croquettes, they each had another. He didn't really want the second one – the heavy sweetness of it threatened to make him sick – but he sipped it anyway and tried to relax in his chair.

Her voice by now had become a rich and tireless monologue: ". . . Oh, and guess who I ran into on the bus the other day! Harriet Baker! Remember the year we lived on Charles Street? And you used to play with the Baker boys? They're both in the Navy now, and Bill's in the Pacific; just imagine. Remember the winter we were so horribly broke, and Harriet and I had those awful quarrels about money? Anyway, that's all forgotten now. We had dinner together and had the nicest talk; she wanted to hear all about you. Oh, and *guess* what she told me about the Engstroms! Remember? Paul and Mary Engstrom, that were such good friends of mine that year? And they came out to see us in Scarsdale, too, remember? And in Riverside? Remember the year we all spent Christmas together and had such a good time? . . ."

It went on and on, while he crumbled his chicken croquettes with the side of his fork and made whatever answers she seemed to want, or to need. After a while he stopped listening. His ears took in only the rise and fall of her voice, the elaborate, familiar, endless rhythm of it; but from long experience he was able to say "Oh yes," or "Of course," in all the right places.

The subjects of her talk didn't matter; he knew what she was really saying. Helpless and gentle, small and tired and anxious to please, she was asking him to agree that her life was not a failure. Did he remember the good times? Did he remember all the nice people they'd known and all the interestingly different places they'd lived in? And whatever mistakes she might have made,

5

however rudely the world might have treated her, did he know how hard she'd always tried? Did he know how terribly much she loved him? And did he realize – in spite of everything – did he realize how remarkable and how gifted and how brave a woman his mother was?

Oh yes; oh yes; of course he did – that was the message of his nods and smiles and mumbled replies. It was the message he'd been giving her as long as he could remember, and for most of that time he had wholly believed it.

Because she *was* remarkable and gifted and brave. How else could anyone explain the story of her life? At the turn of the century, when all the sleeping little towns of Indiana had lain locked in provincial ignorance, and when in that environment a simple dry-goods merchant named Amos Grumbauer had raised six ordinary daughters, wasn't it remarkable that his seventh had somehow developed a passion for art, and for elegance, and for the great and distant world of New York? Without finishing high school she had become one of the first female students ever enrolled in the Cincinnati Art Academy; and not very many years after that, all alone, she had made her way to the city of her dreams and found employment as a fashion illustrator, with only occasional help from home. Didn't that prove she was gifted, and didn't it prove she was brave?

Her first great mistake, and she often said afterwards that she would never understand what had possessed her, was to marry a man as ordinary as her Indiana father. Oh, George Prentice might have been handsome in a quiet way; he might even have been a little dashing, with his fine amateur singing voice, his good clothes, and the salesman's expense account that made him welcome at some of the better speakeasies in town. It was undeniable too that a girl pressing thirty-four wasn't apt to get many serious proposals; and besides, he was so steady, so devoted, so eager to protect her and provide for her. But how could she have been so blind to the dullness of the man? How could she have failed to see that he thought of her talent as a charming little hobby and nothing more, that he could get tears in his eyes over the poetry of Edgar A. Guest, and that his own highest ambition in life, incessantly discussed, was to be promoted to the job of assistant divisional sales manager in some monstrous and wholly unintelligible organization called Amalgamated Tool and Die?

And on top of all that, as if that weren't enough, how could she have foreseen that as a married man he would disappear for three and four days at a time and come home reeking of gin, with lipstick all over his shirt?

She divorced him three years after the birth of their only child, when she was thirty-eight, and set out to become an artist of distinction – a sculptor. She took her son to Paris for a year of study; but that particular year turned out to be 1929, and the shock of economic necessity brought her home in a little more than six months. From then on, her artistic career became a desperate and ever-thwarted effort played out against the background of the Great Depression, a hysterical odyssey that she always said was made bearable only by the "wonderful companionship" of her little boy. On the slender combination of alimony and child support that was the most George Prentice could spare, they lived at first in rural Connecticut, then in Greenwich Village, and then in the Westchester suburbs, where they were always in trouble with the landlord and the grocer and the coal dealer, never at ease among the oppressively neat families that surrounded them.

"We're different, Bobby," she would explain, but the explanation was never needed. Wherever they lived he seemed always to be the only new boy and the only poor boy, the only boy whose home smelled of mildew and cat droppings and plastilene, with statuary instead of a car in its garage; the only boy who didn't have a father.

But he had loved her romantically, with an almost religious belief in her gallantry and goodness. If the landlord and the grocer and the coal dealer and George Prentice were all against her, they would have to be his enemies too: he would serve as her ally and defender against the crass and bullying materialism of the world. He would gladly have thrown down his life for her in any number of ways; the trouble was that other, less dramatic kinds of help were needed, and none came. Pieces of her sculpture were sometimes shown in group exhibitions and very occasionally sold, for small sums, but these isolated triumphs were all but lost under the mounting pressure of hardship.

"Look, Alice," George Prentice would say on the rare and dreaded occasions of his visitation rights, plainly forcing his voice to sound calm and reasonable. "Look: I know it's important to make sacrifices for the boy – I agree with you there – but this just isn't realistic. You simply have no business living in a place like this, running up all these bills. The point is, people have to live within their *means*, Alice."

"All right. I'll give up sculpture, then. I'll move to the *Bronx* and get some wretched little job in a *department* store. Is that what you want?"

"No, of course that's not what I want. I'm simply asking for a little co-operation, a little consideration – damn it, Alice, a little sense of responsibility."

"Responsibility! Oh, don't talk to *me* about responsibility . . . "

"Alice, will you please keep your voice down? Before you wake the boy?"

Life in the suburbs came abruptly to an end with a frightening lawsuits for unpayable debts when he was nearly thirteen; and it was three years later, after a series of increasingly cheap city apartments, that Alice made a final plea to her former husband. She would never be a burden on him again, she promised, if he would only agree to finance Bobby's enrollment in what she called a Good New-England Prep School.

"A *boarding* school? Alice, do you have any idea how much those places cost? Look: let's try to be reasonable. How do you think I'm going to be able to put him through college if I—"

"Oh, you know perfectly well the whole question of college is three years away. Anything can happen in three years. I could have a one-man show and make a *fortune* in three years. I could have a one-man show and make a fortune six *months* from now. Oh, I know you've never had any faith in me, but it happens that a good many other people do."

"Well, but Alice, listen. Try to control yourself."

"Ha! Control myself. Con*trol* myself . . ."

The school she chose was not exactly a good one, but it was the only one that offered to take him at half tuition, and the victory of his acceptance filled her with pride.

His first year there – the year of Pearl Harbor – was almost unalloyed in its misery. Missing his mother and ashamed of missing her, wholly out of place with his ineptness at sports, his cheap, mismatched clothes and his total lack of spending money, he felt he could survive only by becoming a minor campus clown. The second year was better – he gained a certain prestige as a campus eccentric and was even beginning to win recognition as a kind of campus intellectual – but in the middle of that second year George Prentice dropped dead in his office.

It was a stunning event. Riding home on the train for the funeral, he couldn't get over the surprise of hearing his mother weep uncontrollably into the telephone. She had sounded as bereaved as a real widow, and he'd almost wanted to say,

"What the hell, Mother – you mean we're supposed to *cry* when he dies?"

And he was appalled at her behavior in the funeral parlor. Moaning, she collapsed into the heaped flowers and planted a long and passionate kiss on the dead man's waxen face. Recorded organ music was droning somewhere in the background, and there was a long solemn line of men from Amalgamated Tool and Die waiting to pay their respects (he had an awful suspicion that her histrionics were being conducted for *their* benefit). And although his first impulse was to get the hell out of there as fast as possible, he lingered at the coffin for a little while after the conclusion of her scene. He stared down into the plain, still face of George Prentice and tried to study every detail of it, to atone for all the times he had never quite looked the man in the eye. He dredged his memory for the slightest trace of real affection for this man (birthday presents? trips to the circus?), and for the faintest glimmer of a time when the man might have known anything but uneasiness and disappointment in the presence of his only child; but it was no use. Turning away from the corpse at last and taking her arm, he looked down at her weeping head with revulsion. It was *her* fault. She had robbed him of a father and robbed his father of a son, and now it was too late.

But he began to wonder, darkly, if it mightn't be his own fault too, even more than hers. He almost felt as if he'd killed the man himself with his terrible inhuman indifference all these years. All he wanted then was to get away from this sobbing, shuddering old woman and get back to school, where he could think things out.

And his father's death brought another, more practical kind of loss: there was no more money. This was something he wasn't fully aware of until he came home the following summer, not long after he'd turned seventeen, to find her living in a cheap hotel room for which the rent was already in arrears. She had put all her sculpture and what was left of her furniture into storage, and the storage payments were in arrears too. For months, with a total lack of success, she had been trying to re-establish herself as a fashion illustrator after a twenty-year absence from the field. Even he could see how stiff and labored and hopelessly unsaleable-looking her drawings were, though she explained that it was all a question of making the right contacts; and he'd been with her for less than a day before discovering that she didn't have enough to eat. She had been living for weeks on canned soup and sardines.

"Look," he said, only dimly aware of sounding like a ghost of George Prentice. "This isn't very sensible. Hell, *I'll* get some kind of a job."

And he went to work in an automobile-parts warehouse. On the strength of that they moved into the furnished apartment in the West Fifties, and the "wonderful companionship" entered a strange new phase.

Feeling manly and pleasurably proletarian as he clumped home every night in his work clothes, he saw himself as the hero of some inspiring movie about the struggles of the poor. "Hell, I started out as a warehouseman," he would be able to say for the rest of his life. "Had to quit school and support my mother, after my dad died. Those were pretty tough times."

The trouble was that his mother refused to play her role in the movie. It couldn't be denied that he was supporting her – she sometimes had to meet him outside the warehouse at noon on payday, in fact, in order to buy her lunch – but nobody would ever have guessed it. He kept hoping to come home and find her acting the way he thought she ought to act: a humble widow, gratefully cooking meat and potatoes for her tired son, sitting down with a sewing basket as soon as she'd washed the dishes, darning his socks in the lamplight and perhaps looking up to inquire, shyly, if he wouldn't like to call up some nice girl.

And he was always disappointed. Night after night was given over to her talk about the contacts she was certain to establish soon in the fashion world, and about the fortunes still to be made out of one-man shows if only she could get her sculpture out of storage, while the canned food burned on the stove.

Once he found her posing for his admiration in a stylish new dress, for which she'd spent more than half the week's grocery money, and when he failed to be enthusiastic about it she explained, as if she were talking to a retarded child, that no one could possibly expect to get ahead in the fashion world wearing last year's clothes.

"Oh, yes, Bobby's fine," he heard her telling someone on the telephone, another time. "He's taken a summer job. Oh, just a little laboring job, in some dreadful warehouse – *you* know the kind of thing boys do in the summertime – but he seems to enjoy it, and I think the experience will do him a world of good . . ."

He had assumed, with mixed emotions, that he wouldn't be going back to school for his senior year; but when September came around she told him not to be ridiculous. He *had* to graduate; it would break her heart if he didn't.

"Well, but look: what're you going to do?"

"Dear, I've explained all that. Something's bound to happen soon with this fashion work; you know how hard I'm trying. And then just as *soon* as I can get my sculpture out of storage there's no telling what good things are going to come our way. Don't you see?"

"Well, sure, but I'm not talking about 'soon.' I'm talking about now. How are you going to pay the rent? How the hell are you going to eat?"

"Oh, I'll always manage; that's not important. I'll *borrow* some money if I have to. That's nothing to—"

"Who from? And anyway, you can't go on borrowing forever, can you?"

She looked at him incredulously, slowly shaking her head with a world-weary smile, and then she said it: "You sound just like your father."

The argument went on for hours, in ever-rising spirals of unreasoning shrillness, until at last, after hearing one more time and at great length about the invaluable contacts that were certain to be hers, he turned on her and said, "Oh, bullshit!"

And she burst into tears. As if shot, she then clutched her left breast and collapsed full length on the floor, splitting an armpit seam of the dress that was supposed to be her means of advancement in the fashion world. She lay face down, quivering all over and making spastic little kicks with her feet, while he stood and watched.

It was a thing he had often seen her do before. The first time, long ago, had been when one of their landlords in Westchester had threatened to evict them, after she had called George Prentice to plead for whatever sum it was they needed to settle the debt. "All right!" she had cried into the telephone. "All right! But I'm warning you, I'll kill myself tonight!" And rising from the slammed-down phone she had grabbed her breast and fallen to the carpet, and her little boy had tried to put both fists in his mouth to stifle his panic until she roused herself at last and took him sobbing into her arms. It had happened often enough since then, in various crises, that he knew she wasn't really having a heart attack; all he had to do was wait until she began to feel foolish lying there. Before long she turned over and pulled herself up into a tragic sitting position in the nearest chair, hiding her face in her hands.

"Oh, God," she said with a convulsive shudder. "Oh, God. My *son* calls me 'Bull Shit.' "

"No, now wait a minute. I didn't 'call' you – you don't 'call' people – look, it's just an expression. Don't you see? I just said – look, I'm sorry. I didn't mean it. I'm sorry."

"Oh, oh, oh, God," she said, rocking from side to side in her chair. "My *son* calls me 'Bull Shit.' "

"No, look. Wait a minute. Please . . ."

In the end, a week before school started, she took a job – not the "wretched little job in a department store" she had so often threatened George Prentice with, but something more wretched even than that: she went to work in a factory that made department-store mannequins.

The surprising thing was that his senior year turned out to be a kind of success. Through whatever subtle process it is that turns school outcasts into offbeat school leaders, he became one; not until the triumphant year was nearly over did he come to grips with the knowledge that his tuition had gone unpaid for a year and a half.

There were many telephone calls between his mother and the headmaster, during which she probably wept and pleaded and promised, and there were sober talks between the headmaster and himself ("It's a very difficult situation for all of us, Bob") until at last, on the very eve of Commencement Day, the headmaster explained tactfully and with some embarrassment that his diploma would have to be withheld until the account was paid.

By that time his mother had been laid off from the mannequin factory and gone to work in a small, nonunion defense plant that made precision lenses. She described it solemnly, to everyone she knew, as "War work."

A month later he was in the Army, with his mother listed as a

Class "A" dependent; and now, sitting across from her in the ample cleanliness of Childs, he was letting her words flow past his hearing. With a grim, tender patience, he had begun to watch for the first signs of her drunkenness to show: the thickening and slurring of her speech, the tendency of her upper lip to loosen and bloat, the slowing clumsiness of her gesturing hands.

". . . and then suddenly," she was saying, corning to the climax of a long story about some people she'd recently met, "suddenly his eyes went very big and he said, 'You mean you're Alice Prentice? Alice Prentice the *sculptor*?'" She had always taken a child's delight in telling anecdotes that allowed her to speak her own name, and those that allowed her to add "the sculptor" were much the best. "And it turned out they'd been admirers of mine for years. So they asked me in for coffee and we had — oh, we just had the most wonderful time."

He knew he was supposed to join in her pleasure at this, but he abruptly decided he wasn't up to it tonight. "Oh yeah?" he said. "Well, that's interesting. Where'd they heard of you?" And he was fully aware that the question was cruel, but aware too that he had to ask it just that way.

"What? Oh—" Hurt feelings flickered in her face, but she recovered. "Oh, well, friends of theirs had bought a garden piece from one of my exhibitions years ago, or something of the kind. I don't remember exactly. Anyway, they—"

"Your exhibitions?" He couldn't let it go; he was bearing down on her like a prosecuting attorney. He knew damned well that for all her lifelong talk about one-man shows she'd never had one. (And did they really call it a "one-man show" when the artist was a woman? What kind of nonsense was that?) He knew too that the number of pieces she'd sold from group exhibitions could be counted on pitifully few fingers; most of her sales had been made through a garden-sculpture gallery that carried her work on consignment, and even at that they had nearly always been bought by friends, or by friends of friends.

"Well, I *think* they said an exhibition," she said impatiently. "It may have been a gallery sale; anyway that's not important."

He conceded the point, but only to draw back to a new line of attack: "And how did you say you'd met these people?"

"Through the *Stewarts*, dear; I explained all that."

"Oh, I see. And the Stewarts were probably friends of the other people too, the people who bought the sculpture. Right?"

"Well, I suppose so, yes. I suppose that must've been the way it happened." She fell silent for a little while, looking daunted, poking her fork around in the ruins of her chicken croquettes. Then, bravely, her voice went to work again and brought the story around to what had evidently been its point from the start. "Anyway, they're awfully nice, and of course I've told them all about you. They're dying to meet you. I told them we might drop by tomorrow after church, if you feel like it. Would you mind doing that, dear? Just to please me? I know you'll like them, and they'll be terribly disappointed if we don't come."

It was the last thing in the world he wanted to do, but he said yes. And by implication he'd said yes to church, too, which he would also much rather have avoided. He was ready to say yes to anything she wanted now, to atone for the harshness of his questioning. Why had he grilled her like that? She was fifty-three years old and lonely and oppressed; why couldn't he let her have her illusions? That was what her wounded, half-drunken eyes had seemed to be saying throughout his interrogation: Why can't I have my illusions?

Because they're lies, he told her silently in his mind as he champed his jaws and swallowed the cheap food. Everything you say is a lie. You're not Alice Prentice the Sculptor and you never were, any more than I'm Robert Prentice the Prep-School Graduate. You're a liar and a fake, that's what you are.

He was shocked by the force of his own secret invective but carried helplessly along with it, holding his mouth shut tight and allowing his fingers to twist and tear a raddled paper napkin in his lap.

You're Alice Grumbauer, his soundless voice went on. You're Alice Grumbauer from Plainville, Indiana, and you're ignorant and foolish in spite of all the "art" crap you've been spouting all these years, while my poor slob of a father was breaking his back for us. And maybe he *was* "dull" and "insensitive" and all that, but I wish to Christ I'd had a chance to know him because whatever kind of a fool he was I know damn well he didn't live by lies. And you do. Everything you live by is a lie, and do you want to know what the truth is?

He watched her with murderous distaste as she fumbled with her spoon. They had ordered ice cream, and some of it clung to her lips as she rolled a cold mouthful on her tongue.

Do you want to know what the truth is? The truth is that your fingernails are all broken and black because you're working as a laborer and God knows how we're ever going to get you out of that lens-grinding shop. The truth is that I'm a private in the infantry and I'm probably going to get my *head* blown off. The truth is, I don't really want to be sitting here at all, eating this goddam ice cream and letting you talk yourself drunk while all my time runs out. The truth is, I wish I'd taken my pass to Lynchburg today and gone to a whorehouse. *That's* the truth.

But it wasn't, exactly. He knew it wasn't, even while taking deep breaths to fight back the words that, wanted so urgently to burst from him. The real, the whole truth was something far more complicated. Because it couldn't be denied that he'd come to New York of his own free will, and even with a certain heartfelt eagerness. He had come for sanctuary in the very comfort of her "lies" – her groundless optimism, her insistent belief that a special providence would always shine on brave Alice Prentice and her Bobby, her conviction, held against all possible odds, that both of them were somehow unique and important and could never die. He had *wanted* to be with her tonight: he hadn't even minded her calling him her "big, wonderful soldier." And as for the whorehouse in Lynchburg, he knew deep down that he couldn't blame his mother for his own lack of guts.

"Isn't this good?" said Alice Prentice of her ice cream.

"Mm," said her son, and they finished their meal in silence.

On their way back to the apartment she kept swaying against him – her grip on his arm at each street crossing was a little spasm of terror – and as soon as they were upstairs she poured herself a hefty drink from the bottle of whiskey she had probably been working on all afternoon.

"Would you like a drink, dear?"

"No, thanks. I'm fine."

"Your bed's all made up, whenever you're ready. I'm so – tired" – she brushed a loose strand of hair away from her brow – "so tired, I think I'll just go to bed now, if you don't mind. You're sure you don't mind?"

"No, of course not. You go ahead."

"All right. And tomorrow we'll have a lovely long Sunday together." She came up close, smelling of food and whiskey, and raised her arms to give him a kiss. "*Oh*, it's so good to have you here." She clung to him for a moment, and then, swaying, steadying herself against the wall, she blundered into her bedroom and closed the door, which had to be closed several times before it clicked shut in its warped frame.

Strolling alone with his hands in his pockets, he went over to the black window and looked out. Far down the block, where the lights of a bar and grill spilled out across the sidewalk, a couple of soldiers were standing with their arms around a couple of girls. One of the girls was laughing, making high, lewd little sounds that floated up the street. Then one of the soldiers shouted something that made them all join in her laughter, and they walked away and were lost in the darkness.

He loosened his collar and tie and sat heavily on his bed, which also served as the living-room couch and which exhaled a fine cloud of dust. From the cluttered coffee table he picked up the only thing in the room that looked expensive and new: his school yearbook. Leafing through its heavy, creamy pages, he found a pleasurable little shock in discovering one familiar face after another, slicked-up and posing for the school photographer, each looking very young and vulnerable compared to Army faces. And there were the autographs: "Good luck in the service, Bob. It's been great knowing you – Dave."

"Bob, I know you'll go far in whatever you do. I'll always value your friendship – Ken."

By the time he'd finished with the yearbook it was hard to remember that he'd waked before dawn this morning to scrub his cartridge belt for inspection, jostled in the stinking latrine by men who told him to get the lead out of his ass. It was hard to remember his nine hours on the bus and the train, and he was only dimly and guiltily aware of the cruel silent rage that had poisoned his dinner at Childs. The deep, slow, sibilant rhythm of his mother's snoring came in from the bedroom now, and he listened to it with a sense of great tenderness as he undressed and carefully arranged his uniform on a wire hanger. Getting into bed he found that the sheets were surprisingly fresh and clean: he could picture her scurrying to the laundry with them during her lunch hour, in preparation for his coming – or possibly even going to Macy's and buying new ones.

Tomorrow she would wake him late and gently. They would have some kind of messy, inadequate breakfast together, and then they would go to church. The Episcopal service, which she'd discovered only a few years ago after a lifetime of paganism, would make her weep ("I always cry in church, dear; I can't help it. I don't mean to embarrass you"), and then, spiritually restored, they would take a subway or a bus somewhere to visit the people who were supposed to be dying to meet him – the people who'd said "Alice Prentice the *sculptor*?" and who would probably turn out to be as mild and bewildered and pathetically pleasant as she herself.

The deadly realities would be there to reclaim them both soon enough, on Monday morning – the infantry and the lens-grinding shop – but in the meantime . . .

In the meantime he could drift off to sleep feeling privileged and safe, cradled in peace. He was home.

PART ONE

Chapter One

"Com-mence – fire!"

The blast of rifles shocked his ears, right and left; he squeezed the trigger and felt the stock of his own rifle drive hard into his shoulder and cheek, and then he fired again.

They were lying prone on a damp Virginia ridge, firing down across a dismal slope of weeds at a simulated enemy position several hundred yards away – a group of crude wooden house fronts flanked by clumps of trees. Gray silhouette targets darted in and out of view at the windows and came irregularly up from foxholes among the trees, and at first Prentice didn't aim at them very precisely: the main thing seemed to be to keep firing, to get off as many rounds as the men on either side of him. But after a few seconds the tension eased off and he became both careful and fast. It was exhilarating.

"Cease fire! *Cease* fire! All right, fall back. Everybody back. *Second* squad, let's go. *Second* squad up on the line."

Prentice locked his rifle, got up, and stumbled back down the ridge with the others to where a small, painstakingly built campfire was struggling for survival. He made his way into the huddle of men surrounding it and found a place to stand beside John Quint.

"Think you hit anything, Deadeye?" Quint asked him.

"A couple, I think. I'm pretty sure I got a couple, anyway. You?"

"Hell, I don't know."

It was the last afternoon of the week's bivouac that was the climax of their training. Any day now they would be shipped out for overseas processing, and the company's morale could not have been lower, but Prentice had begun to feel an unreasonable elation. It pleased him to know that he hadn't bathed or changed his clothes for six days, that he was learning to handle his rifle as an extension of himself, and that he'd taken part in elaborate field problems without doing anything noticeably absurd. A pleasant little spasm of shuddering seized him; he squared his shoulders, set his feet wider apart, and briskly rubbed his hands together in the woodsmoke.

"Hey Prentice," said Novak, who had been watching him from the other side of the fire. "You feeling pretty sharp today? You feeling like a real fighting man?"

This caused a chuckle around the group, and Cameron, a big Southerner who was Novak's friend, did his best to keep it going. "Old Prentice gunna be a regular tiger, ain't he? Jesus, I'm glad he's on our side."

He tried to ignore them, continuing to rub his hands and stare down into the weak flames, but the sound of their bored, easy laughter had spoiled his mood.

Hardly any of the men in his platoon were less than five years older than Prentice; some were thirty and a few were nearly forty, and a more surly, less amiable crowd he could never have imagined. Like him, they had all come to Camp Pickett from other branches of the service – this whole training regiment, in fact, was what the Army called an Infantry Re-Tread Center – but there was a considerable difference between his case and theirs. He was a veteran of nothing more than six weeks of mild and pampered training as an Air Force recruit, followed by a shapeless month of work details in something called a Casual Company; the others were all old-timers. Some were from recently dissolved Anti-Aircraft units, in which they had idled for years at the gun emplacements around West Coast defense plants; some were from Ordnance or Quartermaster depots; there were ex-cooks and ex-clerks and ex-orderlies, and there were washouts from various officer-candidate schools. Many of them were noncoms in line or technical grades and continued to wear their impotent chevrons, but all of them – every foul-mouthed, hard-drinking, complaining one of them – had in common the miserable fact that their good deals, their months or years of military safety were over. They were replacement riflemen.

And if Prentice had entertained any notion of being called "Bob" or "Slim" or "Stretch" by these men, of relaxing with them in the easy camaraderie of his Air Force days, it was a hope he'd had to abandon at once. They called him "Kid" or "Junior" or "Prentice" or nothing at all, and their general indifference had soon turned into a contemptuous amusement.

On the very first morning, late for Reveille and sleepily fumbling with his unfamiliar infantry leggings, he had put the damned things on backwards, with the hook lacings on the inside rather than the outside of his calves; he had taken four running steps across the barracks floor before the lacing hooks of one legging caught the lace of the other, and down he came – all gangling, flailing six-foot-three of him – in a spectacular lock-legged fall that left his audience weak with laughter for the rest of the day.

And thereafter he had gone from bad to worse. He was incurably clumsy at close-order drill; he couldn't perform the manual of arms without an unsightly dipping of his head when he wrenched open the rifle's chamber; in the field his spindly, ill-coordinated body was put to tests of reflex and endurance that seemed wholly beyond its powers, and he repeatedly floundered and failed.

Worse still, he found himself unable to accept his defeats with any kind of grace. He would rise from each humiliation with a mouthful of shrill obscenities, trying by sheer verbal unpleasantness to beat these laughing bastards at their own game, and the result of this was to lower him still further in their esteem. An all-around incompetent was bad enough, and a wet-behind-the-ears young twerp of an incompetent was worse; but when he turned out to be a little wise guy too – when he swore not only in bad temper but in what sounded like the clipped, snotty accents of a spoiled rich kid – that was too much.

And then one morning after bayonet drill, when the company was marched into a stifling clapboard building for its weekly I. and E. lecture, he found a way in which his luck might possibly begin to change. The lecture was as tedious as ever: first a documentary film, thunderously identified on the screen as one of the *Why We Fight* series, which explained the evils of Nazi Germany in simple-minded words and pictures; then a droning talk by a bored-looking second lieutenant who explained it all over again, and then the question period.

A man several seats away from Prentice got up to raise a question – a quiet ex-Ordnance man from Idaho whom he'd sometimes noticed smoking a pipe in the post library, a man named John Quint – and from the moment he began to talk Prentice sat spellbound.

"I'd like to take issue, sir, with one or two of the points made in the movie just now. Actually, they're things I've noticed cropping up time and again in the Army's indoctrination

26

program, and I think we might do well to examine them a little more closely . . ."

It wasn't what he said that mattered, though all of it was interesting and thoughtful; it was the remarkable ease and confidence of his delivery. Here was a man who couldn't have been more than twenty-four or five – and a bespectacled, almost prissy-looking man at that, a man whose vocabulary and enunciation clearly marked him as "cultivated" – and without the slightest compromise, without any hint of talking down to them, he was holding the respectful attention of every muscle-headed slob in the room. He even got a few laughs – not by any clumsy descent into G.I. humor, but by urbane and witty turns of phrase that Prentice would have thought to be miles over their heads. Hooking his thumbs in his cartridge belt, courteously turning from one section of his audience to another as his glasses gleamed in the lights, he was using words like "ludicrous" and "corruptible" with the dark sweat of the day's bayonet drill still staining his back: he was proving that you didn't have to be a lout to be a soldier.

When he finished and sat down, there was a spatter of applause.

"Yes," the lieutenant said. "Thank you. I think that was very well put. Are there any other questions?"

That was all, but it was enough to give Prentice a sharp new focus for his yearnings. He knew what he wanted in the Army now. The hell with this childish nonsense of being "liked" or "disliked," of being "accepted" or not. All he wanted now, beyond a certain basic competence, was to be as intelligent and articulate as Quint, as independent as Quint, as aloof from the Army's indignities as Quint. He very nearly wanted to *be* Quint, and at the very least he wanted to get to know him.

But the fool of the platoon could hardly buddy up with its one and only intellectual – not, at least, right off the bat. It was a thing that would have to be pursued very cautiously, and with no visible effort at pursuit.

It began that very evening, when he strolled over to Quint's bunk for a desultory chat and was careful to walk away again before there could be any hint of his imposing. Several nights later he saw Quint reading in the library but thought better of going over to start another conversation, though he was careful to display the title of the rather highbrow book he was carrying, in case Quint happened to look up as he passed by on his way to the charge-out desk. Then, luckily, the company began its week of training on the rifle range, marching out there before dawn each morning for a nine-hour session with the targets, and this routine left long conversational openings in the middle of the working day. There were whole half-hours with nothing to do but sit around and wait for your turn on the firing line, and there was even more leisure during the noon meal, which was served in mess kits from a mobile field kitchen. Prentice made the most of those chances; it wasn't long before he and Quint were pairing off at each break, almost as a matter of course. Then when the company went out on bivouac they pitched their shelter halves together and shared the cramped, wet, two-man discomfort of a pup tent in which they both developed chest colds.

By now they had grown as close as members of the same unhappy family, but Prentice knew they couldn't yet be accurately described as friends, let alone as "buddies." They didn't even look right together: Prentice was at least nine inches too tall, with a small, large-eyed face still nakedly eager for approval; Quint was solid and settled in chronic exasperation.

As they trudged side by side in a column of twos for the five-mile march back to the barracks, under full field packs, Prentice was determined not to open any conversation. If they were going to talk at all, Quint would have to start it; and at least two and a half miles of silence went by before Quint said, "Cherrystone clams."

"What?"

"Just thinking about a meal I had once in San Francisco." Quint winced in tiredness as he eased his rifle sling into a more comfortable place on his shoulder. "Best damn restaurant I've ever been to in my life, only I can't remember the name of it. You ever have cherrystone clams? On the half shell?"

And soon they were engaged in what promised to be a long, wistful discussion of the ultimate and perfect dinner, a dinner presumably to be shared some day after the war in the best damn restaurant in the world. It would begin with cherrystone clams and proceed to a celebrated kind of soup that only Quint had ever tasted.

"Okay," Prentice said, "and then what? A big steak, I guess, or a big piece of roast beef with—"

"No. Hold on a second, Prentice; don't let's bolt the whole meal at once. You're forgetting all about the fish course."

"Okay." And as they debated possibilities for the fish course it was all Prentice could do to keep his voice from rising and giggling in pleasure like a girl's.

"Then we're agreed on fillet of sole, right?" Quint said. "All right, now it's time for the main dish. And listen, don't let's be too hasty about the steak or the roast beef – there's plenty of other things. Let's think a minute."

Prentice thought a minute, and while thinking, he allowed one of his worst military habits to repeat itself. His toe scraped the heel of the man walking ahead of him, an ex-Engineer corporal named Connor whose heels, as he often and loudly told everyone, had been stepped on by Prentice every God damned time Prentice followed him in the marching order. And because

Prentice had long since learned that no kind of apology would work with Connor, he could only assume a grave and self-protective look of idiocy when Connor turned around and said, "God *damn* it, Prentice, will you watch your *feet*?" There followed a silence of ten or twelve paces, while Prentice wondered how soon it would be all right to resume the talk of the ideal dinner.

It was Quint, gratifyingly, who broke the silence, "Come to think of it," he said, "I guess you're right, Prentice. There isn't anything better than a steak. Let's make it two filet mignons, then, medium rare. And what'll we have on the side? French fries, I guess, but I mean what kind of vegetable? Or would you rather skip the vegetable and have a salad?"

"Right. Let's do that. Let's just have a big sal—" and then, hating himself, he stepped on Connor's heel again. But there was barely time for Connor to turn around and say, "Prentice, will you watch your fucking *feet*?" – there was barely time for that before Prentice saw something funny in the movements of the men ahead. Far up in front, where the captain was, they had all hunched over and broken into a trot, and they seemed to be taking off their helmets. Nearer, just ahead of Connor, some of them had stopped and buckled over as if in pain; and then, before he could bring his mind into focus, something small and indistinct fell into the dust at his feet and exploded with a soft little noise – *Pluff*! – and his eyes and throat were attacked by fire.

He couldn't see and he couldn't breathe. He crouched, both hands grabbing for his eyes as his rifle swung clumsily loose at his elbow.

"Keep moving, men," somebody was calling. "Keep moving . . ."

Stumbling and pushed heavily from behind, he lost his

balance and fell on the road and rolled, legs in the air – all this happened before the first clear thought occurred to him: *Tear gas.*

And it was an agonizingly long time after that, while he scrabbled on all fours to retrieve his rolling helmet, before he thought of what to do about it – before his right hand clawed at the canvas pouch that had ridden under his left armpit for weeks, tore it open, and pulled out the wobbling rubber paraphernalia of his gas mask.

"Keep moving, men . . ."

Remembering something of gas-mask drill, he squeezed the snout of the thing with one hand and exhaled mightily as he pulled it over his head, and then he slobbered into it, coughing and retching as he opened his eyes and began to see the world through its cloudy plastic goggles. His helmet had come apart on the road, the liner rolling separately away from the steel bowl. He caught them up and fitted them back together, and then he found that this whole part of the column had broken up: he was surrounded by crouching, staggering, helmet-dropping men.

"Keep moving . . ."

Far up ahead – impossibly far, it seemed – the forward part of the column was still intact and marching in good order, and he could see that the last man in that section, plodding along as if nothing had happened, was Quint. He bounded and ran, carrying his rifle at the balance as he tried to keep from vomiting into his mask, which smelled of mildew and rubber and his own breath. They walked another fifty yards before the command came down:

"Test for gas!"

He pulled the sopping rubber away from his cheek and took in a mouthful of sweet fresh air.

"Remove your masks!"

His face was free at last, and he was stuffing the mask back into its pouch as if it were a squirming snake. Then the company was brought to a halt and re-formed into squad and platoon formations in a clearing, away from the road, while the captain climbed a slippery pine-needled rise to address them.

"At ease, men," he said, wiping his own streaming cheeks with a khaki handkerchief. He was lean and austere and hawk-nosed, a veteran of Anzio and widely reputed to be a tough son of a bitch. "Will the ambush party please come forward?"

They were coming forward already, four old-time Camp Pickett cadremen led by a hefty staff sergeant whose fatigues were faded almost white. They had lain in wait for this company all afternoon, ready to throw their tear-gas capsules and assess the results. Now it was over, and they were plainly anxious to get back to the post for supper.

"Sergeant," the captain said. "How'd it look to you?"

"Well, sir, I can't say it looked too good. There was a good deal of confusion and hesitation when the capsules went off – more so 'n usual, I'd say. Seemed to take your men a long time to figure out what was goin' on. Lot of 'em just stood there kind of hunched over, and a lot of 'em lost their helmets. I saw one man go ass-over-teakettle—" there was a faint tittering at this, and somebody said "Prentice" – "one man go ass-over-teakettle before he got his mask on. Your front part of your column did seem to get through pretty well; they kept moving right along; but in the overall, sir, I'd have to say it didn't look too good."

"Thank you." And the captain laboriously blew his nose. His eyes were still red and weeping, and he had to clear his throat several times. "I wonder," he said, "I wonder if you men realize that if this had been poison gas, more than half of you would be dead or dying by now. Think about that. And think about this. You men will be going into combat within a very short time.

32

We know your enemy probably won't use gas, but you can be damn sure of one thing. You can be damn sure your enemy is going to employ the tactic of ambush, the element of surprise, whenever it suits his purposes. That means you men are going to have to cultivate the habit of alertness, and you're going to have to cultivate it in one hell of a hurry."

He put his handkerchief away and drew himself straight. "Now, nobody needs to remind me that you men are re-treads. I'm well aware that you'll be going over with six weeks' training, instead of the minimum sixteen weeks a combat rifleman is supposed to have. If any of you feel that's not fair, I'll agree with you. It's not fair at all. My point is simply this. My point is simply that your enemy is not likely to make allowances for that fact. All right."

The column of twos was re-formed, and soon they were marching at route step again, wiping their eyes and the skin of their faces and necks, which felt as though it had been lightly brushed with nettles. Prentice gave most of his attention to the avoidance of Connor's heels, but from time to time he glanced down at Quint's profile, which was half hidden under the curve and shadow of his helmet. Had Quint seen him go ass-over-teakettle? Other conversations had broken out in the column, but he waited a long time before he felt it would be safe to resume his own.

"Quint?"

"What."

"How do you feel about dessert?"

"What?"

"I said what do you think we ought to have for dessert?"

"Oh. Hell, I don't know. Let's shut up about it now, and try to stay on the ball."

Back in the company street, as they stood waiting to be

dismissed, the first sergeant announced that there would be a Battalion Retreat Parade in fifteen minutes; and this caused an explosion of groans and swearings. Prentice joined in the complaint as the formation broke up and ran jostling for the barracks, but he did so only for the sake of appearances. The truth, which he would never have dared to admit, was that he didn't really mind Retreat Parades. He didn't even mind the outrage of there being one this evening, with no time to take a shower before changing. In fifteen minutes, they had to climb out of their sweated pack harnesses and fatigues and go straight into the dress uniform of woolen O.D. pants and shirt, necktie, brass-buttoned blouse, clean shoes, and overseas cap; they had to detach their cartridge belts from their packs, unhook their bayonet scabbards and affix them to the belts; they had to readjust the frogs of their rifle slings to pull them taut and give the rifles a cursory wiping down with Blitz cloth (they'd have to clean them properly after supper), and if there was any time left over they used it to pick clods of mud off their belts before putting them on and hooking them shut. Then:

"Fall out!"

Sullen and sweating, with a week's grime under the prickle of their clean woolen clothes, they shaped up once again in the company street to be called to attention, given dress-right-dress and parade rest. Within each platoon the lieutenant and platoon sergeant moved in muttering conference to rearrange the men in the order of height, and this always meant that Prentice, to his secret pleasure, had to be put in the first place of the first rank because he was the tallest. Then the command group came hurrying from the Orderly Room to take their places at the head of the company: the captain (looking very natty in his dark, tailored uniform with its brilliant campaign ribbons), the executive officer, and the first sergeant; and with them came

Quint, carrying the long shaft from which hung the guidon, a bright pennant of infantry blue bearing white crossed rifles, the company initial, and the regimental number.

"Any of you old Army men know how to handle a guidon?" the first sergeant had demanded of his newly assembled company on the first day of training. Half a dozen men had lethargically volunteered, and Quint had been chosen for the job. He did it well: he knew how to hold the shaft of the banner at parade rest, at attention, and on the march; he knew how and when to snap it down in salute, pointing it straight out parallel to the earth, and how to whip it up again without letting it wobble.

"*Cuppadeep!*" the captain called, and each of his platoon leaders said, as if in parenthesis, "Patoon—"

"Tetch – *hut! Right* shoulder – *homms!* Right – *face!* Forrad – *hotch!*"

And following the guidon they set off down the company street. They made a column right and fell neatly into place behind the other two companies of the battalion, just in time to hear the opening drumbeats of the regimental band as it stood waiting at an intersection with the color guard. Then they moved in full battalion strength toward the parade ground, and the band, whose drums by now had made it no trouble at all to keep in step, broke into music. The tune they played on the way to Retreat Parades and back was always the same, the Colonel Bogey March, and a tired sotto-voce chorus behind Prentice always gave it the same words:

> "Hitler
> Has only got one ball;
> Goering
> Has two but very small . . ."

On the parade ground the battalion drew up at attention before its commander, a small ruddy major whom they never saw except at this precise distance and under these circumstances. Far behind him, along the opposite border of the field, the regimental commander and his aides stood waiting to review the troops; and beyond that, away up past the flagpole in the haze of a gentle hill leading back into the pines, there were always a number of parked civilian cars surrounded by women and children – officers' families come out to watch the parade before supper. In the abrupt silence after the band had stopped the little major threw back his head to yell, "Battally-*awn!*" Then, bellowing the commands with such force that it seemed his red neck might burst with every syllable, he put them through a massive manual of arms.

And nobody ever noticed it, but Prentice was very nearly perfect on parade. He was never out of step, his posture was impeccable, and his eyes always where they were supposed to be; he performed his manual of arms with a speed and precision he could never achieve in the company street, where it mattered so much more, and he took a craftsman's pride in making his own small role indistinguishable from the mass. He wanted it to look good for the women and children on the hill.

When the arms drill was over there was a long, stock-still wait until they were called to attention to hear the faraway notes of the bugler sounding the Call to Retreat, and the pause after this first, intricate part of the call was filled with nothing but silence.

"Pre-sent – *homms!*"

All the rifles snapped vertical at chest height, the company guidons whipped earthward, the major wheeled to join his superiors in a hand salute, and the bugle took up the simpler and more melancholy strains of "To the Colors" as the flag came down.

Then it was time to pass in review. The band started up again, proclaiming Hitler's deformity to all Virginia; the color guard led the musicians out across the field and back, and the companies fell in behind them at shoulder arms. There was a left turn and then a difficult left flank, a long moment of tension as they passed the reviewing party at eyes right, each man trying mightily to stay in line; then they turned eyes front again and another left-flank command put them back into easier marching order, and then it was all over.

All they had to do now was get back on the road and back to the barracks. At the intersection the music dwindled quickly as the band disappeared down its own street; then the other companies peeled away until only the single company was left, marching to the distant sound of the drums.

"Bunch of God damned chickenshit Boy Scouts," somebody muttered, and somebody else said something about playing tin soldiers. Soon the grumbling and the bitter laughter had become so general that the first sergeant had to turn around and call, "*At ease back there.*"

But Private Robert J. Prentice was not among the offenders. Even without the music he was marching well in the gathering dusk, his face very sober and his eyes straight ahead, fixed on the high, fluttering infantry blue of the guidon.

Chapter Two

Late in December, just after the German breakthrough in the Belgian Ardennes, long trainloads of infantry replacements began to arrive many times a day at Fort Meade, Maryland. The men were counted off and formed into long shuffling columns, and they stood in the snow waiting for everything – to eat, to be medically examined, to receive new issues of clothing and equipment, and to be told where to go next. In the overheated barracks there were hours of preparation for full-field inspections that didn't, at the last minute, take place after all, and there were full-field inspections that took place hysterically on ten minutes' notice; and there was such a continual breaking up and re-forming of groups that everybody said you were lucky if, by the end of your several days at Meade, you had any friends left at all.

Prentice was lucky: owing to the alphabetical proximity of their names he got to stay with Quint, and he was lucky too in that most of the more troublesome men from Camp Pickett were alphabetically sheared away. He and Quint came to share a double-decker bunk in a squadroom full of strangers from other training camps, and he knew that if his luck held they might stay together through all the separations and re-groupings of the days to come: they might well ship out in the same replacement draft and end up in the same outfit.

After a day or so at Meade they made a third friend, or at least a third companion, a portly Arkansas farmer of twenty-nine named Sam Rand who had arrived with a detachment from some Texas camp and taken the lower half of the bunk beside theirs. He had looked forbiddingly grim and sour as he went about the business of unpacking his gear; then, still unsmiling, he had stepped across the narrow space between the bunks and held out a hand from which the index finger was missing. "Sam Rand's my name," he said. "I'm happy to meet you boys." He had served for three years in a noncombatant Engineer outfit until a power saw sliced off his finger; when he got out of the hospital he found that his unit had been dissolved and all its members transferred for re-tread training as riflemen. "I thought the finger'd keep me outa th'infantry; didn't see how I'd be much use to th'infantry without a trigger finger, but they said it didn't make no difference. Said I could farr with my social finger instead."

Quint seemed to take unfailing pleasure in his company, to be consistently amused by his sayings and respectful of his country wisdom; he began at once to call him "Sam," though he never called Prentice by anything but his last name, and the two of them would sometimes leave the barracks together without asking Prentice to come along, which made Prentice a little jealous. So it happened that Prentice sat alone on the top half of the bunk one afternoon, not knowing where Quint and Sam Rand were and determined not to care. His new equipment was heaped around him in a muddle and he knew he ought to do something about getting it organized, but first he had something more important to do: he was trying to answer a letter from Hugh Burlingame, who had been his roommate in his senior year at school.

Letters from Burlingame came only about once a month and

required serious reading, for Burlingame had made it plain that he had no patience with the trivia of ordinary correspondence. "If we're going to write to each other," he'd told Prentice when they were still at school, "let's at least try to *say* things in our letters. If I ever get one from you about what the weather's like, and hoping I'm well, and making a lot of little dumb-assed jokes, I can guarantee I won't answer it, and I'll expect the same from you. Agreed?"

"Agreed."

And the result was that Prentice had spent hours over each of his letters to Burlingame, first in the Air Force and then at Camp Pickett, copying and recopying his manuscript, going to the post library to check his literary references, making sure that each paragraph made its own trenchant point and that the finished product could be read without apology as part of a continuing intellectual dialogue. It was hard work.

Burlingame was now in the Navy, or rather in something called the V-12 Program, which allowed bright students to attend civilian universities in naval uniform, and he seemed to have plenty of time for prose composition:

. . . You speak of your Army comrades as "brutally stupid." I too am surrounded by the type, and can find little compassion for them. Have you read Farrell's *Studs Lonigan*? Do so, and you will find the majority of my classmates in its pages. They are without minds; they are without purpose. They think it "Hot shit" to roll in the bed of some downtrodden whore and to talk of it lasciviously afterwards. I am not shocked by their antics – they amuse me – but I find it depressing to realize that these are specimens of the finest America has to offer in her young manhood. And if this is what one encounters in the V-12,

I can imagine that the caliber is still lower in a unit such as yours, which must include the very dregs of society. Well, *C'est la guerre.*

With regard to religion, I suppose this will startle you (remembering our talks at school about Schopenhauer, etc.) but I am no longer an atheist. In the past several months I have taken honest stock of my philosophical attitudes, and have found to my surprise that Christianity is no longer the anathema I once thought it to be. I can understand now why the greatest thinkers, the most enlightened minds in all of our Western culture have propounded the Christian ideal and the Christian ethic in one form or another . . .

It went on for several more pages, but Prentice felt he had read enough. He carefully wiped his fountain pen and went back to work on his partially finished reply. "As for Christianity," he wrote, "I continue to distrust it, as I distrust all dogma and all moral and/or spiritual certainties." That sounded right – it had the right tone – but he would have to compose three or four more sentences in the same vein before he earned the right to copy out his final paragraph, which he had already scribbled in a burst of inspiration: "I don't imagine you'll be hearing from me for a while because I'm in the process of being shipped to Europe, where I expect we'll all be rather busy for some time – the dregs of society, Studs Lonigan, and me."

He was still working over the intermediate sentences when Quint and Sam Rand came clumping up to the bunk, smelling of beer. "Prentice, old buddy," Quint said, "if you ever got out of that sack and looked at the bulletin board, you'd have found out we've got eight-hour passes tonight. We're going to Baltimore. How about getting off your ass?"

And Hugh Burlingame was instantly forgotten. It was the first time Prentice could remember Quint's calling him "old buddy," even in sarcasm, and it was pleasing to know that he and Rand had come back to the barracks to get him before taking off. As they started down the snow-blown company street, turning up their overcoat collars against the wind, he felt uncommonly jaunty. His new uniform seemed to fit much better than his old one, and he was delighted with the new-style "combat boots" they had been issued at Meade: he had already learned how to darken their tawny color by singeing them with a flame and then applying many coats of polish. They made his legs less spindly and put a new, manly authority into his walk. Neither Quint nor Sam Rand had bothered to darken their boots and they walked as if their feet hurt; for that reason, as the three of them set off for what promised to be a rollicking night on the town, Prentice felt he looked much the most trim and soldierly of the group. And he allowed his rising sense of camaraderie to embrace Sam Rand as well as Quint, for he could see now that Rand posed no serious threat: there was reassurance in the very fact that Rand was so simple and unschooled, so "colorful," like a character actor in the movies. He could serve both Prentice and Quint as a kind of homely, comic relief from the more serious aspects of their friendship, and in that way could safely be welcomed. In combat, when Sam Rand lay wounded, Prentice might run out under heavy fire to bring him back and carry him all the way to the aid station, as Lew Ayres had done with the other man in *All Quiet on the Western Front,* not realizing he was already dead. And Quint, unashamed of the tears in his eyes, would say, "You did all you could for him, Prentice" (or better still, "Bob"). But in the meantime he had to ask them both to stop and wait for him at the PX near the bus station while he called his mother; and when he was folded into the phone booth, dialing for long distance, he didn't feel soldierly at all.

"Oh, *dear*," she said when he had explained that the pass wouldn't give him time to get to New York and back. "Well, but do you think they'll give you any leave from the other place? The one near here?" She meant Camp Shanks, New York, which was the port of embarkation and was said to be shrouded in secrecy.

"No," he said. "They don't even let you make phone calls from there. But anyway, I'll write. And listen, promise not to worry, okay? I'll be fine." The receiver was slippery with sweat in his hand.

"All right, dear. But you *will* be careful, won't you? I know that sounds silly, but I just—"

"Sure I will. I'll be fine. You just take care of yourself and – *you* know – promise not to worry. Okay?"

When he'd hung up he had to sit quiet in the steaming booth for a few seconds, wondering why he had called her at all. And when he came out, stamping to arrange his pants over the boot tops, he found Quint waiting alone.

"Where's Sam?"

"He took off. Ran into some friends of his who had a taxi, and he went along with them. Said he'd try to meet us later in town. You all set?"

In the bewildering civilian disorder of Baltimore they found the hotel bar where Sam had said he'd try to meet them; but Sam wasn't there, and their predicament was compounded when the bartender refused to sell Prentice a drink.

"Oh, what the hell," Quint said. "He's in the *Army*, for Christ's sake. He's going *overseas*. What kind of bullshit is this?"

"Watch your language, soldier. The law says twenty-one, and swearing don't change it none. I serve him, I lose my job."

"Hell, go ahead, Quint; you have one anyway."

"No. The hell with it." And they stood aimlessly near the bar for a while, gazing at tables full of civilians or of officers and girls, or of enlisted men and girls, until Quint said, "Let's get out of here."

"To tell the truth," he said when they were out on the street again, starting to walk without any idea of where they were going, "to tell the truth I didn't really expect Sam to show up. I don't think old Sam wants anything to interfere with the serious business of getting himself laid tonight."

And Prentice chuckled, but it disturbed him a little. He hadn't fully dared to expect that they'd go to a whorehouse tonight, or pick up girls in a bar or whatever it was you did, but what else was worth the effort of doing on your last night of freedom in the States? Did Quint believe that only simple, "colorful" soldiers did things like that? Was it possible that Quint, for all his twenty-four years, was as shy of girls as he himself?

Now they were in what seemed to be the garish, Times-Square part of the city; they were standing under the marquee of a burlesque theater, and Quint, with a frown and a shrug, said they might as well go inside. It was better than going to a movie, anyway; but the show was a disappointment. Most of the women didn't look really desirable, and their stripping was a meticulous concession to police restrictions. The comedians weren't funny, and the whole performance kept coming to a stop so that vendors could patrol the aisles with boxes of candy in which, according to the master of ceremonies, were secreted many valuable prizes including silver cigarette lighters and genuine leather wallets.

"Well," Quint said, when the tedious show was over and they were out on the freezing sidewalk again. "Hell, let's get a drink somewhere. Maybe we can at least get a drink in this cruddy part of town." And the first bar they tried served them bottled beer without a question. It was narrow and bleak, with green walls and a smell of disinfectant, and they settled themselves into a booth just as the jukebox rumbled into the opening strains of "I'll Walk Alone." Most of the other customers were old men lined up at the bar, several of them hawking and spitting on the floor, but there were other servicemen too, and in one of the booths two sailors sat with their arms around two very young-looking girls, the only girls in the place. The beer was stronger than the stuff Prentice was used to in the PX, and by the third bottle he was feeling pleasurably vague: he was ready to decide that this might, after all, be as good and memorable a way as any to spend his last pass, sitting in this strange, squalid bar while John Quint held forth on the larger social and historical aspects of the war. For Quint had broken his moody, pipe-smoking silence and begun to talk – more out of boredom, it seemed, than any real conversational impulse – about economics and politics and world affairs; he was becoming almost as eloquent as on the day of the I. and E. lecture back at Pickett, and the happy difference was that this time he was talking to Prentice alone and allowing Prentice to reply. It was like the old talks with Hugh Burlingame, at school.

"Well, but look at it this way, Quint," Prentice heard himself saying, impressed with the timbre of his own voice. "Look at it this way . . ."

". . . right. You're absolutely right, Prentice." And although Prentice could never afterwards remember what it was he had said, he knew he wouldn't forget the solemn, nodding approbation in Quint's face. "You're absolutely right about that."

" 'Scuse me for buttin' in, fellas," said a stranger's voice through the veils of smoke, and they looked up to find a young, drunken sailor hanging unsteadily over their booth. "Here's the thing. Me'n my buddy got these two li'l gals all loved up, only we gotta be back at the base in twenty minutes. Okay if we turn 'em over to you? I mean I figured you fellas looked kinda lonesome here."

Prentice looked at Quint for guidance, but Quint was intently picking the wet paper label off his beer bottle.

"Tell you what," the sailor said. "Just tell me your first names, so I can introduce you. I mean shit, whaddya got to lose?"

Quint looked up at him with what struck Prentice as an odd mixture of contempt and bashfulness. "John," he said.

"Bob," said Prentice.

And in less than a minute, during which Prentice and Quint didn't quite meet each other's eyes, the sailor was back. This time he brought his buddy, a huge red-haired boy who seemed to be asleep on his feet, and the two girls. "Hey there, John," he said heartily. "How's it going? Hey there, Bob. Fellas, I'd like you to meet a couple friends. This here's Nancy, and this here's Arlene. Okay if we join you fellas a minute?"

The next thing Prentice knew both sailors had gone and left them with the girls. The one called Nancy, plump and talkative with tightly curled black hair, sat chattering cozily beside Quint, and the one called Arlene was pressed into the tremulous circle of his own arm. She was very thin and dead silent, and she was heavily perfumed.

". . . no, but tell me one thing, John," Nancy was saying. "One thing I still don't understand. How come you're friends with Gene and Frank when they're in the Navy and you're in the Army?" And Quint made some polite, inaudible reply. He had removed his glasses and was wiping them with Kleenex, blinking at Nancy with his small eyes.

Then suddenly Arlene became talkative too. "You got a nickel, Bob?" she said. "I want to play that song again, 'I'll Walk Alone.' I love that song."

He rose to do her bidding, stamping the pants around his combat boots, and he hoped she was watching as he made his way to the jukebox in his new walk. When he came back she sang the lyrics for him along with the record, sitting erect with her hands in her lap and staring straight ahead to let him admire her profile, which had an oddly sloping forehead and contained several powdered-over pimples.

"They'll ask me why," she sang, "and I'll tell them – I'd rather. There are dreams I must gather, dreams we fashioned the night – you held me tight . . ."

While she sang he had time for some rapid, baffled speculations about these girls. Were they whores? Could it be that the sailors had already had them and taken off without paying the bill? No, no; the girls would never have let them get away. How old were they? Seventeen? But what kind of girls that age would be in a place like this, allowing themselves to be passed around like merchandise?

". . . I'll always be near you, wherever you are; each night, in every prayer. If you call I'll hear you, no matter how far – just close your eyes, and I'll be there . . ."

And where had the sailors found them? Probably they were what the newspapers called "V-girls"; and here he was briefly troubled: would they be carriers of venereal disease?

". . . Please walk alone; and with your love and your kiss-es to guide me—" Arlene closed her eyes and allowed a little tremor of sentimentality to wrinkle her forehead at the climax of the song – "till you're walk-ing beside me – I'll walk alone." Then she opened her eyes and took a dainty but deep drink of beer, leaving lipstick on the glass and foam on her lips. "God, I love that song," she said. "Where you from, Bob?"

"New York."

"You have any brothers and sisters?" This seemed wholly out

47

of character for her: it was a standard conversation opener for the kind of girls who came to prep-school dances. He tried to put things on a more worldly plane by telling her that he and Quint were at Meade and due to go overseas any day, but that didn't seem to impress her: she had evidently met a good many boys from Meade. Soon the conversation threatened to dry up altogether, and he looked across the table for help, but Quint was red-faced and cramped with laughter at something Nancy had said, and Nancy, laughing too, was wearing Quint's overseas cap. Then suddenly Arlene squirmed closer and dropped her hand on Prentice's thigh, massaging it in a light, rhythmic way that sent delightful waves of warmth from his knees to his throat. It was a very small, childish hand with bitten-down nails, and it wore a high-school ring.

"Look," she said. "It's getting kind of late. You want to take me home?"

She lived so many miles from the center of town that her home could be reached only by riding a bus for great, winding distances and then transferring to another bus. He was uneasy about finding his way back and made her repeat the directions several times, until she began to look tired and bored with him as they jolted along in the second bus. Her boredom made a light sweat break out inside the woolen slant of his overseas cap; he pictured her giving him one limp hand to shake at her door and saying something awful – "So long, stupid; it's been real," or something like that – and in an all-out effort to avert such a disaster he settled his arm more closely around her, bravely working his hand up and somehow around inside her open coat until it held the meager shape of her breast. This caused her to nestle against him with a little purring sound, rearranging her coat to hide his hand; and after bending to touch his lips to her powdery forehead, he rode on into the

Baltimore night feeling like the very devil of a soldier.

But his boldness fled him when they got off the bus at last to walk up a silent block of looming, close-set, ominously dark frame houses. "You live with your parents?" he inquired, and he suddenly hoped the evening might end in a family kitchen scene: a jovial father in suspenders who would want to tell him about the last war and a soft, smiling mother who would thank him for bringing Arlene home safely, who would wish him luck and kiss his cheek and send him on his way with a warm paper bag full of homemade cookies.

"Yeah," she said. "But it's okay. My father works the night shift and my mother sleeps like the dead. Here, it's this next one. Now for God's sake be quiet." She led him down an alley and through a side door, up a creaking flight of stairs, and down a linoleum hall to the door of her family's apartment. Her key scraped in the lock, and then, saying "Sh-sh!", she led him into a room and turned on a light switch.

There was flowered wallpaper, an ornate sofa of green velvet, and a cold fireplace containing a clay-filament gas grill. There were several religious pictures on the walls, as well as a dark reproduction of "The Reaper," and on the mantelpiece were a number of knicknacks including a paperweight model of the Trylon and Perisphere from the 1939 World's Fair and a big kewpie doll with feathers. Arlene stepped out of her shoes and left him alone while she padded out another door, whispering that she'd only be a minute. He took off his overcoat and cap and sat experimentally on the sofa. He started to light a cigarette but decided against it: he would wait until she came back so that he could put two cigarettes in his lips, light them both and then slowly remove one and hand it to her, looking at her with narrowed eyes, the way Paul Henreid had done with Bette Davis in the movie called *Now, Voyager*.

"It's okay," Arlene said, closing the door behind her. "She's out cold." And she came to the sofa bringing a quart bottle of beer and two glasses. "You got a cigarette, Bob?"

He went carefully through the Paul Henreid trick, but she was pouring the beer and didn't notice. "Thanks," she said. "Here, let me put this thing on." And squatting ungracefully she set a match to the gas fireplace, which popped and hissed. Then she turned off the lights and sat beside him in the soft orange glow.

Could you just start necking with a girl, without saying anything first? He guessed you could, and he was right. Once he broke away to stand up and take off his stifling tunic, and when he came back he avoided her while he reached out and swigged at his beer, as if he were an interestingly jaded alcoholic who absolutely had to have a drink or else be bored to death with the whole idea of sex; then, having drained his glass, he tried the *Now, Voyager* business again with two more cigarettes, though their first two were lying almost untouched in the ashtray, but again she didn't notice. She was unhooking her brassiere for him. He wondered if he could say, "Look, Arlene, let's not; you're too nice a girl for this," and if she might then weep in his arms and say, "Oh, Bob, you're the first boy who's ever really respected me," and if then they might cling romantically together at the door with tender goodbyes and promises to write. The trouble was that her tongue was in his mouth and her little naked breasts were in his hands, and her fingers, with their high-school ring, were expertly unfastening the buttons of his fly. Only then did he remember the pack of Army condoms that had ridden in his wallet for weeks; he struggled to get one of them out but wasn't at all sure if he knew how to put the damned thing on until Arlene helped him. She helped him, in fact, to do everything else that was required: she positioned their two bodies on the sofa and gravely, carefully

50

guided him into herself with both hands. He knew it was supposed to take a long time, but it was frantically over in almost no time at all.

"You done already?" she asked, not exactly in irritation but in something dangerously close to it; and so by way of reply, instead of apologizing, he buried his face in her neck with what he hoped would sound like the deepest possible groan of satisfaction. And the surprising thing was that she then seemed as eager as he was to pretend it had been a success: she stroked his back and nibbled at his ear. Could it be that she was used to settling for this kind of performance? He could only hope so.

Then they were sitting up, while she put her clothes and her hair in order. "God," she said. "Look at all those cigarettes. Did you light all those cigarettes?"

Quint and Sam Rand were heavily asleep when he crept back into the barracks, and he took that sleepily to heart as a point of pride, a suggestion that he'd made out better than either of them.

But there was no chance to mention it in the morning, or even to drop sly hints about it, because it was their last morning at Meade and was filled with hectic activity: packing and inspections and roll calls by short-tempered noncoms.

Well before noon they were marched out into the snow – many hundreds of them, well over a thousand – and herded into a northbound train. In the cramped, overheated day-coach Prentice had ample opportunity for letting it be known that he'd made out last night, but he couldn't find the words and wasn't at all sure he would say them if he could. He was afraid that Sam Rand might say something like, "Well, I guess that makes you a big man now, don't it, Prentice?" And Quint might only draw his mouth to one side and shake his head in mild, derisive amusement. Maybe all Quint had done with the other girl,

Nancy, was to pay for her beer and put her on the bus for home; maybe that was all you were *supposed* to do with girls like that, if you had any pride. And now he allowed his mind to dwell on another, uglier aspect of the thing. Hadn't the V.D. movies all made it clear that a rubber was never really enough protection? Shouldn't he have gone to a pro station afterwards? He hadn't even – Jesus! – hadn't even taken a shower. He felt naked and tender under all the layers of winter clothing and long underwear, crawling with loathsome germs. And how long did it take for the first symptoms to show?

Camp Shanks, deep in the woods northwest of New York, turned out to be a maze of long, low tarpaper huts whose air was heavy with coal smoke from pot-bellied stoves and with the sweet smell of cosmoline in which the factory-new rifles came embedded. Once you had cleaned and oiled your rifle at Shanks there was nothing to do but sit around and talk, or listen to the talk, and almost all the talk was of despair.

". . . hell, I wouldn't mind if I was *trained*. Get your full sixteen weeks' basic, join a regular outfit for your advanced training, get to know your job and your buddies, and *then* go over. I mean that's soldiering, you know what I mean? This way, shit – grab your ass and throw you into the line with a bunch of goddam strangers and use you for cannon fodder; that's all they're doing. I don't mind telling you, I'm scared shitless."

"Who ain't, buddy? You know anybody who ain't?"

". . . shit, though, why *not* go over the damn hill? What's the worst they'd give a man? Ten years in Leavenworth, and then get it commuted to six months when the war's over? That ain't so bad."

"Leavenworth, my ass. You'd never see no Leavenworth, buddy. M.P.'s 'ud shove your ass on the next boat, that's all they'd do."

". . . fella over in the next barracks, he was tellin' me they got this one ole boy over there put his foot up on a stump? Just like 'at? Put his foot up on a stump and commenced askin' fellas to hit his leg with a rifle? And you know, that's pretty smart? Get your leg broke here, you'd sure as hell save yourself a mess of trouble later on."

"She-it. Put *your* foot up on a stump, Reynolds! I'd like to see *you* have guts enough to let me hit your leg with a rifle."

"I never *said* I would! *Damn*, you get things twisted around! I never *said* I would! . . ."

Everyone seemed determined to outdo everyone else in boastful claims of cowardice, and Prentice found it disheartening. He stayed as close as possible to Quint and Sam Rand, who avoided the talk, and he spent most of his time trying to finish the letter to Hugh Burlingame. But he couldn't make the paragraphs work out right, and in the end he tore it up and dropped the pieces into the coal stove.

On the second day a harassed little buck sergeant came storming into the hut to announce that he personally didn't give a pig's shit whether anybody paid attention to him or not, but that anybody who didn't, and who missed the boat, would find his sweet little ass up for a general God damned court-martial. He then chalked numerals on each of their steel helmets and told them all to stand by because they'd be moving out any minute. But they didn't move out until long after dark; when they did, it was to become part of an endless column slipping and sliding down an ice-covered hillside that seemed to fall away for miles, and despite the cold they were soaked with sweat by the time they filed into another train that took them to the Weehawken ferry slip, from which they were borne out into the gentle midnight silence of the Hudson. They floated downtown, heading east across the river, and the ferryboat drew up beneath the enormous gray hull of the *Queen Elizabeth*. Then they labored up into the pier and onto the ship, where tired British voices guided them down curving, tilting corridors and stairways until they found the impossibly small canvas bunks, hung in vertical tiers of four, whose numbers matched the numbers on their helmets. And when they woke up in the morning – when they struggled out half seasick to stand with their mess kits in the freezing wind of the open deck, waiting for breakfast – there was no land in sight.

"Only you don't call it the Clyde River," Quint explained as they stood at a railing of the stilled ship, six days later. "You call it—" and here he broke into a prolonged coughing fit. Both he and Prentice had chest colds that were getting worse. "You call it the Firth of Clyde," he said when he'd recovered. "I don't know what the hell 'Firth' means, but that's what you call it. It's supposed to be the biggest shipbuilding center in the world, or something."

"Don't look like much," said Sam Rand. "Them hills is real pretty, though."

It took them all night and most of the next day to ride through Great Britain on a train that pleased Prentice because it was exactly like the trains in British movies, a series of cozy compartments with a connecting corridor. He had a window seat, and long after the other men were asleep he stared with fascination at the dark passing landscape of Scotland and then of England. Being in England made him think of a man whose name hadn't crossed his mind in years – Mr. Nelson, Mr. Sterling Nelson; a man who had once said, "I'll expect you to take good care of your mother while I'm gone" – and for a little while he could almost feel his mother riding beside him ("Oh, isn't this exciting, Bobby?") so that it came as a little shock when the person who slumped heavily against his shoulder, groaning in sleep, turned out to be John Quint.

In the morning, along with the passing out of cold K rations, bright rumors flew up and down the corridor to the effect that this particular trainload of replacements wasn't heading for combat at all. The battle of the Ardennes, which everyone by now had learned to call "the Bulge," was virtually won. The war in Europe would soon be over, and there were enough men now on the Continent to finish the job. Their own destination was to be a camp in the south of England, near Southampton, where they would join a new division in training for service as occupation troops in Germany. All afternoon there was a holiday mood on the train as they sped through the English countryside – there was talk of English girls and English beer and furloughs in London – but there were several skeptics, too.

"Hell, it's the old story," said Sam Rand. "Don't believe anything you hear and only half of what you see. I say we're goin' straight to Belgium."

"Sam, old man," said Quint, "I hate to say it, but I've got a feeling you're right."

And he was. When they walked heavy-laden through the streets of Southampton it was still possible to believe the rumors – their camp was supposed to be *near* Southampton, wasn't it? – but no Army trucks were there to meet them and no jeep drove up with orders to turn them away from the waterfront. The hike went on, past numberless English civilians whose stares made it plain that they were bored half to death with the sight of Americans, and it didn't end until they had filed aboard a British troopship that smelled of fish and vomit. And the ship, under conditions of strict blackout and radio silence, crept out into the Channel that night.

Then they were in Normandy, rolling eastward in a train of

shuddering French boxcars, the floors of which were thickly embedded with straw that caused a good deal of sneezing and complaint until it proved to be comfortable. Prentice woke up coughing and feverish soon after dawn and squirmed around to lie with his head near the partly opened door, even though he knew it probably wouldn't be good for his cold. He wanted to see the snow-covered fields and hedgerows where all the fighting had taken place last summer. Again it seemed that his mother was riding with him – "Oh, look at the *colors*, dear; aren't they lovely?" – but he fell back to sleep and awoke much later to sounds that would certainly have baffled and distressed her: the clamor of commercial bargaining. They had come to a stop near some town, and a number of ragged men and boys were swarming under the boxcar with offers of money and wine in exchange for cigarettes.

". . . *How* much?"

"Vanty-sank, he says. That's twenty-five francs for the pack. Go ahead, what the hell."

"*Shit* no; don't be an idiot – that's only half a buck. Make him give you a buck a pack."

"Comby-ann for the wine, hey kid? Hey! Buster! You with the runny nose – yeah, you. Comby-ann for the veeno?"

"*Pardon, M'sieur? Comment?*"

"I said comby-ann cigaretty do you want for the veeno? No, damn it, the *veeno!*"

Then they were moving again. Prentice would gladly have spent the rest of the day talking with Quint – they could have discussed the countryside and tried to figure out what part of France this was – but Quint said he felt lousy and stayed deep in the straw, either sleeping or trying to sleep. Sam Rand was there to talk to, but he showed no interest in the passing scene. "I just want to get where we're goin'," he said, "wherever the hell it is."

The phrase "replacement depot" had a comfortingly solid sound – it seemed to promise at least a semblance of garrison life, a place with decent accommodations and decent food and medical attention – but the First Army's replacement depot proved to be a jumble of barns and hastily pitched squad tents around a badly shelled Belgian village. Prentice's group got a barn to sleep in instead of a tent, but it leaked wind and snow; the only way to make it bearable was to walk half a mile to where a Belgian farmer sold armfuls of straw for packs of cigarettes, and straw soon became a matter of furious importance:

"Hey, you're takin' all my *straw*!"

"Fuck you, buddy – this is *my* straw."

In the morning they were marched out to a makeshift target range to zero-in the sights of their rifles, and in the afternoon they were given overshoes – ordinary black civilian galoshes which bothered Prentice a little because they looked so unmilitary. Then they were loaded into open trucks and driven away toward an uncertain place from which, it was said, they would be assigned to combat divisions within twenty-four hours.

"Why the hell don't they have covers on the *trucks?*" Prentice demanded in the wind, and Quint, who seemed to know a good deal about the First Army from his reading of *Time* magazine, explained that open trucks had been a regulation since the outbreak of the Bulge: the idea was to enable men to get out of them faster in case of enemy attack. The trucks let them down into an encampment of frozen squad tents, and they spent a coughing, sleepless night there before convoys of other open trucks began to arrive from various First Army divisions to claim their men. Prentice, Quint, Rand, and several hundred others went into the trucks whose drivers wore a shoulder patch of a design worked around the numerals "57."

"Is this supposed to be a good outfit, the Fifty-seventh?" Prentice asked.

"How the hell should I know?" Quint said. "Am I supposed to know everything?"

"Well, Jesus, you don't have to get sore. I just thought you might know, is all."

"Well, I don't."

And there was no more talk in the truck for a long time, as they drew deep inside their snow-encrusted overcoats and tried to expose as little flesh as possible to the wind.

"I wonder if they'll put us out into line companies right away," Prentice said, "or if they'll keep us at division head-quarters a while first."

Quint's round, stubbled, wind-chapped face turned slowly to stare at him as if at a tiresome child. "God *damn* it, Prentice," he said without opening his teeth, "will you quit asking *questions*?"

"I wasn't asking a question. I just said I wondered."

"Well, quit wondering, then. Try shutting up for a while. You might learn something."

They learned all they needed to know about the division that night, against a distant boom and rumble of artillery fire, when they were assembled in a barn to hear a welcoming talk by an earnest, pulpit-voiced chaplain. "You men are now members of the Fifty-seventh Division," he said, standing with his thumbs in his pistol belt and his paunch sucked in, "and I think you'll soon find you have every reason to be proud of that fact." He went on to say that the 57th was not an old division, even by standards that measured a division as old if it had served in Normandy last summer. The 57th had still been in the States last summer. It had come overseas in October, taken advanced training in Wales, and been committed to action here in Belgium a little less than a month ago. But the chaplain pointed out, with a righteous quivering of his cheeks, that in the past month the boys of the 57th had become men. They had "engaged in some of the bitterest fighting yet known in the Second World War, and in some companies the casualty rate has been as high as 60 per cent." He then said a number of other things, using phrases that could have been lifted whole from *Yank* magazine or *Readers Digest*, and Prentice paid more attention to the sound of the artillery than to his voice.

The place they were assigned to sleep in was the second floor of an abandoned grain mill, an ice-cold room with wind humming steadily through its broken windows. Prentice and Quint went on sick call and received a supply of aspirin and some dark, foul-tasting pellets that were the size and texture of rabbit turds.

"Actually they're damn good medicine if you can stand the taste," Quint said. "Hold it in your mouth till it dissolves; let it coat your throat." But Prentice couldn't. He would swallow the thing after a minute and go on coughing, with the awful taste still in his mouth and nose.

On the second night Sam Rand found a farmer down the road who agreed to let the three of them sleep in his kitchen in exchange for three packs of cigarettes, and it was unbelievably warm. They sat with their socked feet on the fender of a great iron stove, drinking K-ration coffee and listening to the artillery. But Quint said they'd better stay here only for the one night: it was risky because they might miss their orders to move up to the line. They had drawn their company assignments that day, and it pleased Prentice to know that they would all three be in the same unit – "A" Company of the 189th Regiment.

"What are the other regiments again?" he said.

"One ninetieth and One ninety-first."

"Right. And there's only those three, right?"

"Oh, for Christ's sake, Prentice. Yes, there are three regiments in a division." And Quint went on in the chanting, singsong tone of a grammar-school teacher, closing his eyes. "There are three battalions in each regiment, three companies plus a heavy-weapons company in each battalion, three platoons plus a weapons platoon in each company—"

"I *know*," Prentice said.

"—three squads in each platoon, and twelve men in each squad."

"I *know* all that."

"Well if you know, why do you keep asking half-assed questions?"

"I *don't* keep asking. I *didn't* ask."

"And for God's sake don't start forgetting where you belong. You're in 'A' Company, First Battalion, One eighty-ninth Regiment. You'd better write it down."

"Goddam it, Quint, you don't have to talk to me that way. I mean I'm not exactly an idiot, you know."

"I know you're not—" and Quint went into a violent spasm of coughing. When it was over he said, "I know you're not. That's why it's so goddam depressing when you keep acting like one all the time."

"You know what's even more depressing? The way you keep acting like a real, royal, first-class little pain in the ass."

"Now, now, children," said Sam Rand. "Quit your fussin'." And there was a long, simmering-down silence around the stove, until Rand said, "How old're you, Prentice? Eighteen?"

"That's right."

"Damn. My oldest boy's half your age. Don't that seem funny?"

And Prentice said he guessed it did. "How many kids do you have again, Sam? Three, is it?"

"Three, yeah. The girl's seven, and then we got another boy four." He eased one buttock off his chair and reached tentatively for his wallet. "You seen their pictures?"

"No, I don't believe I—"

And out came a snapshot of them, blond and serious, lined up against the side of a bright clapboard house with the sun in their eyes.

"Then this here's my wife," Sam said, and turned the plastic frame to reveal a thin, pleasant-looking girl in a flowered dress and a new permanent wave. Prentice examined both pictures long enough to make approving comments and then passed the wallet to Quint, who scowled at it, mumbled something agreeable, and handed it back.

"And then look at this here," Sam said, probing carefully in another part of the wallet. He pulled out a piece of ruled school paper, many times folded and stained brown from the sweated leather. "Somethin' the oldest boy wrote in school."

It was an essay, written in pencil with many erasures and with periods that were almost as big as the letters:

MY DADDY

I love my Daddy because he is so kind to us. He gives us rides on the cultavater and takes us to the Fair and hardly ever gets mad. Now he is in the Army and I pray he will come home soon. He is a very good man. He is very fair. He is smart. This is why I love my father. Vernon Rand Grade 3.

The teacher's red pencil had corrected the spelling of "cultivator" and written "A" at the top of the page.

"Well, I'll be damned, Sam," Prentice said. "That's pretty great. I mean, really, that's great."

Rand's face was stiff with shyness as he stared at the stove, fiddling with his cigarette, picking a shred of tobacco from his lips with his social finger. "Well," he said, "I mean, it's pretty good writin' for a nine-year-old. Or eight, I guess. That's all he was when he wrote that, was eight."

"*Very* good, Sam," Quint said, handing the paper back. "That's really very good."

All the tension was dissolved; they were ready for sleep, and as Prentice settled into his bedroll on the floor he began to draft the opening lines of a letter he might one day write: *Dear Vernon: I want you to know that your father was one of the finest men I have ever . . .*

On the following night both Quint and Rand were assigned to guard duty on the divisional headquarters perimeter, which left Prentice with nothing to do but sit cold and alone in the grain mill until a man named Reynolds came over to squat beside him and to confide, in a half whisper, that he knew a nice warm house down the road that was "bigger'n Dallas." That was Reynolds's favorite phrase: having gotten a laugh with it several times among the strangers at Fort Meade and Camp Shanks, and having found that it won him goodwill in all the ensuing disorders, he had grown addicted to it. He had shrilly announced that the *Queen Elizabeth* was bigger than Dallas, that the water power in the toilet bowls aboard ship was bigger than Dallas, that the space left by the removal of somebody's duffelbag from under his feet in the boxcar would be bigger than Dallas; and he was still saying it even now, after more than a few men had told him to take Dallas and shove it up his ass.

Don't tell nobody else," he said, "'cause we don't want to louse it up. There's this real nice lady lives there, her husband's a prisoner in Germany. She's got these two little kids and this old granny – the granny's real nice too. They let us sleep there last night, me and a couple other boys, and we aim to do it again tonight. Plenty of room for one more."

"Well, thanks," Prentice said, "but I don't know. Don't you think we ought to stay here, in case they call us out?"

"Shit, I ain't worried none. They say the One ninetieth ain't movin' till tomorra night. You're in the One ninetieth, ain'tcha?"

"No. One eighty-ninth."

"Well, suit yourself. Real nice house, though. They give you wine to drink and everything."

And Prentice decided to go, though he wouldn't take his bedroll. He would stay for the wine and get warmed up, and then he'd come back here to sleep. The house was some distance farther away than the one he had stayed in last night, and he took careful note of the journey in order to find his way back.

The ladies were, as Reynolds had promised, real nice: the grandmother, tiny and toothless and wearing many sweaters, kept saying something about his being *un grand soldat,* rolling her eyes upward in disbelief at his height, and the younger woman urged a glass of wine on him even before he was out of his overcoat. She was plump, brisk, and competent-looking, clearly used to keeping order in her house. A tinted photograph of her husband, in uniform, was displayed on the wall along with other family pictures that included one of a priest; and the children, girls of five or six who looked enough alike to be twins, were seated in the laps of Reynolds's two friends, whom Prentice knew only by sight. Soon they had all formed a quietly jolly party around a big table, and despite the language barrier they had managed to agree on certain basic issues: that it was a fine thing to be in a warm house on a cold night, that the wine was good, that Roosevelt and Churchill and Stalin were good, that Hitler was so bad as to be worth describing only in facial contortions of disgust, and that the buildings of New York were extraordinarily tall. The ladies kept laughing and nodding and pouring more wine, and there was rivalry among the men to prove that each knew best how to behave in a decent home: they frequently reminded one another to use the ashtray, to watch their language, whether it mattered or not, and not to tilt back in their chairs. At the children's bedtime their mother urged them to sing an American song for the soldiers, and they were shy but willing. Holding hands and standing very straight in the middle of the room, they sang:

> "Ipp's a long way to Tipperary
> Ipp's a long way to go . . ."

There was great applause, and nobody had the heart to point out that it wasn't really an American song. Then another bottle of wine was brought in, and another. Other friends of Reynolds's friends came in to drink and spend the night, until the whole downstairs of the house was so crowded that Prentice couldn't have slept there even if he'd wanted to. By the time he got up to leave, with many thanks and goodbyes, it was well past midnight.

He let himself out through the blackout curtain, and as soon as the cold air of the vestibule hit him he was crippled over in a paralyzing cough. The spasms went on and on, while he crouched and swayed and leaned against the wall. Little colorless specks hung and danced before his eyes in the darkness, and in the depths of one cough he felt a knifelike pain over his heart – a pain he had first felt on bivouac in Virginia, a month ago, and which Quint had admitted to feeling too. Finally it was over, but not before the younger of the ladies had come out and put her arm around him. She was chattering in French, much too fast for him to follow, but he needed no translation to know what she meant: that she wouldn't let anyone leave her house on a night like this with a cough like that.

She led him back through the kitchen, where the other men were laying out their bedrolls, and with motherly insistence she steered him upstairs. It was useless to protest, even if he could have found the words. Before he fully realized what she was doing she had spread blankets and quilts for him on the floor of the children's room, along the wall opposite their two small beds. Then she instructed him in sign language to leave his rifle in the hall, and to lie facing the wall as a precaution against infecting the little ones. *"Voilà,"* she said. *"Bon nuit."*

"Modom," he told her, pleased with himself for getting the words right, "vouse et tray, tray jonteel. Maircee bo-coo."

When she was gone he spread his overcoat on top of the blankets, took off his overshoes and boots, and crawled under the covers as if relinquishing himself to all the luxury in the world.

He awoke to the smell of urine – one or both of the little girls had used the chamber pot that stood close to his head – and to the sounds of shouting and heavy movement in the road below. He wrestled with the blankets and bolted to his feet, pulled the blackout curtain aside, and looked out. It was blinding white daylight, late in the morning, and the road was filled with a double column of men trudging past under packs and duffelbags. He buckled on his boots and overshoes, grabbed his helmet and overcoat, and was halfway down the stairs before he remembered his rifle. He ran back and got it, and then he was downstairs and outside in the street.

"Hey!" he called in a voice that came out as a croak. "What regiment is this?"

"One eighty-ninth!"

"Which battalion?"

"Second!"

"Where's the First?"

"Way the hell up ahead!"

There was no point in waking the men downstairs; they were all in the 190th. He broke into a run, his overcoat open and flapping, and ran all the way back to the grain mill. He clambered up to the second floor, which was empty and dead silent, and there, all alone in a heap against the wall, were his field pack and duffelbag. He knelt, sobbing for breath, struggled into the pack harness and buckled it. He hoisted the duffelbag to his shoulder, which sent him reeling, and staggered down and out into the road again, just as the last of the replacements were disappearing around a bend. He chased them, slipping and sliding in the trampled snow, and by the time he'd caught up with them it seemed that the effort of speaking was almost beyond his strength.

"Which – which battalion is this?"

"Third."

And he lurched into his stumbling, rubber-legged run again. At first, as in a nightmare, he seemed unable to move faster than the pairs of walking men; then he slowly began to overtake them, one pair after another. Once he was seized with a coughing fit and had to drop his bag and stop, crouched and hawking phlegm into the snow, and when it was over a good many of the Third Battalion replacements had passed him again. He was soaked in sweat.

Finally a voice answered "Second" when he asked which battalion it was.

"Can you – can you tell me how far ahead the First is?"

"Quite a ways, buddy. You better haul ass."

And no sooner had he resumed hauling ass than he slipped and fell headlong in the snow, which set off cheers of delight in the passing column. Then he was up and running again, aware of the column only as a slow brown blur beside him. He had developed a mindless pounding rhythm to his running now; he felt he was about to faint, and that if he did his legs would somehow go on running.

"Which – which battalion?"

"First."

"Where's – where's 'A' Company?"

"Up ahead."

And so he was almost there, but the line of men still looked endless. He let himself slow down to a walk until the white landscape stopped turning and swimming in his eyes; then he started running again, and at last, some six and then four and then three men ahead, he saw the short, trudging figures of Quint and Sam Rand.

"Well, Jesus God, look who's here," Quint said. "Where the Christ have you been?"

"I – I—"

"First thing you'd better do is report to the sergeant up ahead. He's got you down as AWOL."

The sergeant was a big, neat regimental headquarters man, swinging athletically along, setting the pace, unencumbered by pack or duffelbag.

"Sergeant, I – I just got here."

"What the hell's your name?"

"Prentice."

"Where the hell you been?"

"I was – I overslept."

"Well, swell. That's getting off to a great start, isn't it? You know how close you came to a court-martial? Okay, fall on back where you belong."

And Prentice stood slumped and gasping until Quint and Rand came abreast of him.

"Prentice, you take the God damn cake," Quint said, and that was all he said until the march was over, half an hour later.

They were in a wide, flat field beside a railroad track, with a black forest far in the distance. The "A" Company replacements had been taken out to a seemingly arbitrary place in the field, close to the tracks, and told to stand by. Farther away down the tracks the men for "B" and "C" Companies made similar little clusters in the snow.

Prentice sat sprawled on his duffelbag with his helmet off and his throbbing temples in his hands. He felt almost good, proud at least that he'd made it. After a while he lit a cigarette, but it made him cough and he threw it away. Shyly, he got up and walked over to where Quint and Rand were sitting. "So what's the deal?" he asked. "Are we going up to the line now, or what?"

Quint looked up, annoyed, as if a stranger were bothering him. "Damn it, Prentice, if you'd made the formation this morning you would've heard the announcement. Now I've got to explain everything to you, as usual." He sighed. *"No,* we're not going up to the line. They're coming back *off* the line. We're supposed to meet them here, and then we're all going up to the line somewhere else."

"Oh. I see."

While talking, Quint had been unwinding the tin strip of a can of C rations; and Prentice saw now that Rand and all the others were eating, chewing crackers and spooning up cold meat-and-vegetable stew. The sight of it made him know he was terribly hungry, and he saw at once that Quint had caught him watching.

"And of course you missed breakfast, didn't you," Quint said.

"And of course you didn't draw your rations, so now you've missed lunch too. And do you know what that is?" He rose slowly from his duffelbag and stood blinking in fury behind his glasses. "Do you know what that is, Prentice? It's tough shit, that's what it is. You think Sam and I are going to give you any of ours, you're crazy as hell. And I'll tell you something else." He was shaking in anger now. Other men were looking at them with smiles of embarrassment, and Sam Rand was looking stolidly down at his can of stew. "I'll tell you something else. It's going to be just tough shit for you from now on, until you start learning how to take care of yourself. Is that clear? I've been looking out for you and cleaning up after you and wiping your goddam *nose* for you for about three God damned months, and I've had it. This is to let you know that I resign. You're on your own. Is that clear?"

A warm swelling had begun in Prentice's throat, and he was afraid he might start to cry like a child, right here in this Belgian field, in front of all these men. It was all he could do to keep his face straight.

Quint sat down on his bag again and dug his spoon savagely into his food. But he wasn't finished yet. "And now if there are any other questions," he said, "please keep them to yourself. I'm through. I've had it. I'm through being your goddam—" he hesitated over the final word, and when he brought it out it seemed calculated to be the cruellest word he could have chosen: "—your God damn father."

Chapter Three

When the men were throwing away their ration cans and lighting up cigarettes, not long after Prentice had managed to swallow his tears, it began to snow. Big, soft flakes came down at first from the darkening sky; then they thinned out into tiny points of white that whirled in the wind until the snow was flying rather than falling, making it hard to see anything except at close range, making it necessary to squint and blink to see anything at all.

Out of this white confusion a train of empty boxcars drew up to a stop on the tracks beside them. And soon, from far away across the field, came one and then another and then another of a long line of open trucks, each packed with standing men. The First Battalion, after its month in combat, was coming back off the line. There was an uneasy stirring among the replacements, most of whom got to their feet as the trucks came closer. What would they be like, these veterans? How would they feel about meeting men and boys fresh from the States, with the chalked numerals of Camp Shanks still plain on their helmets? Would they be friendly? Or would they laugh and point and shout obscenities?

Prentice began trying to make out individual faces in the first truck when it was still many yards away, but all he could see were their dull helmets, which were covered with combat netting. Then the trucks had drawn up and stopped, parallel to the tracks, and the men were shockingly visible as they dropped off over the tailgates and milled around in little groups of their own.

Most of them had beards. Some wore grimy woolen hoods under their helmets, and others had used towels or pieces of blanket for the same purpose. Most of their overcoats were burned at the hem and hanging in blackened shreds, probably from standing too close to campfires, and none of them had combat boots. Some wore old-style canvas leggings, stiff and shrunken; some had improvised their own leg wrappings with torn strips of cloth, and others let their pants hang indifferently in or outside the loose tops of their galoshes. Their faces were all brownish gray, with black lips that slackened occasionally to disclose surprisingly pink interiors, and these inner lips were the only clean parts of each man's face except for the bright, blank eyes. If they felt anything at all on seeing the replacements, they gave no sign.

" 'A' Company replacements over here," the headquarters sergeant called, holding his clipboard aloft in the whirling flakes. Beside him stood a ragged man who looked no different from the other veterans, and whose eyes seemed to be counting the replacements as they gathered around. "Shit," he said. "Is this all I get?"

The sergeant mumbled something apologetic, and when he backed away it was odd to hear him call the ragged man "sir."

"All right," the ragged man said, raising his voice to address the group. "My name's Lieutenant Agate, and you won't have any trouble remembering that because I'm the only officer left in this company." It was a high, rasping voice, and as he talked he kept taking a few steps forward and a few back, like a man in a cage. "We're gonna get on this train now, and it's no use

71

anybody asking me where we're going because I don't know. We're going south, I know that much, and we'll be going up to the line again very shortly. I'll try to get around and talk to you on the train, get you oriented a little bit; meantime I'll give you some advice. I'll advise you to keep your eyes and ears open and your mouths shut around my men. They're all sore as hell and so am I. We were supposed to be going back for a rest this morning, and now they've sprung this new shit on us. All right, that's all I've got to say."

In the boxcar, which had no straw on its splintered floor, the replacements huddled together to give the veterans most of the room. Prentice sat cold and hungry in a corner, as far away as possible from Quint, and he spent the afternoon watching the veterans and trying to figure them out. It was apparently the first time any of them had seen their duffel bags since before going into combat – the bags were all either soaked or frozen from having lain for a month in some supply dump – and most of the veterans who stayed awake were clawing through their moldy possessions like haggard ragpickers. The most conspicuous was a skinny, awkward man with the face of a clown and a voice that rose to falsetto shrieks of laughter. Probing in his bag, which bore the faded stenciling of the name Mays, he had pulled out a clean overseas cap and set it rakishly on his tangled head; then he found his wrinkled brass-buttoned tunic and pulled it on over his filthy field jacket.

"Hey, you guys ready to go on pass?" he kept shouting, delighted with the comic effect of his costume. "You guys wanna go to town and get laid tonight? Looka me, I'm all ready. Let's go!" And no matter how many times he said the same thing it drove him into uncontrollable giggles. "Let's go, hey! Let's go get laid tonight! Everybody ready? Let's go to town. Looka me, I'm all set to go!"

But however annoyingly shrill he grew it was clear that he commanded respect: the other veterans either ignored him or smiled at his antics; nobody told him to shut up. He was evidently a noncom of some kind, possibly a squad leader, though there were no chevrons on his old tunic; in any case he was someone who had proved himself and could therefore play the fool as much as he liked.

At the other extreme was a square-jawed man who seemed to want nothing more than a chance to sleep, and who incurred the merciless scorn of everyone around him:

"Hilton, move your useless ass."

"Damn it, Hilton, get your feet off my stuff."

"What the hell does Hilton need sleep for? Ain't he been sleeping his life away all month?"

Hilton would only blink and obey his tormentors with a mild, drugged smile of chronic humiliation, and Prentice watched him with a terrible sense of foreboding: it *was* possible, then, to be one of a handful of combat survivors and still be despised.

Soon after dark the train came to a stop and a pair of hands slid a carton of C rations into the car. It would be the first time Prentice had eaten all day, but he knew he would have to wait until one of the veterans opened the box and distributed the cans, and none of them seemed hungry. Most of them dropped out into the snow at the cry of "Piss call!" to take advantage of the stop. And it was during the same stop that Lieutenant Agate climbed into the car with a flashlight, followed by a big stout man who was evidently the first sergeant.

"All right, all you new men," Agate said. "I want to get your names and find out something about your background. First man, over here. What's your name?" And the flashlight beam fell on the squinting face of Sam Rand, who identified himself.

"How much infantry training you had, Rand?"

"Six weeks, sir, is all. Before that I had three years in the Engineers."

"Okay. Next man." And he went through the replacements that way until the light came full into Prentice's face, making him wince and feel the stares of everyone in the car.

"Prentice, sir. Six weeks' infantry training. Before that I had six weeks in the Air Force."

"Where were you before that?"

"Nowhere, sir." And as the laughter rose and broke around him he said, "I mean I was a civilian before that."

"Son of a bitch," said Lieutenant Agate, and the flashlight went away. He conferred quietly with the first sergeant for a while, and then the flashlight swept the replacements' end of the car again. "Weapons Platoon needs a man or two. Any of you men familiar with the light machine gun?"

"I am, sir."

"Who's that again?"

"Quint, sir."

"Okay, Quint; you report to Sergeant Rolls, soon as we get off the train, tell him you're assigned to his section. Got that? R-o-double l-s."

Another man was singled out to serve with a mortar section; the rest of them were to be riflemen. Then, as an afterthought, Agate said: "Oh, hey, wait. Second Platoon needs a runner. Anybody?" The flashlight came into Prentice's eyes again. "You want the runner's job?"

"All right, sir." And he was told to report to a Sergeant Brewer. He wasn't wholly sure what a runner's job was, but he suspected it was something easier and safer than being a rifleman; he suspected too that Agate had picked him because he was the youngest, or maybe because he looked the least competent. Still, it had a nice individual sound to it – the runner – and apparently there was only one for each platoon. Didn't that mean it might carry a certain amount of responsibility?

"All right, here's the story," Agate said, raising his voice to include everyone in the car. "We're going into the Seventh Army sector, down in Alsace. Looks like we're turning into one of these bastard divisions they shove all over the map to plug up holes. Anyway, we'll be under the command of the French First Army, whatever the hell that means, and we'll be going up to the line tomorrow some time. We'll be relieving the Third Division. That's all I know for now. There's gonna be trucks waiting for us when we get off the train. Meantime you better get as much sleep as you can."

Prentice was lucky enough to find Sergeant Brewer soon after the train had stopped, and he was lucky too in that Sergeant Brewer turned out to be a big, kindly Westerner with pleasant manners. "You're the new runner, right?" he asked, standing in the snow with his gloved hand enfolding Prentice's in a painfully reassuring clinch. "What's your name again? Okay, Prentice, I'll fix it for you to meet the squad leaders and everything later on, soon as we're settled." And Prentice had to fight an impulse to cling to Sergeant Brewer, whimpering for protection. "Right now, though, you better hurry along and get into that truck."

The slow ride in the truck convoy, whining in first and second gear over endless mountain roads – somebody said they were in the Vosges – was unbelievably cold. After a while Prentice could feel nothing of his legs from the knees down; it was useless to try flexing his toes or stamping his feet. It could have been two hours or five hours or eight that they traveled; he had lost all sense of time in the cold that held him sitting as stiff as a corpse. When they stopped at last it was almost impossible for him to stand and move. He dropped off and fell in the snow, and it was several seconds before he could get up.

They were quartered for the rest of the night in a big shelled-out factory deep between the slopes of two great hills. It was better than sleeping outdoors, but not much, for all the factory's windows and ragged sections of its walls were open to the wind. Working in the glow of matches and candle stubs, they made their beds on long waist-high work tables that were cluttered with metal scraps and bits of broken glass.

It was still dark when Prentice woke up in a convulsion of coughing, hearing a loud, tearful voice across the room that sounded remarkably like his own:

"Oh Jesus, *help* me, somebody, I'm *sick*! I can't *breathe*! Oh Jesus – please – Medic! Medic! Somebody *help* me; I'm *sick* . . ."

His coughing had forced him upright on the work table. He began to retch and leaned over to drop clots of phlegm on the floor; then all at once, still retching, he felt hands gripping his arms and a flashlight was blazing in his face, and he dimly saw that one of the men holding him wore the white-encircled red cross of the medics on his helmet.

"What's the matter, kid? You the one that called out?"

"No – somebody else – over there."

". . . Oh Jesus, somebody please *help* me . . ."

The flashlight and the hands went away, and in a minute he saw the medics helping a tall, stumbling, weeping figure down one of the aisles between the work tables and away into the darkness.

In the morning they were issued ammunition in what seemed unnecessary amounts: enough rifle clips to fill the cartridge belt, many additional clips in three cotton bandoliers that hung crisscross from the shoulders, and two hand grenades apiece.

For half an hour or so they lingered in the factory to work over their gear, each man separating the things to be left behind, in duffelbags and bedrolls, from the things to be carried into the field. Prentice worked not with the Second Platoon but with the much smaller company headquarters group, which was composed of the other platoon runners, the bazooka man, a couple of communications men, and several other specialists whose jobs he didn't understand. The only one who talked to him was a very short boy named Owens — he looked too small to have been taken into the Army — who was the runner for Weapons Platoon.

"Take plenty of cigarettes," Owens counseled him, "and take all the socks you've got, even if it seems like too many. You don't change your socks often enough, you wind up with trenchfoot. And take toothpaste too, if you've got any. I know that seems funny, but toothpaste comes in handy as hell. Sometimes you brush your teeth, it's almost as good as getting a night's sleep." The only toothpaste Prentice could find in his bag was a big Economy-Size tube of Ipana that he must have acquired in the PX at Camp Pickett, and whether it seemed funny or not he stuffed it into one of his shirt pockets, along with his toothbrush.

When they moved out it was to march five miles to something called the Forward Assembly Area. At first the march seemed easy, with so little to carry, and the action of walking helped to keep the cold out, but before long Prentice's knees had gone soft and he felt feverish. The loaded cartridge belt was a heavy drag at his waist and the bandolier straps were cutting into his neck.

". . . Mutt and Jeff!" Lieutenant Agate was calling, walking backwards at the head of the column, and Prentice saw with a start that he was smiling straight at him.

". . . guys look like Mutt and Jeff," he called again, and this time Prentice got the point: that he and Owens, who was walking beside him, made a comic contrast of tall and short.

"How's the cough, kid?" the lieutenant called, and when Prentice tried to say "Okay, sir," he found he had lost his voice. He tried it again, and nothing but a whisper came out. Finally he shaped his cracked lips into a smile and nodded, hoping that would take care of it, and as he walked he tried to clear his throat.

"Hey, Owens?" he tried to say. "Listen. I've lost my voice." And he managed enough of a squeak to make Owens look up.

"What?"

"I've lost my *voice*. I can't *talk*."

"Laryngitis, I guess." Owens had his own problems. He'd said this morning that he thought he had dysentery, and he didn't seem to be feeling any better.

"All right," the lieutenant was calling now. "Spread it out. Five paces apart."

The Forward Assembly Area, somewhere up past the artillery positions, was a thinly wooded field of snow in which they were told to dig two-man foxholes. The digging quickly exhausted Prentice – his quivering jabs with the entrenching tool became less and less effectual – but Owens helped him out, and before long they had a hole deep enough to be considered finished. For what seemed hundreds of yards in all directions the field was ravaged by black holes and mounds of thrown-up earth. Everywhere men crouched and dug, or sat in their holes and waited, or gathered in nervous little groups to talk about what they were heading for, which was said to be something called the Colmar Pocket. First Battalion was to lead the attack, and their first objective was to be the taking of a town called Horbourg, around which elements of the 3rd Division were said to have been embattled for several days. It all sounded unreal to Prentice.

"How long," he squeaked to Owens, "– how long do you think we'll be staying here?"

"Oh, probably till morning. I don't think they'd have us digging in if they figured on moving us out any sooner."

But he was wrong: they moved out that same afternoon. A shelled-out village, some three miles to the rear of Horbourg, was the jumping-off point for the attack. "A" Company arrived there to find the place a jumble of men and machines: the broken streets, strung with many-colored communications wire, were crawling with vehicles of all kinds, and there were men from the 57th, the 3rd, and a French unit, all busy and hurrying in what seemed a state of total confusion. There were a few civilians too, mostly old men and women in black, with shy, bewildered faces. It puzzled Prentice at first that they seemed to be speaking German, and that the spattered road signs were in German too, until a dim store of schoolroom knowledge reminded him that Alsace was only technically a part of France.

"You hear what I heard?" Owens asked him as the column sat resting against a shrapnel-scarred wall, waiting for Agate to finish his briefing with a number of other officers. "They say Horbourg's changed hands three times in the past two days."

"Changed what?"

"Changed hands. Between us and the Germans."

"Oh. No, I hadn't heard that." His voice was still either a squeak or a husk, and he was weak and lightheaded from the day of marching and digging and marching again. He hoped Agate's briefing would take a long time, so that he could stay seated on this wet sidewalk with his back against this wall. He wasn't sure if he'd be able to get up and move again.

The orders, according to Agate, were that they would move out soon after nightfall. An artillery barrage would be laid down on Horbourg at seven o'clock, and then they'd go in. In the meantime, each platoon was assigned to a separate cellar or stable in the village for resting and waiting. The password for the night was "Mickey Mouse."

Prentice was called upon to deliver several routine messages to Sergeant Brewer while they waited, and he found his fever and fatigue dissolving into a kind of appalled exhilaration that felt nothing at all like fear. He hoped he was being noticed as he walked slowly but conspicuously alone down the streets of churned snow, where everyone else was moving in groups, and he took pride in delivering his small messages, even though the effort of speaking made him twist and rise on tiptoe before any sound came out. He hoped the men who overheard him wouldn't think this chirping was his normal voice.

Late in the afternoon the company cooks brought food up to the village for the first hot meal they'd had since Belgium – salmon patties, dehydrated potatoes, and canned fruit salad – and most of the men seemed in high spirits as they sat or squatted over their mess kits in the street.

"What kind of catshit is this?"

"Salmon-patty catshit, that's what kind."

Prentice looked around for Quint but couldn't see him, though he did catch a glimpse of Sam Rand soberly chewing and talking with some other men. It occurred to him that Sam Rand was the only man in sight he really knew, and that of all the others he knew only three or four by name. Even so, he began to feel a sentimental affection for all of them. Very soon now, all these strangers might well be his friends.

But he found he could eat only a few mouthfuls without retching, and after he'd thrown away most of his meal he felt the sickness closing in on him again.

He found a broken slab of concrete to sit down on, and wondered if he dared to light a cigarette. The worst thing about Horbourg now was that it was three miles away: he felt it would take everything he had to walk three miles. The scene around him began to float and blur, and if there had been a place to lay his head he would have fallen instantly asleep.

"Move over, old buddy," said John Quint's voice; and there he came, lugging a machine-gun barrel on his shoulder, slowly strutting out of the crowd with his cold pipe clenched upside down in his teeth. He had apparently forgotten that he and Prentice were not on speaking terms. "You look like I feel," he said, letting himself carefully down on the slab.

"It's funny, you know? I felt—"

"What the Christ's the matter with your voice?"

"I don't know. Laryngitis or something. But I mean it's funny, you know? I felt pretty good just before we ate, and now I'm sick as hell again. I guess it comes and goes."

"That's what's the matter, all right. Same with me. And it's going to come a whole hell of a lot worse before it goes."

It was comforting to have Quint there; it seemed to help things come back into focus. Some men nearby were pointing upward, and Prentice looked up to discover that the rich blue of the sky was intricately marked with white vapor trails. Aerial combat was taking place between fighter planes too high to see except as dots at the head of each trail, like the planes that used to spell out "Pepsi-Cola" high over New York on summer afternoons. But the act of looking up doubled Prentice over in a seizure of coughing that twisted him with pain and left his head hanging between his knees.

"Prentice, look," Quint said, and at first Prentice thought he meant look up at the planes; but that wasn't what he meant. "Look. Let's quit kidding ourselves. You know what I think? I think we've both got pneumonia. Either that or we're pretty far along in the process of getting it. We've got all the damn symptoms."

"Well, but how about all these other guys? How come *they* don't have it? Guys that have been sleeping in the snow for a month in the Bulge?"

"Oh, balls, Prentice. It's got nothing to do with that. People get pneumonia in April and May. Babies get it. Athletes in top condition get it. Old ladies get it walking around the dimestore. It's a disease, that's all, and when you get a disease you're supposed to go to the hospital."

Prentice thought it over. "You mean you want to go back?"

"I mean I think we both ought to go to Agate and tell him we're sick. Tell him we can't make it, and go back to the aid station. Right now. Doesn't that sound sensible?"

And the remarkable thing was that Quint's face, owlish and bespectacled, heavily fringed with beard, had an expression that Prentice had never seen on it before: a look of defiance clearly mixed with pleading. For the first time in all these months, Quint was asking Prentice for guidance, instead of the other way around.

It was an oddly dramatic moment – exactly like a moment in the movies when the music stops dead on the soundtrack while the hero makes up his mind – and it didn't take Prentice long to decide what his answer would be. It didn't even matter that it had to come out in his absurd falsetto. "No," he said. "I don't want to."

Quint put his pipe back in his mouth and looked down at his overshoes.

"I mean, don't let me stop you, Quint, if that's what you want to do; you go ahead. I'm staying, that's all." He knew he was laying himself open to a charge of false heroics, but he didn't care – and whether Quint saw the opening or not, he didn't take advantage of it.

"Okay," he said.

"I mean after this Horbourg business is over maybe I'll go back, but not before. It's just a thing I'd never feel right about doing, that's all."

"*Okay*," Quint said. "You've made your point."

And that was the end of their talk, though the weight of it hung like something palpable between them as they blinked at each other and then avoided each other's eyes.

"A" Company led off in the battalion column that night. Third Platoon went first; then came the command group, or "Headquarters Platoon"; then came the First and then the Second, with Weapons Platoon bringing up the rear. They walked in strict silence most of the way to Horbourg, five paces apart on either side of the road, each man with his eyes fixed on the back of the man ahead. Then they waited, crouched in the dark roadside ditches, for their artillery support.

When it came, in great fluttering rushes overhead that ended in earth-rocking explosions, lighting up the sky, it seemed to go on forever, and when it was over it seemed that nothing could be left alive in Horbourg. Trembling in the ditch, Prentice forced all his attention on the dim shape of Owens's back. When it rose and wavered silently upward he scrambled after it, up to the surface of the road again, hearing a muffled rustle and clink of equipment as the man behind him did the same. He was very conscious of the sound of his own breathing as he walked, a rapid, shallow rasp in and out of his nose in counterpoint to the faint steady hum of the wind through his helmet. He wished he could be close enough to the other men to see if they were still carrying their rifles on the sling, as he was, or if they'd taken them in their hands for greater readiness. He had just about decided to unsling his rifle when Owens's back floated up close enough to reveal the vertical line of the slung rifle beside his helmet, black against the snow; so he kept his own rifle where it was.

Almost before he realized it, the ghost-white fields on either side of the road gave way to the dark shapes of houses – they must be *in* Horbourg by now, or at least on its outskirts – and without worrying about Owens he slid the sling off his shoulder and carried his rifle at port arms with his gloved finger trembling on the safety and slipping experimentally in and out of the trigger guard. Then he thought it might look silly if he were the only man in the column doing that, so he put it back on the sling. But then Owens's back came up close enough to show that *he* was walking at port arms now; and off it came again.

Gradually, and then suddenly, the road ahead was illuminated with a wavering orange glow: it was a house on fire, one of the houses on the other side of the road. As they moved past it, the individual shapes and shadows of the men were clearly visible – for several seconds Prentice could even see the dirty brown nap of Owens's overcoat and the dirty green squares of netting on his helmet – and a thought occurred to him that was instantly put into words by the man behind him: "Jesus, we're perfect targets."

But except for the hiss and crackle of timbers in flames the night remained dead silent until they were well past the burning house, enclosed once more in the protection of darkness. Prentice resumed the difficult job of watching Owens's helmet, until it suddenly came up very close and he realized Owens had stopped. He stopped too, and moved back a few steps. Apparently the whole column had come to a halt.

Glancing down and to the left, he saw the unmistakable shape of a man lying in the snow. It struck him as odd for a second – what the hell was he lying *down* for? – until he realized the man was dead. It was impossible to tell whether he was German or French or American. He looked back at Owens's helmet just in time to see it turn and disclose the pale oval of his face. Owens was whispering something to him, and at first he thought it must be some comment on the dead man. But it wasn't.

"What's that?" he whispered back.

"Send up the First Platoon; pass it on."

And Prentice turned around to face the dark blur of the stranger behind him. "Send up the First Platoon," he whispered. "Pass it on."

Soon, from the rear, there came a scuffle of overshoes and a muted creak and jingle of equipment as the men of the First Platoon moved up to receive their orders.

Did everyone have better night vision than Prentice? It was all he could do to concentrate on the floating shape of Owens's helmet, waiting to see if it would turn again.

It turned. "Send up the Second Platoon; pass it on."

He was pleased that he'd heard it right the first time. He turned back and repeated the words, and in a little while the Second Platoon came plodding up past him in the darkness. Then he waited, studying the helmet, for what seemed a very long time. And the next order came as a stunning surprise:

"Send Prentice up."

He went dogtrotting past Owens with his heart in his mouth, past a number of other shadowy figures and on up to Lieutenant Agate, whose anger was visible even in the dark.

"Damn it, boy, where you been? When I say Second Platoon, that means you."

"I know, sir; I'm sorry, I—"

"All right. Logan, take him and show him where the hell they are. And hurry up."

Logan was the communications sergeant, tall and sardonic. "Christ," he whispered. "Are you gonna start fucking up already? Can't you stay on the ball? You're the Second Platoon runner – can't you get that straight in your head? Now you're holding up the whole fucking works."

"I know; I – I just didn't think."

"Well you better start thinking, kiddo. This is important."

He knew it was important, and he stumbled along as fast as he could beside Logan, weak with embarrassment.

"There," Logan said. "See that house? That's where your platoon is. Now for Christ's fucking sake don't forget it."

And Prentice stared at the dim face of the house for all he was worth. The way he committed it to memory was that its roof, instead of sloping, was built in steps. "Okay," he whispered, and went loping after Logan, afraid he might lose him as they ran back to the column.

He was able to recognize Owens because of his shortness, and fell into place behind him again. But the brief run had winded him and he began to cough wretchedly, trying his best to stifle it; he heard someone say, "Shut that bastard up!" but he had to cough again and again, doubled over with his fist in his mouth. The spasms held him blind and crouching for a long time, until time itself seemed to have stopped, and when he straightened up at last and opened his eyes to the whirling darkness, Owens was gone. He took several faltering steps forward, but Owens wasn't there – and neither was anyone else. There was nothing ahead but snow and blackness. He spun around and looked behind him: nobody; nothing but the empty road and, far in the distance, the glow of the burning house. He was alone.

He ran forward, the straps biting his neck and the two grenades bouncing heavily on his ribs. He had no idea where he was going, but there seemed to be nothing to do but run. Once he tripped and nearly went sprawling over something that felt like a soft log and proved, when he looked back, to be another corpse. Then finally he made out some movement ahead, across the road, and he ran in that direction. It was a trotting column of four or five men – good God, were they Germans? No; Americans – and he ran up to the first of them, gasping for breath.

"Is this – is this Headquarters Platoon?"

The man didn't answer or even slow down.

"I said is this Headquarters Platoon?"

And at that instant the air was split by a high whistling shriek and a tremendous *Slam!* with a burst of yellow in the road. All the men hit the road on their bellies at once, and Prentice fell with them. Another shriek, another *Slam!,* and they all scurried to fall again behind the shelter of a big nameless shape several yards away – it seemed to be a truck lying on its side.

"Mortars . . ." somebody said, but that was all Prentice could hear except the repeated Shriek – *Slam!* Shriek – *Slam!* and the whir and ping of flying fragments. Then from somewhere not far away came a shy, tremulous voice that rose to a frantic childish cry of shock and pain: "Medic? Medic? Oh Jesus – *Medic?* Oh Je-*heesus, Medic! Medic! . . .*"

Five or six more mortar shells hit the road while Prentice and the others lay behind the fallen truck, which had turned out not to be a truck at all but an armored halftrack; and finally there was an abrupt, ringing silence. One by one the shadowy men rose into a crouch and ran, and Prentice went up to the first man.

"Where's Headquarters Platoon?"

But the man moved past him without a word.

"Look, excuse me, I – where's Headquarters Platoon?"

But the next man ran past him too, and the next, and the next, and then there was only one left.

"For Christ's sake *tell* me. Where's Headquarters Platoon?"

His terrible voice broke into a womanish wail on the "toon" and he knew it sounded as if he were crying, but at least it was

87

enough to make the man turn around, and he was close enough to be recognized: it was Mays, the clown from the boxcar. Prentice tried to atone for his tearful-sounding voice by staggering a little more than necessary, to prove he was really sick.

"Who do you want? Agate?" Mays said. "Come on, then."

Prentice followed him, deeply ashamed both of the "toon" and the fraudulent stagger. The men led him back some fifty yards down the road, turned in between two houses so abruptly that he almost lost them, and went clambering down a flight of pitch-black cellar stairs. A door opened onto a blanket hung as a blackout curtain, and beyond the blanket, inside the cellar, Agate and all the other headquarters men were huddled in the weak yellow light of a single candle.

Prentice looked quickly around at Mays and his squad, to see if they were laughing at him or looking at him with contempt, but they paid him no attention at all. Mays was talking rapidly now with Agate while the others stood by; then Agate nodded and gave some curt instructions, and they went out again as quickly as they'd come.

The cellar contained a great deal of mildewed furniture, and several of the men were sitting in chairs; that meant it was all right to sit down. He found a deep upholstered armchair and sank into it as if into a morass of self-abasement, staring tragically into the candlelight. He had fucked up badly, twice. If anyone wanted to give him the upbraiding he deserved, now was the time. He would sit here and take it, however it came.

But nobody looked at him, and after a while it began to seem that they weren't ignoring him out of disgust; they simply hadn't noticed he was there, and possibly they hadn't noticed he'd been missing in the first place. He glanced furtively at Logan, ready to accept any kind of derision from him, but Logan was wholly absorbed in his hand radio, speaking in a tense monotone, repeating words that Prentice was now dimly aware of having heard ever since his arrival in the cellar.

"Donkey Nan," he was saying, "Donkey Nan, this is Donkey Dog, Donkey Dog. Do you read me? Over." Then he paused, listening, and started again. "Donkey Nan, Donkey Nan . . ."

A soft moan came from the shadows along the far wall, and Prentice made out the figure of a medic crouched over an inert form on the floor: it must have been the wounded man, the man who'd cried out on the road.

". . . this is Donkey Dog, Donkey Dog. Do you read me? Over." And Logan turned to the lieutenant. "Can't seem to get 'em, sir."

"Shit. Okay, get the runner. Where's what's-his-name? The kid?"

And Prentice bolted clumsily to his feet.

"Go on over to your platoon," Agate told him. "Find out why they're not answering. If their radio's broken or anything, bring Brewer back to me. Got that?"

"Yessir."

"You know where they are now?"

"Yessir," he said, though all he could remember was a house with a stepped roof: he had no idea where it was. As he hurried across the cellar floor the house was jarred by a great *Slam!* and then another, and another.

"That's artillery this time," somebody was saying. "That's eighty-eights."

"No, it's both," somebody else said. "It's mortars *and* eighty-eights."

Prentice paused near the door and looked back at Agate. Was he supposed to go anyway? In the middle of all this? Or was he supposed to wait until the barrage was over? But Agate had turned away and was talking to someone else.

Go anyway. At least it was better than going back to ask. A grizzled, old-looking man named Luchek was standing wide-eyed with his back to the wall, beside the blackout curtain. "Jesus, kid," he said. "You going out *now?*"

"Guess I've got to," Prentice said, beginning to feel very much like the hero of a war movie, and he stood with his hand on the blanket, waiting for a pause in the shelling. He looked back once again at Agate, but Agate was still turned away. Then he slipped out around the curtain and ran up the steps.

There was nothing but silence as he ran down the path to the road, and not until he'd almost gained the road did he fully realize, in a panic, that he didn't know which way to turn. Right or left?

He decided desperately on left. But how far away was the house with the stepped roof, and how would he know how far to go before giving it up and trying the other direction? He had just made the turn into the road, heading left, when a rapid fluttering rush of air sent him sprawling heavily on his chest, and *Slam!* It was louder than the mortar shells: this must be artillery. Then came another fluttering rush and another *Slam!* and a number of small objects, hard but not heavy, fell across his buttocks and thighs. They couldn't be shell fragments; they were chunks of broken roof or wall.

He was up and running again, looking urgently at the dark passing face of each house. Shriek-*Slam!* Shriek-*Slam!* Those were mortar shells – he was numbly proud of being able to tell the difference now – and they were clearly so far away that he didn't even bother to hit the ground. But then came the rush of an eighty-eight so shockingly brief that its huge explosion caught him still on his feet: he felt the jolt and saw the flash of it as he fell headlong on his grenades, and he heard the fragments zip and whine away very close to him. He was still lying there, uncertain whether to wait or get up and run again, when he lifted his helmet away from his eyes and saw the house with the stepped roof, no more than ten or fifteen yards away. He got up and ran.

"Who's that? Is that Prentice?" said Sergeant Brewer's voice from a dark cluster of men standing just inside the door.

"Yes." And Prentice went stumbling in among them. Only later did he realize that they probably should have said "Mickey" and "Mouse."

"The lieutenant," he said, and started coughing. "The lieutenant wants to know why you're not answering the whad-dyacallit, the radio. He says – says if it's broken—"

But it wasn't broken: Brewer's radio man was crouched and fussing with the dials, and before Prentice could finish his sentence he had made contact. "Donkey Dog," he was saying, "Donkey Dog, this is Donkey Nan, Donkey Nan. I'm reading you loud and clear. Over."

Brewer took the radio and started talking into it, probably to Agate; Prentice couldn't follow the words and wouldn't have been very interested if he could. He leaned panting against the wall and gave in to a sense of triumph. He had made it.

The jogging run back to the headquarters cellar was very short and uneventful; only a few mortar shells came in far down the road, probably at the place where the ruined halftrack lay. He hadn't exactly expected anyone to shake his hand and say, "Nice work, Prentice," when he got back to the cellar, but still it was faintly disappointing that nobody did, and that nobody even seemed to notice he was back as he dragged himself over to his easy chair and sat down again.

Then suddenly both Agate and Logan were looking at him with stern faces. "How far away are they, kid?" Agate said, and Prentice felt his chest go tight, as if he were a suspect on a witness stand.

91

"About a hundred yards, sir. To the left."

"A hundred *yards?*"

"A hundred feet, I mean. Thirty yards, something like that. Maybe fifty."

They both turned away again, and only after several minutes did he realize that they hadn't been grilling him: they hadn't been trying to find out if he'd really made the trip or faked it, or to see if he would exaggerate the distance. They wanted to know how far away it was, for reasons of their own; and this was such a great relief that he felt free to relax for the first time all day. He even felt free to take off his helmet and tenderly finger his scalp, where the roots of his matted hair were sore from wearing the helmet so long.

The odd coughing noise of American mortars began from somewhere near the cellar: the mortar section of Weapons Platoon had opened up to return the enemy shelling. As he listened, it occurred to him that this was the first time anyone in "A" Company had fired a shot – he hadn't yet heard any machine guns or rifles. Could this be all that was meant by an "attack"? A duel of mortars and artillery, while you sat in an upholstered chair by candlelight?

Gradually, sitting there, he became aware of an oddly familiar, civilian smell in his nostrils – a yellow, minty smell – and of a wet glutinous mass that had fastened the left side of his shirt to his chest, under one of the grenades and deep inside the layers of winter clothing. It was the Economy-Size tube of Ipana, crushed and ruptured from his falls on the road.

There wasn't much sleep to be had in the cellar that night, and Prentice got almost none. He had to stand his share of guard duty outside the cellar door – more than his share once, when Owens came moaning about having dysentery and having to lie down –

and when he wasn't on guard he lay awake on the floor, coughing and sweating in fever, listening to the intermittent sounds of the shelling. Once, during a lull in the noise, Logan roused him to take the lieutenant over to the platoon for a conference with Brewer; another time, after an incendiary shell had crashed through the roof of the house, he had to join in the general staggering upstairs and help put out the fire.

Just before dawn he dozed off long enough to have some kind of grotesque, instantly forgotten dream, and the first thing that hit him when he woke up was the smell of frying eggs. Lieutenant Agate had found a stove and a frying pan in the cellar. He had also found three fresh eggs, which he was solemnly cooking for himself, and a bottle of wine from which he took long, relishing swigs as the eggs smoked and spattered in the pan. He had taken off his helmet and all his equipment: he looked cozy and self-indulgent and not at all like a company commander as he went about his breakfast.

"Donkey Oboe, Donkey Oboe," Logan was saying into his radio, and then "Donkey Nan, Donkey Nan" and "Donkey Key" and "Donkey Easy." He was calling all the platoons and telling them that they'd be moving out at oh-six-hundred – and that, according to Prentice's watch, was five minutes from now.

The lieutenant stood up, wiped a trickle of egg yolk from his chin, and lobbed the wine bottle crashing into a corner. Then he put his helmet on over his dirty hair, buckled himself into his gear, and said, "Okay, let's get going. No overcoats. Leave 'em here and we'll send back for 'em later."

Prentice hated to leave his overcoat. He knew the idea of not wearing it was to assure greater maneuverability in action, but this seemed hardly to apply in his case: he felt unable to maneuver at all, overcoat or not.

When they moved cautiously out of the cellar, toward the

road, he was grateful for every chance to stop and lean against the wall. The rifle hung heavy in his shaking hands, and the equipment sagging from his shoulders and waist seemed an intolerable weight. Was it possible that he'd run and fallen and gotten up and run again, only last night?

The early morning light revealed several new and surprising things about the road, or street: that all its houses were maimed, with shattered windows and ragged walls, and that a cluster of three dead Germans lay in shocking stillness directly in front of the headquarters house. They had apparently been dead for days: their hands and faces seemed to be made of putty, and their eyes were like dusty marbles. A little farther on, two or three house away, they came upon a dead American. He was face down at the roadside, partly covered with snow thrown up by passing vehicles, but enough of him was exposed to show that he had curly brown hair and a snub-nosed, full-lipped profile. His skin was the same color as the Germans', skin that looked incapable of ever having been alive. But it was his uniform that affected Prentice most: how could anyone be dead who wore these terribly familiar clothes and straps, with this terribly familiar canteen against his right buttock?

There was an intermittent crack and stutter of small-arms fire now in another part of town, probably another company's sector; and Agate and the other Headquarters men were moving with a stealthiness that showed they expected a burst of fire at any moment. They hugged each wall and hurried, one at a time, across the open spaces between each house. Second Platoon was following close behind them, with equal slowness and care. As they approached the ruined halftrack Prentice saw that its markings were French, and that the body of a very small French soldier, wearing a G.I. field jacket, lay primly on his back six feet away, apparently blown from the wreckage.

When they came to the corner of an intersection Agate stopped, motioning for his men to stop too and stay close to the wall. Then he beckoned for the Second Platoon to come forward: evidently the platoon would brave it into the new street while the command group held back. Sergeant Brewer held back too, crouched against the wall with Agate, while his rifle squads moved on around the corner. Only after the last of the squads was out of sight – a group that included the portly figure of Sam Rand – only then did he go after them, followed by his radio man and his platoon medic, and this troubled Prentice a little. Weren't platoon leaders supposed to lead? But then, company commanders were supposed to lead too, and so were battalion commanders, and so were generals; it was too confusing to think about. He lowered his rifle and allowed the butt to rest on the ground, which brought a small relief to the muscles of his right arm, and he looked down at the trampled snow with longing, wishing he could let his knees go slack, slide forward against the wall, and lie down in it.

From around the corner came a stunning sound straight out of the movies: the *B-d-d-rapp! B-d-d-rapp!* of a German burp gun. There was silence, then shouting, then the slower, louder, chugging fire of an American B.A.R. and the irregular crack of several rifles. The burp gun opened up again, or maybe it was another one, and an instant later it was impossible to pick out the separate sounds: the whole street had become a solid uproar of gunfire and spanging, whining ricochets.

Prentice brought his rifle up to a trembling port arms and fixed his eyes on the lieutenant. What the hell was he going to do now? Just stand here? He just stood there, and it wasn't long before the noise was over. Then he moved on around the corner and led Prentice and the others into the new street, which was lightly filled with smoke and brick dust. Riflemen were crouched in doorways or running in both directions and shouting at each other, their faces pink with excitement; halfway down the block the medic knelt beside a man who sat smiling against the wall with his pants leg torn open to expose a red blotch high on his thigh. And nearer, across the street, three German soldiers were slowly approaching with their hands locked over their bare heads, followed by a B.A.R. man who held his weapon pointed at their backs. One of the prisoners, with very long blond hair that hung against his cheeks, was bleeding from the face.

Apparently, for all the noise, it had been only a minor skirmish, a token resistance by the Germans before they surrendered; and the man with the leg wound – a "million-dollar wound," somebody called it – was the platoon's only casualty.

"Donkey Oboe," Logan was chanting, "This is Donkey Dog, Donkey Dog . . ."

Riflemen, working in twos, were forcing their way into houses now, smashing doors open with their rifle butts: apparently the idea was to search each house on the block for enemy soldiers. But that was as much of the logic of the morning as Prentice could follow. Agate and the other headquarters men were moving back and around to another block now, evidently to check on the progress of another platoon; and as Prentice swayed in their wake, repeatedly stopping to cough, he grew less and less able to make sense of the sights and sounds around him. Things seemed to happen out of sequence, as in a movie that someone has mindlessly cut and scrambled and spliced together at random. The only continuity was the problem of keeping up, and this soon became a matter of studying Agate's overshoes as they rose and fell in the snow, sometimes slowly, sometimes flying into a run, sometimes stopping for long, long waits.

Once, when they stopped for a while in a little courtyard,

Prentice let his head sink against the wall to rest, and he didn't realize he'd gone to sleep on his feet until a distant burst of machine-gun fire made his eyes pop open to see a German soldier coming straight at him, less than five yards away. It took him a second of dodging back and fumbling with his rifle before he saw that the German was unarmed: he was another prisoner, flushed from one of the houses, and behind him came four or five more, under the guard of a rifleman who chuckled in passing at Prentice's surprise.

He whirled around to look for Agate and found him still there, but over on the other side of the courtyard now, talking with some of his men. An ambulance was there, too, with its doors open – it must have driven up while he was sleeping – and litter bearers were bringing a wounded man toward it while Agate and the others watched. Prentice went over to join them as they slid the stretcher gently into the ambulance. The man lay very still under a blanket, wide-eyed and white-lipped, his face powdered with brick dust. From the muttered talk around him Prentice gathered that he was an officer, a battalion artillery observer, and that his wound was very severe. But then the whole scene swam and vanished as he went into another of his coughing fits; when it was over he found Agate looking at him in a speculative way.

"Why don't you get in there too, kid?" he said. "Go ahead, if you want to." And one of the medics was tentatively holding open the ambulance doors.

"No, sir, that's okay. I'll stay." As soon as the squeaking words were out he began to regret them. If only Quint had been there, to say it was all right and to go with him, he would have gone.

"Okay, it's up to you," Agate said as the ambulance doors slammed shut. "Let's get going."

Some time later – or was it earlier? – he followed Agate's

cautious back around a corner into some kind of public square and saw him fall flat on his face. Another man fell with him, and it wasn't until Prentice had instinctively fallen too that he realized they were under fire: the ricochets were among them like hornets. In no time at all he was back safe around the corner, having somehow scrambled up and run with the others. Agate, coming last, was the only one who seemed to know what had happened – there were snipers somewhere high above them – and the only one who'd thought fast enough to return their fire. He came crouching and walking backwards, managing to get off two or three rounds from his carbine.

"Fucking church steeple," he said, and Prentice wasn't even aware of having seen a church steeple. "Some crazy bastards up there tryna pick us off."

Much later, Prentice was able to figure out what the lieutenant chose to do about it – to call for several riflemen to divert the snipers' fire to another part of the square, and then to call up the Bazooka man to do the job from here – but at the time, all he could concentrate on was that the Bazooka man's name was Magill, that Magill looked very dirty and awkward as he knelt at the corner, and that his weapon made an ear-stopping roar when it went off. Then he was following the others around the corner again, and he saw that there was indeed a church with a brutally amputated steeple: the whole rising structure ended in a blunt mass of naked plaster and carpentry from which wisps of smoke were still curling.

And it must have been in the same square that he watched two litter bearers come trotting in perfect rhythmic unison through the rubble, using their legs with the skill and delicacy of dancers so that their upper bodies wouldn't jog the load: from the waist up they could have been men on bicycles. The man on their stretcher rode as smoothly as if he were in a hospital bed, and

Prentice thought with envy of how dreamlike and sweet it must be to be borne that way, floating horizontally away to rest and peace and care. In the middle of the square the bearers came to a halt and eased the stretcher gently to the ground. They rested for a few seconds, standing wide-legged with their hands on their knees, like winded athletes. Then, still moving as one, they squatted to take up their load again; but almost as soon as they'd raised it they set it carefully down, and both of them crouched over the wounded man, tenderly lifting his blanket to feel and scrutinize him. And then, with a terrible abruptness, they tore off the blanket, tipped the stretcher high on its side, and sent the man rolling hideously out into the slush. They didn't even look down at him as they turned and ran, heading back to wherever they'd come from, one of them hauling the collapsed stretcher on his shoulder and the other humping along at his side. All their unanimity and grace was gone: they ran with the heavy-footed clumsiness of exhausted laborers.

By noon the day had turned mild and almost warm. The snow was melting rapidly, there was a continual dripping from the roofs, and there were spoors of sweat on Agate's dirty face. Little clusters of civilians had begun to appear on the streets, looking oddly out of place. They would venture bashfully up to the sidewalks and try to speak with the soldiers, apparently trying to explain that all the Germans had left town, until they were shouted and gestured back into their cellars.

Some time in the afternoon, while Agate's overshoes plodded along some other street, a brief barrage of enemy mortar shells sent everyone clambering and tumbling into the cellar of the nearest house. Prentice, almost fainting from the effort of it, heard somebody yell "Yeeow!" and thought at first that the man was hit, but it turned out to be a cry of joy: the far wall of the cellar was packed to the ceiling with bottles of wine. And for what seemed a disgracefully long time after that, long after the mortars had stopped, Lieutenant Agate and his men sat guzzling on the floor with all the furtive pleasure of boys playing hooky from school. Someone had handed Prentice a bottle and he gulped it as if it were the only medicine in the world that could save him. It made him shudder but it sent a wonderful strengthening warmth through his chest and back, and he knew that if Agate didn't get him out of here soon he would drink and drink until he lay insensible on the floor. But just when he'd begun to wish for this very thing to happen – when he'd begun fervently to hope that maybe, somehow, this might mean the whole "attack" was over and they could stay here celebrating for the rest of the day – Agate was up and leading them out into the sunshine again, and Logan was babbling more of his gibberish about Donkey Dog and Donkey Oboe and Donkey Nan.

It must have been soon after that, when he was still enriched by the wine, that Prentice was put to use as a runner for the first time all day; and he thanked God that his reeling memory had retained, as if by chance, a dim knowledge of where Brewer's Second Platoon was likely to be. The trip involved a long dogtrot, alternating with a fast walk, down a street on the perimeter of the town that he guessed was supposed to be the main line of defense against the possibility of a counterattack: it was the place where the company's machine-gun positions were set up. And he was walking weakly back along the same street, having delivered his message, before it occurred to him that this must be where Quint was. The first gun emplacement he passed was manned by strangers; but then he saw him, standing alone in a ground-floor window with the snout of his gun protruding over the sill. He was wearing a maroon bed quilt wrapped around him, like an Indian, and he was smiling.

"Hey there, runner!" he called in a hoarse voice.

100

Prentice went over close to the window and stopped, looking up at him. "How you feeling?" he said.

"I don't know; about the same, I guess. You?"

"Little better maybe; I don't know."

"I saw you barrel-assing past out there," Quint said. "I'm glad as hell they let me stay in one place, anyway."

"Yeah."

"I hear the artillery spotter was killed."

"No, he wasn't killed; I saw him." It gave Prentice a small thrill of pride to be able to give this information. "He was pretty badly hit, though." Then, after a pause, he said, "Listen, what do you think? You think there's going to be a counterattack, or not?" He knew at once it was the kind of question that might exasperate Quint ("How the Christ should I know, Prentice? Will you quit asking questions?") but instead, surprisingly, he got a straight answer.

"Hard to say. I doubt it, somehow. I know *I* sure as hell wouldn't try it, if I were them."

"Me neither. Well; I better get back."

"Look, Prentice." Quint reached down behind the window sill and brought up a clean strip of G.I. blanket. "I got hold of an extra blanket and I cut it into thirds, to use for mufflers. You fold it this way, you see, and then you put it around and cross it over your chest. That's what I'm doing with mine, anyway. Or you could wear it over your head, if you'd rather. I know it's not very cold now, but it might get cold again."

"Well, thanks. That's – that's very good." Prentice took the scarf and arranged it around his neck. "Thanks a lot," he said.

"Then I thought I'd give the third piece to Sam, if I can find him."

"Good. That's a good idea. Well." He lingered there, looking down at his feet. He felt a great rising temptation to say, "Look,

Quint. I'm ready now. If you still want to go back to the aid station, I'll go too." But the unfamiliar wealth of Quint's respect for him was still too new and too valuable to risk losing. All he said was, "Well. I'll see you around. Take care of yourself."

"You too," Quint said.

And Prentice did his best to put an easy, old-combat-man swing into his walk as he moved away down the street, very much aware that Quint would stand there watching him until he was out of sight. Once he turned back to make sure of this, and it was true. He waved and Quint waved back, letting the maroon quilt fall away from one shoulder.

But that one welling of strength, that one brief time of lucidity was the first and last of the day for Prentice. For the rest of the oddly warm, wet afternoon he would hear bursts of machine-gun fire and feel no curiosity or interest in where they came from; he would watch Agate's talking face with no idea of what he was saying, as if all words had become as meaningless as Logan's droning donkey talk. At one point, following Agate up an alley and out across an empty lot filled with rubble, he discovered that Agate was drunk. A bottle of Hennessy cognac hung from his hand as he walked, and he was singing, to the tune of "One O'Clock Jump":

> "Spread your legs
> You're breakin' my glasses,
> Baby, won't you please lay still . . ."

He sang it over and over, until the song became the only thing Prentice was truly aware of, the only thread of coherence among turning, shifting images of broken houses and running men and brick dust and smoke and dripping water. Once he saw a vivid close-up of Logan's face shouting at him – apparently scolding him, as he'd done last night on the road – but he could make no sense of the words.

>"Spread your legs
>You're breakin' my . . ."

He awoke as if from a dream to find himself standing up against a chest-high plaster wall, flanked by two riflemen he had never seen before, looking out over an expanse of gray fields and black trees; and he had no knowledge of how he'd gotten there or what he was supposed to be doing. "Spread your legs" still rang in his head, but Agate and the others were nowhere within sight or hearing. Through a slow, fuddled process of deduction he figured out that this must be part of the defense perimeter: someone must have posted him here with these two men, either to give him a rest or because every available man was needed on the line. But had he been told to report back to his runner's job at some specific time? Or would someone come and relieve him here? And where the hell was company headquarters now? Was he supposed to know?

He glanced sideways at each of the two men, who were staring out at the horizon, one of them chewing gum. Was he supposed to know them? He did his best to concentrate on the horizon too, but he had to blink again and again to keep the landscape from swimming in his vision.

And he guessed he must have fallen asleep at the wall, because he had a dream in which he and the whole company command group were seated in class, in some brown and chalky school-room of his childhood. Agate was at the teacher's desk, sweeping all the books and papers onto the floor to make room for his helmet, his carbine, and his bottle of cognac. Prentice was squeezed into one of the child-size pupil's desks on which a number of hearts and initials had been carved, and Magill was slumped in the desk beside him with his big, ungainly Bazooka balanced across its top. Logan, in another desk across the aisle, was saying something about Donkey Oboe into his radio.

"Will the class please come to order?" Agate called out in a mincing, womanish voice. "Will the class please come to order? The first lesson today will be – oh, let's see, now. Spelling." He leaned back against the cloudy blackboard, picked a piece of chalk from its shelf, and threw it at Magill's head. "All right for *you*, Billy Magill," he cried. "You stay after school!" And he broke up in a spasm of giggling laughter.

Then Prentice saw a couple of men hanging up blankets to black out the windows, and he began to understand that it wasn't a dream: this schoolhouse was to be the company's command post for the night.

Agate seemed to tire of his teacher impersonation. He took a swig of his brandy and began to stalk moodily around the classroom, studying his field map, only a little unsteady on his feet as he got down, at last, to business. Sitting on the top of Logan's desk he talked soberly with battalion headquarters on the radio, and then with someone else, and the monotone of his voice put Prentice to sleep for what seemed many hours.

". . . hey, *kid*!"

His eyes came open to see that Agate, still hunched on Logan's desk, had turned away from the radio to call to him across the room.

"Wilson's bringing up the bedrolls. You want to ride on back with him? Let him drop you at the aid station?"

He tried to speak but no voice came, so he shook his head to mean No, and Agate went back to the radio.

"Okay, Prentice," said Logan, who had turned around in his seat to look contemptuously back at him, exactly like the

104

brightest boy in class addressing the dunce. "It's your funeral. But if you want to stay you're going to damn sure have to get on the ball."

Then he was asleep again, dreaming that his bandolier straps were caught in some kind of machine that painfully pulled and pushed, pulled and pushed . . .

"*Prentice,* God damn it. Come *on.*"

It was Logan, gripping his shoulder and rocking it back and forth.

"Okay," he whispered. "I'm awake." He wiped away the saliva that had spilled from his sleeping mouth and tried to understand what Logan was saying. It was something about having to "go back for the coastal ranges." Only after he'd struggled up out of the desk and followed Logan out through the door of the schoolroom was he able to grasp that it wasn't "coastal ranges" but "coats and rations" – the stuff they had left in the cellar this morning.

There were three of them on the detail – Logan, Prentice, and another runner whose name was either Conn or Kahn. They started out three abreast, and Prentice was dimly amazed that the others seemed to have no trouble finding their way back through the ruined town. But what amazed him even more was that they were able to walk so fast. He began to fall behind almost at once, stumbling and coughing; the distance between them lengthened to as much as ten feet, and then it was more like ten yards.

"Come *on,* Prentice."

Walking on rubber legs, hating Logan with all his heart, he watched the two of them get smaller and smaller as they moved inexorably ahead in the thin yellow light of late afternoon. They turned a corner, going out of sight, and then they disappeared around another corner just when he'd found them again. He knew that if he didn't find them this time he'd be lost, unable to get back to the cellar *or* the schoolhouse: he would go on stumbling alone through these heaps of rubble all night, until he fell among the dead. Only once did he find himself in a familiar place – the square where the knocked-off church steeple was, and where the litter bearers had dumped their corpse – and he caught a glimpse of Logan and the other man vanishing down one of the streets at its opposite end. Gathering all his strength he took lumbering, running steps across most of the square; then he had to walk again, and it was some seconds before he could see anything clearly through a red fog that went thin and thick, thin and thick in cadence with the beating of his heart.

At last, toward the end of one more impossibly long street, he saw the overturned French halftrack. He had his bearings on the cellar now; all that remained was to stay on his feet and keep them lifting and falling, like a man on a treadmill, and he would somehow close the distance.

In the gloom of the cellar he found Logan squatting over a pile of overcoats, counting them. Conn or Kahn was tying up the corners of a blanket into which he'd dumped all the K rations, and there was also another load to carry: half a dozen bottles of wine and a great many tall mason jars of fruit preserves that they'd looted from the shelves of the place. Prentice looked with longing at the armchair he had used last night – surely it would be all right to sit down, just for a minute – and in creeping through the shadows toward it he almost fell over two bodies. They were lying asleep on mattresses – Owens and the gray-haired man, Luchek – and only now did he realize that he hadn't seen either of them all day. They had both complained about their bowels last night: could it be that they'd simply stayed behind this morning? Then why the hell hadn't he done the same? Another, empty mattress lay not far away, and Prentice sat in his armchair, looking down at it.

"Owens," Logan was saying. "*Owens*. God damn it, will you lift your feet?" He was pulling at an overcoat that had become entangled with Owens's legs. "You've been goofing off here all day," Logan told him, wresting the coat free. "The least you can do is move your God damn feet."

Owens's eyes came open. "Blow it out your ass, Logan," he said. "Don't tell *me* about goofing off, you shithead." Then, with no change in tone and certainly without a trace of humility, he said, "Listen. Will you find out what happened to the medics? They were supposed to send up for us, hours ago."

Prentice expected Logan to answer this with something like: "Maybe they got more important things to do," or "Tough shit" – but all he said, wearily, was: "Okay. I'll put in another call. Hey *Prentice. Take* this stuff."

And Prentice struggled out of the armchair, slinging his rifle; but he wasn't wholly on his feet before Logan flung a load of six or seven overcoats into his arms, which knocked him back. Very slowly he managed to force his way up out of the chair again, carrying the coats, and to take three steps toward Logan, the rifle sling slipping from his shoulder.

"And here," Logan was saying. "Take these too, and these . . ." He was planting mason jars firmly on top of the load of coats, building them up against Prentice's chest like cordwood. Conn or Kahn was already heading for the door, hauling an immense burden, and Logan was nimbly picking up his own share of the load, a stack of coats slung over one shoulder and a burlap bag bulging with food and wine in the other hand. "Okay," he said, turning away. "Let's go."

And that was when Prentice gave up. He moved his feet, but instead of going forward they went back – three tottering steps – and he was sprawled in the armchair again with the load on his lap, his helmet coming down hard on the bridge of his nose. One of the mason jars slid off and rolled away across the floor with a dull, gritty sound.

"Logan," he tried to call, but no sound came. "Logan . . ."

"Oh, for Christ's sake." Logan's voice was very far away. "What *now*?"

"I'm sorry, I – listen. Tell the lieutenant I can't – I can't make it. I'm—"

"And who the fuck do you think is going to *carry* all that?"

"I'm sorry. Tell the lieutenant I—"

"Shit." There was a distant clink and thump as Logan set his own load down, and then Prentice felt the weight on his lap decrease as the jars and overcoats were angrily snatched away. When his trembling arms were free he reached up and tipped off his helmet, letting it fall to the floor with a terrible crash. Then he slumped forward out of the chair on one knee, his head hanging, and used his rifle stock as a staff to help him walk on his knees across the swaying floor to the edge of the mattress, where he crawled and squirmed his way into total collapse.

Logan was still there, moving around somewhere above him, probably still chewing him out, but he could no longer hear the words. He knew, though, that there was one final thing he had to say, and that it would have to be said if it took his last breath.

"I know—" he croaked. "I know you think I'm goofing off, Logan. But get this – get this straight. If I'd wanted to goof off, I'd have – done it – a week ago."

There was no way of telling whether Logan made any reply to this, or even whether he'd heard it, or even whether he was still in the room.

Then there was nothing but a silent, spinning darkness; and soon there was a dream in which his mother appeared, saying: "Just rest, now, Bobby. Just rest."

PART TWO

PART TWO

Chapter One

Sometimes in dreams there are visions of the past. For that reason Alice Prentice had always welcomed sleep, but she suffered an insomniac's dread of the time just before sleeping, the act of falling asleep itself, the perilous twilight of semi-awareness when the mind must struggle for coherence, when a siren or a cry in the street is the very sound of terror and the ticking of the clock is a steady reminder of death.

Now, with Bobby gone in the Army, she had found that whiskey was a great help. Under its protection she could allow her memory free rein: she could dwell without chagrin on the tenderest, most painful times in her life and draw comfort from the belief that nothing was ever as bad as it seemed – that everything, somehow, worked out for the best.

She could even remember Bethel, Connecticut – the long, bleak time after coming home from Paris, when it seemed every day and every night that she couldn't possibly be more lonely. Her fine old colonial house was a pleasure – at least it would have been a pleasure if she'd had a man to share it with – and she had made a studio out of the old barn behind it, where she was managing to get a good deal of work done. But she couldn't work all the time. In the evenings after Bobby was asleep she would listen to the radio – the big floor-model

Majestic that had been her one great extravagance since coming back from France – but even the most entertaining programs were seldom enough to divert her from the knowledge of what she was really doing: she was waiting for the telephone to ring.

On the increasingly rare occasions when it did ring it was most often her sister Eva, calling precisely because she knew how lonely Alice was. An old maid, six years her senior and forever bossy and meddlesome and condescending, with the best of intentions, Eva was the only other member of her family to have fled the Middle West: she was a nurse in a New York hospital and seemed to have nothing better to do with her free time than to pester Alice with kindly disapproval. She had disapproved of her marriage to George and then disapproved of the divorce; now she wasn't at all sure if she could approve of Alice's new way of living.

"But you're so remote out there," she would say. "There can't be very much for you in the way of – well, social life. Really, dear, I can't help being concerned."

And Alice would try, unsuccessfully, to explain that no concern was warranted. It was after one of these dismal conversations that Alice began to toy with the idea of calling up some of the people she and George had known in New Rochelle. The trouble was that everyone they'd known there was happily married – or almost everyone. When she first thought of Harvey Spangler, the doctor who had brought Bobby into the world, she knew at once that she ought to know better. Harvey Spangler was married, but that had never kept him from enjoying a reputation as a ladies' man around New Rochelle – nor had that reputation kept Alice from confiding in him more than once. It was in the privacy of Harvey Spangler's office, in fact, that she'd first breathlessly poured out the news of her intention to leave George and go to Paris; and Harvey, calm and solicitous, had seemed to understand.

Still, it would be indiscreet to call him now, and so she didn't. She waited until several days later, when she called him at his office to inquire, in as neutral a way as she could manage, if he could recommend a general practitioner in the Bethel area.

"Well, *Alice*," he said. "It's good to hear from you."

And the very next evening, his voice enriched with what she suspected was several drinks too many, he called her back to ask if he might drive out to see her.

She knew it was a mistake to say yes, and that was only the first of her mistakes. Bustling around the house to make it ready for him, taking a bath and changing her clothes, tiptoeing into Bobby's room to make sure he was asleep, bringing out a bottle of whiskey on a tray with two glasses, waiting for the sound of his car – oh, there was no excuse for it; no excuse at all.

She had no one but herself to blame when he took her in his arms almost at once, and when he took her impatiently and almost roughly to bed. And that was only the beginning: he stayed all night, which meant that she had to find some acceptable way of dealing with him in the morning.

She let him sleep while she fixed Bobby's breakfast, and she was careful to keep Bobby quiet so as not to disturb him. Even so, she knew there would be an awkward confrontation when he came downstairs, and there was. He came into the kitchen wearing his wrinkled gaberdine suit with the vest unbuttoned and held together with his watch chain. His hair was combed but his shirt was wilted and he hadn't shaved; he looked weak with hangover and badly confused.

"Good morning," she said, and she was aware that Bobby, looking up from his Cream of Wheat, had fixed him with a malevolent stare.

"Well," Harvey said. "Who's *this* big fella?"

"Say good morning to Dr. Spangler, dear," she said, and then, "I guess he doesn't remember you."

"He looks fine, Alice." Harvey was clearly grateful for a chance to dispense a professional opinion. "Little underweight, but otherwise fine."

"What would you like for breakfast, Harvey?"

"Oh, just coffee'll be fine for now."

And the three of them were seated at the table, if not quite companionably at least in a state of truce.

"Mind if I smoke a cigar?" Harvey inquired, withdrawing one of the White Owls that crowded his vest pocket, and Bobby watched with mixed fascination and distaste as he filled the kitchen with its acrid smoke.

"Isn't it a wonderful day?" Alice said. "They said it was going to rain, but it's just lovely – the sky is so blue and clear. Bobby, if you're finished why don't you run outdoors for a little while?"

"I don't feel like it."

"But it's too nice a morning to stay indoors. Don't you want to go and see what the other children are doing?"

"No."

Eventually, though, he slid down off his chair and sidled out of the kitchen, pausing to look back at Harvey Spangler with suspicion.

"He really does look well, Alice," Harvey said when he was gone. "Looks like you're taking good care of him."

"He's wonderful. I don't know what I'd do without him."

Thoughtfully stirring his coffee, Harvey ventured to ask a delicate question. "Does George get to see much of him?"

"Of course he does. As often as he wants to. He had him just last weekend – three whole days at Atlantic City."

"Atlantic City? That must've cost a lot."

"I suppose it did. It was his idea, not mine."

That was the only time they mentioned George, though they sat talking for another twenty minutes or so. Or rather, Alice talked, while Harvey Spangler listened and nodded and seemed to be waiting only for a decent chance to leave. Why couldn't she stop talking? Did all lonely people have that problem? She was telling him about Paris, trying to make it sound exciting but fully aware from the clumsy, hesitant way she pronounced French names that she was betraying how confused and unpleasant a time she'd had there.

". . . And you see there are two railroad stations with names that sound almost exactly alike," she was saying. "One is the Gare de Lyon and the other is the Gare d'Orléans, clear over on the other side of the city; only I didn't *know* that. So if it hadn't been for that taxi driver I might have ended up goodness knows where."

And Harvey Spangler managed an appropriate chuckle, examining the ash of his cigar.

Then with relief she left off talking about Paris and asked him to admire the unusual width of the floorboards: she wanted to point out features of the house that she hadn't had time to show him last night. "Only the real pre-Revolutionary houses have floorboards like that," she said. "And do you see the old pegheads? Instead of nails? And did I show you my wonderful old Dutch oven? In the fireplace? Come and look. Careful of your head, now."

Crouching low, for he was a tall man and all the doors were short, he followed her into the creaking silence of the living room, where he joined her in a respectful scrutiny of the Dutch oven.

"It's quite a place," he said. "How much you paying for it, Alice?"

And when she told him the rent he was astounded. "Can you *afford* that much?"

She gave a nervous little laugh. "Well, just barely. But it really is a bargain, when you think how few of the old Colonials are available at all. Over in Westport they're a lot more expensive."

"Well, but that's Westport," he said. "That's fashionable. This is kind of out in the middle of nowhere."

"Well," she said, "anyway, we like it."

"It certainly is – attractive; I'll say that for it."

"And the main advantage," she said, brightening again, "the main advantage is the studio. It's really just an old barn, but I remodeled it and put in a skylight. Come and look."

Then he was following her out into the sunshine, across the expanse of unmowed lawn that led to the barn.

"Isn't it wonderful?" she demanded. "Look at all the *space* I've got."

"Not bad," he said, pacing the rotted wooden flooring. "Not bad at all; I can see you've really fixed the place up. Must've been a lot of work."

"Oh, not really; the skylight was the main thing, and I had a carpenter do that. All I really did was clean it out and paint it, and fix the door. And I got electric wiring put in from the house, so I can work at night sometimes."

Most of the sculpture was hidden under muslin cloths, which spared her from showing it to him. The only exposed pieces were two lifesize garden figures – the Goose Girl, which she had recently cast into plaster, and the one she was currently working on in clay, the Faun.

"I'm afraid the Goose Girl isn't at her best," she said. "She really shouldn't be seen until I get her painted. She's going to be green, you see, to look like bronze."

"Looks fine to me."

"Well, but they always look so garish and chalky when they've just been cast. Anyway, I think it's a nice composition. But the one I'm really excited about is this new one, the Faun. I've done quite a few of these garden things and they've all been girls, because I guess girls are more traditional in garden sculpture, but then it occurred to me to do something with a boy. It suddenly struck me that I've got this wonderful little *boy* for a model, and I've simply been letting him go to waste."

"Mm. I can see that. I mean, I can see where you've put a lot of Bobby into it."

"Well, I wasn't trying for a likeness in the face. I wanted the face to be sort of – well, elfin, and *you* know, like a faun. But it's Bobby's body. It's Bobby's little arms and back and tummy. Of course it's still unfinished – here, look, you can see what I'm getting at in some of these drawings." And she showed him her sketch pad, where her conception of the Faun was complete: a boy of Bobby's age from the head to the thighs, holding a bunch of grapes in one arm and eating an apple with the other hand; but from the thighs down his legs were an animal's, with fetlocks and cloven hoofs.

"Do you like it?"

"Well, you know me on the subject of art, Alice," he said. "I mean I'm certainly no judge or anything. It looks fine to me. It's very – fanciful."

"Oh, good. That's just what I was hoping you'd say. And I've got a wonderful idea for the next one: the next one's going to be Pan. Let me show you." And she turned a page to reveal a drawing of a little boy kneeling in shrubbery, playing the pipes of Pan.

"Well," Harvey Spangler said. "That looks fine, Alice." A bumblebee was trapped inside the skylight, buzzing loud and frantically against the brilliant pane, and Harvey stared up at it as if in the hope that it might excuse him from looking at any more sculpture or making any more comments. Then he said: "Well, I guess I'd better be getting started, Alice; it's a long drive."

Back in the kitchen he gathered her up in a cozy, awkward embrace, kissing her hair and the tip of her nose, and she rested her head against his chest for a moment; then he stood apart from her and straightened his clothes. "Take care of yourself, now," he said.

"I will, Harvey. You too."

She walked out to the car with him and stood watching while he got it started and backed it out into the street. A little group of neighborhood children stood watching too, with wide-eyed, expressionless faces, and one of the smaller ones was Bobby.

When he was gone, heading back for New Rochelle, there was nothing for Alice to do but sit in the studio and hold her head in both hands with her eyes closed tight. Harvey Spangler! A dull, humorless, middle-aged New Rochelle doctor; a man with a wife and four children! And as if her behavior last night wasn't bad enough, there was the shame of her performance this morning: running around the kitchen like a bride on a honeymoon, smiling at him while he blew his horrible cigar smoke in Bobby's face. And taking him to the studio! Showing him her work, asking for his opinions, being pleased – yes, pleased – when he said he liked something. Harvey Spangler! But soon she got up and began walking around smoking a cigarette, trying to pull herself together. It was almost time to go in and fix lunch.

"Where's Dr. Spankler?" Bobby inquired while she worked at the stove.

"Dr. Spangler," she corrected. "He went home, dear. He was only here for breakfast."

"Oh. Where does he live?"

"In New Rochelle, dear. Where we used to live."

"Did I live there?"

"Of course you did. That's where you were born."

"Did Daddy live there?"

"Of course. Hurry and wash your hands, now. The soup is almost ready."

When lunch was over she went back to the studio and tried to work, but it went badly for nearly an hour before she realized what was wrong: the children were playing just outside the barn door, and the noise of their voices made it impossible to concentrate. She took several deep breaths so that her voice wouldn't sound shrill; then she went to the door and opened it. "Would you children mind playing somewhere else?" she said.

There were four or five of them. Bobby and one of the little Mancini boys were the smallest, and the older Mancini girl was the biggest, a gangling nine-year-old with a sly, insolent face.

"We weren't making any noise, Mrs. Prentice," she said.

"Well, I can't work as long as you're playing here. Please, children; I've got some important work to do. Just find some other place to play."

"Can we watch you, Mrs. Prentice?"

"Some other time you can. Not just now."

"Even if we don't make any noise?"

"No. Please, now, children. Just do as I say."

And finally, laggardly, they moved away to another part of the yard. Watching them go, she felt a tremor of dislike for the Mancini girl. The child was too much like her mother, whom Alice suspected of being a malicious gossip, and it was a pity because the father was so nice – a rough, jovial Italian who worked in one of the Danbury hat factories and who'd gone out of his way to be neighborly when Alice first moved in.

There were no more interruptions for nearly two hours and she got some good work done. Or so it seemed, at least, until she stopped to look at it from across the room. Then, with a terrible suddenness, it seemed that there was something very much the matter with the Faun's left arm, the one that held the grapes. She had labored too hard over it; it was stiff and lifeless with overwork, and so was the left hip. But it wasn't hopeless: she could still save it if the daylight lasted long enough and if she allowed herself to concentrate on nothing else. She went quickly out across the yard to where the children were.

"Bobby," she called. "Can I see you a minute, please?" And he detached himself from the group and walked toward her. He looked reluctant, which prompted her to be especially nice when she got him alone. "Dear, would you mind posing for me again this afternoon? Just for an hour or so?"

He was willing.

"It'll be just like the other times," she said when they were back in the studio and she was helping him get undressed, "except that this time we won't use the apple and the grapes. But if you pose very well, and don't move, you can have all the apples and grapes you want afterwards. How would that be?"

She took him to the right spot under the skylight and positioned his feet, one a little forward and one back. Then she arranged his arms, one crooked as if holding the grapes and the other raised with his hand to his mouth. "There," she said. "That's fine. Oh, this will be such a help to me, if you'll just hold that pose. You really are a wonderful model."

The light was perfect, and in a little while she felt she was getting the arm right. "That's wonderful, dear," she would say abstractedly from time to time, shifting her gaze back and forth from his sunlit flesh to the clay, and "You're doing fine," and "Hold still, now – don't move."

What a pleasure it was to work when the work went well! It was a pleasure that took care of everything else, that made everything else fall away in unimportance, and it always took her back to Cincinnati and to her second year at the Academy – the year she'd abandoned painting and discovered sculpture.

"See how you like it." Willard Slade! Sometimes she could go through whole weeks without thinking of him, but he was always there to remember at times like this. And that was what he'd always said – "See how you like it," in a casual, offhand way – when he introduced her to something that would enrich her life forever.

The funny part was that she hadn't even liked him at first: a sarcastic, unkempt, and almost loutish young man, with his hands usually dirty from working on his dreadful motorcycle – not at all the kind of boy her parents would have liked. She couldn't understand why all the other boys either despised or admired him, and why the boys she liked best were the ones who admired him most. He never seemed to pay attention in class and he made fun of most of the instructors. She thought him rude and spoiled, and she didn't like to be around him for fear he might say something awful; but that was before she'd begun to learn what everyone else seemed to know instinctively: that Willard Slade was a genius.

It wasn't that he was always brilliant. Sometimes he would work and work over a piece and it would turn out to be as dull and forced as everyone else's, and he'd throw it away. But there were other times, and they'd begun to happen more and more frequently – times when, as he would have said, he was feeling right – when what he did was apparently effortless and was much, much better than good, and the teachers would look at him in open envy.

He was wonderful. "See how you like this," he'd said to her once and handed her a copy of Keats's poems, and she'd taken it home and studied it for days, memorizing several of the more obscure poems so as to be able to surprise him; and in the end, when she went carefully through her recitation of one of them as they sat in Lytle Park, he said, "Yeah, that's nice, but it's one of the sissy ones. I like the later stuff better. Try this one." And he handed the book back to her, open at the page of "Ode on a Grecian Urn," which she'd skipped because she'd thought it was too famous to bother with. "Read it out loud," he said, and so she read it, really read it, for the first time:

> "Thou still unravish'd bride of quietness,
> Thou foster-child of silence and slow time . . ."

And when she got to the end, to the overwhelming final two lines, she started to cry.

Oh, there had been nothing at all she wouldn't do for Willard Slade. He asked her to marry him, and her life took on an unbelievable richness until October 8, 1914, when Willard Slade ran his motorcycle into a trolley car and was instantly killed.

It was years before she got over it – years spent first back in Plainville, then breaking into the advertising business in Cleveland, and then in New York, where Willard Slade had always wanted to go – and sometimes, like this afternoon, it seemed that she hadn't gotten over it yet and never would.

"Mommy?"

"What, dear?"

"My nose itches."

"Then you'd better scratch it, silly boy. I'll wait while you do."

He scratched it and then resumed his careful pose.

"Move your hand just a little higher, dear – no, the other one; there. That's fine. You're really helping your mommy a lot. Would you like to talk while you're posing?"

"All right."

"Fine. Why don't you tell me about what you did in Atlantic City."

"I *told* you."

"You didn't tell me hardly anything at all. You told me about the big waves and the saltwater taffy, and that's all you told me about."

"And I told you about the chairs on wheels."

"Oh, that's right, you did."

"And I told you about me and Daddy and Uncle Bill getting up on each other's shoulders."

"That's right." A small, querulous part of her mind was annoyed that George had taken his brother along on the trip: Bill Prentice was loud and coarse and drank too much, and she hated him.

"And Uncle Bill was so funny, we kept laughing and laughing. And Irene said Uncle Bill was the funniest man she'd ever met in her whole life. And then me and Daddy and Brenda and Irene covered him all up with sand, so just his head was sticking out."

"That must have been fun. And who were Brenda and Irene? Were they some children you met on the beach?"

"No, Mommy, they're *ladies*. They're the ladies we *stayed* with."

"Oh. I see." She was at a difficult place now, a juncture of arm and shoulder on which there was a subtle play of light, and she allowed herself to think about nothing but that.

"And we kept covering Uncle Bill up with sand and he kept saying 'Hey! Let me *outa* here!' and we kept covering him and covering him."

"Hold still now, dear. Maybe we'd better not talk any more for a little while. This is a hard part."

The ladies they stayed with! She was doing her very best not to think about it, to think only of the tip of her modeling tool and the clay, but it was impossible.

"And were they nice ladies?" she inquired.

"Is the hard part over?"

"What? Oh, yes, the hard part's over. Were they nice ladies?"

"Yes. I liked Irene best because she smelled so pretty and she played with me a lot. Brenda was nice too but she kept wanting to hug and kiss me all the time."

"I see."

She put down the tool and got out her cigarettes, and she was just about to say, "Let's rest a minute, Bobby," when she heard a startling sound from somewhere in the wall behind her – an erupting, burbling sound that she was a little late in identifying as a lewd giggle of children. In the split second of her confusion she whirled to look at the wall, and she saw them: three or four pairs of eyes peering in through an inch-wide crack in the wallboards – eyes that vanished, leaving only sunlight in the crack, as soon as she discovered them. The sound of their laughter rose up louder as they ran away, and when she turned back to Bobby he was round-eyed with humiliation, hunched over with both hands hiding his genitals.

She wanted to get hold of the Mancini girl and beat her – hit her across the face – but by the time she got to the door the children had disappeared. She stood looking out across the bright grass for some time before realizing that there was nothing she could do. She couldn't call up Mrs. Mancini without telling her what it was the children had done, and that would mean having to explain what she and Bobby had been doing.

"They're gone, dear," she said, turning back to him. "Let's not worry about those silly children."

She persuaded him to pose again, but he was clearly uneasy

about it; in a little while she let him get dressed and went on working alone until the light began to fade. It was nearly five o'clock, and when she went back to the house she found she was exhausted.

She went to the living room first and turned on the radio for the five o'clock news. It was something unintelligible about President Hoover and the Treasury deficit, but she listened to it anyway because she always enjoyed Lowell Thomas – his voice was reassuringly steady and baritone, and there was something nice about the way he always said: "So long until tomorrow." She turned the volume up in order to hear it in the kitchen while she got the dinner started; she had begun to scrape a carrot when Lowell Thomas went off and Kate Smith came on:

"When the moon comes over the mountain . . ."

And the ridiculous thing was that it made her cry. "Every beam brings a dream, dear, of you . . ." She had to put the carrot and the knife down and stand with her forehead pressed against the kitchen window until her sobs abated, and afterwards, though she felt refreshed and much better, she was ashamed of herself. Keats could make her cry but so could Kate Smith.

Neither she nor Bobby were very hungry, so dinner didn't take very long. She got the dishes washed and Bobby put to bed a little earlier than usual, and then there was nothing to do.

She listened to the radio and then tried to read, but thoughts of Harvey Spangler kept obtruding on the page. After a while she got up and began walking around the room, smoking one cigarette after another. If only there were some way to escape the evening hours!

When the telephone rang it was such an unexpected, exciting event that she let it ring three or four times before answering it, knowing it would probably be Eva but savoring the fact that it might be anyone at all. It was George.

"Did I get you up?" he inquired.

"No. I wasn't in bed."

"Listen, Alice," he began in a tone that warned her of unpleasantness. "I'm calling because there's something very important that we've got to discuss."

"All right."

"They're putting through another cutback in salaries and commissions next month. That means I'll be making an awful lot less money, and in fact I'm lucky to have a job at all."

"I see."

"So what it amounts to is that we're simply going to have to economize, Alice. I'm afraid you'll have to give up that place in the country."

"But it's cheaper here than in the city."

"Alice, I know what that place is costing you in rent alone. Do you know what other people are paying for rent? Do you know what *I'm* paying for rent?"

"And how much—" she started to tremble and had to hold the phone in both hands. "How much did it cost you to take your lady friends to Atlantic City?"

"I – look, Alice. That has nothing to do with – Please try to be reasonable."

And she did her best. She listened while he explained about good, inexpensive apartments in Queens, and while he offered to find her such a place himself; and she knew that by her silence she was concurring in his wishes, or at least expressing willingness to abandon the house in Bethel.

But then it was her turn, and she gripped the phone in both hands again. At first she was scarcely aware of what she was saying; she knew only that she wanted to hurt him as badly as possible, and she knew that the force and rhythm of her words were building to an inevitable climax.

"... and I don't care *how* many lawyers you get; I'll never *ever* let my child be exposed to you and your – your little whores again, do you understand me? Never!"

She hung up the phone, and when it rang again a moment later she didn't answer it; she let it ring ten times, and then it stopped.

She thought she heard Bobby crying and went quickly upstairs to see, but he seemed to be sleeping peacefully. She tucked the covers more securely around him and moved his Teddy bear closer to his head, just in case.

Downstairs again, she walked around the living room twisting her hands together, going over and over the things she wished she had thought of saying to George; then, as her breathing and her blood slowed down, she sat quietly in a chair.

After a while she started thinking about the Faun again and wondering how it looked. Sometimes, if you looked at a piece of sculpture under artificial light, after working on it all day, you could see new things in it.

There was a full moon, which made it easy to walk to the barn, and once she was inside there was enough blue-gray glow from the skylight to show her the outlines of the Faun. It didn't look bad at all. Then she switched on the lights, and after the first shock of brightness she had to stand biting her lip for a full minute before she could admit how disappointed she was: all the work she'd done today looked crude.

But then, moving back a few steps and squinting, she was able to see the beginnings of something promising, and she began to breathe normally again. She knew better than to touch it now, but if she had a good day tomorrow she might still be able to bring it off.

She looked at several other pieces, seeing things she could improve in all of them, but she had to leave the studio soon because she kept thinking of Harvey Spangler standing there with his gaberdine suit and his awful cigar, saying: "Well, you know me on the subject of art, Alice."

Instead of going back to the house she went up into the field behind the barn – she wanted to be as far as possible from thoughts of Harvey Spangler, and of the Mancini girl, and of George, and even of Bobby.

And no sooner was she standing in the tall, windswept grass of the hillside than she was crying again, but this time there was no pleasure in it. All she could think of was another poem Willard Slade had liked:

> Perhaps the self-same song that found a path
> Through the sad heart of Ruth, when, sick for home,
> She stood in tears amid the alien corn . . .

Well, she was sick for home, all right; and she didn't mean New Rochelle or New York or Cleveland or Cincinnati, and she certainly didn't mean Paris. She was sick for Plainville, Indiana, and for her dead mother and father and for all her sisters – even Eva – and for a lost and innocent time when everybody knew she was the baby of the family.

Chapter Two

After Bethel there were three trying but hopeful years in Greenwich Village. They moved to a different studio apartment each year, Alice seeking a new peace and a brave new foundation for her career with each move, and it wasn't until the end of the third year that all her loneliness dissolved with the advent of Sterling Nelson.

Never, in the most wistful of her longings, had she imagined that a man like Sterling Nelson might exist for her. She had long been resigned, in fact, to the idea that no man would ever exist for her again, not in any kind of responsible, durable way; she had come to accept the probability that the rest of her life would be spent in what Natalie Crawford called "a state of single blessedness."

Natalie Crawford was her neighbor on Charles Street, a twice-divorced, childless woman who had some sort of job with an advertising agency, who burned incense in her apartment and believed in her Ouija board and liked to use words like "*simpatico*," and who habitually found respite from her own state of single blessedness with any man she could get her hands on. Alice didn't like her very much, or at least didn't wholly approve of her, but for lack of other friends she had come to rely on her – to spend excessive amounts of time with her and attend her frantic parties, and even to borrow small sums of money from her at times when she couldn't make her income stretch through the month.

And the ironic thing was that one of Natalie Crawford's parties should have been the occasion of her meeting Sterling Nelson. He was nothing at all like most of the men Natalie knew – men who drank too much and delighted in their rudeness and got into raucous quarrels. He was tall and dignified and aristocratic, with graying temples and a little graying moustache; he was talking quietly in a small group of other nice-looking people she had never seen before, aloof from the mainstream of the party, and from the moment she saw him she wanted urgently to find some way of breaking through all the noise and smoke and getting close to him, of reaching out to touch the sleeve of his handsome suit (for he was beautifully dressed in tweeds that could only have come from England) and of letting him know that she was different too.

But a dreadful man named Mike Driscoll, who had recently been fired from a publishing house, had her backed into a corner and was demanding to know how she felt about the C.I.O., and she had scarcely escaped him before she got involved in a drunken argument between Paul and Mary Engstrom. "Do you know what you are when you're like this?" Paul asked his wife, who had been supporting him for nearly a year since he'd lost his job on the New York *Sun*. "I mean seriously, do you know what you are? Because I'll tell you."

"I don't have to take this, do I, Alice?" Mary said. "Is there any reason why I have to take this from him?"

"*Listen*, God damn it. You know what you are? You're a God damn little snot-nosed Jewish bitch, that's what you are."

And that was when she heard Natalie's voice rising up behind them. "Come along over here," Natalie was saying. "I want you to meet these nice people. Paul and Mary Engstrom; Alice Prentice. This is Sterling Nelson."

And the first thing he said to her was the least expected, nicest, and most encouraging thing she could have imagined: "I hear you're an artist."

She talked to no one else for the rest of the evening, and Sterling Nelson talked to no one but her. He was indeed English, and from his quiet, reticent talk she learned several other things about him: that he was in New York to represent a British export firm – a businessman with far too much sophistication to take his business seriously – that he was an art lover, and that he had evidently traveled all over the world. (It wasn't until later that she found out more specific and still more impressive details: that he'd been decorated as a submarine commander during the war and had later held important positions with the Colonial Service in places like Burma.)

The trouble was that she couldn't stop her voice, or even control it. Helplessly, she heard herself saying one inane or pretentious thing after another while his polite, lightly sweating face continued to nod and smile and the rest of the room swam around them in a dizzying blur. All she knew was that if she stopped talking he might go away, and then she began to fear that if she stopped talking he might be better able to notice all the things she knew were wrong with her: her dress, which was neither new nor wholly clean and which she was almost sure was visibly wet under the arms, and her hair which badly needed combing, and the fact that she was wearing too much lipstick too hastily applied. She wanted to escape to Natalie Crawford's bathroom and work on herself at the mirror, composing herself, but if she did that there was a terrible chance that he'd be gone when she came back; so there was nothing to do but stand there, gripping her warm, sticky drink with both hands, and go on talking. Then suddenly the people he'd come with were gathering their coats to leave, and he cordially excused himself and was gone. And no sooner had the door closed behind him than Natalie Crawford was bearing down on her through the smoke. "Isn't he wonderful?" Natalie demanded. "I can't imagine where they found him, but isn't he marvelous?"

And Alice began sidling away, trying to leave before Natalie could say he was *simpatico;* all she wanted then was to get her own coat and get out of here, to go home alone and make sure Bobby was all right and then go to bed and weep, and that was what she did.

So it was much, much more than a delightful surprise when she picked up her ringing telephone the very next day and heard: "Mrs. Prentice? Sterling Nelson here."

When he came to visit her studio she was a little anxious that he might not like her sculpture, but he was kind and respectful about the few pieces she dared to show him, and soon she found herself wholly at ease. She knew she looked better this time – she had bought a new dress for the occasion and spent a long time over her make-up – and her self-confidence was so improved that she let him do most of the talking. She was aware that most of what few things she said came out exactly right – cool but promising – and one or two of her phrases even seemed to strike him as witty.

He took her to the sidewalk café at the Brevoort, where nobody had taken her for years and which she now decided was the finest restaurant she'd ever been to in her life. Sitting at that elegant table as the final glow of sunset gave way to darkness, with their heads just visible to passers-by beyond the neat little potted shrubs, she kept hoping someone she knew would walk past and see them there: she even hoped for strangers to notice them and to wonder, enviously, who they were.

Then he took her home to his own place, which turned out to be a spacious apartment on Gramercy Park that was filled with wonders. Its walls were heavy with books and with dark paintings of kinds and periods that she wouldn't ordinarily have responded to, except that each was so clearly a gem in its own right, framed in gilt and lighted with a little museum lamp. "This is a Poussin," he was saying, "and this over here is a Murillo, one of the early Murillos. I've always liked the Spaniards of that school; of course I expect you know a good deal more about these things than I do." But the pictures were only the beginning: every piece of furniture was a valuable-looking antique – Moorish and Italian and French – and there were two charmingly roughhewn three-legged chairs that were primitive relics of Elizabethan England. The mementos of his years in the Orient included a heavy ivory-hafted sword that he called a "Burmese dar," and one long wall of his bedroom was emblazoned with a great bright tapestry that he explained was a "purdah." "If you follow the figures in it, you see, it tells a kind of pictorial narrative: it's meant to portray the rite of exhuming and reinterring the fingerbones of Buddha. Whole thing's a bit garish by our standards, I'm afraid, the colors and whatnot; that's why I've consigned it here to the bedroom." He was standing in the bedroom doorway when he said this, pouring brandy into two snifters, and he looked up briefly and shyly while she studied the purdah. "Hate to part with it, though. It was given me with a good deal of ceremony when I left the colony, as a sort of token."

"Oh, I don't think it's garish at all," she said, accepting one of the snifters. "I think it's beautiful." Then she moved delicately past him to re-explore the other rooms, while he hovered close behind her. "Really," she said. "Really, Sterling, this whole apartment is beautiful. All your things are so different from each other, and yet you've managed to make them all harmonize. Oh, that's not the right word; that sounds like an interior decorator or something. What I mean is that you've made everything – made everything *whole*. You've achieved – you've achieved—"

But Sterling Nelson gave her no chance to finish telling him what he had achieved. He had taken the brandy glass away from her and set it down on a table; he had taken her by the shoulder and turned her around and kissed her hard and full on the mouth.

Within a very few weeks his apartment had become the warm center of her world. There were difficulties – it would have been too good to be true if there hadn't been – but there were times when it seemed that no difficulties in the world could fail to be resolved if only good fortune allowed her to stay with this wise, calm, splendid man.

The main difficulty was that Sterling Nelson had a wife in England from whom he wasn't yet technically divorced, and he sometimes talked of the brief voyage he would have to make next fall to make it final. She never knew what to say when he mentioned that, but he always managed to make it clear that the whole business was a matter of tiresome legal details, to be taken care of and dismissed with as much dispatch as possible.

Another difficulty, at least at first, was Bobby. She knew it was only natural for Bobby to resent her spending so much time away from home, and she understood too that Sterling, with no children of his own, might find himself uncomfortable in the presence of a child. Even so, it troubled her that they were so awkward with each other. Bobby was always good about saying "Hello, Mr. Nelson" and "Goodnight, Mr. Nelson," and it always pleased her to see them solemnly shake hands, man to man; but one evening Bobby made a terrible scene. He had been tense and irritable all afternoon, claiming his stomach hurt, and he kept getting in her way while she was trying to dress; then he sat down in the middle of the floor and started to cry and said: "I don't *want* you to go out!"

She didn't know whether to scold or mollify him; she tried both, which only made him worse. "I *hate* Mr. Nelson!" he cried, fighting her off when she tried to put her arms around him, and he was still in the full heat of his rage when Sterling came in and stood watching, looking bewildered.

"Sterling, I'm sorry about this. He's just – he's upset because I'm – because we're—"

But Bobby, hiding his face in shame at being seen in tears, scrambled up and ran tragically to his room and slammed the door behind him.

Sterling sat down uneasily. "Is he sick?"

"No, I don't think so. He said his stomach hurt, but I think it's mostly just a tantrum." And she looked helplessly toward the slammed door.

"Bit old for that sort of nonsense, isn't he?" Sterling said.

"I suppose he is; I don't know. But the point is I *have* been spending a lot of time apart from him, and he feels – I think he feels neglected."

"Mm," Sterling said, shifting his feet and folding his hands in his lap. "Well. In any case I expect Mrs. what's-her-name can look after him tonight, can't she? The woman who sits with him?"

"I suppose so." But she still yearned toward the silent bedroom door. She could picture him flung face down across his bed, exhausted and ashamed and alone in the deepening shadows, too miserable now even to cry, and she knew he would be waiting for her. "Sterling," she said, "why don't you fix yourself a drink, and I'll just go in and talk to him. I won't be a minute."

135

" 'Talk' to him? I must say I fail to see the point of that, Alice. Wouldn't you just be starting up the whole silly business again?"

And then her own voice came close to tears: "Oh, Sterling, *please* try to understand." It was the nearest thing to a quarrel they'd ever had, and as her voice rose before his blinking face she was touched with panic: what if he *couldn't* understand? "I *can't* just leave him in there, don't you see? Oh, if he had a father it'd be different, but I'm all he has in the *world* – can't you see that?"

In the end they took him out to dinner with them, to the Brevoort. He had washed his face and put on his best clothes, and in the aftermath of hysteria he was by turns chagrined and over-exhilarated. At first they couldn't get a word out of him: he hung his head and kept avoiding Sterling's patient, kindly eyes; then all at once he started talking as if he would never stop. He had made a mess of his dinner plate, mixing everything together with his fork into an unsightly mush, and he explained this procedure at shrill and elaborate length.

"I don't really like peas, you see," he said, "and I don't like this kind of potatoes and I don't much like this kind of gravy, so you see what I do is, I just mix them all up together and then they don't taste so bad. I always do that whenever I get a whole bunch of different kinds of food I don't like, and it makes everything taste a whole lot better. Just mix 'em all up together, and you don't even taste the things you don't like. I mean it tastes *good* this way . . ." He went on and on, while Sterling stoically endured the monologue, while Alice tried ineffectually to quiet him down and people at neighboring tables glanced over in open irritation at the spectacle of such an ill-behaved little boy.

He didn't stop talking all the way home, except to break away from them on the sidewalk to demonstrate his prowess at leap-frogging fire hydrants; he didn't stop talking, in fact, until Alice had managed to get him into bed and put out his light and shut his door.

Then she said, "Oh, Sterling, thank you so much. I know it was awful for you but you were – really, you were wonderful."

And after that, Bobby became more and more a participant. They didn't take him to the Brevoort again, but they began going to the Brevoort less frequently themselves. More often Alice would fix dinner for the three of them at home, and they'd usually wait until Bobby was in bed before going to Sterling's place. Sterling didn't seem to mind; he was consistently kind and fatherly and stern without ever being harsh, and he seemed to enjoy the increasing evidence of Bobby's attachment to him. One evening he brought an illustrated book for boys, *British Submarine Service in the Great War*, and Bobby sat silent and spellbound, turning the pages, while Sterling explained the pictures and told tantalizingly cryptic anecdotes about his own submarine service. And Alice, watching them from the kitchen doorway, allowed herself to indulge in a happy daydream of the three of them together forever, of Bobby grown tall and disciplined and calling Sterling "Dad."

When the heat of the city grew unbearable that summer, Sterling sent them both away for a week to a cool lake in New Jersey, where they learned – or almost learned – to catch perch and sunfish with the rod and reel that Sterling had equipped them with, and where they sat for hours under a great shade tree while Alice read aloud from Sterling's volume of *Great Expectations*. And when the vacation was over and she felt that neither she nor Bobby could face the wretched city school system again, it was Sterling, one unforgettable night in his bedroom, who first suggested she might consider moving out to Scarsdale. He knew about Scarsdale because one of the items his company imported was lead-casement windows, which had enjoyed a vogue in the wealthier, Tudor-style homes of that town before the Depression. "Matter of fact we're still doing a fair amount of business out there," he said. "Seems to be a little isolated pocket of prosperity. In any case I understand the schools are first rate; be a good thing for Bobby. And of course the town itself is charming – green grass and fresh air and all that; get you away from all the bother of the city."

"It sounds lovely," she said, "but I'm afraid I could never afford it. George keeps saying I'm 'living beyond my means' as it is."

"Well, but some of the rentals aren't as high as you might think, Alice; it's a curious thing. Some of the older houses along the Post Road are rather rundown, and they're vacant – as long as they're vacant the owners are losing money, willing to lease them quite cheaply. It's a thing you might be wise to look into."

"You make it sound so easy." But that was one of the wonderful things about Sterling Nelson: he could make any difficult thing sound easy, and the only other man she had ever known who could do that was Willard Slade. All the others, George, for example, had made easy things sound difficult.

"Might well be simpler than you think," he said, sitting up on the edge of the bed and reaching for his dressing gown. "Pay a reasonable price and still have all the advantages." He walked across the room to get a cigarette and refill their brandy glasses, and when he came back, she allowed herself a thrill of girlish pleasure at how handsome he looked in his dressing gown. On any other man it would have been a bathrobe, but the way Sterling wore it made it a dressing gown. He sat on the edge of the bed again and looked at her, still silently inquiring if a move to Scarsdale mightn't be a good idea. And because his eyes were so considerate she was emboldened to tell him why the plan held so little appeal for her. She reached out and smoothed the silken lapels over the hairs on his chest.

"But Scarsdale's so far away," she said, "and I don't think I could bear being that far away from you."

And instead of betraying even the faintest sign of distaste at this confession, he took her in his arms and kissed her as though it had been the very thing he'd hoped she would say. "Actually," he said against her ear, "that brings up something else I thought I might suggest. Point is, there's really no reason why we'd have to be apart."

Then he released her, letting her sink back into the pillows, while he began to explain his plan. His lease here on Gramercy Park was soon to expire, and he'd realized for some time that he'd be unwise to renew it – the place was really too expensive, and he would be still less able to afford it after his costly trip to England; in other words it was only sensible for him to find a new place to live, and he wondered – "It's only a suggestion, mind you; just something I thought we might discuss" – he wondered if she might consent to their moving out to Scarsdale together. Mightn't it turn out to be a good thing for both of them? For all three of them? And there would, of course, be a distinct economic advantage – sharing the expenses, and so on. Oh, it was only a suggestion, but how did it strike her?

"Sterling," she said. "Oh, how do you *think* it strikes me? Don't you know it's the most wonderful, beautiful idea I've ever heard? Whatever made you think I'd – how could you possibly have thought I'd say no?"

He looked pleased but also deeply serious. "Well," he said, "it's not as if I could offer you a formal proposal of marriage. Point is, I can't do that; at least—" and here he squeezed her hand "at least not yet. Not until this England business is cleared up. All I can offer you now is – well, myself, and my love."

And she spent the rest of the night assuring him that she would never ask for anything more.

Within a few weeks the house had been found and rented, and the Neptune Moving and Storage Company had been contracted to move the contents of their two apartments out to Scarsdale. Alice and Bobby rode out on the train in the early afternoon of the moving day, to be there in plenty of time before the van arrived. And as she stood on the front porch, watching the great truck approach through the trees along the Post Road, she was almost ill because she could scarcely contain her happiness.

First came a barrel of china and kitchenware, and the men tracked bits of excelsior across the floor as she guided them through to the rear of the house. Then they began unloading her furniture – the ugly, once expensive sofa and upholstered chairs, the unwieldy parts of the big dining room table and the mahogany dresser with the drawer that didn't work – plain, middle-class things that she and George had bought for New Rochelle, things now grown shabby with the lonely years in Bethel and New York, things that looked somehow all the more forlorn for being heavily bumped and hauled through the Scarsdale sunshine. The men were mincingly gentle with the Majestic radio, but they didn't quite know how to deal with her sculpture, which she steered into the garage that was to serve as her studio. Then came several trunks and any number of sloppy cardboard boxes filled with odds and ends and Bobby's toys; that was all there was of their own belongings, and the great padded cavern of the moving van was still far from empty: the rest of the load was Sterling Nelson's treasure.

"Oh, *please* be careful!" she cried when one of the men allowed the delicate leg of a rosewood table to scrape against the doorjamb, and she scurried around in nervous supervision as they brought in one priceless object after another.

"Where d'ya want this, lady?" they would ask, swaying and grunting under their loads, and "Where d'ya want this?" And she did her best to make decisions about the placing of the most important pieces. But how could the perfection of Sterling Nelson's apartment be sorted out from this jumble and restored to any kind of coherence in these big, strange rooms? And her distress was compounded when Bobby came in from outside to claim her attention. He was acting as helpless and silly as if he were four instead of eight, and it wasn't until she happened to look out a front window that she understood why. Some other boys of about his age were clustered and idling near the van in the driveway. They had appeared from neighboring streets to watch the unloading, and to watch Bobby, and his shyness had driven him indoors.

"I want to help the movers," he said.

"The movers don't need any help. Please, dear; can't you see I'm busy?"

"Where d'ya want this, lady?"

"Over there – no, wait; over here, in this room, next to the big cabinet. Bobby, *please* stay outside."

"I don't feel like it."

"Is it because of those boys? Is that it?"

"No."

She sighed and raked back a wet strand of hair from her heated face. "Dear, they only want to be friendly. Why don't you go out and make friends with them?"

"I don't feel like it. My stomach hurts."

"Oh, Bobby, please. Can't you see how important it is to make everything nice for when Mr. Nelson comes?"

Because that was the whole point. Sterling's commuter train would arrive before dusk, and she wanted to make it a home-coming. It wasn't only a matter of putting the house in order; she wanted to be bathed and fresh and wearing clean clothes when his taxi drove up, and when he came striding up the porch steps. She wanted to have a real dinner ready, with candles and wine.

But she was still frantically unrolling carpets and struggling with boxes long after the movers and their van had left, and the house was still a shambles. No sooner would she get a table or a chest established in what seemed its proper place than it would turn out to be all wrong. Then at last, with the time running out, she found an alcove that made a perfect setting for the two little Elizabethan chairs. In the same swift burst of inspiration she laid the Burmese dar on the mantelpiece, and the rest of the living room was suddenly easy. Or at least it seemed that it *could* be easy: everything would fall into place if only she could get the whole splendid length of the purdah hung on the wall opposite the fireplace. She found it rolled up in one of the cardboard boxes, but it turned out to be much heavier than she'd thought. Then, in the depths of another box, she found some brackets that looked strong enough to hold it, if she used enough of them, and she found a hammer and a kitchen chair to stand on for the job. But she would need help.

"Bobby, will you bring another chair and help me, please? We've got to get this up before Mr. Nelson comes, and I can't do it alone. You stand on that side and hold that end of it, and I'll start putting in the brackets. All right?"

"All right. What is it, anyway?"

"It's a tapestry, dear. It's Burmese. It belongs to Mr. Nelson and it's very, very valuable. That's why we'll have to be careful." And they stood on their chairs at opposite ends of the purdah, Bobby doing his best to keep the weight of the thing held high while Alice carefully hammered in one bracket after another in what she could only hope was a straight line, hooking each bracket into the burlap backing of the tapestry and inching her chair along toward Bobby's as she made progress.

"That's wonderful, dear; you're really being a great help. Just keep holding up your end, and we'll be done in no time."

"What're they doing, anyway?"

"Who, dear?"

"The people in the tapestry."

"Well, you see they're Burmese people, and they believe in a god called Buddha, and they're performing a religious ceremony. Can you hold it up a little higher? There, that's fine."

"How do you mean, a religious ceremony? I mean what're they doing?"

"Well, actually, it's very interesting. They're transplanting Buddha's fingerbones."

"Doing *what?*"

"Transplanting – oh, that's not the right word. They're taking the fingerbones of Buddha from one grave, you see, and putting them into another."

"Oh. How come you don't get to see them?"

"Get to see what, dear?"

"The fingerbones."

"Well, because it's all symbolic. I mean they're not really – It's just a ceremony, you see. Mr. Nelson can explain it to you."

The hammering in of each bracket caused a little crumbling hole in the plaster and the brackets wobbled as she hooked them into the burlap, but she felt that with luck they would have enough collective grip to hold. When she was finished, when she'd moved her chair up next to Bobby's and put in the final bracket, she felt a sense of triumph. It was up.

But when they got down and walked away to look at the purdah, the first thing she saw was that it wasn't quite straight. Then there was a slight, loose sputtering sound as one after another of the brackets gave way, and down it fell, the whole purdah lumped in a hideous heap on the floor, spraying brackets as it came and leaving a row of ugly little sockets in the naked wall.

She began to weep, and at that very moment there was thumping on the boards of the front porch and a cry of "Hello! Hello!"

"Oh, Sterling! Sterling, I'm so sorry. I wanted to have everything ready for you and we *did* try, but *look* at everything. Just *look* at it!"

He did his best to comfort her, but he was as damp and unsteady as she herself: his shirt and suit were rumpled from the train and there was an anxious, bewildered look about his eyes.

"I thought at least I'd get the purdah hung before you came, and we tried and tried but we couldn't make it stay *up*. *Look* at it."

"It wants a rod," he said.

"A what?"

"A rod. Quite a heavy curtain-rod sort of thing, with heavy screws; must be packed somewhere. Those little hooks won't take the weight, you see."

"And now look at those awful little *holes* in the wall. Oh, Sterling, I'm so sorry."

"We can fix the holes later; putty them up. We've plenty of time. Look what I've brought."

Only then did she notice that he'd come in laden with packages. He had brought a bottle of Scotch and a bottle of champagne, and he'd brought what struck Bobby as the perfect gift: a fielder's glove from Spaulding's and a regulation baseball.

And so they made the best of it. Alice and Sterling strolled talking with their drinks through all the rooms, pausing some-times to sit down on chairs or to stand at a window looking out at Bobby's antics in the yard. He would throw the ball up in an inexpert, underhand way and then run desperately under its flight and try to catch it. He always missed, and when he'd retrieved the ball he would pound it firmly into the glove, standing with his legs apart in a manly, athletic pose; then he'd make another throw and race to miss the ball again.

"Doesn't seem to have the knack of it," Sterling said.

"Oh, he'll be all right. He'll learn."

"Afraid I won't be of much use to him there; whole subject of baseball's rather a blank to me."

"The other boys will teach him. He'll be fine. Why don't you take your drink out to the porch, and I'll get dinner started."

If nothing else, she was determined that their first dinner would be a success. The kitchen had an unpleasant smell from the previous tenant's garbage and the refrigerator made an alarming drone, but she worked with the kind of efficiency that had eluded her all day. From the kitchen door she called out to Bobby, "Come in and wash, dear; hurry, now." Then, taking her time, she walked proudly through the dining room and living room and out onto the porch, where she pressed a kiss into the back of Sterling's neck and whispered: "Dinner is served."

"Marvelous," he said.

He helped her into her chair and stood expertly unwinding the wires of the champagne cork and working it loose with his thumbs. It went "Flup!" in exactly the way champagne corks were supposed to go, and they all three laughed in a way that brought the house to life.

"Here's to Scarsdale," Alice said, raising her glass. "Here's to the future. Here's to everything."

"Right," Sterling said, sitting down. "I must say you've done all this beautifully, Alice – the table, the food – everything looks delicious."

Less than a second later he was on his feet and dabbing urgently at his trousers with his napkin: Bobby had knocked over his glass of milk, and the quick white flood of it had spilled into Sterling's lap.

"Oh, *Bobby*," she cried, and she was ready to slap him. "Can't you be more careful? Now look what you've done."

"It's all right," Sterling was saying. "Suit wants a cleaning anyway."

But the rest of the meal was almost devoid of conversation.

Later, though, in the calm after they'd gotten the dishes washed and Bobby put to bed, there was a peaceful time while they sat on the porch in the darkness, watching the fireflies and the lights of cars going by on the Post Road.

"Doesn't the air smell wonderful?" she said.

"Mm."

"I just can't believe it. Here we are, and everything's going to be so – did I tell you Bobby's starting school on Monday?"

"No."

"Well, he is. The third grade. Three-B."

There was a long silence while the cars droned past, going toward and away from White Plains, and Alice willed herself not to talk. If Sterling wanted to sit here quietly, that was what they would do.

Then at last he started talking. The husky British resonance of his voice was enough to bathe her in reassurance; it didn't even matter that he was discussing the trip he would soon have to make to England. While he talked she curled up in her wicker chair and felt protected.

"Would you like a drink, Sterling?"

"Yes, that might be nice. A little Scotch."

When she went inside to fix it, moving through the unfamiliar rooms and working at the ice trays of the strange refrigerator, she felt a chill of foreboding about how it would be when she and Bobby were alone here. How long had he said he'd have to be in England? Six weeks? But that could be endured, and anyway he wouldn't have to go for a little while. She carried the tinkling highballs out to the porch.

"I don't expect it'll be a very lively community, Alice," he said. "Rather a change for you after living in town."

"Oh, but I don't care. Do you?"

"I expect you'll miss your friends."

"I didn't really have any friends; not real ones. Anyway, we'll make new friends."

"May not be easy. I imagine they'll be rather dull business people for the most part. Homeowners and all that; Roosevelt haters. Rich and dull and probably a bit – inquisitive about our arrangement."

" 'Our arrangement.' You make it sound like a play."

Sterling was silent for a moment in a way that caused her to bite her lip, and she wished she could see his face in the darkness. Then he said, "Won't you find it a bit awkward being called 'Mrs. Nelson' and so on?"

"Not if you don't."

He gave a little chuckle and reached out across the arms of their chairs to squeeze her hand. "I suppose we'll be all right."

And she supposed so too.

The question of whether or not she would find it awkward being called "Mrs. Nelson" remained unresolved; nobody in Scarsdale called her anything at all.

Electric trains drew the men away to the city each morning and the children were swallowed up by school. The women, alone in their big, impeccable houses, let their days slip away in endless rounds of triviality – or at least, that was the way Alice

147

saw them in her mind's eye. She pictured them idling through easy household chores or giving instructions to their maids, and painting their fingernails and fixing their hair and compounding their lassitude by spending hours on the telephone with one another, talking of bridge clubs and luncheons and functions of the P.T.A. If their lives included anything more interesting than that she didn't learn of it, for none of them ever called her up or dropped in for a neighborly visit – nor, apparently, did any of their husbands ever strike up an acquaintance with Sterling on the train. Scarsdale behaved as though Alice and Sterling didn't exist.

She didn't care. She had her mornings and part of her afternoons free for sculpture in the garage, and she was doing new, exciting work: she had abandoned garden sculpture and was making sculpture for its own sake – sinuous torsos and semi-abstract animals – things that would make excellent exhibition pieces as soon as she had enough of them to warrant a one-man show.

A little after three o'clock each day she would go out across the Post Road and wait for Bobby's coming home. The school was within easy walking distance, but it was on the other side of the road, and she didn't want him crossing that wide, hectic highway by himself: she took him across each morning and went across to wait for him each afternoon. He didn't seem to mind when he came home alone, which was most of the time – for the first week or so, in fact, he would break into an eager run for the last few yards and let her hug him, to prove how much he'd missed her all day – but later, when he began walking home in a cluster of other boys, it seemed to embarrass him.

"I can cross the street by myself," he said.

"No you can't."

When Sterling found out about it, one morning after he'd

missed his regular train to the city, he was almost angry with her. "You mean to say you do that every day?" he asked, looking up from the breakfast table when she'd come back to the house. "Take him across the street by the hand?"

"But it's not just a street, it's a *highway*. And the cars come so terribly fast I'm almost afraid to cross it myself."

"Oh, nonsense, Alice. The boy's eight years old. How's he ever going to learn to look after himself if you keep babying him?"

"I don't baby him, Sterling."

"Yes you do. I'm sorry, Alice, but it's a thing I've meant to speak with you about before." He looked grimly at his coffee cup. "Well," he said, "I expect it's none of my business."

In the end she agreed, reluctantly, to let Bobby cross the street alone, even though it meant standing at the window in the grip of anxiety, morning and afternoon, watching until he had looked both ways and run in awkward safety to the other side. She was willing to agree with Sterling on almost everything now because there was so little time left before his trip, and she couldn't bear the thought of any unpleasantness.

And it seemed to her that Bobby, by this time, had become as careful as she was about the importance of pleasing Mr. Nelson. He never whined or made childish scenes or tried to monopolize the conversation; he did his homework promptly and without coaxing, and if there was any time left over before bedtime he would spend it lying prone on the living room carpet, absorbed – or, she suspected, pretending to be absorbed – in *British Submarine Service in the Great War*. One evening, after long preparation, he showed Sterling a slingshot that some boy at school had taught him how to make: a stout and carefully whittled forked stick, with strips of pink rubber cut from an inner tube and a leather sling made from the tongue of an old shoe.

"Oh, I say," Sterling said, examining the thing. "That's really fine. That's a first-rate piece of work." And Bobby, hooking both thumbs in his hip pockets, could only duck his head in bashful acceptance of the praise. "Want to try it out?" Sterling asked him. "Have a little target practice?" And Alice fondly watched from a window as the two of them went outdoors in the gathering dusk. Sterling fixed a scrap of paper to a tree for a target, while Bobby collected pebbles for ammunition; then together they paced off a range and took turns at firing the slingshot.

But the game had scarcely begun before it ended, and when they came back into the kitchen Bobby looked pink in the face and close to tears. "It broke," he told her. "Mr. Nelson pulled it back too far and it broke."

"The rubber was rotted through, you see," Sterling explained. "All we need is a better piece of inner tube."

"But that's the only piece of inner tube I could *find*. It's *hard* to find pieces of inner tube."

"No," Sterling said, "I shouldn't think it'd be all that hard; I imagine I can find one." But he didn't sound at all sure of it, and for a perilous moment Alice felt as if she had two children on her hands.

"Well," she said, "maybe it can be fixed, and anyway it was fun while it lasted. Hurry along and wash up now, Bobby, Dinner's ready."

He did as he was told, after throwing down the broken sling-shot with only the smallest display of temper. He didn't sulk over it, and she was proud to notice that he didn't bring the subject up again in the days that followed, even though Sterling had apparently forgotten about finding a better piece of inner tube.

When the time of Sterling's departure was only a week away she suggested, shyly, that she might go into the city to see him off – she had a pleasant vision of herself smiling and waving, a little tearful among the cheers and streamers and confetti as the great horn sounded and the great ship drew majestically away from the pier – but he said he thought that would be silly. "These sailings are always such a crush and a bother; lot of overemotional nonsense. I think the less elaborate we make our goodbyes the better, don't you?"

Then suddenly the day itself was upon them, and their good-byes weren't elaborate at all. Breakfast was the same as ever, except that two heavy suitcases stood waiting for removal in the hallway, along with his daily commuter's briefcase. The only other difference was that when they got up from the table he gave her a little hug and kissed her cheek – normally they never kissed in Bobby's presence – and then, with one arm still around her waist, he reached out and shook Bobby's hand.

"Well, old man," he said. "I'll expect you to take good care of your mother while I'm gone."

And Bobby said "Okay."

She knew she couldn't expect a letter for at least two weeks, but even so, toward the end of the second week, she began abandoning her studio every morning at ten to watch for the mailman. He would come trudging along the Post Road while she breathed a silent prayer to him – Oh please, please – and more often than not he would go on past the house; the few times he stopped to deposit something in her mailbox it would turn out to be bills or advertisements – and, once, the familiar ugly business envelope from Amalgamated Tool and Die that contained her alimony check. In the third week he brought her a real letter, but it wasn't the one she was praying for, the one in fragile air-mail stationery with a British stamp and postmark. It was only a letter from her sister Eva, and she was so disappointed that she didn't even open it until there was nothing else to do in the tedious hours of the afternoon. When she did, she found that it contained startling news: Eva was getting married. Fifty-year-old Eva, the everlastingly plain and bossy big sister, the meddlesome old maid of the family, was announcing her engagement to someone named Owen Forbes from Austin, Texas. And the funny thing, the touching thing, was that Eva sounded so shy and formal about it.

". . . Owen is naturally eager to meet the members of my family, so we plan to spend much of our wedding trip in Indiana, before settling in Austin. But I've been wondering if it might not be possible to spend a little time with you before we leave. Do you suppose you might come into the city some evening next week, and we could all have dinner together at some nice hotel like the Commodore? . . ."

So it was pity and curiosity, as much or more than affection, that prompted her to pick up the phone and call Eva that very night.

". . . I think it's wonderful news, Eva," she said. "Really, I'm so pleased, and so happy for you."

"Well, I'm very – well, thank you, dear. It was good of you to call." Eva was as shy on the phone as in the letter, as if she'd been afraid Alice might think the whole idea of her marriage was ludicrous. And when Alice sensed this and felt guilty about it (because she *had* thought it ludicrous, in a way) it made her even more effusive than she'd planned to be.

"I'd love to meet him," she heard herself saying. "But look: instead of meeting in the city, why don't you bring him out here? Wouldn't that be nicer? And we've got plenty of room, in case you'd like to spend the night. You'd be more than welcome. Really."

More than welcome. That was the phrase that kept ringing in

her memory while she readied the house for their visit. This house, filled with Sterling's belongings and horridly vacant of his presence, had become all but intolerable; and therefore the idea of receiving Eva and Mr. Owen Forbes of Austin, Texas – or anyone else in the world, for that matter – was more than welcome.

"Guess what," she said to Bobby at breakfast. "Remember your Aunt Eva? Well, Aunt Eva is getting married, and this evening she's going to bring her fiancé out here to meet us, and we'll all have dinner together and they might even stay the night. Won't that be fun?"

"What does that mean?"

"What, dear?"

"Fiancé."

"Well, it means the man she's going to marry. His name is Mr. Owen Forbes and he comes from Texas. After they're married he'll be your uncle."

"Oh." Bobby thoughtfully stirred his spoon around in the remains of his Cream of Wheat, and she could tell from the averted, almost sly look on his face that his next remark would be something less than wholly ingenuous. "Mommy?" he said. "Is Mr. Nelson your fiancé?"

"No, dear; don't ask silly questions. I've explained all that to you before. Mr. Nelson and I are very dear friends. We care very much about each other and we both care very much about you."

"You mean you're in love with each other, or what?"

"I mean exactly what I said. Now will you please just finish your cereal and stop asking silly—"

"I'm *not* asking silly questions. All I mean is, if you and Mr. Nelson are in love with each other, and if you get married when he comes home from England, then what'll he be? My father, or what?"

"Oh, Bobby, I know you know better than that. He'd be your stepfather."

"You mean he couldn't ever be my real father because Daddy's my real father. Right?"

She sighed. "Yes, dear, that's right."

"Then how come Aunt Eva's husband's going to be my uncle? Won't he just be my stepuncle?"

"He'll be your uncle by marriage. Hurry along, now, or you'll be late for school."

The mailman passed her by again that morning, but she forced herself not to mind; she was fully composed by the time the taxi turned into the driveway that evening. The house was clean and she and Bobby were both in their best clothes, wearing fixed, vulnerable smiles, ready to make their visitors more than welcome.

Owen Forbes turned out to be big, ruddy, and hearty, so engagingly forceful and masculine a man that Alice was surprised into thinking, How did Eva ever get him? And Eva was radiant. She was as plain and heavy-legged as ever, but she had bloomed into a new womanliness that was all the more impressive because she seemed conscious of it, and proud of it.

"Heard a lot of very fine things about you, little lady," Owen Forbes said when he took Alice's hand, and he bent to give her a respectful little kiss on the cheek. Then he turned to Bobby, but instead of shaking hands he made a fist and gently cuffed it across the tip of Bobby's chin. "Been hearing some pretty good things about you, too, Buster," he said. "How's it going?"

His booming voice and lumbering frame filled the house with authority: in the first few awkward moments of choosing chairs and getting the conversation started he took command of them all, as if the house were his own and he were the host, and he put them all at ease.

154

"None for me, thanks," he said firmly when Alice offered cocktails. "You girls go right ahead, though." And a moment later: "Hey, listen," he said to Bobby. "You got a football? Thought we might get in a little catch outside, before it gets dark."

Bobby replied that he didn't have a football but did have a baseball and a glove; would that do?

"Great," said Owen Forbes, standing up and stripping off his coat for action. "And if you've only got one glove, you wear it. Then you can kind of just lob 'em over to me and I'll really burn 'em into you. Okay?"

"This really is a remarkable room, Alice," Eva said when they were alone together. "Did you rent the house furnished?"

Alice was prepared for that question; she had already rehearsed her careful lie, and she was glad Bobby wasn't there to hear it. "Well, no; most of these things are very valuable. They belong to some friends of mine who've gone to Europe for a while."

"And what's that?" Eva inquired of the purdah. "Is it Persian?"

"It's Burmese. These people are English, you see, and they lived in the Orient for some time."

"Well, it's very — striking," Eva said. "It's really very decorative."

And now that these amenities were out of the way they could get down, over the pouring of second drinks, to the serious business of discussing Owen Forbes. He had been a patient at the hospital where Eva worked — that was how they'd met. "He's not as strong as he looks, you see," she explained. "Actually, he's still in quite delicate health." That was why he'd had to give up his strenuous position as a history professor at N.Y.U., and that was why they planned to settle in Austin. There, in the gentler climate and the slower pace of life, in semi-retirement, he would find the leisure to finish the book he'd been planning for years:

155

a scholarly treatise on the role of the A.E.F. in the War. He himself had served in the A.E.F. with distinction, emerging as a major; he'd been wounded and severely gassed, which was the origin of his ill-health. He'd been married before to a woman who never understood him, who had divorced him and demanded an exorbitant alimony until her own remarriage; now he was free at last, and he had chosen to share his new life with Eva Grumbauer. "He needs me, Alice," Eva said as her embarrassed, old-maid's eyes began to fill with tears. "That's the wonderful thing. I've never known anyone who's really – really needed me before."

And Alice found it necessary to wipe her own eyes – not only out of gladness for Eva and not only because of the gin and vermouth, but because she had been touched with an ache of envy. To be needed: that *was* the wonderful thing. And even if she had been able to tell Eva about Sterling Nelson, could she honestly have said that Sterling Nelson needed her?

But there was no more time for sentimentality, because Bobby and Owen Forbes had come banging and, thumping back into the house – a couple of laughing, winded athletes, ready for a solid meal.

Owen Forbes took full charge of the happy dinner table, though he refused his share of the wine. He kept urging more meat and potatoes and milk on Bobby – "You got to build yourself up, if you want to develop that arm" – and long before the evening was over he had Bobby calling him "Uncle Owen."

"Okay, Champ," he said at Bobby's bedtime. "Get yourself a good night's sleep, and I'll see you in the morning."

"You know what, Mommy?" Bobby said when she went upstairs to tuck him in. "Uncle Owen taught me how to throw. It's *easy*; what you do is, you do it with your whole body. You

156

kind of put your whole body into it instead of just your arm. I mean I haven't quite learned how to do it yet, but it's *easy*."

"Well," she said. "Isn't that nice."

But they were gone by noon the next day, after another morning in which the mailman passed her by; they were gone in a flurry of kisses and promises to write, bound for Indiana and then for Texas, and they left the house emptier than before.

Toward the end of the fourth week she considered telephoning Sterling's office in New York to inquire, discreetly, if they'd heard from him, and to ask if they had an address in England at which he might be reached. But she dismissed the idea, after more than a day of thinking about it and after getting as far, three or four times, as to pick up the phone and begin to place the call.

It wasn't until a rainy day in the fifth week that she decided she could bear it no longer. When the mailman retreated up the road in the rain, leaving nothing in her box, she settled herself at the telephone with a fresh pack of cigarettes beside her for courage.

She had called his office any number of times before, and always it had been a simple matter of saying "Mr. Nelson, please" to the switchboard operator, and then of hearing his secretary say "Mr. Nelson's office," and then of hearing Sterling. Now she didn't quite know how to begin.

"I'd – I'd like to speak with Mr. Nelson's secretary," she told the switchboard girl.

"Mr. Nelson's no longer with us."

"No, I said his secretary. I know he's abroad, but I'd like to speak with his secretary, please."

"Oh; you mean Miss Breen. She's working for Mr. Harding now. Just a moment."

There was a buzzing and a clicking and then another voice said: "Mr. Harding's office." It was the same cheerful, Brooklyn-accented voice that used to answer for Sterling.

"Are you Miss Breen?"

"Yes."

"I'm calling to inquire about Mr. Nelson."

"Mr. Nelson's in London. Mr. Harding's handling all his accounts now; perhaps he can—"

"No, no; this is a personal call. I just wanted to find out when Mr. Nelson is expected to return."

There was a pause. "Well, as far as I know he isn't *expected* to return. I mean I believe he's been transferred to London on a permanent basis."

Alice was patient. "No," she said. "I'm sure there must be some mistake. He was expected back in four to six weeks."

"Oh. Well, as far as I – perhaps you'd like to speak with Mr. Cameron, our managing director?"

"Yes. Yes, please."

There was more buzzing and clicking and another secretary to deal with; then at last a thunderous British voice said: "Cameron here."

"I'm – I'm calling to inquire about Mr. Sterling Nelson. I wondered if you could tell me when—"

"If this is Gramercy Realty, I've nothing further to say. I've made it perfectly clear to you people that we are in no way responsible—"

"No," she said. "I'm not – this isn't – Please, I—"

"Well, if you're another of his creditors my answer's the same. We are in no way responsible for any debts he may've—"

"No, look, please. This is a personal matter. I'm a – personal friend of Mr. Nelson's, and I simply wondered if you could tell me when he's expected back."

Mr. Cameron sighed audibly into the phone, and when he spoke again he was less harsh, as if beginning to sense that this might indeed be a personal matter – perhaps even a delicate one. "I see," he said. "Well, there seems to've been a good deal of confusion about Mr. Nelson's activities, to say the least. Matter of fact, you might be able to help us. Have you any knowledge of his whereabouts now?"

"His whereabouts?"

"Have you any address in England where he might be reached?"

"No. No, I don't have—"

"And you say he told you – it was your understanding that he planned to return to this country?"

"That was – yes, that was my understanding."

"Well, I'm afraid you were misinformed. Mr. Nelson's American visa had expired and we chose not to arrange for its renewal. Then after he left there began to be no end of nuisance here from his creditors, so I cabled London. The London office has replied that directly after reporting there he severed his connection with the firm, and since he left no forwarding address we're quite unable to trace him. Puts the firm in a most awkward position but there's nothing we can . . ."

Alice could never afterwards remember how she managed to conclude the conversation; all she knew was that when it was over she sat paralyzed at the telephone table for a long time. Then she began walking through the house looking at Sterling's things, touching them, not crying and not even wanting to cry, realizing in wave after wave of pain that the gift of these things had been Sterling's way of saying goodbye. "I think the less elaborate we make our goodbyes the better, don't you?" – and he'd known even then that it was forever. He'd known – he must have known even before the move to Scarsdale, and God

159

only knew how long before that – he must have known she would one day be walking alone and bereft among his gifts, and he must have hoped, in his quiet, knowledgeable way, that she would understand.

But she didn't understand – that was what made it impossible to cry. All she could do was walk and sit and get up and walk again, with the voice of Mr. Cameron echoing in her head; all she could do was fail and fail and fail to understand.

A little after three o'clock, still walking, she began to know what she would do. She would go to the front window and wait for Bobby – no, better still, she would put on her raincoat and go out across the Post Road to wait for him, and when he came he would say, "How come you're here?" and she would say, "Just waiting for you." And they would cross the road together and go into the house. Then Bobby's eyes would get very round and he'd say, "What's the matter, Mommy? Is something the matter, or what?"

And she wouldn't tell him right away. She would carefully put both of their raincoats on hangers to dry, and she would inquire how his day had been at school. But when he asked her again if something was the matter, she would break: she would go down on her knees and take him in her arms. She would gather him in and press him close, and then – she knew that by then she'd be able to cry – then she would say, "Oh, Bobby, he's gone. He's gone from us, and he's never coming back . . ."

That was how she planned it, and that was the way it happened.

Chapter Three

If Scarsdale was, as Sterling Nelson had promised, an isolated pocket of prosperity, the town of Riverside, only a few miles away in the Hudson Valley, was an isolated pocket of grandeur. It was like no place Alice had ever seen before, and she knew at once that she wanted to live there. It would change her life.

It wasn't really a town at all, or even a village, but a colony of handsome dwellings built as close as possible to the high-walled borders of a great private estate called Boxwood. Both the estate and its careful environs were the work of a self-made Wall Street tycoon named Walter J. Vander Meer – a man whose eagerness to erase his own beginnings on a small Missouri farm had made him seek to establish a new dynasty here, among the ghosts of the colonial Dutch whom he believed, on slender evidence, to have been his ancestors.

He had spared nothing in creating Riverside: he had equipped it with two tasteful churches, Episcopal and Presbyterian; he had made certain that its Riverside Country Club would have the finest golf course in Westchester County; and had taken considerable pains over the founding of Riverside Country Day School, on the high marble panel of whose main hall were engraved the words:

MANNERS MAKETH MAN

But the full flowering of his zeal had gone into the creation of Boxwood. Its grounds were a marvel of professional landscaping in that every vista was pleasing to the eye – wide, rolling lawns, tall trees, rich hedges, and deep gardens. In addition to a number of servants' quarters and guest cottages, there were four substantial homes intended for the families of his four sons, and all the winding roads and pathways led eventually to the high ground on which he'd built his own mansion, which might have been named Boxwood Manor if it hadn't always been called "The Big House." All the tall western windows of the Big House, and the marble-flagged esplanade beneath them, commanded a majestic view of the Hudson, a view only partially blemished by another and more famous Big House less than two miles upriver in which more than a few of Walter J. Vander Meer's early business associates had spent their final days: the squat, ugly structure of Sing Sing Penitentiary.

Vander Meer had died of old age and bewilderment soon after the Crash, but enough of his millions remained to ensure a long and sound survival for his aristocratic widow, his progeny, his Boxwood, and his Riverside.

"Isn't it something?" Maude Larkin inquired, moving through the summer breeze of the esplanade with the proud and stately tread of a pathfinder, and Alice had to agree, in something close to reverence, that it certainly was.

They paused to rest against the balustrade, and Maude Larkin said, "See? Those are the Palisades. That big one's High Tor, the one Max Anderson wrote the play about. And look here—" She called Alice's attention back from the mountains and away from the intermediate hulk of Sing Sing; she was pointing to the balustrade on which their forearms rested. "All this marble was imported from Italy, piece by piece. Can you imagine what that must have cost? And you see he never did quite finish it. He built this whole beautiful place all through the Twenties, and the esplanade was meant to be the crowning glory; but you see it was supposed to go all the way across the lawn, all the way to the poplars over there. And you see what happened instead?" She took Alice by the hand and led her out to where the esplanade came to an abrupt amputation, and with a theatrical flourish she pointed to five Italian marble columns lying corpselike in the grass. "Nineteen twenty-nine," she said in a stage whisper. "Isn't that something? I mean really, Alice; isn't that something?"

In the long, lonely time since Sterling Nelson's desertion – almost three years now – Alice had found a small measure of comfort in spending two afternoons a week as a teacher of sculpture in the Arts and Crafts Guild, a community enterprise that occupied the basement of the Westchester County Center, in White Plains. The money she earned from it was scarcely worth counting – most of the other teachers were volunteers – but she thought the experience would be valuable, and she hoped it might be a way of meeting people. It was: all her students were women of her own age or older, prosperously married and vaguely dissatisfied and "looking for something," as more than a few of them put it, and they tended to make a pet of her. They would take her into their homes, in Scarsdale or in other nearby towns just like it, to meet their polite if baffled husbands; but more often than not those evenings would end with her riding home in the embarrassing silence of the husbands' cars, her mouth dry and swollen from too much talking about "art" and "form" and "Paris" and "Greenwich Village" (and when would she ever learn not to monopolize a whole evening's conversation?) while the husbands shifted gears and groped for pleasantries about how "interesting" it had been.

Then toward the end of the third year Maude Larkin had enrolled in her class, and she knew from the start that Maude Larkin was going to be different. Not only did she seem more talented than the others, or at least more responsive to criticism, but everything else about her suggested the kind of person Alice really did want to know, and to have for a friend. One day Maude shyly asked her out for a drink after class and they sat for hours in a White Plains cocktail lounge. For once it wasn't Alice who did most of the talking, and all the things Maude said revealed more and more clearly that Alice hadn't been wrong about her: Maude Larkin *was* interesting. She didn't live in Scarsdale or in any of its stifling vicinities; she lived in Riverside, of which Alice had never heard. And her husband wasn't an insurance man or a lawyer or a business executive like the others, but a writer: he wrote scripts for three of the evening radio serials to which Alice had long been addicted.

"You mean you really like them?" Maude asked, her eyes as bright as a happy child's. "Oh, I can't *wait* to tell Jim that; he *hates* them; he'll be absolutely delighted." Her witty, knowledgeable talk went on through round after round of relaxing Manhattans for which she insisted on paying; Alice had to excuse herself twice to telephone Bobby with promises to be home soon, and when Maude drove her back to Scarsdale at last they lingered in the parked car for an exchange of affectionate declarations:

"Oh, it's been so nice, Maude. Please come in and have dinner with us."

"Dear, I'd love to, but I've got to get home or Jim and the kids'll kill me. But listen: I'm not letting you out of this car until you promise me one thing. Do promise to come see us soon. Bring your little boy and spend the weekend. Next weekend."

"Well, I'd love to, Maude, but really I—"

"Promise. You've got to promise. I'll come and get you, all right? I'll call you tomorrow. And another thing, Alice – I know this may sound drunk and foolish, but there's one other thing I *must* say before I let you go. I simply can't tell you how much this sculpture class has meant to me. Honestly. I feel – it's what I've always – well, I just feel you've opened up a whole new world for me, and I want to thank you, that's all."

And now in return, by bringing her to Riverside and guiding her through the splendors of Boxwood, it seemed that Maude was opening up a whole new world for Alice.

"Are you sure it's all right for us to be here, Maude?" she asked when they'd left the esplanade and started back down one of the winding paths.

"Of course it's all right. The old lady and I are on first-name terms. Well—" and here she laughed in the candid little self-effacing way that was one of her most winning traits – "I guess that's not *exactly* true. She calls me 'Maude' and I call her 'Mrs. Vander Meer.' I don't think anyone in the whole world uses *her* first name. Anyway, she seems to approve of me, and I know she'd approve of you. The only one you ever have to worry about is Walter Junior, the oldest son. He can be nice sometimes, but he's essentially a pompous ass. Jim calls him a capitalist piglet – says he isn't big enough to be a capitalist pig. He's the whaddyacallit of the whole business, you see – the executor? Is that what you call it? I don't know. Anyway, he's the man in charge, and he takes it all very seriously. But look: here's what I've been dying to show you. Come along."

And Alice followed her in pleased bewilderment. They were heading around toward the rear of one of the splendid houses Maude had pointed out earlier in the tour – the one built for Howard Vander Meer, the second son, which had been vacant since the Howard Vander Meers' divorce some years before – and Maude walked boldly up to one of its rear doors and opened it. "Just wait till you see this," she said.

"You mean you're going inside? Do you really think we—"

"Not the house itself, that's all locked up. Just the basement. Come along."

Even the basement looked rich: clean concrete corridors along whose walls were piled the incidental refuse of the broken family (expensive wardrobe trunks, racked pairs of skis, cardboard boxes bearing the trade names of Bergdorf Goodman, Brooks Brothers, Abercrombie and Fitch) – but Alice scarcely had time to notice these things before Maude drew her over to a door that couldn't have been more than five feet tall. "You'll have to duck going in," she said, "but just wait till you see what's inside."

The tiny door let them into an enormous, absolutely bare white room that was flooded with daylight. Its walls were of lacquered white wood, flecked all over with hundreds of little gray-black smudges, as if they'd been daubed with licorice, and they were windowless: all the light came from the high ceiling, which was made wholly of wired glass, "What *is* it?" Alice whispered.

"It's a squash court. Howard was crazy about squash, you see, so his daddy built this whole gigantic thing right into the house. *That's* the kind of money they had. But Alice, don't you see what I'm driving at? Look at the lighting; look at the walls. Don't you see what it *could* be?" Her eyes were gleaming. "A sculpture studio. *Your* studio. You could hold private classes here – my God, you'd have room for three times as many students as you have now, and still have plenty of room for your own work. Wouldn't it be priceless?"

It would indeed. Alice was instantly able to picture herself at work here – teaching people as congenial as Maude, doing sculpture of her own that would be better than anything she'd dreamed of in the past. "Well, but how could I possibly – I mean how could I ever—"

"Wait." And Maude placed a rigid forefinger against her lips. "Don't say another word. I just wanted you to see this place, and now there's one more place I want you to see, and then we'll go home and have a drink. I *told* you I was full of plans, didn't I? Come on.

"If you're going to work here you'll have to live here," she said. "And I've got just the right house picked out for you. The perfect home for the artist in residence."

It turned out to be an elegant little house of white stucco, attractively set in the extreme northeast corner of the estate, surrounded by trees and beds of rhododendron, with a flagstone path leading up to its front door. "They call it the gatehouse," Maude explained. "It was built for one of Mrs. Vander Meer's relatives, but it's never been occupied; actually it's still unfinished, but I happen to know Walter Junior's been planning to fix it up and rent it this year. And why shouldn't it be yours?"

It was locked, but they could see the whole of its interior by moving around and peering through windows: a big central room with a spectacular fireplace, a kitchen and dining area, two ample bedrooms with a connecting bathroom in the rear. "Can't you just see it?" Maude demanded. "Wouldn't it be the absolutely perfect home for you and Bobby?"

By the time they had let themselves out through one of the heavy iron gates and strolled back to the Larkins' home that afternoon, to have a drink and talk it over with Jim, Alice was completely enthralled with Maude's plan. It had become her own plan, as firm and settled as any decision she had ever made. She and Bobby would live in the gatehouse; Bobby

167

would attend Riverside Country Day; they would be among stimulating people like the Larkins, instead of the stuffy mediocrities of Scarsdale, and the whole charming new life would be made possible by her role as "artist in residence." She would have a generous new income from teaching private classes in the squash court, and if that didn't wholly solve the financial side of things she might well find other sources: she could sell some of her old garden sculpture – possibly even sell some of it to the Vander Meers – and once she was established in this brisk new environment there was no reason why she couldn't turn out enough new work to warrant a profitable New York exhibition once a year. Anything seemed possible in Riverside.

Jim Larkin was a little doubtful. "Well, I don't know, Alice," he said. "I wouldn't want to see you get involved in more than you can handle."

"But she'll be *able* to handle it, Jim," said Maude. "That's the whole point. She's an exceptional woman. She's an artist of the first rank, she's an inspiring teacher, and she's been hiding her talents under a bushel long enough. This place was *made* for her. She's going to *thrive* here."

"I certainly don't mean to question any of that,' he said, "but before you girls get carried away there's one or two practical points you ought to consider."

And Alice was willing to hear him out. Jim Larkin had frightened her a little the evening before by saying he was a communist, but he wasn't at all like the communists she'd known in New York. He was quick and funny and brusque in a nice way; he seemed embarrassed to be making so much money out of radio but he wasn't boringly apologetic about it, and he was clearly a man of intellectual substance. Hundreds of books had overflowed the shelves of his study to be strewn in attractive disorder around the living room; he knew Maxwell Anderson well enough to call him Max, and once he had even hinted at knowing Thomas Wolfe well enough to call him Tom. Alice guessed she liked him very much, enough to be patient while he went over the one or two points they ought to consider.

"In the first place," he said, "how do you know old Walter Junior won't take a dim view of having sculpture classes in the squash court?"

"Oh, where's your imagination, Jim?" Maude said. "We won't *deal* with Walter Junior. We'll go directly to the old lady, and I know she'll approve it. I know she'll love Alice, that's a foregone conclusion. And I know she's dying for some way to express herself besides writing out all those checks to hospitals – I'll just bet the idea of being a Patroness of the Arts is going to knock her for a loop."

And Jim chuckled. "Well, you may be right about that. Knock her for a loop. All for art; art for art's sake. Maybe she'll be a pushover. God knows if anybody can talk her into it, you can. But still, even assuming that part's okay, won't it be a little hard for Alice to swing the rest of it? You can be sure they're going to ask a nice little rent for that house, for one thing, not to mention the tuition at Riverside Country Day. This is a pretty expensive town for a woman with a limited income."

"Her income won't be limited for long," Maude assured him. "And anyway we don't know how much rent they'll ask – they might make it reasonable for her. As for Country Day, you know perfectly well half the children go there on scholarships." And she explained this point to Alice. "That's the way most of these smaller private schools operate, you see: they've got heavy endowments, but in order to justify their existence they've got to keep their enrollments up to a certain minimum. The result is that an awful lot of the kids go free. Ours don't, but that's because Jim makes so much money. I should certainly think Bobby might qualify for a scholarship."

"Somebody ought to tell you it's a pretty silly little school, though," Jim said, and Maude turned on him.

"It is *not*, Jim. It's a *fine* school."

"Oh, come off it, sweetheart. What the hell's 'fine' about Riverside Country Day? You mean it's 'fine' because our kids get to mix it up with the landed gentry? It's a ridiculous school."

"Don't listen to him, Alice. *Please* don't listen to him when he gets like this."

"Gets like what?" he demanded. "It is a ridiculous school. Everybody knows that."

"Jim, darling, will you please keep your voice down? Before the children hear you?" And she turned to Alice in urgent appeal. "Alice, all I can tell you is that our children love it." But by this time Jim Larkin was laughing, touseling his wife's hair, proving that it hadn't been a quarrel at all, or even an argument, but only another surprising facet of this remarkable family, another aspect of the wonderfully free and easy way these people lived. "Sure they love it!" he was saying. "Sure they love it! That doesn't mean they're not smart enough to know it's ridiculous, does it? Whoever said you can't love ridiculous things? God knows I love you, and you're the most ridiculous woman I ever met!"

The Larkin children, a boy and a girl in their middle teens, had puzzled Alice the evening before because they seemed so aloof and unmindful of the rudiments of courtesy. They hadn't been openly rude to her or to Bobby; it was just that they'd seemed withdrawn into some private, unsmiling social pattern of their own. Their demeanor was loose and slumbrous, and they were dressed like workmen in sloppy flannel shirts and blue denim trousers, which had made Alice wonder if, to their expressionless eyes, her own and Bobby's clothes might look too careful, too neat and middle-class. But now in the second evening she felt she was beginning to understand them, just as she'd begun to understand Jim. At dinner they teased their father and joined him in teasing their mother, all in a kind of affectionate wit that was precocious without being offensive. And afterwards, with no trace of showing off, they performed an impromptu musicale. Jim started it, slouching over to the piano and hammering out some quick, frivolous popular song by way of introduction; then the girl produced a guitar and the boy a clarinet, and they played and sang delightfully for more than an hour. They were gifted children; they were interesting children; they were children quite capable of loving their school and finding it ridiculous at the same time; they were, she decided, children of exactly the kind she had always wanted Bobby to be.

"Oh, Maude," she said, riding back to Scarsdale much later that night, "I can't tell you how much we've enjoyed it. It's just been the nicest weekend we've had in years and years."

"Then it's all settled, isn't it," Maude said. "I'll speak to Mrs. Vander Meer tomorrow – or I guess I'd better not promise tomorrow; getting into the Big House is like getting an audience with the Pope or something – but anyway I'll speak to her this week, and try to fix it for you to meet her next weekend. She'll probably invite us both for tea, and you can take it from there. I just *know* it's all going to work out."

And it did.

"Will you have cream or lemon?" Mrs. Walter J. Vander Meer inquired the following Saturday in what was, beyond question, the most magnificent room Alice had ever seen.

"Lemon, please." Alice felt a drop of sweat creep out of her armpit and slide down her ribs, and at the same moment she saw that the long ash of her cigarette had fallen into her lap. Would crossing her legs hide it, or would it be better to hide it with her napkin? In either case, how could she hide it when the time came to stand up? "Thank you," she said, accepting the hot, delicate cup and saucer from Mrs. Vander Meer and trying to keep them from chattering in her hands. Without Maude's comforting presence beside her, she was sure she would have fumbled and spilled everything on the floor. Maude had carried most of the conversation so far, sparing her from any direct involvement, but now all the talk had stopped and she looked up to find herself under the full weight of the old lady's scrutiny.

Tall and thin and remarkably erect in her chair beside the tea service, Mrs. Vander Meer seemed to speak from a great distance. "Maude tells me you're a very courageous woman, Mrs. Prentice."

And how in the world could she reply to that? "Well," she said, "that's very kind of Maude." And it seemed, from Mrs. Vander Meer's small, qualified smile, that she'd passed the first test. But she didn't want to risk a sidelong glance at Maude for fear that Maude might wink at her, or raise and shake her clasped hands over her head like a victorious prizefighter.

"Please excuse me," Mrs. Vander Meer said. "I'm afraid I've forgotten to give you an ashtray. Could you hand her that one, Maude? From the table?"

There was nowhere to put the ashtray but in her lap, which was already filled with the trembling cup and saucer; after a little agony of hesitation she set it on the carpet and stubbed out her cigarette in it, and then she was touched with terror. Had anyone ever put an ashtray on the floor in the Vander Meer house before?

Mrs. Vander Meer's gaze had indeed followed the passage of the ashtray to the floor and now was fixed on it with a little frown; but it turned out to be only a frown of concentration on the difficulty of forming her next sentence. "It's always seemed to me," she said at last, "that it must require a great deal of courage to be an artist, if only because the creative process is such a lonely one. I should imagine it must be all the more difficult for a woman."

And Alice let the tension of her spine and shoulders subside a little into the upholstery. She had known from the start that Mrs. Vander Meer was imposing, that she was stately and beautiful, that she was an embodiment of every admirable connotation of the word "aristocratic"; now, for the first time and with enormous relief, she began to believe that Mrs. Vander Meer was nice.

"Tell me, Mrs. Prentice. Do you think you might enjoy working here? And living here?"

"Yes, I believe I would," she said. "I believe I'd enjoy it very much."

"I'll be speaking to my son in the morning," she said. "I'm sure something can be arranged."

"Oh, you were marvelous!" Maude Larkin said when they were alone and free of The Big House at last. "You couldn't have been better. I know she fell in love with you."

But Alice didn't need to be told: she could still feel the old lady's approval around her like a warm cloak.

Mrs. Vander Meer apparently did speak to her son in the morning, and her son apparently didn't find the plan bizarre. An interview with him took place that same week, in his office, again with Maude coming along for moral support; and though Alice found him not very likable – a plump, small-eyed, high-voiced man who seemed to have inherited none of his mother's qualities – it was clear that she had, as Maude put it, "passed muster" with him as well.

There were two more people for her to pass muster with: a Mr. Frank Garrett, the real estate agent, and a Dr. Eugene Cool, who was the principal of Riverside Country Day. And neither of them, according to Maude, presented any obstacle. "Treat Garrett like an employee," Maude advised her. "After all, that's all he is. He's just a little Yonkers mick who knows damn well he's lucky to be making a living at all; he'd do pick-and-shovel work if the Vander Meers told him to. As for old Cool, just keep calling him 'Doctor' instead of 'Mister,' and let him talk about the virtues of progressive education for half an hour, and you'll have him eating out of your hand."

But neither of those interviews was a success. Mr. Garrett, who didn't look even faintly capable of pick-and-shovel work as he sat behind the wide desk in his office, told her that the rent for the gatehouse would amount to more than she had ever paid for living quarters before.

"And that will include the utilities, will it? The heating and so on?"

"No, it won't, Mrs. Prentice. Utilities are extra."

"I see."

And she had nothing to say but "I see" to Dr. Eugene Cool, a few days later, when he explained that Riverside Country Day would be unable to give Bobby a scholarship. The best that could be arranged was what he called "a partial scholarship," and that meant she would pay almost as much as full tuition.

Everything now depended on the income she hoped to earn in the squash court; but a surprising number of her students declined to transfer from the Arts and Crafts Guild. Some said Riverside was too far from home, others said they couldn't afford the fees. In the end she received commitments from only eight students out of a possible fifteen.

"Well, that's a nucleus, anyway," said Maude Larkin, without whom it would have been a nucleus of seven. "We can recruit plenty of others from around here – probably a lot more interesting students than that damn Scarsdale crowd anyway. Really, dear, I'm sure it'll all work out once you get settled."

But Jim wasn't sure at all: "How's she ever going to *get* settled, with bills like that coming in? If I were you, Alice, I'd think twice before you take on any of this. You're much better off in Scarsdale."

He didn't seem to understand that there was no turning back. The new life *would* be possible, in spite of everything. It had to be: Alice was committed to it now with a desperate optimism that left no room for argument. She had faith in the essential rightness of it.

There was still the problem of making it all sound feasible to George. She had told him only that her work at the County Center had led to the establishment of new, private classes in a studio of her own, which might soon make her self-supporting, and that this would require their moving to Riverside, which she'd described only as "Quite a small, nice community, with a fine school for Bobby." Now she had to confess that the rent would be much higher than in Scarsdale, and that the fine school was in fact not a public one; soon he was exploding with questions on the phone.

A *private* school? A private *estate?* What did she mean, private estate? Vander Meer? Walter J. Vander Meer? Good God, didn't she know those people were millionaires? And in the end it was deadlock.

"Alice, it sounds to me like you're biting off an awful lot more than you can chew. I don't like any part of this."

"I'm not *asking* you to like it. I'm not asking you to interfere in any of my affairs, and I certainly don't have to ask your approval. It's none of your business."

And she gained courage, after she'd hung up on him, from the very firmness with which she'd made that final statement. It *was* none of his business. It was entirely her own, and Bobby's. If it wasn't the kind of venture George Prentice could understand, that only proved how incapable he was of understanding her at all. Nothing could stop her now.

They made the move in September of 1937. They hung Sterling Nelson's purdah over the fireplace and found attractive settings for Sterling Nelson's paintings and furniture, and soon their home was far more than rich and cozy – it was interesting, in a way none of their homes had been before.

Maude and Jim Larkin came over to praise the house, bringing friends of theirs who praised it too, and it wasn't long before Bobby began bringing boys home from school – boys whose manners were as cool and strange as the Larkin children's, and whose parentage Maude was quick to endorse.

"The little Jennings boy? Oh, that's R. *Philip* Jennings; he's very big at *Time* and *Life*." Or: "The Ferguson boy? Oh, they're a marvelous family. Horace Ferguson was old Vander Meer's private secretary for years until he got to be a partner in the firm; now he sort of tells Walter Junior what to do. His wife's kind of a bore, but Horace is really sweet; Jim's quite fond of him, even though they argue politics all the time."

And soon there were evenings in the homes of these people – evenings in which she was instantly accepted as the Larkins' friend, Alice Prentice the sculptor; the men were flattering and solicitous and the women expressed interest in becoming sculpture students.

One of the first things she did was get a good supply of personal stationery printed up –

ALICE PRENTICE

BOXWOOD

RIVERSIDE, NEW YORK

– and she wrote enthusiastic letters to everyone she knew who might be glad of her good fortune: her New York friends, several people in Scarsdale, and all of her sisters: The longest and most enthusiastic letter was for Eva – Mrs. Owen Forbes of Austin, Texas – and Eva was quick to reply:

". . . I can't tell you how much I admire your spirit, dear. You are indomitable. I know it will be a wonderful new life for you and Bobby. Owen joins me in sending . . ."

The phrase "You are indomitable" occurred to her more than a few times during her long mornings in the squash court, for she was producing a good deal and working like a professional. Art *did* require a congenial environment. The squash court and the new life of Boxwood, with its aura of wealth and ease, seemed to have freed her talent from a kind of bondage. Ideas that had seemed intractable in her makeshift Scarsdale studios now proved capable of swift and competent fruition. Casts of some of her old garden figures were grouped in the far end of the studio, respectable relics of a period she had outgrown; but much of the experimental work she'd done in Scarsdale was now hidden from view under muslin cloths because it no longer pleased her. She had taken up a new medium: direct stone carving. It was a thing she had tried several times before, in an amateurish way, but only now was she beginning to discover its potentialities. There was something more vital, more elemental about stone; it made modeling seem artificial. She didn't abandon clay – some pieces *had* to be modeled – but in both media she was moving into a brave new freedom of expression. She felt she was approaching a mastery of sculpture for the first time in her life. Willard Slade would have been proud of her. Even her less successful efforts were promising; she was developing pieces worthy of submission to the Whitney Annual, as well as to other lesser exhibitions, and she felt that she might have enough

177

finished work to warrant a one-man show in New York by spring.

And the teaching, three afternoons a week, was anything but a conflict: she found it stimulating, and she moved among her students with a calm authority she had never been able to achieve in White Plains.

"All sculpture is a matter of form in relation to form," she would say, and coming to pause over someone's half-finished piece she would find an example. "Now, you see, this shape doesn't fully relate to *this* shape – not in a really dynamic way. Perhaps if this shape were made more forceful, if we could feel its thrust into this shape, we might find a more satisfying statement." Then, moving on, she would say, "We have to develop a sense of *mass* in our work; we can never allow ourselves to look at the composition from a two-dimensional viewpoint. . . ."

She had never known teaching could be such a pleasure, nor had she ever more consistently enjoyed the feeling that she was holding her students spellbound.

Once, in the middle of a particularly full afternoon, she looked up from her criticism to find that Mrs. Vander Meer had come quietly through the tiny door and was observing the class.

"Please don't let me interrupt you, Mrs. Prentice," she said. "I just wanted to come and watch. I must say it's most fascinating."

By the beginning of the winter she was running into debt: the class had gained only three new pupils, and the bills were mounting.

But at Christmas time she received a formal note requesting the pleasure of her company at the home of Mrs. Walter J. Vander Meer, and an excited talk with Maude, who had also received one, confirmed that it was indeed a social triumph: only a very few people were ever asked to the Big House Christmas parties, and "the rest of the town practically commits suicide every year."

Maude and Alice bought new evening dresses for the occasion, and the occasion itself left nothing to be desired. Yuletide logs were ablaze in great fireplaces, making hundreds of tiny reflected fires in crystal and silver; white-coated servants carried trays of hot hors d'oeuvres and punch, and Mrs. Vander Meer moved slowly and regally among her guests. Jim Larkin looked crude and out of place in his tuxedo – he kept saying things like "Where the hell's the food?" and "Why don't they put out any decent booze?" – so Alice was glad that he and Maude weren't standing nearby when Mrs. Vander Meer came over to her and extended one elegant hand.

"I've seen so little of you since you moved in, Mrs. Prentice," she said. "I hope everything's been satisfactory?"

"Oh, yes, thank you. Everything's been fine."

"Has the squash court been adequate for your purposes?"

"Oh, much more than adequate; it's a wonderful studio."

"I'm so glad. Have you met Dr. Hammond?"

And there was a tall, emaciated, beautiful old man who turned out to be the rector of Trinity, the Riverside Episcopal church. Mrs. Vander Meer drifted away and Alice spent almost an hour talking with Dr. Hammond, aware from time to time that Mrs. Vander Meer was observing their conversation with approval. She found herself saying: "I've always been fascinated by the Episcopal service" (which wasn't really a lie: Episcopalians had been the people she admired most in the town of her childhood, and more than a few times in recent years she had spent tearful Sunday mornings in the dark, cool nave of St. Luke's in New York), and before he cordially withdrew she had promised to become a member of his parish.

"I saw you were really hitting it off with old Hammond," Maude said on their way home. *"That's* playing your cards right. He and the old lady are thick as thieves – she calls him her 'spiritual adviser.' If they both weren't so ancient I think the whole town would suspect the worst."

"He seemed very kind," Alice said with some severity, and she didn't care if Maude laughed or not. It was one of the first times – there would be others later – when she had reason to wonder if Maude might in some ways be a trivial person.

From then on, she and Bobby never missed a Sunday at Trinity. Mrs. Vander Meer was always there in her private pew near the front, sometimes with Walter Junior and his wife and sometimes alone; Alice and Bobby would make their way down the aisle to take their places at a respectful distance, under the red and purple stained glass windows and the heavy tones of the organ. Dr. Hammond made a slow pageantry of the service. She found it hard to follow his sermons – she would allow her attention to wander to the shapes and colors of the altar, the windows, the choir loft, and sometimes she would plan pieces of ecclesiastical sculpture in her mind – but she joined wholeheartedly in the psalms and hymns, and certain of the ritual prayers, intoned in Dr. Hammond's deep and melodious voice, would always make her weep.

"O God, who hast prepared for those who love thee such good things as pass man's understanding; pour into our hearts such love toward thee, that we, loving thee above all things, may obtain thy promises, which exceed all that we can desire."

When the recessional was over and Dr. Hammond stood in the sunshine of the front door, shaking hands, she would say,

"That was wonderful, Doctor; thank you so much." If she happened to catch Mrs. Vander Meer's eye among the departing parishioners she would nod and smile with dignity, and Mrs. Vander Meer would always return the greeting.

She enrolled Bobby in the Confirmation Class, which was conducted by Walter Junior's wife, and the most memorable, most ennobling Sunday of her spring was when she watched Bobby kneel at the rail to take his First Communion, having received the Laying-On of Hands from no less a personage than Bishop Manning of New York. Soon after that she learned that one of Dr. Hammond's altar boys had dropped out, and she arranged to have Bobby fill the vacancy.

He became the crucifer. Erect and solemn in a flowing white surplice, bearing the long shaft of the bronze cross, he would lead the singing choristers in from the vestry at the beginning of each service and lead them out again at the end, while Dr. Hammond reverently brought up the rear. It was a spectacle that never failed to fill her with pride and hope. Nothing, not even the pleasure of her days in the squash court, gave her a greater sense of being exactly where she belonged.

In June she was summoned to Walter Junior's office for what he called "a talk about your plans for the future. I mean," he said uneasily, "do you plan to stay here indefinitely?"

"Yes I do. My work in the studio hasn't been as profitable as I'd hoped, but I'm confident it will be soon."

"I see. Well, I don't mean to press you, but quite naturally we've been concerned. For one thing there's the matter of your rent, which Mr. Garrett tells me is three months in arrears, and quite naturally . . ."

For another thing there was the matter of Bobby's tuition, also in arrears, and that led to another small ordeal in the office of Dr. Eugene Cool.

". . . Well, but the point is, Doctor, I was rather hoping – that is, I wondered if we might discuss the possibility of his receiving a full scholarship next year."

"Mm. I see. Suppose we take a look at his – at his—"

Dr. Cool fingered through a drawer in a filing cabinet and produced a manila folder, which he opened and spread before him as he fixed his tortoise-shell glasses into position. The record disclosed that Robert Prentice's Intelligence Quotient had been assessed at slightly above average, and that he had done reasonably well in the fields of Social Adjustment and Personality Growth. But his Capacity for Self-Discipline had received the rating of Poor, and of the six Units of Study assigned to him during the academic year he had failed two, had received the grade of Incomplete in one and the passing grade of C in the other three. There was also a brief note by one of his teachers under the heading of Remarks, which Dr. Cool chose to real aloud: "Robert may eventually turn out to be as precocious as he seems to think he is, but if he expects to prove it to me he will have to buckle down."

"So you see, Mrs. Prentice," he said, closing the folder and removing his glasses, "under the circumstances, any question of extending his scholarship is really quite out of the – quite out of the question."

Both interviews were upsetting, and she went to the Larkins' house for cocktails and sympathy, dimly hoping that the Larkins might help her find a way out of the problem. But she found them both surprised to learn how bad things were: Maude had apparently assumed that the sculpture classes were paying for everything, and Jim, having, warned her against Riverside in the first place, had apparently given it no further thought.

"Well, but even so," Maude said. "It does seem outrageous that they should be *dunning* you. Don't you think so, Jim?"

Jim Larkin was laboriously lighting a cigar. He had explained when Alice came in that he was "feeling lousy" because he'd been "up working all night," and now, unshaven and wearing a sweatshirt, he looked irritable. "I don't see what's so outrageous about it," he said. "She does owe the money, after all."

"But Jim, it isn't fair. Alice is an *asset* to this place, and they ought to realize it. They ought to be *proud* to have her here."

"Oh, I agree," he said. "I agree one hundred per cent. Trouble is, the bills still have to be paid, here the same as anywhere else. Guess I can't expect you to see that because you never earned a dollar in your life, but if you had my headaches you'd see it fast enough. You'll have to excuse my wife, Alice; I guess I've spoiled her. She doesn't quite understand the facts of life." And he reached over to pour a martini into Alice's glass. "So they're kind of ganging up on you, are they? Isn't there some way you can raise a little dough?"

Staring down into her bright drink, Alice mulled over a thought that had often occurred to her before. Why couldn't Jim Larkin himself, with his embarrassment of riches from radio – why couldn't *he* lend her money?

"Alice, there *is* a way," Maude said, and Alice hoped she would say, *We'll* help you. But instead she said, "By selling some of your work. Oh, I don't mean the things you're doing now – those are museum pieces – but some of your garden things. The Faun, the Pan, the Goose Girl – all those things are lovely in their way. And is there any reason why the Vander Meers shouldn't be prime customers? Have you ever noticed how many little dells and glades in Boxwood are crying *out* for garden sculpture?"

"Sounds great," Jim said. "Personally, though, if I were old Walter Junior I don't think I'd really be in the market for any Pans or goose girls right now."

And Alice knew he was probably right. This was clearly the time to come right out and ask him for a loan – she would never have a better opportunity – but if words existed for the making of such a request they had eluded her. All she could do was sit here and drink the Larkins' gin, beginning to dislike them both.

In the end, as usual, she got the money from George – enough to settle the rent bill and the fuel oil bill and to make a token payment on the tuition. But he warned her that this was "absolutely the last time" he could so exceed the divorce agreement. "Alice, I just don't see where this is going to end. My only advice to you now is that you'd better get out of that place before they throw you out."

"No one's going to throw me out, George."

"Why not? You go on running up these impossible debts and they'll sue you. They can do that, you know. They can sue you and attach your income."

"George, I know you've never understood this, but I know what I'm doing. Next year's going to be entirely different. My classes are bound to expand, for one thing, and I happen to be doing a great deal of very good, very important work that's bound to be profitable. I know these problems won't go on much longer."

"They'd better not. They can't."

For the rest of the summer she managed to pay the rent, which gave her an illusion of solvency until the beginning of the school year. After that the illusion was harder to sustain, but she hoped the tuition question wouldn't come to a crisis until February, and that seemed comfortably far away.

She gained no new students in the fall, but her own work was going so well as to promise great things: she had visions of a one-man show in the spring that might rescue her financially and make her famous at the same time. Even on bad days she was comforted by faith: God, as invoked by Dr. Hammond's rich voice every Sunday, would not fail to provide for her.

Maude's enthusiasm was waning – "I don't know *what* to suggest, dear; I honestly don't know *what* I'd do if I were you" – and Jim was by now openly advocating that she leave town. "You can't fight arithmetic, Alice," he said. "I feel Maude and I more or less got you into this mess, and I'm sorry for that, but it does seem only sensible for you to get out while the getting is good." By saying that, he made it harder than ever for her to ask him for money; and she hated him for it.

The only person who seemed to understand her, however distantly, was Eva, and she began to draw strength from the phrasing of Eva's letters:

"If you believe that what you are doing is right, then stick to it. Nothing ventured, nothing gained – that's always been your way, and the way of all brave and forthright people. And please remember, dear, that Owen and I stand ready to offer you whatever help we can. Financial help is impossible, I'm afraid, but in a real emergency we can always offer you and Bobby a temporary home . . ."

By December she was three months in arrears with the rent again, and she owed a terrible amount of money to the oil dealer. "Let's not answer the doorbell, Bobby," she would say when they saw Mr. Garrett's car in the driveway, or the car of the man who collected for the oil company, and they would hide like thieves until the car went away. Bobby was a willing accomplice: he was doing as badly in school as she was in her financial affairs, and with a twelve-year-old's sense of justice he seemed to feel it appropriate that they should both be fugitives from authority, threatened with expulsion.

"I don't care if we have to leave," he told her.

"Well," she said, "we don't have to leave yet."

Shortly before Christmas there was another, more unpleasant interview in Walter Junior's office. "We have to expect you to fulfill your agreements, Mrs. Prentice," he said. "This kind of thing really can't go on. I feel it's only fair to warn you that we may be obliged to take legal action."

And he evidently told his mother how matters stood, for the old lady became noticeably cool toward Alice at church, and did not invite her – this was a terrible blow – to the annual Christmas party.

In January she imposed on one of the Larkins' friends, a photographer, to take dramatically lighted pictures of some of her best new work, and she took the photographs to New York to make the rounds of the 57th Street galleries. It was a project that consumed four days and yielded no tangible results – one gallery manager asked her to leave her name, but that was all.

Then one sleeting afternoon, after she and Bobby had managed to avoid a visit from Mr. Garrett, a desperate final measure occurred to her: they could sell some of Sterling Nelson's things. From the Manhattan telephone book she found an antique dealer and an art appraiser, and she arranged for them to come out to Riverside on two successive days.

The antique dealer came first, a heavy young, man with a simpering manner. He pronounced some of the furniture "interesting, but not in good enough condition. If we were in town I'd offer you a hundred dollars for the lot and take my chances, but out here it's impractical: I'd spend very nearly that much just to move it."

And what about the purdah?

"I don't know what I'd do with something like that. It's an unusual curio, but I don't know where I'd find a market for it."

And the art appraiser was even worse. An old man, blotting his leaking nose with a dirty handkerchief, he scrutinized the

186

Murillo and the Poussin and all the other dark, heavy paintings and said they were "fakes. Not even very skillful fakes." And so Sterling Nelson had come back over the years to deceive and desert her again.

The end came early in March – not with a final visit from Mr. Garrett or an ultimatum from Dr. Cool or harsh words in Walter Junior's office, but with the dizzying suddenness of matters gone wholly out of control. A man appeared at the door one day, identified himself as a deputy sheriff, and handed her a document with the heading: "Original Notice of Action Pending Against You in the Supreme Court of Westchester County."

She had never been sued before and had no idea of what to do. Her first impulse was to call George, but instead she fled to the Larkins' house.

The Larkins' daughter answered the door, eating an apple.

"Is your father home?"

"Well, yes, Mrs. Prentice, but he's working."

"Is your mother home?"

"Yes, but she's resting."

"Oh, *please*!"

The girl looked startled and backed away, apple juice shining on her lips.

"I'm sorry, but this is *terribly* important," Alice said. I've *got* to see them. *Please*."

"Well, I – I don't know what to—"

But then Jim Larkin emerged blinking from his study, wearing his sweatshirt.

And she turned on him. "You!" She hadn't planned this burst of anger, but she couldn't control herself. "You could have helped me! You could have helped me months and *months* ago, and now it's too late! *Look* at this! *Look* at this!"

187

He took the document, put on his glasses, and frowned over it.

"It's too *late!*" she cried. "Oh, it's too late, it's too late."

Maude came hurrying downstairs in a housecoat, with her hair in curlers. "Alice," she said, "what's the—"

"And *you!* My *friend! Ha!* Oh, you've been a fine friend to me, haven't you?"

In the silence that followed, while Jim handed the paper to Maude, there was a crisp, moist chomping sound: the girl had taken another bite of her apple.

Alice sat down on the sofa and covered her face with her hands. "Oh God," she said. "Oh, oh, oh God."

"Alice," Jim Larkin said. "I really don't see why you're attacking us about this. Frankly, I think you're way out of line."

"Oh, oh, oh God."

"Well, but what can she *do,* Jim?" Maude inquired.

"Looks to me like the best thing to do is disappear," Jim said. "I imagine that's all the Vander Meers really want anyway – they must know they can't collect. Isn't there somewhere you can go, Alice? Somewhere out of the state? Somewhere good and far away?"

And the only place she could think of, in all the world, was Austin, Texas.

Chapter Four

Mr. and Mrs. Owen Forbes lived in a brown, one-story house on a highway five miles west of Austin. The house was set well back from the road and there were no close neighbors – there was, in fact, nothing at all nearby except parched fields, a small abandoned barn, and a chicken yard in which a dozen hens and two roosters pecked and cackled in the sun.

It might have been a comfortable home if Owen had held a job: with him gone all day, Eva could have done enough housework to make the place cool, inviting, and pleasurable when he came back in the evening. As it was, their roles were reversed: Eva went out to work, at the hospital, while Owen stayed home to work on his book. And the house simply wasn't big enough for that: it couldn't accommodate the intensity of his brooding and his restless pacing all day, and at night the rooms seemed to reverberate with his pent-up energy as much as they smelled of his cigarette smoke.

It was technically true that they had enough space to take in two guests – there was a spare room for Alice and a couch in Owen's study that could be made into a bed for Bobby – but it was far from practical. When Eva suggested it – "We can always offer you and Bobby a temporary home" – she had no idea that Alice would accept the offer; then when Alice telephoned from

New York there was nothing to say but yes, and when she and Bobby arrived in Austin they all four had to make the best of a difficult situation.

Alice knew the house was too small the moment she saw it, though she tried to cover her disappointment by chattering brightly with Eva and Owen – "Oh, I think it's a charming little house" – as they made the turn into the driveway. They were pressed three abreast in Owen's eight-year-old coupe, with Bobby riding in the rumble seat with the luggage, and Alice hadn't stopped talking for a minute since getting off the train: it was as if the awkwardness of her position – a homeless, penniless refugee, wholly dependent on their charity – could be eased only by the sound of her own voice. "And what a beautiful *view* you have," she said, getting out of the car. "The sky seems so much bigger out here – I suppose that's what they mean by wide-open spaces."

While Owen and Bobby were unloading the rumble seat – four cardboard suitcases containing everything they owned that hadn't been consigned to storage in New York – she followed Eva inside to explore the rooms, which were plainly furnished and papered in dark tones of brown and green. "Oh, this is *very* nice," she said.

"May be a little crowded," Owen said, "but I guess we'll manage. Here, fella; take your mother's bags into her room, and then we'll get your stuff stowed away in here."

"Why don't you two get washed up," Eva said, "and unpack if you like, and then we'll all go out to the front porch and have something cool to drink."

Alone in her room, Alice did her best to feel a sense of safety, of rescue and hope. She had fled thousands of miles from her adversity to find this resting place; now she was here, sheltered and protected by her own sister's love, and she knew she ought to be grateful. But she couldn't escape the knowledge that she was here only because she had absolutely nowhere else to go, and for a minute, as she stared at herself in the streaked mirror above the dresser, she was touched with panic. How could she possibly live here, in this cramped bungalow under the alien Texas sun, half a continent away from her own life, from her work, from anything she could consider home?

But she forced herself to be calm. Her plan, after all, was to stay here only for a few months – three or four, six at the very most. With her regular monthly checks coming in and no money at all going out, it would be no longer than that before she had saved enough to return to New York, to find a place to live and get her things out of storage. In the meantime, the only thing to do was take this new life as it came, a day at a time, an hour at a time; and now it was time to go out to the front porch for something cool to drink.

"Oh, isn't this pleasant," she said when she'd settled herself on the porch. Eva, Owen, and Bobby were already there, in wicker chairs. There was a pitcher of iced tea, and also, she saw with a rush of relief, there was a bottle of whiskey.

"This is the time of day when Owen and I just relax," Eva said. "We just sit out here and watch the sun go down, and we're grateful for all our blessings. Would you like iced tea, dear, or will you join Owen in a drink?"

"I think I'd like a drink, thanks." The first swallow of whiskey and water warmed her at once, and soon she was able to recapture the feeling of adventure that had sustained her on the long Pullman journey. There was no telling what the future might hold. Alice Prentice the sculptor might be temporarily out of commission, but Alice Prentice the free spirit, the exceptional person, was still functioning. Anything was possible.

The view from the house *was* beautiful, or at least it was

remarkably spacious: miles of flat, gently rolling land led away to a shimmering horizon beneath a sky emblazoned with red and gold. Vague sculptural yearnings were awakened in her as she gazed into the distance and sipped her whiskey, and she almost said, *"Oh,* what wonderful work I'll be able to do here," before she remembered that she wouldn't be able to work here at all. Instead she said, "Oh, I wish I had some water colors; that's such a lovely sunset."

"I could get you some paints in town, if you'd like," Eva said.

"No; I'm not really much of a painter. What I'd really like is some clay, but of course I'd need a studio for sculpture. I don't really mind, though; I'm looking forward to taking a real vacation." She wasn't at all sure what she meant by this – what *was* she going to do with her time here? – but it sounded like the right thing to say.

"And what've *you* been up to since I saw you last?" Owen demanded of Bobby. "Playing much ball?"

"Not too much, no," he answered. "I'm not very good at it."

"You're not? How come? You don't enjoy it?"

"I don't know. I'm not very well coordinated, I guess."

Owen stared at him briefly in evident disappointment, and Bobby shifted bashfully in his chair, rattling the cubes in his glass of iced tea.

Owen had aged a good deal in the past five years: she had scarcely recognized him at the railroad station. His hair was white, he had developed a heavy paunch, and there was something haggard about his eyes. Now she tried to draw him out by asking about his book – she dimly remembered Eva's telling her it was something about the World War – and he said it was going slowly. It was a big job; might not be done for years.

"It does sound very interesting," she said.

"Interesting for anybody who likes to read about wholesale slaughter," he said. "Way the world's going now it won't be long before we're in the middle of another one."

"Another war? Oh, don't say that."

"Not saying it won't keep it away. Probably happen in time for this young fella to see a little action."

"Oh, *dear*, no. You don't really think so, do you?"

"Owen's very disturbed about the situation in Europe," Eva said.

"So's everybody else who's in his right mind," Owen said, and poured himself another drink. He made it a stiff one, and Alice began to suspect he'd been drinking all afternoon, since before meeting the train. This was odd, because she was almost sure she remembered that he'd made a point of turning down drinks that time in Scarsdale.

"There'll be no stopping it and no staying out of it," he was saying, "and it's going to be worse than the last one." Then he turned on Bobby again. "How do you think you'd like that?" he asked. "Think you'd enjoy being a soldier? You know, they'll take you in the Army whether you're well coordinated or not. Stand up. Let's have a look at you."

And Bobby got shyly to his feet, smiling, holding his iced tea.

"Put the glass down. Heels together; toes at an angle of forty-five degrees; knees as close together as the nature of the man will permit. Thumbs along the trouser seams. Shoulders back. No, throw 'em *back*. That's better. Suck that gut in. Wipe that smile off your face."

"Oh, Owen, please," Alice said, trying to laugh. "He's only twelve."

"I'm almost thirteen," Bobby said.

"They're training 'em at that age in Germany right now. Maybe we ought be doing it too. All right, at ease, soldier. I said

'At ease.' That means you can relax." And when Bobby slumped he reached out one heavy hand and cuffed him on the upper arm. "God bless you, boy," he said. "I hope it never happens to you. Probably will, though."

"Oh, please," Alice said. "Can't we talk about something more pleasant?"

Owen drained his glass and stood up. "Tell you what. You girls stay out here and find pleasant things to talk about. I'll go read the paper till suppertime."

"Owen's very tired," Eva explained when he'd gone inside.

He remained very tired through dinner – he hardly said a word while Alice and Eva talked of their sisters – and he went to bed soon afterwards.

"We live very quietly, as you see," Eva said when they were washing the dishes together. "I imagine it'll be quite a change for you."

And it was quite a change indeed. All the next day, with Eva gone and Owen secluded in his study, she and Bobby were left with nothing to do. They went outside to inspect the chickens; then they took a long aimless walk across the fields; then they came back and sat around the house reading magazines. Owen emerged at lunchtime and Alice fixed sandwiches for the three of them, which they ate in near silence; then there was nothing to do but wait for Eva to come home. And that, more or less, was the way things went for nearly a week.

The high point of the day – every day – was the hour when they congregated on the front porch to relax and be grateful for all their blessings. Alice tried again and again to lead the conversation along light, uncontroversial channels, but Owen repeatedly made that impossible. Once she remarked on how "different" Texas was from the East, meaning the landscape, and Owen said, "It's different, all right. You're in the United States of America now. This part of the country hasn't been taken over yet, thank God."

"Taken over?"

"By the Jews."

"Oh."

"New York's not fit for a white man any more," he said, and he held forth in that vein for what seemed an hour, until Eva managed to change the subject.

The menacing rise of the American Negro was another of his favorite topics, as was the cancerous growth of communism in labor unions, and still another was the reckless irresponsibility of President Roosevelt in both domestic and foreign affairs. They heard him out on all of these matters in the course of several evenings, following days of almost unbearable idleness during which they could hear the frequent clink of bottle on glass through the closed door of his study.

Then it was Saturday, with a welcome change in the day's routine: Eva stayed home. It was as if Alice had never before had anyone to talk to. She talked and talked, following Eva around as she went about her housework, accepting small tasks of dusting and polishing, grateful to be given anything to do with her hands as long as it meant the talk could continue.

Late in the afternoon Owen went out alone, taking the car, and stayed away. Eva prepared and served supper as if nothing were amiss; later she sat talking pleasantly with Alice and Bobby until bedtime, and it was well past midnight when Owen woke them all up by coming home – slamming the kitchen door, bumping into the table and cursing, stumbling and staggering through the house until he fell asleep.

On Sunday morning, mostly because she wanted to get out of the house, Alice asked if Eva could drive Bobby and herself to the nearest Episcopal church.

"Certainly," Eva said, glancing uneasily at Owen. "That sounds like a very nice idea."

The church was disappointing – it was small and hot – and the sermon was a dull fund-raising appeal ("Be ye doers of the Word and not hearers only"). But Eva sat politely with them throughout the service, and afterwards said she had found it "very instructive." Like Alice she had been raised a Methodist, but she hadn't been to a church of any kind for years.

"It *is* a more interesting ceremony, isn't it?" she said when they were home again. "I really enjoyed all the singing." This caused Owen to look up sourly from the Sunday paper. "I mean," she said, "assuming one does have a religious bent, I can see how the Episcopalian service would be more appealing."

"I thought it was a little dull," Alice said, "but of course I've been spoiled by the wonderful service we had at Trinity, in Riverside. We had such a fine minister there, Dr. Hammond, and the church itself is so beautiful. Oh, and I *wish* you could have seen Bobby as the crucifer."

"As the what?" Owen inquired, squinting his eyes.

"The crucifer. He carried the cross and led the whole procession, at the beginning and the end of each service. And he did it with such *feeling*. When he'd come to a stop in front of the altar, to let the choir file past him into the choir loft, he'd raise the cross way, way up high and just stand there—" she pantomimed the raising of a shaft high over her head – "*Oh*, it was so impressive; and then he'd lower the cross and turn around, and there'd be the most wonderfully dedicated, ethereal expression on his face – I wish you could have seen it."

Owen looked at her for a moment, and then at Bobby, who ducked his head in discomfort. Then he made a little snorting sound in his nose, gathered up his newspaper, and went into his study and shut the door.

Owen stayed away from them for the rest of the day. He went out again that night, after dinner, and again they were awakened by his homecoming. He lurched against the kitchen table and knocked over one of the chairs, and then they heard his voice.

"Jabber, jabber, jabber," he was saying as he moved toward bed. "Jabber, jabber, jabber, jabber, jabber . . ."

By the end of the third week Alice had decided that the situation was impossible. She and Bobby couldn't stay here: the whole idea of coming here had been a mistake. Her next check from George would give them enough to get back to New York, which now rose in her mind's eye as a city of magical promise, and once there they would find a way to survive. She would make a desperate appeal to George for enough money to tide them over until they were settled, and if that didn't work she guessed she could get some kind of a job. In any case, they would find a way.

"I think we'd better go home," she told Eva as they washed the dishes together one evening. She tried to keep the tone of her voice neutral. "We can leave as soon as I get my next check from George; that ought to be in about a week."

"Well, but where will you go, dear? What will you do?"

"We'll manage somehow. Perhaps I'll take a job or something; anyway, we'll get by."

"But I thought you were planning to stay here for some time, until your savings built up." Eva sounded a little hurt.

"I was, but it really isn't at all practical for us to live here. I think it would be better for all of us."

And whether Eva's feelings had been slightly hurt or not, she was clearly relieved by the news.

So was Bobby; and so, apparently, was Owen: he stayed relatively sober and polite for several evenings in a row.

Now that she was soon to be gone from here, Alice was filled with impatience. The days seemed even longer, and being deprived of sculpture was worse than ever. She knew she might soon be able to work again, but in the meantime she would have given anything for some clay and tools and a studio.

Then one afternoon as she and Bobby sat reading in the living room, she had a wonderful idea.

"Dear," she said. "Could you turn your head a little this way? No, wait; the light isn't quite right. Could you move over to that chair? Near the window? There. That's fine. Now, look up a little – there. Oh, that's wonderful. Do you know the first thing I'm going to do when we get back to New York? I'm going to do a portrait of you. I know just exactly how I'm going to do it. I can *see* it."

And she could. It would be the best thing she had ever done. She would call it "Young Boy," or "My Son" – or, better still, "A Portrait of the Artist's Son." She could picture it exhibited in next year's Whitney Annual, and perhaps even photographed in *The New York Times*.

"You really do have a wonderfully sculptural head, dear," she said. "I can't imagine why this never occurred to me before."

She asked Eva to bring her a sketch pad and some drawing pencils from town the next day, and she began sketching Bobby's head from every conceivable angle.

On the morning she expected to receive her check there was something else for her in the mail instead: a densely worded letter from George's lawyer. She had to read it through several times before she understood it, and then it was sickeningly clear. She had violated the terms of the divorce agreement by taking Bobby out of New York State without George's consent;

accordingly, all payments would be suspended as long as she stayed away.

"Well, that *is* unfortunate," Eva said when Alice showed her the letter. "Still, I imagine you can write to George and explain. I imagine he'll send you the money if he knows you'll use it for going back."

But Alice wasn't so sure. How could she explain what she planned to do when she *got* back? She spent all of one day and part of another writing and rewriting her letter to George: she was trying to make him feel guilty for his action and at the same time trying to persuade him that one month's payment was all she would need to re-establish herself in New York. But she knew, even as she mailed the final draft, that it probably wouldn't do any good.

"Are we just going to stay here forever, then, or what?" Bobby asked her.

"No, dear. We'll go home just as soon as we can find a way. And a way will come; I know it will. We mustn't lose faith."

"Lose faith?"

"Faith in God, dear. Have you forgotten what you learned in church?" And she was able to quote, from memory, her favorite Collect from the Book of Common Prayer: "'Oh God, who hast prepared for those who love thee such good things as pass man's understanding; pour into our hearts such love toward thee, that we, loving thee above all things, may obtain thy promises, which exceed all that we can desire.'"

"Well," he said, "okay, but doesn't that mean getting good things in Heaven? After you're dead?"

"Not necessarily. Besides, there's another one that says 'Grant that those things which we ask faithfully we may obtain effectually.' And there's another one – oh, how does it go? Something about God's ordering all things both in Heaven and earth, and then it says, 'We beseech thee to put away from us all hurtful things, and to give us those things which are profitable to us.' We can't always know exactly what it is God wants for us, but we know He wants what's right. We know He wants us to find a way. That's what 'The Lord is my shepherd' means."

Even so, her own faith was sorely tested by the long, idle days.

It was only May, but as hot as August. The heat rose in shimmering waves over the fields, and the house was like an oven. A few hundred yards away, on the way into town, the highway was under repair: men were cutting through the surface with jackhammers, the powerful noise of which clattered all day, and a heavy pall of white dust hung over the excavation, eclipsing the distance.

"Hot!" Owen Forbes exclaimed, coming out of his study one afternoon. Alice and Bobby were in different parts of the living room, reading detective stories that Eva had brought home from a local lending library, and they looked up at him in apprehension.

"Sweet *Jesus*, it's hot," he said. He tore off his soaked shirt, flapped it in the air, bunched it into a ball and used it to mop his armpits, one after the other. He threw the shirt into the laundry hamper in the hall; then they heard him banging at the refrigerator in the kitchen, and he reappeared with a cold bottle of beer in his hand. He went to stand near Bobby's chair, in front of a small electric fan that slowly turned its buzzing head from side to side. "Damn thing doesn't do any good at all," he said. "Doesn't even stir up the air. What're you reading, boy?"

"Just a mystery," Bobby said. "It's by Erle Stanley Gardner."

"You enjoy books like that?"

"I don't know; I guess so."

"You ought to be in school," Owen said. "You ought to be studying math and Latin and history. Pretty nice how you got

out of half a year's school by coming to Texas, isn't it? What're
you going to do with him in the fall, Alice? Put him in school
out here?"

It was impossible for Alice to think that far ahead. "If we're
still here," she said, "I suppose so, yes."

"What grade you in? Seventh?"

"I'll be starting the eighth."

"You mean you'll be starting the eighth assuming they give
you credit for the seventh. If you ask me, that isn't a very safe
assumption. And you'll find they don't just fool around in the
school system here: it won't be much like your fancy little
private academy for young ladies back East."

He took a deep swig of beer and let all the air out of his lungs
in a long, harsh sigh of satisfaction that ended in a belch. He
wiped his mouth with his forearm, then let his hand fall to his
hairy, protuberant belly and slowly scratched himself.

Watching him, Alice decided she had never seen so gross and
ugly a man. He was hideous in his massive half-nakedness,
and she shuddered with the knowledge that she hated him. She
hated his sour face; she hated his damp, pale, flabby-breasted
torso; she hated his moving around this room with his cruel stare
and his bottle of beer. Let him just say one more thing, she
silently vowed; let him just say one more hurtful, bullying thing
to Bobby and I'll – I'll—. She didn't know what she would say,
but it would be final. She wouldn't stand for any more of this.
She saw herself rising to confront him with a controlled, well-
worded, withering remark – she wouldn't lose her temper – and
then quietly instructing Bobby to go and pack his suitcase. She
would go unhurried to her room and pack her own belongings;
then without another word they would simply walk out of the
house and down the driveway. The trouble was that her fantasy
took her only as far as the road. She had something less than a

dollar in her purse – not enough for calling a taxi. Where would they go? How far would they get, walking with four suitcases in this dreadful heat?

"All right," Owen said, starting back toward his study. "All right, have it your way. Stay indoors, laze around the house all your life, let your brains rot. Turn into a goddam *woman* if you want to."

"That's enough, Owen," she said, getting to her feet. "I won't have you picking on him this way."

"Can't he stand up for himself? Do you have to answer for him?"

"Owen, *please*. He's only a child."

"And you're going to make damn sure he stays that way, aren't you?" He went into the study and shut the door behind him.

Bobby looked hurt and embarrassed. "You shouldn't have *said* anything," he told her, keeping his voice down. "That only made it worse."

"But he has no right to talk to you that way. I won't allow it."

"Don't pay any *attention* to him," Bobby said. "Just ignore him when he gets like that."

"All right, dear; I'm sorry. Where are you going?"

"I don't know. Outside, I guess."

She watched him leave; then from the window she watched him walking aimlessly around the yard, hands in his pockets, kicking up little puffs of dust.

When she heard the car in the driveway – Eva coming home – she went into her room and shut the door. She decided not to go out to the front porch for drinks: if they wanted her, they could come and get her. She decided further that she would say "No, thank you," when Eva stood outside the door and asked her to join them, and if Eva said, "What's the matter?" she would try to explain, as calmly as possible, that Owen had behaved very badly and she wanted nothing more to do with him for one day. "And it hasn't been only today," she would say. "He's been absolutely impossible ever since we *came* here. Either he will start acting like a gentleman or we're leaving. I mean that."

She sat in her room pretending to read, silently rehearsing her speech as she listened to Eva's bustling around the kitchen, and she waited. But in the end it wasn't Eva who came to the door: it was Bobby.

"Aren't you coming out to the porch?" he asked.

"No, I'm not, dear. I'd rather stay here."

"Why?"

"Never mind why."

She would have stayed there through dinner, too, except that the sounds Eva made in the kitchen made her hungry. When she did go in to the table she was careful to meet no one's eyes. She looked soberly at her plate and said nothing, determined to speak only when spoken to.

"Alice?" Eva said after a while. "Are you all right?"

She said she was fine.

"I think this heat is making us all a little – out of sorts," Eva said, and that was the end of the dinner conversation.

When he had finished eating, long before the others were finished, Owen pushed his plate away and scraped back his chair. "I'm going out for a drive," he said, and then he turned to Bobby. "Want to come along?"

Bobby said "Okay" and Alice said "Oh, no!" at the same moment, which caused them all to turn and look at her.

"Please," she said to Bobby. "I don't want you to go."

But Bobby had already left his chair and started toward Owen? and Owen was glaring at her, "What's the matter?" he demanded. "You scared to let him out of your sight?"

"Of course not; that's not the point. I just—"

"It's okay," Bobby said.

"Do him good to get away from the house for a while," Owen said, and he turned to Bobby again as he moved toward the door. "You coming, or not?"

Bobby followed him, glancing back once at his mother with an imploring look, as if to say *Please* don't interfere with this.

There was nothing for Alice to do but watch them go. "Well, do be careful," she called, and they were gone. She heard the car doors slam, heard the car start with a roar and go moaning down the driveway. "Oh dear," she said. "Do you suppose they'll be all right?"

"Of course. What do you mean?"

"Well, but where are they going? He didn't even say where they were going."

"I don't know. Probably just for a drive in the country. Or perhaps they'll visit friends. Owen has a number of friends around town. I certainly wouldn't worry about it, if I were you."

"Well, but isn't he – do you think he'll be able to drive safely?"

"What do you mean?"

"Oh, you know what I mean. He *has* been drinking heavily."

Eva stood up and began stacking the plates. "He's perfectly capable of driving a car," she said. "I think you're being very foolish." And she carried the plates into the kitchen. When she came back a moment later her face was set in a look that Alice remembered from earliest childhood: a look that meant trouble. It meant that Eva would stand for no more nonsense and was about to lose her temper, and it had the same effect on Alice that it had always had when they were children: it goaded her to press her advantage.

"He's drunk and you know it," she said, standing up for

emphasis. "He's drunk every night, and even when he's not drunk he's hateful – he's crude and stupid and *hateful*."

"He's my husband. I'll not allow you to speak that way." And it was just like Eva to say "I'll not" at such a time instead of "I won't."

"He's hateful. I *hate* him, I've never hated anyone so much in my life, and I'm glad I said it. I'm glad I said it. I *hate* him! I *hate* him!"

"Alice! I want you to stop this at once. You're hysterical. I'll not listen to another—"

"Ha! Hysterical! *I'll* show you how hysterical I am. If that boy isn't back here in half an hour I'll call the police!"

"You'll do nothing of the sort. I'll not listen to another word of this."

"Yes you *will* listen. I've kept quiet long enough. Your husband's a beast, do you hear me? He's a *beast*. Oh, I know you only married him because he was all you could get, but you're a fool! He's a *beast!*"

That had the sound of a good exit line, so she went quickly into her room and slammed the door. But Eva followed right behind her, wrenched open the door, and stood facing her, quivering with anger.

"You'll regret this, Alice," she said. "I'll never forgive you for this."

And the quarrel went on and on. It drove them back into the living room, then into the kitchen, and back into the living room again.

". . . and to think," Eva said, "to *think* what we've done for you. To *think* what Owen and I have sacrificed to give you a home!"

"I *hate* your home! I promise you I'll leave your home tomorrow! I won't spend another *day* in this wretched place!"

205

In the end they collapsed crying in their separate rooms, and the house settled into silence as they both lay listening for the car in the driveway.

It was almost midnight before they heard it. The sound of it made Alice sit up, leave her bed, and stand close to her closed door, listening still more intently. With a sense of revulsion she heard Owen's heavy tread pass the door, and then she heard Bobby. She opened the door a crack and called to him in a whisper.

"What's the matter?" he said.

"Nothing. Just come in here a minute, please." When he was inside the room she drew him close in a tight hug. Then she released him and said, "Where did he take you?"

"No place special. First we went to a bar down the road where there were some men he knows, and he talked to them for a while. Then we went to another bar and played the pinball machine."

"Is he drunk?"

"Not especially. I mean – you know – no more than usual."

"Well, at least you're back. Listen, dear: I want you to sleep in here tonight."

"In here? Why?"

"Can you bring your cot in?"

"It's too big. Why do you want me to—"

"All right, never mind. You take my bed and I'll sleep on the floor."

"But why? What's the matter?"

"Just do as I say. I don't want you sleeping out there tonight, that's all. I want you close to me."

She finally persuaded him to use her bed, and when he was in it she stretched out on the carpet with a blanket. The hardness of the floor suited her bitter mood; but some time before dawn she woke up, chilled and cramped, and got into bed with Bobby. He was so warm, and the bed so soft, that she started to cry again as she pressed against him. He woke up and stiffened in her arms.

"What's the matter?"

"Nothing, dear. I'm sorry. Go back to sleep."

She awoke again with the hot sun of morning in her face, and Bobby was now up and dressed and sitting in a chair, looking at her.

"What time is it, dear?"

"I don't know; a little after eight. What's the matter, anyway?"

She sat up, feeling gritty from having slept in her clothes. "Eva and I had a dreadful quarrel last night," she said. "I don't want to see her. Let's just wait here till she goes to work."

"Well, but she's not going to work. It's Saturday."

"Oh dear; that's right. Let's stay here anyway, though. You don't mind, do you?"

"What about breakfast?"

"I'm not hungry. I'll go out and get you something to eat, though, when I'm sure they're out of the kitchen."

"You mean you want to just stay in here? What's the point of that?"

"Dear, *please* don't torment me with questions. Just please do as I say."

"Okay." He sat looking uncomfortable, and after a moment he said, "What was the quarrel about, anyway?"

"I don't know; everything." She went to the dresser mirror and began trying to do something about her hair. "Are they in the kitchen now?" she asked. "Can you tell?"

"I don't think so. I think they're out in the living room. I'm not sure."

"Let's wait till we're sure. You can go to the bathroom if you want."

"I already did."

One of the doors in her room opened onto the bathroom, which in turn led to the hall near the kitchen. She tiptoed through, spent a long time listening at the hall door, and finally risked it outside. There was nobody in the hall and nobody in the kitchen. On the stove she found a pot of coffee that was still warm, and she poured herself a cup with trembling hands; then she found a box of dry cereal, a bowl, and some milk, which she carried back through the bathroom for Bobby. He ate hungrily, and when he was finished he said, "Are we going to hide in here all day, or what?"

"We're not 'hiding,' dear; we're simply keeping to ourselves. We're minding our own business."

Some time later they heard Eva's footsteps approaching outside the door, which caused Alice to stiffen. The door couldn't be locked: Eva could walk right in if she wanted to. But she stopped outside and knocked. Then they heard her voice, sounding stern but shy, as if she had forgotten nothing of last night but was tentatively willing to make amends. "Alice? Are you all right?"

Alice said nothing and placed a forefinger over her lips so that Bobby would keep quiet too.

"Is Bobby in there with you?"

Neither of them answered, and the footsteps went away; but soon they were back.

"Alice," Eva called. "Owen is driving into town to do some shopping. Is there anything you'd like him to bring you?"

They remained silent, though Bobby smiled in embarrassment, showing he thought it was silly. Then from the window they saw Owen go out to the car and drive away. Alice felt relieved to have him out of the house; she almost felt she could deal with Eva as long as he was gone.

But she was wholly unprepared for what happened next. The door swung open and Eva came walking in, carrying a tray that held three tall glasses of milk with ice cubes in them. "This has gone on long enough," she said. "Why don't we all have something cool to drink." She set the tray down on a table and confronted Alice with her hands on her hips, looking wounded and patient and ready to accept apologies.

Alice had never seen anyone put ice cubes in milk – she knew Eva must really have been rattled to do a thing like that – and she was infuriated by the look on Eva's face. "Please leave us alone," she said. "I have nothing to say to you."

"Oh, Alice. Don't you think you're being childish?"

"No."

"Well, you are. You said a great many cruel things last night. It's not easy to forget those things. It's not easy to forgive you, and I—"

"I'm not *asking* your forgiveness. I meant everything I said and I'll say it again. Your husband is a dirty, filthy—"

"Alice! As long as you're a guest in my house I—"

"Ha! A guest in your house! I'm a *prisoner* in your house!"

"You're nothing of the sort. You're perfectly free to leave at any time."

"Then I'll leave today. I'll leave right now." And she swept dramatically around to face Bobby. "Go and pack your things," she said. "Quickly."

"Alice, try to control yourself. You know you don't mean that."

"I most certainly do mean it." She pulled one of her suitcases from under the bed, opened it, and began stuffing clothes into it with spastic haste. "Go *on,* Bobby," she said, and he went.

"Alice, this is ridiculous. Where will you go?"

"I don't know. Please get out of my way." She swept an armload of dresses from the closet, pressed them into the suitcase, and snapped it shut. Then she started packing her other two bags, and not until all three were packed did she begin to realize the weight of what she was doing: now they would *have* to leave. Where in the world would they go? But her passion carried her along on its own momentum. She took two of the suitcases into the living room and Bobby followed her with the other two, wearing a bashful smile. He apparently didn't believe what was happening, and neither did Eva.

"Come back here at once, Alice," she said. "You're making a complete fool of yourself."

"I'll never come back." Alice took a new grip on the suitcase handles and pushed out through the screen door. On the porch she turned back, aware that this was the moment for some crushing last word, but she couldn't think of anything to say. She licked her dry lips. "And I hope I'll never see you again," she said. Then she crossed the porch, went down the front steps, and out into the hot sunshine. She looked back only once to make sure Bobby was coming; he hurried to catch up with her and they walked side by side down the driveway.

"Where're we going, anyway?" he asked.

"Never mind. Just come along."

"You mean you don't even know where we're going?"

"We're going into town. It's only five miles. We'll go to a hotel." How they would ever get out of the hotel was a problem she would deal with later.

They had gone only a few steps up the highway when she had to stop and rest. Her hands were sore from the suitcase handles and she was soaked with sweat. "Let's rest a minute, Bobby," she said.

Not far ahead of them now was the beginning of the place where the highway was under repair. The noise of the jack-hammers was loud and persistent, and the cloud of white dust looked impenetrable. They would have to walk through it.

"Why don't you give me the big bags," Bobby said, "and you take the little ones."

"No, that's all right. I'll manage."

"Come on, *give* them to me," he insisted. "I'm stronger than you."

And she let him take them, surprised and pleased by what he'd said. He *was* stronger than she, and as they lifted the suitcases and trudged on into the heat she felt comforted and protected. She was no longer a woman alone with a little boy. He was someone she could depend on, someone who would take command in a crisis like this.

Her main difficulty now was that she was wearing high heels: they wobbled and threatened to turn her ankles with every step. And her only other pair of shoes, riding in one of the suitcases, had heels that were just as high.

"I'm sorry I have to go so slowly, dear," she said. "It's these shoes, you see. I can't—"

"That's okay," he said with his new authority. "You're doing fine."

When they reached the excavation they were enveloped at once in the white dust. "I'm going to have to stop again, dear," she said, but he couldn't hear her over the noise of the jackhammers. "Bobby, *wait*," she called, almost in tears, and he turned back, stopped, and put his own suitcases down.

"We'd get there a lot sooner if we didn't stop so often," he said.

"I know, dear, but I can't keep up with you. I've got to rest a minute."

"Okay."

"Isn't this dust dreadful?"

"What?"

"This dust I can hardly *breathe*."

"It's caliche."

"What?"

"The dust. It's called caliche; sort of like chalk. It's all through this area, just under the topsoil. Uncle Owen told me."

"Oh."

"Let's pretend it isn't happening," he said.

"What?"

"I said let's pretend it isn't happening. Let's pretend it's real cold and we have to walk as fast as we can to keep warm."

"I'm not very good at pretending, I'm afraid."

"Come on. And we'll pretend the dust is a big snowstorm, a blizzard, and we have to get through."

She was about to say, "Oh, Bobby, *please*," in irritation, but when she looked into his earnest, sweating face she was won over. What a cheerful, heartening companion he was, and what a good sport! If he could pretend it wasn't happening, so could she. "All right, dear," she said.

"Br-r-r!" He shuddered, hugging himself. "We better not stay here any longer or we'll freeze to death. Let's get going."

And hefting their suitcases they set off again, Bobby in the lead. Watching his narrow back as he moved ahead of her in the whiteness, she knew it was a sight she would never forget. An ordinary boy might have complained, might have whined and lagged behind and been a hindrance, but Bobby was no ordinary boy. He was brave and lighthearted and imaginative; he was her own.

"How you doing?" he called back.

"All right, dear." And she was able to smile. "I'm doing fine."

Pretend it isn't happening! And the funny part was that it almost worked. Dizzy and nearly suffocating, with sweat running in streams down her back, she did her best to imagine she was cold, and it almost worked.

One lane of the highway was open for traffic; a steady stream of cars moved eastward, and then, after an interval, the westbound traffic came through. She was afraid that each westbound car would be Owen Forbes on his way back from town, but the cars all proved to contain strangers, some of whose heads swiveled around to stare at the odd spectacle of a woman and a boy toiling along with suitcases in the blaze of afternoon.

"Bobby," she called. "I'm going to have to stop again."

"Okay."

She sat on one of the bags to rest her aching feet. "I think we've come about two miles," she said, "don't you?"

"I don't know; it's so cold it's hard to tell."

"Oh, Bobby, you're wonderful. How would I ever get through this without you?"

"Aren't you freezing?" he said. "Let's get moving again."

And they did. They passed very close to one of the workmen and he stopped his terrible automatic hammer to stare at them: a Mexican or a half-breed of some kind, short and brutal-looking, his face and clothes powdered white. She knew that she herself must be coated white by now – she could taste the dust and feel it in her eyes and nostrils – and when Bobby turned back to call "You okay?", she saw that his face and hair were white too.

She always said afterwards that God was watching over her that day, giving her the strength to go on; and it was certainly true that she prayed as she walked. "Oh, please, dear God," she said aloud against the noise of the jackhammers. "*Please*, dear God, help me through this." And with her teeth clenched tight against the dust she recited: "Oh God, who has prepared for those who love thee such good things as pass man's under-standing . . ."

The noise gradually diminished and the dust began to clear: they had come to the end of the excavation. The road ahead had turned into a street now, with close-set houses and shops on either side. They were still far from the center of town, but they were within its outskirts.

A sign a block ahead – CAFÉ – made her wonder if they dared to stop there: they would at least be able to sit down, and to drink cold Coca-Colas. But her purse contained exactly seventy-five cents; they had better save it.

Then another sign drew her attention – TEXACO – because there would be toilets there. "Bobby," she said. "Let's stop at the gas station. We can at least get some water."

The eyes of the Texaco attendants followed them with curiosity and perhaps suspicion as they trudged around to the back of the station toward the two white "rest room" doors, MEN and LADIES.

The ladies' room stank and was unbearably hot, but she stood at its dirty sink for a long time, cupping up handfuls of warm, sweet water and drinking it down as if her thirst could never be slaked. There was no soap and the paper-towel dispenser was broken, but she managed to wash her face anyway, getting rid of most of the dust, and dried it with toilet paper. Her face, in the spattered mirror, was a shocked and wild-eyed ruin.

When she picked up the suitcases and pushed out into the sunshine again she had a dizzy spell and nearly fell down. Bobby was waiting for her, his face gleaming and his wet hair sticking up and out at all angles.

"Are you okay?" he asked her.

"Yes, dear. I was just dizzy there for a minute. I'll be all right. It can't be very much farther, do you think?"

"Probably not. Let's get going."

But there was no way of telling, as they labored down block after block, whether they were heading for the center of town or only moving around its periphery. Sometimes there were glimpses of distant tall buildings ahead; sometimes not.

"I think we *must* be going in the right direction, don't you?" she said. "Do you remember any of this part of town?"

"No. Let's just keep going, though."

And at last, as they reached the end of still another block, they came upon three taxicabs parked at the curb around the corner. "Oh, look, dear," she said. "*Taxi*cabs!" She scuttled ahead of him, wrenched open the passenger's door of one of the cabs, dropped her suitcases, and crawled, nearly collapsing, into the wide back seat. The driver, hustling around from the front of the cab, looked worried.

"You all right, Ma'am?"

"Yes. Will you help me with these bags?"

He took them and stowed them briskly in the front seat; then he took Bobby's two bags and put them in the trunk of the car.

Bobby was still standing on the sidewalk, looking doubtful. "Get in, dear," she said, and he climbed in beside her, sitting stiffly erect as if he were afraid to relax in the upholstery.

"Driver," she said. "Can you recommend a hotel?"

"Well, Ma'am, there's the old Stephen F. Austin, that's supposed to be the best, but if I was you I'd try the Hilton. That's brand new, and it's air-conditioned."

"All right, fine," she said. "Take us there." Air-conditioned! She had thought only movie theaters were air-conditioned. Imagine a whole hotel! "But wait," she said.

"Ma'am?"

She closed her eyes. "Can you tell me approximately how much it will cost you to get there?"

"Well, Ma'am, I figure that'll run you about thirty-five cents."

And she had seventy-five. That meant she could tip the driver fifteen cents and still have a quarter left for the bellhop at the hotel. "Fine," she said. "That'll be fine." And she lay back and closed her eyes again.

At the elegant entrance of the hotel a uniformed doorman sprang forward to seize all four suitcases, leaving her with nothing to carry but the twenty-five cents change she had received from the driver. She felt that everyone on the sidewalk was looking at her – were her clothes all right? was her slip showing? – and she wished there were some way of improving her appearance before she went into the lobby. But then they passed through a heavy plate-glass door, and the cold air enveloped them like water.

"Wow!" Bobby said, and his exhausted face broke into a smile of pure delight. "Isn't this something?"

They seemed to float as they walked across a great expanse of deep, soundless carpet to the front desk, where a kindly gentleman stood waiting to bid them good afternoon.

"And how long will you be staying with us, Mrs. Prentice?" he asked when she'd filled out the registration form.

"A few days – I don't know. We haven't made definite plans."

Then they were riding in a big, silent elevator, and then they were being shown into their suite, which was blue and unbelievably sumptuous. "Don't open the windows," the bell-hop told them, "or you'll interfere with the air-conditioning. And look here." He pointed to the bathroom sink, which had three instead of two faucets. "That middle one's for your ice water. You've got a continuous supply."

The first thing she did when they were alone was to draw two glasses of ice water. "There," she said, handing one to Bobby. "Now let's just relax."

And that was all they did for nearly an hour. Lolling in the deep cushions, they kicked off their shoes and laughed together in an ecstasy of rest and relief.

"Will you ever forget that awful caliche road?" she asked him. "Wasn't that just the most dreadful experience you can imagine?"

"Well," he said. "At least we made it."

"We certainly did. And do you know something? I never would have made it without you. You were wonderful."

They both took long baths and changed into the best clothes they could find. Then, feeling fresh and clean, they went without haste to the dining room. In the first shock of reading the menu she thought she'd better caution him to order only the least expensive things, but then it occurred to her that this would be a false economy. If they were going to run up a bill here it might as well be a big one. "You have anything you want, dear," she said. "Doesn't it all look good?" And she started the meal off on a festive note by ordering two Manhattans for herself.

"Are you going to call Daddy now, or what?" Bobby asked when they were back in their blue suite.

"Yes, dear; there's nothing else we can do."

But she knew it would be an unpleasant telephone call, and she didn't want Bobby to hear it. She sent him down for a walk around the lobby before she picked up the phone and asked for the long-distance operator.

George's voice sounded very far away. "Alice? Did you get my letter?"

"Your letter? No."

"Are you all right? Is the boy all right?"

"Yes, we're fine; no thanks to you."

He sighed into the phone. "Alice, I was following my lawyer's advice. I followed his advice because frankly I didn't know what else to do."

"So you jumped at the chance to punish us. You took advantage of a legal loophole to rid yourself of all responsibility."

"Alice, it wasn't like that at all. If anything, I simply wanted to teach you a lesson."

She gripped the phone with both hands. "What lesson?"

"That people have to live within their means. Alice, after your behavior up there in Riverside I felt I was entirely justified. Do you know how much I've paid out in excess of the agreement over the past two years?" His voice had taken on a rich and familiar texture now. It was the voice of exasperated reason, of aroused common sense. It was the voice of people who said "No, I'm afraid that's not practical," or "You should have thought of that before you got into this trouble" – the voice she had been hopelessly contending with all her life, and which promised, always, that it would have the last word.

"My lawyer couldn't believe it," the voice was saying. "He said I must be crazy. And even at *that* you ended up with a lawsuit for more than you'll ever be able to pay. Have you heard from your friends the Vander Meers, by the way?"

"No."

"Well, you're lucky. They could easily serve you a judgement through the Texas courts, if they wanted to. Anyway, you'll probably get my letter tomorrow. I've offered to send you enough to get back to New York, providing that we have a clear and definite understanding from now on. No more nonsense, Alice. No more exorbitant rents; no more private schools. I want you to read it very carefully and think about it."

"All right. But I won't get it now because we've moved out. We're not living at Eva's any more."

"You're not? Why?"

In the end she persuaded him to telegraph enough money to settle the hotel bill and buy train tickets, and she listened patiently while he explained once more about the clear and definite understanding they would have from now on.

When Bobby came back, looking worried, he said, "Is it all right?"

"Yes, dear. It's all right."

But she couldn't sleep. For an hour or more she turned and twisted in the cool hotel sheets; every time she drifted off there was a terrible vision of Eva's weeping face, or of Eva saying "I'll not allow you to speak that way," or of Eva bringing glasses of milk with ice cubes in them.

At last, sitting up and smoking a cigarette, she decided it would be possible to apologize to Eva one day. Not now, not soon, but sometime in the future she could write a letter of apology – a letter thanking Eva for her kindness and asking her pardon for the way things had worked out. It wouldn't be easy and it might not be a very good letter, but it would probably be good enough for Eva.

She stole softly into Bobby's room and sat beside his bed for a while, watching his sleeping face. The awful events of the afternoon seemed far away now, far in the past. Nothing had ever been that bad before, and nothing would ever be that bad again. For years, whenever they were faced with any ordeal, she would gain strength from saying "Remember the Caliche Road?" And if anything ever did turn out to be that bad, or worse – if even "Remember the Caliche Road" should fail as a rallying cry – she could fall back on Bobby's advice for enduring the intolerable: "Let's pretend it isn't happening." She felt quiet and brave and well armed for the future.

Bobby turned and thrashed his limbs in his bed, and his face was contorted as if he were having a nightmare. Then his eyes came open.

"It's all right," she said, and his eyes closed again. "Just rest now, Bobby. Just rest."

PART THREE

Chapter One

It was diagnosed as pneumonia, and it took five weeks to cure. After the first few days of pain and drugged sleep it became an exquisitely peaceful time for Prentice, a time of warm sponge baths and clean sheets, of low, courteous voices and regular meals. The hospital, miles farther back from the line than evacuation hospitals for the wounded, was set up in an old stone building that had once been a Catholic school for girls, and its pneumonia ward overlooked a scene of gently rolling hills, gray and brown in the February thaw.

Very soon after his arrival, on the first day he was truly awake, he lay propped up in bed to watch an endless convoy of muddy Army vehicles crawl past beneath the window, and the news spread quickly through the ward that this was the 57th Division, relieved from the line in Colmar. They were going up to Holland, where they would rest and take on new replacements until they were restored to combat strength; and this meant there need be no sense of guilt about lying here, clean and warm and sipping hot chocolate. By the time they were restored to combat strength, Prentice would be too.

Meanwhile he could devote whole mornings to the delicate task of finding the most comfortable arrangement of his feet, which burned in the aftermath of a mild case of frostbite; he could read Armed Forces Edition paperbacks until the effort of reading became tiresome; he could strike up listless, casual friendships with the other patients; he could write letters.

He explained to his mother, several times, that he was hospitalized but not wounded and not really very sick, and he devoted much of one letter to a conscientious description of how the Normandy countryside had looked from the train.

He wrote a very different kind of letter to Hugh Burlingame, full of cryptic references to snipers and death and heavy shellings, managing to imply that he no longer had time for the gentle boyish pursuit of intellectual abstractions; and at the end he made a pointed remark to the effect that the V-12 Program must be tough.

And he wrote to Quint, hesitating for a long time over the salutation "Dear John." It wasn't an easy letter to write.

Sorry I didn't get to see you again that day in Horbourg, before I went back to the medics . . .

But in his revision of the letter he changed that sentence to read "before they took me back to the medics." It wasn't really a lie – they *had* taken him back. Besides, hadn't Lieutenant Agate made two separate offers to let him go back earlier that day? And hadn't he refused them both?

It proved to be pneumonia, just as you predicted. Guess you probably had it too, and hope they've taken care of you. I've been sort of expecting to see you turn up here, but am told there's more than one hospital in the area, so maybe you went somewhere else. Or maybe you stuck it out until the outfit pulled back to Holland, as I'm told they did a few days later. Anyway I hope you're well again, wherever you are.

We both probably should have gone back when you first suggested it, before the Horbourg business.

After that ticklish part of the letter was written, it was hard to think of anything else to say. The last few sentences had a falsely hearty sound, like some civilian's idea of the way old Army buddies ought to talk, and he concluded it with: "Regards to Sam R., if you see him, and the best of luck." It was as strange to sign "Bob" as it had been to write "John." Then he put:

P.S. – There seems to be an unlimited amount of your damn Bond Street tobacco in the PX supplies here. Soon as I'm out of bed I'll try to grab as much as I can for you.

He got four packages of the stuff and tied them up with a strip of red ribbon torn from the Catholic girls' school curtains, and he wrote out a little card that said "Merry Christmas." By that time, when he was padding around in a bathrobe and cotton slippers, the news commentators on the ward radio had begun to talk about a Marine Corps landing on an island called Iwo Jima; and not long after that there was another news item that set off whoops and hollers throughout the ward: the First Army had found a German bridge intact and had crossed the Rhine. There were giddy predictions that the European war might be over in a matter of weeks, and this was a little troubling. What if it ended before he got back to the line? Would he then be able to say he'd been in the war, or not?

But there still seemed to be plenty of war left on the day he got his discharge and his clothes. Saying goodbye to his ward acquaintances, and later as he rode in a truck to the Seventh Army Replacement Depot, it pleased him to know that he looked like a combat man: his boots looked used, his field jacket and pants were still stained with the mud and the brick and plaster dust of Horbourg – even the toothpaste stain on his breast was faintly impressive – and Quint's blanket scarf gave the whole costume a rakish, nonregulation touch. He felt healthy, if still soft and weak from the hospital, and the smell of spring in the air was exhilarating.

At the depot he learned that the 57th had finished its spell of limited duty in Holland: they were now in the Ninth Army, in Germany, holding a long defensive or "screening" position on the west bank of the Rhine, and they were expected to make their own crossing soon.

"How soon do you think you'll be able to get me up there?" he asked a fat personnel clerk.

"Shouldn't take long," the clerk said, stacking his papers. "We'll have you out of here in a couple of days." Then he looked up with a loose-lipped, effeminate smile. "Anxious to get back to your buddies?"

Unsettled, Prentice turned away from the desk, only to find his discomfort compounded by glances of shy admiration from two very clean, fresh-from-the-States-looking soldiers who stood waiting in line behind him. How easy it was to play the hero in a setting like this! Here in this room, so many miles from danger, any fool and any coward could saunter across the floor in a golden aura of celebrity as long as his clothes were dirty enough to suggest that he'd been "in combat." It wasn't fair, and the unfairness of it made him tighten his face under the scrutiny of these other, newer replacements – yet he was aware too that the very tightening of his face, like the dust and toothpaste stains, had the effect of enhancing his false image.

The clerk was right: they had him out of there in a couple of days. They had him riding north in a crowded truck, with a brand-new rifle between his knees, rolling along through the tender browns and yellows of the early spring countryside, rumbling through any number of gray, broken towns where old men stared bewildered at the passing truck and children waved.

They had him in and out of the Ninth Army Replacement Depot in a couple of days too; then they had him riding east through the Rhineland in another truck to division head-quarters, then east again to Regiment, and at last they had him standing on a great windless plain in the afternoon, waiting for a jeep from "A" Company to come and pick him up.

The driver of the jeep turned out to be Wilson, the supply sergeant, a gaunt, bespectacled man with a long neck, a jutting Adam's apple, and a look of chronic displeasure. Prentice remem-bered him shouting and quarreling over the distribution of ammunition in the factory, just before Horbourg. But Wilson, plainly, had no memory of him. He walked right past him, calling, "Where's the man for 'A' Company?" and when Prentice was pointed out to him, his eyes went as blank as his glasses.

"You a new man?"

"Not really, no. I joined the outfit in Belgium, right after the Bulge."

"Yeah? Funny; I don't recognize you at all."

In the jeep, as they hummed along over seemingly endless flatland, Wilson's profile drew up into a squint. "Which platoon you in?" he asked.

"I'm the Second Platoon runner."

And Wilson briefly turned away from the road to give him a testy look. "You can't be. McCann's the Second Platoon runner. He's been Second Platoon runner ever since we left the States."

"Well," Prentice said, "maybe he was out for a while or something. Anyway, I was—"

"No, he's never been out. Not to my knowledge. You sure you've got the right company?"

"Of course I'm sure. I was Second Platoon runner down in Colmar, up until after Horbourg."

"Well," Wilson said. "I'm damned if I remember you." He rubbed his chin. "Wait a minute. Were you the kid that took sick in the factory?"

The kid that took sick in the factory! That moaning, shamelessly weeping boy!

"No," Prentice said. "That wasn't me. The factory was before Horbourg. I stayed until afterwards."

"You get hit then, or what?"

"No, I had—"

"Dysentery?"

"No. Pneumonia."

"Oh. Well, anyway, don't say you *are* the runner. You won't be the runner now. Coverly'll probably put you in one of the squads."

"Who?"

"Lieutenant Coverly. He's the new platoon leader."

"Oh. And is Brewer still platoon sergeant?"

"No, Loomis is. Brewer was hit, back in Colmar."

"Jesus, I didn't know that," Prentice said. "Where?"

"The hip; bad, but not too bad."

"No, I mean *where?* In Horbourg?"

"Appenweier. That was the second town we took. Shit, Horbourg was a breeze compared to Appenweier."

"Oh." There was a pause. "And is Lieutenant Agate still—"

"Yeah, he's still CO. Only it's Captain Agate now."

"Oh." And from there on they rode in silence across the plain, which was so long and wide and level as to give very little sense of speed. They passed several artillery positions, far out in the slowly turning land, and then they passed an anti-aircraft gun emplacement. By now Prentice could make out the separate shapes of distant houses that had been mere dots on the shimmering horizon a minute before, and he could see that the land stretching out beyond the houses met the sky in a new horizon that was probably the west bank of the Rhine.

When they'd reached and overtaken the houses, Wilson swung the jeep into a left turn and they drove slowly down the road on which the houses faced; and now, passing one of them after another, Prentice saw soldiers lounging in their yards and looking out of their windows. All of them were carelessly dressed, and some wore the black silk top hats, looted from German closets, that had lately become an Army fad.

"This here's the C.P.," Wilson said, and brought the jeep to a stop outside the largest house.

Agate was there in the yard, laughing and talking with some men Prentice had never seen before. He looked about the same except that he was clean and shaved and seemed to have gained some weight. Captain's bars gleamed on the shoulders of his washed and shrunken field jacket, and over his left breast, crookedly pinned on, was the rich little ribbon of the Bronze Star.

Approaching him, Prentice wondered if he ought to salute; then in fear of looking silly he decided not to.

"Excuse me, sir. I'm just reporting back from the hospital. My name's Prentice; I don't suppose you rem—"

And by that time Agate's eyes had come slowly into a focus of recognition. "Oh yeah,' he said. "You're the fella lost your voice, right?" He didn't offer to shake hands – was that a bad sign? – but his voice and manner were courteous, and Prentice felt a little warmed. "Well, good," he was saying. "We've been having it pretty soft up here lately, but I expect things'll be getting noisy again very shortly . . ."

As he listened, Prentice thought he could see the strolling

figure of Logan from the corner of his eye, and he stared fixedly at Agate's face in order to avoid whatever greeting Logan might have for him. Then he risked a full glance in that direction and found that Logan, or whoever it was, had vanished.

"Let's see, now." The captain rubbed the side of his red neck. "Afraid we can't use you as a runner any more. You'll find your platoon in the third house down the road; ask for Lieutenant Coverly. Only first you better go inside here and check in with the first sergeant, for the Morning Report."

"All right, sir. Thank you." And turning away he wondered again if he should have saluted, but it was too late. There were no familiar faces in the C.P. – even the first sergeant himself, fat and partly bald and stupid-looking, was a man he only dimly remembered and who didn't remember him at all.

"How do you spell that?" he asked when Prentice gave his name, and he had to have it spelled out for him several times as he hunched over his paperwork, his heavy fingers using the pencil as slowly and gingerly as if it were a surgeon's scalpel.

"Dysentery, was it?"

"No. Pneumonia."

"How do you spell that?"

There were no familiar faces on the road, either, as he made his way down to the Second Platoon. A number of men were loitering in the doorway of the platoon house, some of them wearing top hats, and they all stared at Prentice, blocking his way. Most of them looked no older than himself.

"Is Lieutenant Coverly here?"

"Inside. In the kitchen." And two of the men, or boys, moved aside to let him through. There were other watching strangers in the vestibule of the house, and in the shadowed living room, and in the hall. In the kitchen doorway the slanting rays of the afternoon sun hit him full in the face: he had to stand there blinking and trying to shade his eyes before he could see that four men were sitting around the bright kitchen table, drinking coffee out of flowered china cups. All their heads were raised to look at him.

The man who seemed to be in charge was dressed in a light, old-style zippered field jacket with no insignia. He was burly and bull-necked, with small eyes set close together in a truculent face; and Prentice was about to address him when he saw that the narrow and much less imposing man beside him was wearing lieutenant's bars.

"Lieutenant Coverly?"

"Right. What's up?"

And Prentice labored once again through the announcement of his identity.

"Well." The lieutenant stood up, revealing that he was short as well as thin. "Welcome aboard." His small blond head was delicately handsome and his voice was Southern. His hand was moist, and all its fingernails were bitten to the quick. "You know Sergeant Loomis? Our platoon sergeant?"

The burly man was on his feet now, crushing Prentice's knuckles. "I don't seem to remember you," he was saying in a deep, theatrical baritone. "Were you with us before?"

"Just for a few days, is all. Back in Colmar, when Sergeant Brewer was in charge. Only I was the platoon runner then, you see."

"That so? I would've said McCann was our runner right along. You must've been one of the people joined us on that train in Belgium, then. Right?"

"That's right. From there to Horbourg. Through Horbourg, actually."

"Then what? You get hit?"

"No, I – I had pneumonia." And he wondered why he had to stumble in saying it. What was so shameful about having pneumonia? Was he afraid that Loomis, like Wilson, might mistake him for the kid that took sick in the factory?

"I see," Loomis said. "Well." And he nodded toward the other two men at the table. "This is Klein – uh, Joe Klein, the radio man; and this is Ted Bankowsky, the medic."

They couldn't have been more different. Klein was swart and rat-faced, dapper in a grubby way, with a carefully shaped pencil moustache showing black against the gray of a three- or four-day growth of beard, and his smile was yellow. Beside him Ted the medic looked very clean and fair and healthy: he could have been an Eagle Scout or the president of a Polish-American youth club. And the most attractive thing about him now, as he held out one strong and shapely hand, was a dawning of recollection in his eyes.

"Oh yeah," he said. "I think I do remember. Didn't you have laryngitis or something?"

"That's right, yes."

"Where'll we put him?" the lieutenant was inquiring of Loomis. "Which squad's the most shorthanded?"

"Hell, they could all use another man. I guess Finn's the worst off, though. Okay, Prentice, we'll put you in the first squad. Klein, run out back and get Finn in here."

"Right." And the radio man scurried obediently around the table and out through the back door, wearing the earnest frown of a habitual toady. Then there seemed to be nothing to do but stand there and wait – nobody had asked him to sit down – while the men at the table resumed some interrupted conversation of their own.

In a little while the door opened again and the talk stopped. Klein was back, and with him came a slight, cave-chested man who wore a flat yellow straw boater that might have been the pride of some Rhineland dandy in the early 1900's.

"Finn, we got a new man for you," Loomis said, "so you can quit your bitching. Prentice, this is Sergeant Finn, your squad leader."

Sergeant Finn did not smile while shaking hands, which made Prentice feel foolish for having smiled himself, and the next thing he discovered was that Sergeant Finn was surprisingly young – nineteen or twenty at the most. But his thin, homely face was filled with self-assurance, and his squint made it clear that he was sizing Prentice up. This caused Prentice to lick his lips and lower his eyes like a girl, and in self-defense he began furtively looking for flaws in Finn's excellence. For one thing he was as skinny as Prentice himself, and a good deal shorter. And the antique straw hat was not the only touch of absurdity about him: he was wearing a pair of green special-issue combat pants that were many sizes too big for him, and they were held up by blue-striped civilian suspenders worn over the outside of his tight, dirty G.I. sweater. If you just looked at his clothes, at his odd slouch and sunken chest, it might be easy to see him as a possible fool and butt of jokes – nobody to be afraid of, certainly. But there was his calm face again, and there were his cool, evaluating eyes.

Finn had him so preoccupied that he didn't notice the entrance of another man – let alone see who it was – until he heard Loomis say, "And this is your assistant squad leader, Sergeant Rand."

"*Sam!*" And Prentice was filled with elation, grabbing and pumping the familiar four-fingered hand, punching the familiar solid shoulder, while Sam Rand allowed his poker face to break, for once, into a smile of old acquaintance.

"Good to see you, Prentice," he said, and then he explained the outburst to the others: "We come over on the same boat."

"I'll be God damned," Prentice was shouting with a

salesman's enthusiasm. "So it's *Sergeant* Rand now – how about that!" He knew it sounded a little excessive, but it did seem important to let them all know, and especially Finn, that this good and valuable man was his friend.

"Want to come upstairs, Prentice?" Sam said. "We'll find you a place to sleep." And he turned respectfully to Finn. "There's another bed in Walker's room; okay to put him in there?"

Finn shrugged, causing the suspenders to hike the loose waistband up and down. "Don't matter," he said.

As Prentice followed Sam down the shadowy hallway full of watching eyes, he hoped they would all notice that Sam was carrying part of his gear for him and asking interested, old-buddy questions: "How're you feeling, Prentice? . . . Where'd they have you hospitalized? . . ."

It was turning out to be all right, after all. As soon as he had unpacked his stuff and received permission to leave the house, he would go over to Weapons Platoon and find out about Quint.

"How's Quint?" he asked, starting up the stairs behind Sam's slow, laboring buttocks, and at first he thought he hadn't heard him. "Hey Sam? How's Quint?"

Sam paused on the stairs and looked part of the way back over his shoulder, not quite as far as Prentice's face. "Well," he said, "that's not so good." Then he went on climbing.

"You mean he's still sick?"

"No; worse'n that."

"You mean he was hit?"

"Come on along in the room," Sam said.

In the room, which smelled of old wallpaper and damp plaster and rifle-cleaning fluid, Prentice sat on the edge of a quilted bed and Sam sat on a delicate antique chair.

"It was right after we pulled out of Horbourg," he said. "On the way to Appenweier – that was the next town we took down there. Anyway, we had to go acrost this big-assed field. The thing is, there was land mines in the field. Not many, but some. Now, I didn't see this happen – Weapons Platoon was followin' some distance behind us, and away over to the left – I didn't see it happen, but I heard about it later. They say Quint stepped on a mine. Now, they say he wasn't hurt too bad – not then. This medic run over and commenced tendin' to him; only just then this other medic comes runnin' over to help, and this other medic set off another mine right up close. They say all three of them was killed outright."

There was a long silence, during which the sound of laughter floated up from the kitchen and died away: someone had evidently told a joke.

"Real sorry, Prentice," Sam said. "I know you and him was good friends." He probed inside a pocket of his woolen shirt and brought out a pack of cigarettes. He gave one to Prentice and took one for himself, and he ponderously lit them both with a tiny, expensive-looking lighter that he'd probably looted from a German home. Then he shifted his weight in the creaking chair and blew a long jet of smoke at the floor between his boots. "I saw him only a day or so before it happened," he said. "I told him about you bein' hit; he felt real bad about that."

"You told him I was *hit*? Jesus, Sam, I wasn't hit. I went back with pneumonia, that's all."

And Sam looked up in mild surprise. "That so? Well, I must of had the wrong information, then. I heard you was hit in Horbourg." There was another silence, and then Sam got up from the chair and mumbled that he would see him later.

"Wait a second." Prentice was suddenly in terror of being left alone. He wanted to say: Wait a second. Listen. Do you know he would have gone back even before Horbourg, if it hadn't been for me? I talked him out of it! And do you realize I went back the next day without even telling him? Without even *telling* him? And do you see how awful it is that he thought I'd been hit? Sam, for Christ's sake, do you realize I killed him?

But he didn't say any of those things. Instead he said, "Wait a second. I – I've—" he rummaged in his bag until he found the four packages of Bond Street tobacco, but he didn't bring them out until after he'd torn off the red ribbon and the tag. "You smoke a pipe sometimes, don't you?" he said.

"Sometimes, yeah. Well, that's – that's real nice of you, Prentice. I 'predate it." And Sam Rand stood there holding the stack of packages in both hands, straightening their edges with his social finger.

Then he was gone, and Prentice was alone in a silence that rang with all his shrill, unspoken words. He was so alone that the only thing to do was lie back on the bed and roll over and draw up his knees like an unborn baby, staring with dry eyes at a cluster of pink flowers on the wallpaper, knowing he had never been so alone in his life.

After a while he rolled off the bed and got to his feet, gazing at the ceiling as if beseeching God for punishment; then he let his head fall forward and clasped his temples with both hands – a gesture as melodramatic as any that Alice Prentice had ever achieved – and he was still doing that when the door burst open and a husky boy in a top hat stood staring at him.

The only thing to do was reshape his tragic features into a wince of discomfort and begin scratching his scalp with all ten fingers, as if he were a man bedeviled with dandruff who could sure as hell use a good shampoo.

"You Prentice?" The boy's big face was so expressionless that Prentice couldn't tell if the scalp-scratching ruse had worked or not. "Here's your mail. It just come over from the C.P." And he slung a thick, twine-bound sheaf of letters onto Prentice's bed.

"Oh," Prentice said, still scratching and wincing. "Thanks." Then he smoothed his hair, shook his fingers as extra proof of dandruff, and hooked his thumbs manfully into his belt.

"My name's Walker," the boy said. "I got the other sack in here."

"Oh. Glad to meet you."

But Walker only mumbled something about being on duty and having to haul ass. He snatched up his web equipment from the bed and buckled it on, exchanged his top hat for a helmet, picked up his rifle, and was gone as quickly as he'd come, leaving an almost visible trail of unfriendliness.

It was the first mail Prentice had received since coming overseas. The letters were mostly from his mother – she seemed to have written three or four a week – and he sorted out the one with the most recent postmark and opened it first, to make sure she was all right.

Dearest Bobby:

I do try so hard not to worry and I know the hospital must be a safe place to be, as long as you say you're not "very" sick, but even so I am just worried half to death!!! Everybody says the war will soon be over, and I do so hope and pray . . .

He let his eyes slide down the lines of her big, impassioned handwriting until they came to rest on another paragraph: . . .

Oh, how I loved your description of France!!! You made it all so real for me that I feel almost as if . . .

And then he put it back in its envelope. There was a letter from Hugh Burlingame, too, and two others from lesser of his

237

school friends, but he didn't feel like reading them now. The one letter that claimed all his attention, the one he held and stared at for a long time without opening, had not been intended for him. It was very new-looking, written on Red Cross stationery in his own shamefully familiar hand, addressed to Pfc. John R. Quint, and it bore the company mail clerk's pink rubber stamp: RETURN TO SENDER.

Being "on duty" at this position on the Rhine meant walking out across the flatland, twice a day and twice a night, to sit in a foxhole overlooking the mild, surprisingly narrow river. You sat there for two hours on an improvised wooden bench, with a field telephone close at hand, watching for any sign of movement on the opposite shore, until another man came out to relieve you. From half a mile away to the north came the faint, wavering sounds of Engineers at work on a pontoon bridge.

Prentice welcomed his two-hour sittings because they gave him a chance to be as alone as he felt, and only when he was alone could he savor the full enormity of his guilt.

It would have been so easy! If only he had said "Okay" when Quint first suggested their going back – and what, after all, would it have cost him to say that? Or later, in the talk they'd had over the window sill in Horbourg, if only he had said he was ready to go back then. Or later still, after he'd fallen on that mattress under Logan's cursing: how much strength would it have taken, after all, just to have roused himself and gone to find Quint again and said, "Look, I'm ready now; I'm going back." Why *hadn't* he done that one, last, tremendously important thing? Was it really because he'd been too sick to get off the mattress? Or was it – this was the most galling thought of all – was it because of all the God damn wine he had drunk that day?

Once, walking back to the platoon house at midnight, he began to compose a difficult letter in his mind:

Dear Mr. and Mrs. Quint:
   I want you to know that I feel personally responsible for the death of your son . . .

And when he was in bed, huddled with a flashlight under the tent of a blanket so as not to disturb Walker's sleep, he tried to commit it to paper. But all the sentences had to be crossed out and reworked and crossed out again, until, an hour later, he abandoned the job. What could he hope to accomplish with a letter like that? All he'd get back, if anything, would be some formal, kindly words from the grieving parents.

He crumpled it up, turned off the flashlight, and tried to sleep. Then half an hour later he was up and writing again, trying a different kind of letter.

Dear Mr. and Mrs. Quint:
   I want you to know that your son John was the finest man I have ever . . .

But he couldn't finish that one, either.

At last he put the flashlight away and lay still, flexing the writer's cramp out of his fingers, listening to Walker's heavy snore and to the shallow sound of his own breathing. It was hopeless. The only way he could ever make amends was with action, not words – with whatever action might still be possible on the dangerous land beyond this river – and he put himself to sleep with daydreams of heroic combat and rescue and self-sacrifice.

In the meantime there was the daily problem of how to fit in with the men of the Second Platoon, and especially with those of his own rifle squad. More than once he was tempted to walk up to Finn and say: "Look, Sergeant: there's something I want to get straightened out with you. The point is, I think you must have confused me with the kid that took sick in the factory, back in—" But he was never able to do so, and Finn's narrow gaze seemed never to include him except with mild disdain.

And Sam Rand wasn't much of a comfort. With Quint gone, it soon became clear that the two of them had very little in common; besides, it wasn't easy to talk to Sam now without seeming to be currying favor with the assistant squad leader.

Only two of the squad were veterans of the Bulge – Finn himself and a noisy, flat-faced little man named Krupka, who looked seventeen but was in fact twenty-three. It was Krupka who made the first friendly overtures; one morning when Prentice was waiting his turn at the platoon's extra latrine – a straight chair with a knocked-out seat that straddled a slit trench in the back yard (the original latrine, a civilian outhouse, had become too full and foul to use). Krupka was taking his time on the chair, allowing his bowels to move with an unforced animal rhythm, gesturing with a clutched wad of K-ration toilet paper to emphasize the points of his one-way conversation.

"You was with us down in Colmar, right? Well listen, don't let nobody shit you – you ain't missed nothin' since then. All we done since then was go to Holland in a holdin' position; then we come up here and since then we just been quiet. Some a these guys'll try to give you a big line a bullshit; don't listen to 'em. Part of the States you from, Prentice?"

He seemed decent and kindly enough, but Prentice was cautioned by an old and trusted rule of his schooldays: Beware of the first friendly one; he's probably an outcast himself. As it turned out, Krupka was not exactly an outcast – he was apparently too good and reliable a soldier for that – but he was nobody's favorite: despite his lack of any discernible sense of humor he was a tireless kidder and teaser, a wounder of feelings. Once when one of the other squad leaders came into the kitchen to speak with the lieutenant – a tall, stooped, scholarly-looking man named Bernstein – Krupka greeted him with, "Hey there, Suicide? How's Suicide today?" Sergeant Bernstein ignored him, though little flecks of pink appeared in his cheeks, and somebody else said, "Ah, blow it out your ass, Krupka." But Krupka couldn't leave it alone: he kept it up throughout whatever business it was that Bernstein had with the lieutenant, and the minute Bernstein was gone – "So long, Suicide" – he nudged Prentice heavily in the ribs. "Know why I call him that? Back in the Bulge, when Brewer had the platoon. We hadda go acrost this ridge one time; old Bernstein chickens out and starts yellin' at Brewer. He says, 'I won't *take* my men acrost there'" – and here Krupka rolled his eyes in a cruelly accurate imitation of hysteria – "He says, 'It's suicide! It's suicide!' Turns out there wasn't nothin' on the other side of the ridge – no Jerries or nothin'. Anyway, that's why I call him that. Makes him sore as hell; he don't let on, though."

The other five men in the squad (it was a nine-man squad as opposed to the regulation twelve) were all newcomers who had joined the outfit in Holland. All five were Prentice's age or younger, and the husky, top-hatted Walker, Prentice's room-mate, was clearly their spokesman. He and two taciturn, squint-eyed country boys, Drake and Brownlee, were inseparable companions, and it was with these three that Sergeant Finn chose to spend most of his time. He accompanied them on foraging trips down the road for eggs and wine, he sat up late to drink and play cards with them, and he continually looked out for their welfare. It was as if he had decided that these three were the only members of the squad worth bothering with. He seemed to have decided that Sam Rand was all right but that Sam was older and could shift for himself, that Krupka was all right but that Krupka was a pain in the ass; as for the others, though it might be his duty to lead them, his every glance and muttering made it clear that as far as he was concerned they were on their own.

And these others, in addition to Prentice, were two: a small, sad-eyed, homesick boy named Gardinella who constantly tried to ingratiate himself with Finn and constantly failed, and another very young-looking soldier named Mueller, who was so quiet and so rarely in evidence that Prentice at first thought he must belong to another squad. He was middle-sized and stocky, though his weight was more baby fat than brawn, and he had small, tapered, weak-looking hands with dimpled fingers. The surprising thing about Mueller was that he was the B.A.R. man – he would theoretically control the major firepower of the squad – but Prentice hadn't been in the house more than three days before hearing the story of how Mueller had come to be assigned to that job. In Holland, there had been some kind of battalion lecture or briefing after which, in the confusion of re-forming ranks and getting back into trucks, Mueller had left his rifle behind. And Finn, after chewing him out – "You mean you lost your *rifle?*" – had said: "Okay, Buster. From now on you're the B.A.R. man." It was a punishment: the B.A.R. weighed twice as much as an ordinary rifle and required the wearing of a special belt heavy with sagging ammunition magazines. It was generally assumed that when the squad went into action Finn would assign the B.A.R. to some more competent man – Walker, for instance – but in the meantime Krupka gave Mueller a merciless kidding about it. "Hey, you gonna get yourself a buncha Jerries with that B.A.R., Mueller?

You gonna stop a coupla Tiger tanks? Hey fellas, let's get Mueller some armor-piercing ammo, so he can stop a coupla Tiger tanks – okay, Mueller?" The carrying of the B.A.R. was Mueller's cross, and he bore it with a fortitude that Prentice could only admire.

But there seemed to be no way for Prentice to relax among these men – even with Gardinella and Mueller. He kept to himself, and he looked forward to his two-hour sittings in the riverbank foxhole. And it was there, late one afternoon, that he decided to do the thing he had put off for too many days: make a visit to Weapons Platoon. He walked there as soon as he was free.

The first few men he spoke to were of no help – they were new replacements – but then he found a haggard-looking staff sergeant with the dimly remembered name of Rolls who had been with the outfit all along.

"Quint?" said Rolls. "Short fella? Wore glasses? Yeah, I remember him, only I'd forgotten his name." He looked up, squinting in the fumes of cleaning fluid that rose from the stripped-down pistol he was swabbing on an ornate dining room table. "I was there, all right. I was walkin' along right behind him."

"Can you tell me about it? I mean can you tell me exactly what happened?"

The sergeant put down his cleaning rag and applied a match to a flattened cigarette. "Well," he said, "this mine went off. Not exactly up in his face; kinda off to one side; didn't kill him. Then Dave – that was our medic, best damn medic in the company – Dave goes over to help him. And then this other medic – I don't know who the hell he was, never saw him before in my life – this other damn fool medic comes chargin' over outa nowhere. Sumbitch wasn't even *needed*, that's the funny part;

just some eager-beaver bastard couldn't mind his own business. Anyway, this other damn fool medic comes over without watchin' his step, and *Wham!* another mine."

"I know," Prentice said. "I mean I've heard that part of it. What I mean is, there's no question but that all three of them were killed? I mean you're absolutely sure Quint was dead?"

Sergeant Rolls removed the cigarette from his mouth and picked a fleck of paper from his lower lip. "Buddy," he said, "the last time I saw him he was layin' there." One nicotine-stained forefinger pointed to a place on the dining room carpet, while Prentice nodded; then the finger drew a slow arc in the air and pointed to another part of the floor, five or six feet away: "And his head was layin' over there."

On the way back to his own house, Prentice felt his toes curling as if to grip the earth like talons with every step, and he moved as heavily as if he were nearing the end of a ten-mile hike.

When he was still some distance away from the house he heard the noise of laughter and clattering dishware, and only then did he remember what evening this was: the Second Platoon was having a party they'd been planning for days.

A number of chickens had been killed and butchered, many bottles of schnapps and wine had been saved for the occasion, and now the feast was at its height. All the tables in the house had been crowded into the kitchen to form a long, intricate banquet surface. Lieutenant Coverly sat in the place of honor, dwarfed by the hulking presence of Sergeant Loomis on his right, and the rest of the hunched, eating men filled every available inch of table space. As Prentice stood awkwardly in the doorway it was clear that he had nowhere to sit.

"We don't wait for anybody here, Prentice," Loomis called out, his mouth and cheeks shining with chicken grease. "I'm afraid you're out of luck."

"That's okay," he said, and as one chewing face after another turned to look at him, he wished he could dissolve into the wall.

But Ted the medic was on his feet, loading up a plate of food for him. Several of the men had to pull in their chairs to let Prentice sidle past them along the wall toward the stove, and then they had to pull in again to let him make his way back. He ate squatting on the floor, trying to hold his plate steady on one thigh. The elbows and backs and turning heads of the men were high above him, far too high to let him be included in their talk, and he could scarcely taste the food for his embarrassment. The scene was almost too pat, too ludicrous an illustration of his role in this platoon: the one man bound to be late for everything, left out of everything, and finally consigned to a place too low for notice.

At last several men left the table to go belching upstairs, and Prentice slipped into one of their chairs as unobtrusively as possible, nursing his glass of wine. And after a minute or two it no longer mattered that nobody was talking to him, for all the conversations had died away and the talkers had become listeners: Lieutenant Coverly had the floor.

". . . but I mean it isn't an infantry *war* any more," he was saying. "From now on it's going to be one big artillery fight all the way. And I mean maybe their infantry *is* shot to hell, but you know damn well there's nothing the matter with their artillery. And I mean how much chance does a man have against an eighty-eight? You figure it out."

And the nods and murmurs around the table conveyed agreement and sympathy, if something less than respect. Even Prentice had come to know by now, as well as anyone, that the lieutenant was wholly unsure of his command and of himself. His nail-biting, his shyly darting eyes and breathless, almost whispering voice all betrayed him, and so did his insistence that

245

the men call him "Covey," instead of "Lieutenant" or "Sir," as if informality might relieve him of his obligation to lead. His talk was always full of his having been trained as an administrative Signal Corps officer, and of the unhappy transfer and shockingly brief retraining that had brought him to this platoon in Holland; there was a rumor too that he'd recently received a Dear John letter from his wife. Please, his gentle Southern voice seemed always to be saying, please don't expect very much of me. And nobody did, though nobody seemed to dislike him. The men did call him "Covey" without embarrassment, and for the most part they seemed tactfully determined to do whatever they could to help him through his ordeal.

". . . Hell," he was saying now, and his drink-enriched voice was taking on an uncommon authority. "Hell, when you're up against infantry at least it's a fair fight, right? I mean then it's essentially one man against another, kill or be killed. And hell, I'll take my chances in that kind of a situation any day."

Prentice couldn't help doubting this, and looked furtively around the table to see if there were any other doubting faces. Would Coverly really rather take his chances in that kind of a situation any day? It didn't matter: foolish statement or not, he was getting away with it.

"I'll make you a little bet," he was saying now. "I'll bet you not one man in ten of us gets to fire his weapon from now on. Nothing to *shoot* at. No way to fight *back*. Hell, we might as well be going in unarmed, for all the good our weapons'll do us." His eyes were glittering defiantly around the table. "We'll be sitting ducks for their eighty-eights all the way; that's what scares me – and I don't mind telling you men, it scares the piss out of me."

Sergeant Loomis elaborately cleared his throat, and when he began to speak Prentice could understand what it was about Loomis – despite his fine record and despite his being the real leader of the platoon – that made most of the men detest him. It was that he was such a God damn actor: everything he said came out with the ponderous fraudulence of something in the movies; it was as if he had learned how to be a platoon sergeant by watching every Hollywood war picture ever made. "Well, I don't know, Covey," he was saying now, staring at the schnapps he rolled in the bottom of his glass, "at least we're winning the damn war. I'd a hell of a lot rather be winning a war than losing one. For a while back there in the Bulge it looked like we might be losing – that's when you find you really got some trouble on your hands."

And the lieutenant could only lower his eyes in deference; he hadn't, of course, been in the Bulge.

"I agree with Covey, though," said Klein, the unkempt and sycophantic radio man. He had washed and shaved for the party and looked almost clean, except that his white cheeks now called attention to a multitude of blackheads in his nose. When his endless agreeing with Loomis became too obvious, even to himself, the next best thing was to agree with "Covey." "The worst part about artillery *is* just that," he said. "You can't fight back. I mean there's no *sense* to it."

But Klein was ignored, as usual; and the next speaker was the man on the lieutenant's left, who was rising now and gathering up his dishes – a tall, ruddily handsome staff sergeant named Paul Underwood, who was the platoon guide. Underwood rarely stayed around the house for long; he seemed to have so many friends throughout the company that he was always on the move, as if to bestow his presence on a few admirers at a time. When Prentice had first seen him stride into this house to a happy chorus of "Hey, Paul" and "Where you been, Paul?" and "Wait a second, Paul, I got something to tell you," he had felt an instinctive, envious resentment. *Nobody* could be that good-looking, that charming, that much in demand. But then Underwood had strolled over and said, "I don't believe I've met you, soldier; you a new man?" and Prentice had been meekly won over. He *was* perfect; and now, as he sidled away to carry his dishes from the table, he held everyone's attention.

"Well," he said, "all I know is they can't get the damn thing over with too soon for me. I just wish they'd keep us here on this side of the river and let the Russians clean it up; that'd suit me perfectly."

"Buddy," said Ted the medic, "you can say that again." And there were nods and rumblings of agreement all around the table. It would suit them all perfectly – all, apparently, except Prentice, who hid his mouth in the last of his wine.

A faint, faraway buzzing in the eastern sky made them all freeze and look at each other, round-eyed; then it grew louder and lower – an aircraft engine, a lone German plane come to reconnoiter the bridge.

Almost at once the anti-aircraft gun opened up in the fields behind the house, and the men all bolted to their feet, knocking over chairs and spilling glasses: they were clambering out of the kitchen door like frantic children, and then they were all outside and running in the field to watch it, shouting and pointing.

There it was, the plane trying to break away out of range and pursued by the yellow tracers and the flak that burst in little black puffs against the pink of the evening sky.

"*Get* the bastard! *Get* 'im! *Get* 'im!"

"They're firing *short!* Christ's sake, bring it up! Bring it *up!*"

"They *got* 'im! They *got* 'im!"

"No they ain't – not *yet* they ain't – *Get* 'im!"

The plane was still climbing, heading northwest and apparently moving away from the flak, but then it began to cough out a trail of black smoke. It described a long, graceful arc and went into a gliding fall: they saw the small black and orange burst of its crash a mile or more away, and then the sound of it came back across the flatland in the abrupt and ringing silence of the gun.

"Wow!"

"D'ja see that? D'ja see that?"

"Beautiful! Beautiful!"

"Wow!"

"How *about* that?"

Somebody slapped Prentice on the back and he felt the sting of his own hand slapping somebody else's back; he didn't know who either man was. He had been as wholly caught up in the spectacle as anyone else, and it seemed to have made him one of them for the first time.

As they turned and started back to the house in a straggling group, each looking very small and individual in the wide evening landscape, he could look from one walking, talking figure to another – even the frightening Finn, with his absurd straw hat; even Krupka; even Walker; even the kiss-ass Klein – and take pleasure in the simple knowledge that they were the men of his platoon. He knew it probably wouldn't last long, this sense of fellowship, and he knew it was probably the wine as much as the plane that had brought it on, but there it was. This was his outfit; these were the men with whom he would cross the river and find whatever was left of his chance for atonement, whatever was left of the war.

Chapter Two

The day of the crossing began before dawn. It began with a rude, angry jostling of men made weak by the unaccustomed weight of urgency and equipment, with a laggard company formation on the dark road, and a sullen, cursing forward march.

The sky and the land were turning blue by the time the column reached the bridge. The crossing itself was a matter of trying to keep from slipping down a hill of loose dirt that led to the waterline, then of treading carefully and for what seemed a great distance on the steel cleats of a footpath whose shuddering pontoons rode low in the loud black and silver flood of the river, and then of climbing another hill of dirt on the opposite shore.

Soon everything was green and gold. They were walking on a neat macadam road through woodland, and the only sound except for their rubber-heeled boots was the song of birds high in the trees.

Lieutenant Coverly, in what appeared to be a burst of nervous energy, was making his way down the platoon to have encouraging little talks with his men. Prentice saw him up ahead, chatting with Finn. Then he dropped back to spend some time with Mueller, walking with his hand on Mueller's shoulder, and then he exchanged a few words with Walker, who said something that made him laugh.

"And how *you* doing, Prentice?" he said, still smiling from Walker's joke.

"Okay, sir."

"I imagine this is quite a change for you, after the hospital. Well; keep it up."

They marched all morning, with five-minute breaks every hour. At noon they stopped in a clearing beside the road – a clearing that contained two dead German soldiers – to eat their K rations. Most of the men stayed as far away as possible from the corpses, but Krupka seemed to enjoy them. He kicked them in the ribs and stood on them; then, finding a pair of black-rimmed eyeglasses in the grass near one of them, he fitted them back onto the dead man's face as carefully as a little girl playing with a doll.

"Hey, you guys," he called. "I betcha none a ya's got guts enough to sit on one of these bastards and eat. Five bucks. I got five bucks says none a ya's got guts enough."

Nobody took him on, so he did it himself: he sat on the chest of the bespectacled corpse and spooned up his can of dehydrated eggs, which were almost exactly the color of the dead man's flesh.

Then they marched all afternoon. They passed occasional barns and farmhouses, all of which appeared to be abandoned, but for the most part there was nothing in sight but trees and fields and endlessly unwinding road.

Once Prentice looked up to find the jaunty, handsome figure of Paul Underwood walking beside him. "Here, Prentice," he said. "Present for you." And he gave Prentice a hand grenade from which the pin had been removed.

"Jesus!" Prentice held it in one tight, trembling hand while Underwood laughed.

"What's the matter? Hell, it's safe as long as you hold the spoon down."

And Prentice realized now that Underwood, for all his apparent carelessness, had pressed it into his hand in such a way that it couldn't have dropped. "Well, but I mean where *is* the pin?"

"Nobody knows, that's the funny part. Guys've been passing it up and down the column all day. Here, I'll take it back. Careful, now."

And Underwood moved gracefully away up the column to find another victim for his practical joke. A little later Prentice saw him leave the road and go trotting out into a field. When he was about a hundred yards away he stopped and crouched, and Prentice figured out what he was doing: he was burying the grenade, packing earth or rocks around it, and this struck Prentice as an appallingly rash thing to do. What if some farmer – or, for God's sake, some child – should come and stumble over it? But then, what else was Underwood to do with the thing? He certainly couldn't keep it, and he probably couldn't throw it because the enemy might be close enough to hear the explosion. In any case it wasn't something Prentice could afford to think about; all his mind was occupied with walking, making his swollen feet rise painfully and fall, rise and fall, and matching his breath to their rhythm. He had a pain in his chest, but couldn't tell if it was the bad lung or the weight of the bag of six rifle grenades that rode over it. Where the hell did Underwood get the strength to run out there and back?

By dusk, which brought a chilly wind, a number of men were falling behind: the column was bedraggled on both sides of the road, and Prentice kept passing the dim shapes of men sitting on the ground or lying down. The man directly ahead of him, Walker, was showing signs of weakness, sometimes drifting back to within a boot or two of Prentice before he pulled himself forward again. But Mueller, with more to carry than anyone else, was doing well: the steady motion of his plump, baby-shaped back had begun to serve Prentice as a goad. Once Mueller stumbled and fell but clumsily righted himself, using his B.A.R., barrel down, as a crutch to help him back on his feet. The muzzle was probably plugged with dirt after that, but that didn't spoil his performance in Prentice's eyes. If *he* can make it, Prentice told himself, I'll make it too.

They spent the night in a barn, with guards posted around its yard. Most of the Second Platoon was assigned to the loft: they had to climb a wooden ladder to get there and use cupped matches to find their way around in the darkness, but once they were settled they found it very comfortable to stretch out under their raincoats for sleep. It could have been minutes or hours later when they were jolted awake by a Shriek-*Slam!* It might not have been a direct hit on the roof but it sure as hell sounded like one, and so did the three explosions that came rapidly after it. By the time of the second shell the barn loft was a madhouse of shouting, stumbling, colliding men, all heading for the ladder and struggling to climb down.

"Lemme *outa* here . . ."

"Get outa the fuckin' *way* . . ."

Prentice felt a squirm of fingers under his boot on one of the rungs and heard a scream; then another boot crushed his own fingers and someone's swinging rifle butt cracked him across the head. He lost his footing halfway down the ladder and fell scrabbling, hit the concrete floor and rolled, and another man fell heavily into his arms.

"*Easy!*" Sergeant Loomis was calling. "Take it *easy,* for Christ's sake . . ."

Then it was over, and there were no more shells. But nobody wanted to go back to the loft, and the ground floor of the barn was impossibly crowded. A standing man could hardly move without stepping on someone's wrist or ankle, and there were many curses and yelps of pain. But at last, somehow, room was found for everyone to lie down and a kind of peace descended once again.

When Prentice's turn for guard duty came, some time after midnight, he stepped on three men in making his way outside the barn. And when it was over, after two hours of peering into the darkness with the wind in his face and his head ringing from the bruise of the rifle butt, he knew he couldn't find his former sleeping place. Instead, he felt his way along one wall, then went down on his knees to feel along the floor. His hands sank into a heap of straw, or silage, and he lay down in it with a sense of unexpected luxury. Someone else's warm, broad back lay close beside him, and he nestled gratefully up to it. Only when daylight came did he discover that he'd been sleeping in a straw-covered mound of pig manure, and that the back he had pressed against was that of a sleeping pig.

"Where the hell are we going?" the men kept asking each other on the second morning's march. "What the hell's the deal?" But by noon everyone knew what the deal was. Three small towns lay ahead of them within a space of several miles. If they found no enemy resistance in the first town they would go on to the second, and if that town too was evacuated they would take the third.

"Be one damn long walk, that's all," somebody said, "and they'll be laying back there lobbing eighty-eights at us all the way."

Soon they left the road to move out across open fields, and the column was re-formed into a wide, intricate attack formation. Each squad was formed with the two scouts going first, then the B.A.R. man with riflemen on either side of him, then the squad leader flanked by other riflemen, with the assistant squad leader bringing up the rear. That was the way they approached the first town, moving up over the slope of a newly plowed field, with the Second Platoon leading the company and Finn's squad leading the platoon.

"Spread it out, now," Finn kept calling. "Don't bunch up, now. Spread it out."

Moving stealthily along on Mueller's right flank, his rifle at port arms and his finger on the safety, Prentice felt his face twitching in an uncontrollable little tic. The distant line of houses ahead might well be filled with German machine gunners, crouched and waiting for these small green and brown figures to come a little closer across this field; they'd be taking aim now, telling each other to hold their fire, and Prentice himself would be one of their three or four primary targets.

But nothing happened. As they came closer they could see that nearly all the houses had white flags hanging from their windows, and then they saw a cluster of black-clad civilian men coming out into the field with a white flag held high. Two of the civilians broke into a stumbling run to meet the soldiers, calling and gesturing. One of them wore a chain of office over his dusty frock coat: he seemed to be the mayor of the town.

And so there was nothing to do but move on into the streets, which were littered with cast-off German Army equipment – packs, helmets, even rifles – and to make token checks of houses here and there to look for enemy troops. Civilians clustered around them as they entered each house: one old man clutched Prentice by the sleeve and showed him a grubby document, pointing to each printed line of it with a trembling forefinger – it seemed to be legal proof that he was a citizen of some country other than Germany.

"Some of these bastards are Jerry soldiers in civilian clothes," Sergeant Loomis said. "They probably changed 'em ten minutes ago."

A brief artillery barrage came in as they made their way through the town, and Prentice found himself sitting wedged between Mueller and a weeping old woman on the floor of a cellar, but soon the sky was quiet again. Then it was time to move on to the second town, and the second town was so much like the first that the two became blurred in memory. By the time it was cleared, a heavy fatigue had settled over the men. It was only four o'clock in the afternoon, but Prentice wanted nothing more than a chance to sleep. He didn't even want to eat until he'd slept, yet to think about food was to realize he had never been so hungry in his life.

"The third town'll be the bitch," someone was saying. "That's where they'll be holed up and waiting for us." And the third town was another three miles away.

"Spread it out," Finn kept calling. "Don't bunch up, now. I said spread it *out*, Prentice . . ."

They were approaching the third town across a long meadow that led up to a wooded ridge. The town was said to be close on the other side of the ridge, and the word was that "B" Company, moving in from somewhere on the right, would make the initial assault. Finn's squad had gone less than a third of the way across the meadow when the earth was shaken by a great explosion behind them – and whirling around, Prentice saw a spire of dirt and smoke and clutter rising straight up, more than fifty yards high, from a part of the dirt road they had just crossed. It was a mine; and now, among the spinning, falling fragments, he could make out the shape of a pair of automobile wheels. It was a jeep – the company runner's jeep, he heard later – and both jeep and driver had been blown to bits.

Was this the kind of mine that Quint had stepped on? No; probably this was a bigger one. But the mine – the two mines – that had killed Quint and the medics must have gone off with this same shocking abruptness, filling the air with this same brutal flavor of chance.

"Keep it spread out, now," Finn was calling.

Climbing the ridge was an arduous job: there was a thick entangling underbrush, and there were twigs to catch at your equipment straps and whip your face. On top of the ridge they moved cautiously toward the brink of the opposite slope until they could see what lay ahead: a deep flat field, perhaps two hundred yards across, and then another, treeless hill leading up to the densely packed houses of the town – a town in which no white flags were hung.

The two scouts, Drake and Krupka, were crouched in the brush and waiting for Finn, who went forward and began arranging his men in a line across the crest, five or ten yards apart. The second squad was forming a similar line on their left, and the third was in reserve, somewhere behind them in the trees. The platoon command group was over on the right, where the ridge was considerably lower: looking down in that direction Prentice could see Loomis's profiled head and another helmet that was probably Coverly's. Just ahead of them, at the base of the ridge where the field began, there was a small industrial brick structure – an electric power station or something – and Paul Underwood was standing in its shelter, turning back to smile and say something to Loomis.

"Keep it low, now," Finn was saying. "Keep low in the brush. Heads down."

Prentice deepened his crouch and ducked his head lower; then he saw that Walker and Brownlee, on either side of him, were getting into a prone position, and he lay down too, gratefully letting himself relax against the earth. It meant he could no longer see Finn, or Loomis, but he could still see Walker, and Walker could see them. When Walker moved, he would move too; and Brownlee and the others would follow him. In the meantime he would simply lie here, switching his gaze between Walker and the gray, silent town across the field. But he found that when he looked at the town the shapes of its houses tended to swim together in a drowsing mist. Lying down was too damned comfortable: it was all he could do to keep his eyes from closing.

What the hell were they waiting for? Then he remembered: they were waiting for "B" Company to go in first, on the right. And no sooner had he remembered this than there came a ringing sputter of machine-gun fire from the right-hand side of the town, instantly followed by more machine guns and B.A.R.'s and rifles, until all the sounds were blended in a welter of noise. "B" Company! And what the hell were they supposed to do now? Were they just supposed to lie here, while "B" Company got torn apart?

He rose briefly, just enough to see that Finn was still huddled behind a bush, and that down beyond him Loomis's and Coverly's helmets had made no movement. Apparently, no orders had yet been given for "A" Company to advance across the field.

He lay down again and forced himself to watch Walker, who was watching Finn, who in turn was watching Loomis and Coverly. The gunfire dwindled a little and then was resumed; it was steady for a while and it dwindled again. The noise of it began to rise and fall almost rhythmically, like the sound of the sea or his own breathing; it formed a cadence for the silent chant in his mind:

If I watch Walker and Walker watches Finn and Finn watches Loomis . . .

If I watch Walker and Walker watches Finn and Finn watches Loomis . . .

If I watch Loomis, and Loomis watches – no; wait. If I watch . . .

If I watch . . .

. . . *Slam!*

He was awake and on his feet in a split second, and the first thing he saw was that Walker was still there: Walker was getting up and spinning around to see where the shell had fallen. Yellow dust was rising and clods of earth were falling all around them.

Slam!

He saw Walker fall again, get up, run a few steps one way and a few steps another, like a man in panic; and now, turning, he saw Brownlee's face rise up over the brush, open-mouthed and wide-eyed.

Slam!

The branch of a tree came crashing to the ground beside him. Brownlee's head ducked down again, and only now did Prentice see that Finn and Loomis and Coverly were no longer there, nor were they anywhere to be seen in the empty field ahead. Near the little brick structure the grass had been torn away in a ragged shellhole, and close beside it he saw Ted the medic crouched over someone who was lying down. The noise of small-arms fire was so intense that it was impossible to tell how much of it was coming this way: the whole field might be humming with bullets.

Slam!

A lone man was running out across the field now, holding his free arm high in a gesture of "Follow me" – it was Sergeant Bernstein, "Suicide," and Prentice followed him. He felt an exultant animal energy as he galloped through the brush and down the hillside, yelling "Come on!" at the top of his lungs to Walker and Brownlee and anyone else who might still be back there. At the base of the hill he lost his balance and went sprawling, but he was up and running again with the wind singing in his helmet and the rifle-grenade bag pounding his sore chest, convinced that this was the bravest thing he had ever done in his life.

Shells were still coming in but they were falling behind him now, back on the ridge where Walker and Brownlee and God only knew how many others were still huddled; only Bernstein and he himself, it seemed, were crossing the field.

He ran so fast that he'd almost caught up with Bernstein in time to climb the hill with him; Bernstein had just reached the crest and fallen into a crouch, turning around, when Prentice came panting up behind him.

"Where's *my* squad?" Bernstein demanded.

"I don't know – they must be back there. You know where Finn is?"

"No. Well, you'd better stay with me. Come on."

And still crouching, they ran up over the crest into a small, shabby back yard full of rusting automobile parts and piled-up boxes that proved to be rabbit warrens. The gunfire could have been coming from across the street or even from this house itself, but Bernstein seemed to know what he was doing. He ran straight for the back door of the house, and without breaking his stride he raised his rifle butt and brought it down on the knob and lock of the door, shouldering all his weight against it in the same motion, whipping the rifle back up to the ready as he lunged inside. Prentice loped after him, into a prim kitchen that smelled of recent cooking; Bernstein was already disappearing down a dark hall calling, "You take the upstairs!"

Prentice found the stairway and took it two steps at a time with his heart in his mouth, half expecting to find a German machine gunner poised at the top landing or waiting in one of the rooms. He smashed open the first of the bedroom doors and went charging in, badly off balance but with his rifle ready at the hip. There was a neatly made double bed, a flounced dressing table scented with perfume, and a closet that swung open to reveal a mass of men's and women's clothing. Some of the clothes were the uniforms of a German officer, and an officer's high-crowned garrison cap sat on the hat shelf beside several civilian fedoras.

There were two other bedrooms, both empty, and he had just finished with the last of them when Bernstein's voice called, "Okay up there?"

"Okay!"

And they were out in the back yard again, vaulting over a low latticework fence to approach the next house. Where the hell was the fire coming from? This house was bigger, and they took the ground floor together; then they ran upstairs, with Bernstein in the lead. He slammed into the first bedroom while Prentice took the second, and they attacked the third and largest room together. There was a bed in the room with a crude canopy of blankets hanging over it from a length of clothesline strung high on the walls. Prentice wondered what to do about it – tear the canopy down? – and he was still wondering when Bernstein raised his rifle and fired three times into it with an ear-splitting noise, making three little black holes in the quivering cloth. And it wasn't until they were halfway downstairs again that Prentice began to worry about what might have lain under that canopy: what if it was an old man or woman, too sick to be evacuated with the rest of the family? Or a couple of children playing Indian inside their homemade tent?

But they were approaching their third house now, crouching low as they ran across an alley. The kitchen door was standing open, and inside they found three huddled men: Loomis, Coverly, and Klein.

"Donkey Dog," Klein was saying into his radio, plugging one ear with his free hand to block out the noise of gunfire. "Donkey Dog, this is Donkey Nan, Donkey Nan. Do you read me?"

"Bernstein, where the hell are your men?" Loomis said.

"I thought they were *following* me. I guess they're all back on the—"

Klein had gotten through to Company headquarters now and Coverly had grabbed the radio, talking in a high quavering voice that sounded almost on the verge of tears: "I've lost contact with the element on the right," he was saying, "and I've lost contact with the element on the left. I don't know *what* the hell we're doing here, and I don't even know how many men I've got. Most of my men are still pinned down on the ridge."

"Pinned down my ass," Loomis said. "They're scared shitless, that's what they are."

And then Sergeant Finn appeared from the hallway, followed by Mueller and Gardinella and Sam Rand. They were all out of breath; apparently they'd just finished clearing the house.

"Finn," Loomis said. "How many men did you bring over? Just these three?"

"That's right."

"I'm here, Finn," Prentice said.

'Well, where the hell you been?"

"I came over with Bernstein — hell, we've already cleared two—"

"How come you didn't follow me?"

"I didn't see you go. Bernstein was the only one I—"

"All right, shut *up*, everybody," Loomis said.

The lieutenant was still on the radio, wiping his wet face with his free hand. "No, sir, I don't," he was saying. "No, sir, I don't . . ."

The sounds of fire were still close in the street outside. What were they supposed to do now? Just wait here until the rest of the men came across? Bernstein showed no sign of eagerness to move out again, nor did Finn. Edging away from them and trying to make himself inconspicuous, Prentice saw that the oven door of the kitchen stove was open, and now he saw what made the sweet vanilla smell he'd been aware of ever since coming into the room: it was an angelfood cake, set out to cool, apparently abandoned just before the woman of the house had fled. He touched it with his forefinger, making a little dirty dimple in its top. It was still warm.

"Yes," Lieutenant Coverly was saying. "All right. All right, sir . . ."

Ted the medic came blundering in from outside, winded and very red in the face.

"How's Paul, Ted?" someone asked him.

"He's gone," Ted said. "Concussion. There wasn't a mark on him."

"Jesus," said Bernstein, and Loomis said, "Oh, shit." Prentice was dumbfounded. Did they mean Paul Underwood? Did they mean he was dead?

"There wasn't a mark *on* him," Ted said again. Then he came over and sat in a chair beside the angelfood cake and started to cry. It was a terrible thing to watch: he was sitting there with tears dribbling down his dirty face and his hands trying to wipe them away, his lips curling and bloating like a baby's. "There wasn't a mark *on* him. There wasn't anything I could *do* for him . . ."

Then Bernstein was leading Prentice out of the house again, following Finn and Rand and Gardinella and Mueller: they were to clear other houses and set up defensive positions until the rest of the platoon came over. Other doors were smashed open, other empty rooms were disclosed. Was Prentice supposed to go on working with Bernstein now, or should he follow Finn? There was no chance to ask. He was following Bernstein out of another house when Bernstein turned and held him back. "No, wait, Prentice," he said, his scholarly face screwed up in concentration. He was evidently working out primitive tactics in his mind. "You stay here and keep that lot covered. See there?" And he pointed to a window that faced a gray vacant lot, irregularly bordered by other houses. "You stay here. You see anybody run across that lot, use your rifle. Got that?"

He nodded yes and hurried over to kneel by the window.

"Okay," Bernstein said. "Stay on the ball now, whatever happens." And he went jogging out of the house, calling something to someone else.

Prentice did as he was told, pointing his rifle out the window. After a second or two he thrust the muzzle forward and broke out the pane of glass, less because he knew it would make for better aim than because it was what gunmen always did behind windows in the movies. He felt eager and competent as he knelt there: at least he had a specific job to do. The complexity of action outside might be wholly beyond his understanding, but nobody could say he wasn't doing his part; nor could anyone say he hadn't done better than Walker and the others, whether he'd fallen asleep on the ridge or not. They were still back there, "scared shitless" – he thought of Walker's terrified face in the yellow dust – and he had made it across the field. He was here.

The sounds of gunfire were still all around him, interspersed with spells of alarming silence, but nothing happened in the vacant lot. After a while his pride gave way to an almost petulant feeling that he was missing out on everything: he wished Bernstein would come back and relieve him of this apparently useless assignment.

"What the hell are *you* doing, Prentice?" said Loomis's voice, and Prentice turned to find him standing there in the room with Coverly and Klein.

"*Bern*stein told me to stay here. He said to keep—"

"Well, you better get back to your squad."

And by the time he found his own squad again, huddled against a brick wall three houses away, the other missing men were in the process of finding it too. Krupka came trotting up first, then Drake and Brownlee, and finally Walker, whose glance at Prentice was more than a little shamefaced. If Walker *had* caught him in his melodramatic posture that day of their meeting on the Rhine, it seemed to Prentice now that the score was settled.

Gardinella wasn't there, though Prentice didn't give much thought to wondering why, and there was something decidedly strange about Mueller's face – flaming red, with a stunned look about the eyes – but Prentice assumed this only meant that Mueller was scared; he wondered if he looked that way himself.

"Is everybody here now, for a change?" Finn asked. "All right, let's quit goofing off now and stay together."

Prentice wanted to say: "Look, Finn, I haven't been goofing off; Bernstein posted me at a window and I *had* to stay there . . ." but there wasn't time. Motioning for the squad to follow him, Finn ran to the end of the brick wall and out across an open space toward the shelter of another house.

It soon became clear that most of the enemy had either surrendered or withdrawn. Once Finn's squad saw a German soldier running away at the far end of a street and they knelt to fire at him, but he turned a corner and vanished even before Prentice had squeezed off his single, wasted round of ammunition – the first shot he'd fired in the war. For the rest of the afternoon, working in twos, they cleared houses.

Prentice enjoyed it: he liked to smash open doors and lunge

inside in a marauder's stance, ready for anything. In one house he surprised two very clean, frightened young civilians of about his own age. One was wearing earphones and they'd both been seated at a table over a small, complicated-looking radio set. Prentice couldn't tell whether it was a sending set as well as a receiver, but the barest chance of their being artillery spotters seemed to justify what he did next: he tore the earphones from the boy's head, kicked over the table, and brought his butt plate down hard on the fallen radio, smashing it into fragments that skated across the floor while the two boys winced as if in pain. And what if they *were* only amateur radio hobbyists who'd spent months or years building their equipment? The hell with them.

In another house he went charging into a roomful of old men and women – a dozen or more, all stock-still in fear as he whipped his rifle down from high port to his hip. One stout woman in the foreground had screamed and cowered away from him, covering her face with her hands; now she peeped out from between her fingers, let her hands fall, and looked at him with a tearful, motherly smile, saying something that plainly meant she had never expected the invading enemy to be a thin, beardless, exhausted-looking boy. Then she came forward and put both soft arms around him, pressing her head into his shoulder, while with his free hand he reached around and patted her back.

It was in another house that he broke into a shadowy bedroom and found himself confronted by another rifleman, and it took him a moment to realize he was seeing his own reflection in a dark full-length mirror. There was no time to spare – Brownlee was yelling "Come on!" from downstairs – but he moved up close to the mirror and looked himself over, pleased with the picture he made. Maybe it *was* a boy's face, a face to make a mother weep, but the rest of him was every inch a soldier. "Coming!" he called to Brownlee, and he took a last, proud glimpse of himself before he ran from the room.

It wasn't until late that night, as he fought off sleep while standing guard against a counterattack that never came, that he learned what had happened during the five or ten minutes of his kneeling at Bernstein's window that afternoon. In that time, on a street that couldn't have been more than two houses away from where he knelt, Gardinella had been killed and Mueller had become a hero. It was from Sam Rand's droning voice that he heard it, while Sam was relating the story to Loomis. Four of them – Finn, Rand, Mueller, and Gardinella – had been moving down the street when a German rifleman stepped out of hiding less than five feet from Gardinella and killed him with a single shot in the back. Mueller had spun around to face the German, given out a yell, and fallen over backwards, bringing his B.A.R. up and firing steadily: he had stitched a row of bullets up the belly, chest, and face of the German before Rand and Finn were able to see what was happening.

"And then when I turned around," Sam said, "there's old Mueller on his back yellin' his head off and still firin', and there's this big-assed Kraut foldin' up like a God damn paper doll. I don't think old Mueller knew what he'd done till after he done it. Finn says, 'Mueller, you're gonna *keep* that B.A.R.; you've earned it.'"

Prentice didn't know what to feel about Gardinella, that sad, hopefully friendly little man he'd scarcely known, and whose death seemed so much less important to everyone than Underwood's; but what he felt about Mueller was a childish kind of envy, or jealousy: I could have done that; that's the kind of thing *I* could have done, if only I'd had the chance.

And it wasn't until the next morning, on the march again, that he learned what had happened to Bernstein's hastily re-formed squad during that same brief time. They had run into a machine gun that killed two of the new replacements and wounded a third. Bernstein himself had knocked out the gun with a beautifully aimed hand grenade, and his B.A.R. man had dropped another German who was trying to make a getaway.

Both actions already had the unlikely, made-up sound of all second-hand war stories; yet both had taken place right there, within a few yards of him. And it seemed to him now, as he walked and tried to adjust the rifle-grenade bag to ease the ache in his chest, that his own performance yesterday had been ludicrous. What had he done, after all, except to fall asleep on the ridge, to miss out on all the combat, to break a radio, to please an old woman – and even (Jesus!) to admire himself in a mirror?

There was no coherence to the days and nights that followed. There was never a whole night's sleep, and there was never enough to eat. Mile after mile of what was said to be the Ruhr was slowly consumed in the changeless rhythm of walking on heavy, swollen feet; through a haze of exhaustion the broken towns rose up and divided into broken streets and houses, and the houses divided into rooms; then rooms, houses, streets, and towns closed up and fell behind, and there were more roads, more fields and woods and railroad tracks and factories, with other towns waiting.

And there was something called the Dortmund-Ems Canal, which they had to cross at night. One of the other companies was to make the assault, but Finn's squad was detailed to work for Battalion headquarters: their job was to follow directly behind the assault company carrying reels of communications wire. The reels each weighed forty or fifty pounds, and the one Prentice drew was missing its handle: it had to be carried by a looped and knotted strand of wire that bit into the flesh of his hand. Carrying his rifle at the balance in his other hand, he allowed himself to think about nothing but Walker's helmet, which moved ahead of him on the road as they approached the canal in almost total darkness. He wanted to turn around and whisper "Sam?" to make sure that Rand was following him, but he was afraid to turn around even for a second. It was like that other march into Horbourg, last winter, except that then at least there had been snow to silhouette the figures around him.

The first high, fluttering rush of an eighty-eight sent him sprawling into the roadside ditch with the heavy reel falling against his kidneys – *Slam!* Walker was lying ahead of him, and by reaching out his left hand, with the strand of wire hiked up over his wrist, he could touch the sole of Walker's boot.

"Keep moving, men," somebody was calling.

Then came another fluttering rush and another explosion, but Walker's boot stayed where it was and so did Prentice.

"Keep moving, men . . ."

– *Slam!* And this time Prentice felt something clink on his helmet and spatter across his back. From the other side of the road there was a tremulous, almost apologetic voice: "Medic? Medic?"

"Where? Where are ya?"

"Over here – here he is . . ."

"Keep moving, men . . ."

Walker's boot moved and Prentice followed it, scrambling up to the road and running, rifle in one hand and reel in the other. At the next fluttering rush Walker and Prentice hit the ditch in time – *Slam!* – and then they got up quickly and ran again. Everyone was running now.

Across the road a new voice had broken into a scream: "Oh! Oh! Oh! The blood's coming out, it's coming out, it's coming *out!*"

"Quiet!"

"Shut that bastard up!"

"S'coming out! S'coming *out*!"

"Where? Where *are* ya?"

"Keep moving, men . . ."

Walker's back slipped away in the darkness, seeming to turn right. Then it seemed to turn right again, heading for the rear, but Prentice couldn't be sure. He stood hesitating in the middle of the road, turning around, until he saw it moving again straight ahead. But was this the same back? Wasn't it too narrow and too short? There was another fluttering rush and the back fell and Prentice fell beside it, grabbing it by the shoulder. "Walker?" he asked after the explosion.

"Wrong man, Mac."

He was up and running again. "Walker? . . . Walker? . . ." The carrying wire of the reel was a burning crease of pain in his hand. He slowed down to keep in step with a short figure who looked like Sam Rand but who, to judge from the authoritative way he was saying "Keep moving, men," was some kind of an officer. With absurd politeness Prentice said, "Pardon me, sir, can you tell me where the wire detail is?"

And at least the officer, too, was rattled enough to be absurdly polite: "I'm afraid not, soldier; sorry. Keep moving, men . . ."

Prentice pulled ahead of him and ran out across the road. At the top of the road's crown he heard another fluttering rush, and he dove for the other side like a ballplayer sliding home, just in time – *Slam*! A man was lying face down in the ditch beside him. "Hey, Mac – you seen the wire detail?"

There was no answer.

"Hey, Mac—"

Still no answer: maybe the man was dead, or maybe just scared half to death. Prentice got up and ran again, and it wasn't until

270

much later that he thought: Or maybe wounded. Jesus, was I supposed to stop and feel his heart? Or call a medic?

All he did was run, heading back across the road again, only ducking for the shells now and sometimes not even ducking, feeling brave because he was on his feet and everybody else was falling down.

The road ended and he ran with the crowd down a wide slope of muddy earth. The eighty-eights were falling mostly behind him now, or seemed to be; and now he was running on some kind of wooden ramp – it seemed to be nothing more than a plank flung part of the way across the water, sloping sharply downward and shuddering with the weight of many jostling runners. "Take it easy, you guys," somebody was saying. "Take it *easy*!" Then there was an ice-cold shock of water up his legs as the plank ended: he was wading thigh deep. Just ahead of him a man fell forward with a heavy splash, and two others stopped to help him up.

Then abruptly the mud of the opposite shore was rising under his feet; he was on land again, but something high and straight was looming ahead, darker than the sky. It was a retaining wall, stone or concrete, ten or fifteen feet tall. Somebody was saying "Ladders . . . ladders . . ." and he groped ahead to find slick wooden rungs against the wall. He slung his rifle and thrust his other arm through the carrying wire of the reel, to free both hands, and he began to climb, dimly aware of other ladders and other men climbing on either side of him. The rungs ended short of the top and there was an instant of frantic teetering without a handhold until a pair of arms reached down to help him up. "Thanks," he said, getting one knee up over the edge, and the man ran off. He turned back to reach down and take hold of the next man's arms, and the next man said, "Thanks."

All along the top of the embankment there was a babble of

voices, excited and out of breath: "This way . . ." "Which way? . . ." "Where the hell do we go now? . . ."

They were in a plowed field: the ridged, uneven earth gave like sponge beneath their feet. Prentice followed the sounds of voices into the darkness, running again, while the shells rushed overhead to explode well behind him, back on the other side of the canal. And it was there in the field, slightly behind him and to the right, that he heard Sam Rand's voice:

"Prentice? That you?"

"Sam! Jesus, where've you—"

"Where the hell you been?"

"Where've *I* been! My God, I've been looking all over hell for *you*. Where's Walker?"

"Keep your voice down. They're all on up ahead; I hung back to look for you. Got your wire?"

"Of course I've got it. What the hell do you think I'd—"

"Hang onto it, then. And try to keep up this time. Come on."

Jogging along in Rand's wake he felt a bitter sense of injustice; he was angrily determined not to accept whatever reprimand Finn might have for him. God damn it, I *didn't* fall behind, he silently rehearsed in his mind. For all I know I got across the damn canal before *you* guys did . . .

The reprimand came half an hour later, just before daybreak, when the wire detail was over and they were crouched, along a wall of the village that lay beyond the plowed field, waiting to be dismissed and rejoin their platoon.

"Finn wants to see you, Prentice," said Walker in a righteous voice, and Prentice went up to the place where Finn sat against the wall. There was just enough light to see the jaunty angle of his helmet and the thin shape of his angry face.

"Prentice," he said. "What happened back there?"

"I lost sight of Walker during the shelling, that's all."

"Well, why the fuck can't you keep up?"

"Keep *up*?" He knew that a mumbled apology now might save him from worse trouble, but he couldn't stop his voice. "It wasn't a *question* of keeping up, Finn. My God, I crossed the canal when you did – I may even have crossed it before you did. I mean look, Finn, if you want to pick on somebody that's one thing, but don't be telling me I—"

"I ain't pickin' on nobody, soldier."

"All *right*. Don't be telling me I can't keep up, that's all. I got separated, that's all."

"Yeah, and you got a big fuckin' mouth, too, don'tcha? Now you shut up and listen to me."

Shamefaced and dry in the mouth, there was nothing for Prentice to do but listen. All the other members of the squad were listening too.

"I got no use for fuckups, Prentice. And you done a pretty good job of fuckin' up right along, ain'tcha? *Ain'tcha*? Well, as long as you're in this squad you're gonna soldier with the rest of us, and I don't wanna hear any more snotty-assed remarks. Got that straight?"

"Finn, I—"

"Got that straight?"

"Yes."

"All right. Get on back, now."

It could have been two days or three days or five days after that – everyone had lost track of time – when they marched all day in the rain. Their objective for the day was to take the high ground beyond still another town; and to get there, after they'd cleared the town, was to walk across acres of bombed-out factories and warehouses, a flatland of industrial ruin.

"Keep it spread out, now," Finn kept calling as the squad

picked its way over the loose bricks, the snaking wires, and the tilting, seesawing slabs of concrete. They were once again in the point of the platoon and company formation.

Far ahead rose a big undamaged brick structure surmounted by a derrick, and beside it, extending for what seemed half a mile across the horizon, was a mountainous heap of coal, as black and shining as licorice in the rain. Coming closer, they could see that a railroad yard lay along the foot of the coal heap – many parallel tracks and switches and sidings, on one of which stood a train of gondola cars. The big building was evidently a loading station: it straddled the tracks on a forest of brick pillars. Almost any point in this intricate scene – the coal heap or the loading station or any of several smaller buildings around it – would make a good enemy gun emplacement or artillery observation post; and so they moved stealthily, carrying their rifles like hunters.

The first eighty-eights came in just as the squad was approaching one of the smaller buildings beside the loading station; all they had to do was run the last few yards and scurry inside and they were safe. But looking back, they saw the panicky disorder of the rest of the company as the shells burst among them: men were running and falling, getting up and running again; some were trying to take cover in the rubble and others were trying to run it out.

Bernstein's squad made it into the building; so did Loomis and Coverly and Klein, and so did Captain Agate and part of his headquarters group. Much of the rest of the company was safe in the building next door now; others had fallen behind a broken wall a hundred feet back, and only a few could be seen lying in the open: it was impossible to tell if they'd been hit or not.

"Well, shit," Captain Agate said. "We sure as hell can't stay here. Let's get on out across the tracks."

Finn's squad crept around the side of the building to the open place where the brick pillars supported the loading station, and started out across the wide bed of rails. And they were out in the middle of the tracks, halfway across, when a machine gun – no, it was fifty times louder than a machine gun – sent each man leaping for cover behind one of the pillars. In the huge noise of the automatic fire a river of yellow tracers came whipping through, and the bullets – Christ, they weren't bullets at all, but shells – the shells were exploding against the pillars and the sides of the buildings with sharp detonations – *Pok! Pok!* – almost like flak. It *was* flak: it was an anti-aircraft gun firing in flat trajectory.

Prentice's pillar was an inch or two wider than his shoulders: if he stood very straight with his back pressed to the bricks, keeping his elbows in and his rifle butt-down beside his right foot in a rigid order-arms position, he was safe from the shells that streaked past him on either side; but there was no way of hiding from the whining, invisible fragments of flak, some of which flew with a *Whunk!* into the pillar above his head or into the cinders at his feet. From the corner of his eye he could see Sam Rand, equally rigid behind the next pillar, and on the other side was Drake.

Captain Agate was standing some twenty feet away, close to a wall whose angle protected him from the line of fire. His eyes were fixed on Prentice as the firing continued, and suddenly his grave, heavy face broke into a delighted smile. "Hey Prentice!" he called into the noise, and Prentice could understand more by reading his lips than hearing him. "Hey Prentice! Par-rade – *rest!*" And he bent over to slap his thigh at the hilarity of the joke.

It probably wasn't more than half a minute before the gun stopped, but it seemed much longer; and it seemed too that it had stopped only to tease the men away from the pillars. Prentice didn't know what to do until he saw Sam Rand run for the protection of the building where Agate and the others were. He ran after him, with the rest of the squad, and the gun didn't open up again. Drake came last, stumbling and trying to hop on one foot, and Ted the medic went out to help him, half-carrying him back. He had caught a piece of flak in his leg.

"Son of a bitch probably ran out of ammunition," Captain Agate was saying. "Now he'll disable his gun and take off like a big-assed bird. Either that or he'll come out with his fucking hands in the air."

But Finn's squad couldn't linger there to find out what Agate planned to do about the gun: they were sent running off to the left, shielded by the train of gondola cars. They were to go as far as the train would allow and try to cross the tracks from there.

They made it, and then with a good deal of struggling and sliding they climbed the coal heap. There was nothing to see on the other side but an empty wet plain stretching away to a horizon of black trees, and the view to the right was blocked by another coal heap built at right angles to this one: there was no way of looking down to where the anti-aircraft fire had come from. When they slid down the far side of the heap in an avalanche of falling coal, Finn waved them off to the left. At the end of the coal heap they met Bernstein's squad coming around the other side, followed by two machine-gun teams from Weapons Platoon, and Bernstein had a message from Sergeant Loomis. Both squads, with machine-gun support, were now to take up a defensive position at this end of the coal heap. Half the group would dig in on top of the heap, at points that would command the whole stretch of land before them: the other half would rest in a small brick building to the rear. Halfway through the night, the men in the building would relieve the men on the coal.

"Only look, Finn," Bernstein said. "I've only got five men. Can I borrow one of yours? Can I have Prentice here?"

"*Sure* you can have him," Finn said, and Prentice didn't know whether to feel pride or shame. It was pleasing that Bernstein wanted him – maybe it meant he remembered the day they had crossed that field together – but it was galling that Finn was so eager to let him go.

It was decided that Finn's squad would take the first shift on the coal heap. Prentice managed to walk beside Bernstein on the trip back to the building, and to engage him in a pleasant, monosyllabic conversation about what a bitch of a day it had been. He was fearful of talking too much, of seeming to court favor, but Bernstein's kindliness was encouraging. If he did everything right tonight, it was just possible that he might be allowed to transfer to Bernstein's squad.

The little brick building evidently had something to do with the railroad, though its cold and rubble-cluttered interior was too dark for them to see much of it in detail as they felt around the floor for places to sleep. Someone woke Prentice once to stand guard outside the door, and after that his sleep was so deep and peaceful that it seemed to last for many hours. Then Bernstein's voice said, "Prentice? Are you awake?"

"Yes." He got to his feet.

"Okay; come on over here." And Bernstein led him to an old rolltop desk that was illuminated by two candles stuck onto its writing surface. "You got a watch? Okay, here's the deal. You're going to be in charge for a while so I can get some sleep. It's now twelve-thirty. At one-thirty you wake up Kornish to relieve the guard outside. Got that?"

"Right."

"And then at two o'clock you wake us all up; that's when we're supposed to go out to the coalpile. Okay?"

"Okay." Prentice sat down in the swivel chair that faced the desk.

277

"And if anybody comes in bitching from the coalpile," Bernstein said, "tell 'em you've got orders to stick to that schedule. We're not relieving anybody till two o'clock."

"Right."

When he was alone, the quiet and the comfort and the candlelight made him drowsy. He considered resting his head on the desk but decided not to: it was too risky. Instead he took off his wristwatch and laid it on the desk and studied the second hand as it crept around the dial.

In a little while Bernstein came back through the shadows. "Everything all right, Prentice?" he asked.

"Everything's fine."

Bernstein sat down in another chair near the desk. "Can't seem to get to sleep," he said. "Might as well sit up. You can go on back and sack out again, if you want to."

"No, I'll stay awake too." And soon they were conversing as comfortably as old friends.

"You're not getting along very well in Finn's squad, are you?" Bernstein said.

"No; I guess not."

"I'm not surprised; Finn's not too bright. I can see how he wouldn't know what to make of someone like you."

"How do you mean?"

"Well, you *are* a little out of the ordinary, don't you think? Why do you think I picked you out?"

"I thought it was by chance."

"Well, it wasn't. I think you and I are essentially two of a kind, Prentice. We're intelligent, but it's not the kind of intelligence the Army knows how to appreciate. If there were any justice in the Army, people with minds like yours and mine would be officers. I've often thought that. For example, take—"

Suddenly there was a violent gripping and pulling on his arm, which spun him around in the swivel chair – and there was Krupka, soaking wet and black with coal dust, shouting at him.

"What the fuck's goin' *on,* Prentice? Where the fuck's our *relief?*"

Then Prentice was on his feet too, shouting back, feeling immensely powerful. "Now, you just hold your water, Krupka. You'll get your God damn relief when I say so. I'm under specific orders to—"

Only then, with sickening slowness, did he begin to to separate reality from the dream. Krupka was real; the candles and the desk were real, too; so was the fact that his watch read 2:35, and so was the undeniable appearance of Bernstein hurrying forward from the shadows, heavy with sleep, saying: "What the hell's the trouble?"

And the whole conversation had been false. It had taken place only in Prentice's head, and he knew now that his head, until the very moment of Krupka's grabbing him, had been lying on the desk.

For the rest of that night, soaked and freezing on the coal heap, he suffered little spasms of self-loathing that made lumps of coal rattle under his weight.

But that was the last and worst of his humiliations. Whatever mistakes he made after that were mercifully hidden from public exposure; if he remained the worst man in the squad, at least he managed to keep from calling attention to himself. And then one memorable morning, not long after the coal heap, the onus passed from him to Walker.

They had marched all night again. They had followed no road but gone over rough country in the dark, through what Captain Agate grimly told them was enemy territory ("I see one man strike a match, that man's dead"). And they had done it in absolute silence, each of them wearing a strip of white bandage tied to his right shoulder tab, so that the man behind him could stay in line without calling out. By dawn they had reached the place on Agate's map that was supposed to be their destination, and most of the Second Platoon found itself in a warm, clean farmhouse where a woman agreed to heat water for their coffee and more water to wash and shave in. But soon they were out in the fields again, with a bright misty morning as sharp as winter on their scrubbed skin. They were on the outskirts of another town, and they had to approach it across a swamp that led into a number of little hummocks so dense with shrubbery that they couldn't spread out: the squads had to proceed in single file, making crude wet footpaths between the hills. The bright, dripping fog was so heavy that nobody could see more than a few yards, and any object emerging into view as they walked – a tree, a bush, a shed – had a look of ghostly danger. They were on rising ground when a great rectangular shape appeared on their right, and it was just then, when the shape had established itself as a barn, that the silence was shattered by a burst of machine-gun fire on their left.

Everyone hit the ground and wriggled for cover, and there were isolated rifle shots from somewhere ahead. Somebody on the left was shouting, "Fire! Fire!" and Prentice guessed he ought to bring his rifle up and use it; but how could he tell where he was shooting? Bernstein's squad was hidden in the fog to the left, and so was the third squad. Was he supposed to fire anyway, at the risk of hitting his own men?

"Don't shoot, you men – hold your fire," Sam Rand called from close behind him, and that made it all right just to lie there. He looked ahead, where the foreshortened shape of Walker's boots and buttocks lay just beyond his face.

Then Finn's voice came back: "Let's go, my squad – follow me!" And Walker's boots sprang into action. He was up in a crouching run, heading in a wide circle to the right, past a thick hedge and around to the shelter of the barn. Prentice followed him, with Sam Rand close behind, and they got all the way around the corner of the barn before discovering that there were only the three of them: the rest of the squad had disappeared.

"What the hell?" Rand demanded. "Where's Finn? Who was you *followin'*, Walker?"

And Walker's big, breathless face betrayed his guilt. "I thought that's what he *meant*, Sam. I thought he *meant* get behind the barn."

"How come?"

"Well, I mean – Jesus, Sam; I don't know."

"Shit. Now how the hell we gonna find 'em? They go straight on ahead, or to the left, or what?"

They were safe as long as they huddled here behind the barn, but Sam Rand didn't let them huddle for long. First he sent Prentice through the hedge to go back the way they'd come, but the machine gun opened up again and a quick splatter of broken plaster a foot over Prentice's head made it clear that he was the target. He dropped flat and scrambled back through the hedge in what seemed a single frantic motion, and Rand said, "All right. We'll try another way, is all."

He led them around the other corner of the barn, and they were crouched there, wondering whether to risk it into the open, when the noise of fire broke out again: intermittent bursts from the machine gun answered by rifle and B.A.R. fire that seemed to be coming from several directions; and suddenly all the firing stopped after the shock of a single explosion – a hand grenade. Then there was shouting:

"*Get* the bastard!"

"There he is!"

"*Kamarade . . .*"

"Comrade my ass! *Get* the bastard . . ."

Sam Rand was pointing the way into the open now, not toward where the shouting was but to a farmhouse that was now plainly in sight and near which they could see the rising, standing figures of Finn and the rest of the squad.

"God damn it," Finn said, "where you been, Prentice?"

"I – look, Finn, it wasn't my – we were over behind the—"

But Sam Rand came quickly to his rescue. "It wasn't his fault, Finn. Walker led us around behind the barn."

And Finn switched his narrow gaze to Walker. "What the hell d'ja do that for?"

"I – Finn, I *thought* I saw you going—"

It was a great pleasure for Prentice to watch Walker's abasement, and the pleasure increased during the rest of the day, and the next day, and the next, as Walker seemed to go from bad to worse.

Then a few days later there occurred what seemed to be a chance for both Walker and Prentice to redeem themselves: Captain Agate wanted volunteers for a special patrol. "I'm going," Finn announced to his squad. "Anybody else?"

"Shit no," said Krupka. "Volunteer? When the whole fuckin' war's practically over? You oughta get your head examined, Finn, no shit."

Walker and Prentice were the only two other volunteers; with Finn they joined eight or ten other men at the Company command post, and they solemnly listened to their briefing by the captain.

"All right," he said, squinting around the group, and there were uneasy glances among the men as they began to realize he was drunk. "Here's what I want you men to do. I want you to go out through that underpass, turn left, and keep going till you meet the Krauts. We know there's Krauts out there but we don't know how many and we don't know how far. You men are gonna find out. Who's the ranking non-com?"

"I guess I am, sir," said a huge, bearded staff sergeant from the First Platoon named Kovarsky.

"All right. Sergeant Kovarsky'll be in command. Any questions, Kovarsky?"

"Sir, is this a reconnaisance patrol?"

"Hell no, it's no reconnaisance patrol. Whaddya think we're on, maneuvers? This is a *combat* patrol. When you meet those Krauts they're gonna be shootin' at you, and you better gonna be damn sure shootin' back. How the hell else you gonna find out how many they are?"

"Son of a bitch," somebody muttered, "is this ever gonna be a ball-buster."

But instead it was an abortion. They had gone scarcely a hundred yards beyond the underpass when Kovarsky halted them and called them together for a briefing of his own.

"I don't know about you guys," he said, "but personally I never would of volunteered for this deal if I'd known Agate was drunk. I think this here is one patrol we can damn well afford to goof off on. Anybody want to argue with that?"

Nobody did.

"Okay, then. What we're gonna do is, we're gonna go on up as far as those trees. We'll lay down some fire into the woods, and that's it. Then we take off, whether we get any answering fire or not. I'll make the report, and everybody else keep their mouth shut. Okay?"

They did exactly that, robbing Prentice and Walker of any chance for heroism; and Captain Agate accepted Kovarsky's fraudulent report, looking, throughout the brief interview, as though what he really needed now was an hour or two to sleep it off.

★

By now the days and nights were so full of rumors that one story had as much chance of truth as the next. Almost anything could be believed: nothing in the blur and drift of daily events had the power of surprise. One rumor had the northern salient of the Ninth Army on the outskirts of Berlin; others placed it hundreds of miles further west. And there was still neither corroboration nor denial of a story that had been circulating for days: that President Roosevelt was dead. "All right, hold it up here," Sergeant Loomis called one warm afternoon, turning against a shrapnel-pocked wall to address the platoon. They had come through a village that day and across a great expanse of open country without any sign of enemy troops, but it had now become clear that there were a good many of them dug into the side of a high, steep hill that rose beyond this larger town. It had begun to seem, in fact, that this afternoon might bring about the first hand-to-hand fighting of the campaign. But Prentice was too tired to feel either excitement or fear, and as he looked around at the other dusty, sweat-streaked, black-lipped faces it appeared that everyone was in the same listless mood.

"This is going to be the real thing, for a change," Loomis said. "We'll be making contact with the enemy in force this time." He was doing his best to instill a sense of emergency, but his own red-rimmed eyes and dust-caked lips showed that he was as tired as anyone else. For once it must have seemed to him, as it did to others, that his words were something out of a movie.

"Now, we're going to get plenty of artillery support before we go up there, but they're dug in good and solid and you can be damn sure the worst part of the job'll be up to us. When we hit that hill it'll be every man for himself. I don't want to see anybody laying back and chickening out and afraid to use their weapons. All right, that's it. Any questions?"

And they continued to make their laborious way up the steep, white-flag-hung streets of the town, looking ahead to where the hill rose bald and brown in the afternoon sunshine. Nothing seemed real.

At the top of the town they were allowed to rest. The artillery barrage was scheduled to start in thirty minutes, and in the meantime there was nothing to do but wait. Finn's squad sat in a sullen, exhausted row with their backs against a stucco house, looking down over the streets they'd climbed, and there was no talk among them until Sam Rand produced a sleek Luger pistol that he'd taken from the belt of a German prisoner in the previous village.

"Hey-y," said Walker. "Nice, Sam. Mind if I take a look?" And he leaned forward to reach across the laps of Krupka, Brownlee, and Prentice. Sam leaned forward to hand it over, and it was then, at the instant of the pistol's changing hands, that all the world stopped dead.

It was an American artillery shell, half an hour too early and five hundred yards too short, and it plowed into the house six feet above their heads. Later some said it had skip-bombed off the sloping street at their feet before hitting the house; others said it hadn't. At the time all they knew was the overwhelming shock of it, the scorched eyes and stopped eardrums, and the panic that had them instantly up and spinning, colliding with each other, losing their helmets, leaping away in all directions with a blind and breathless urgency.

Prentice ran head on into Walker, caromed away, and made it around the side of the house only to go slamming into a high chicken-wire fence. He spun away from the fence and took off in a sprint down the street after the frantic figure of Krupka, with someone else pounding at his heels. The second shell sent him sprawling on his belly, and he lay wriggling on the pavement as if to burrow down inside it. When he looked up, Krupka was no longer there. Ten yards from where Krupka had been lay a loose heap of green and brown cloth, and only later would he understand that this was all there was left of Krupka. Then the third explosion came, and the fourth. The brief interval of silence that followed was filled with a sobbing falsetto scream that he was now aware of having heard for some seconds, and he raised his head just enough to see who was screaming. It was Lieutenant Coverly, running down the street and waving his arms. Loomis was close behind him, running in a crouch and calling: "Get *down*, Covey, get *down*!" Then there was another explosion, and another, and Prentice hid his face in his arm and embraced the gutter for all he was worth, thinking, At least we won't have to take the hill now; at least we won't have to take the hill. He lay there grinding his teeth and hiding his face in his arm as the earth was rocked again and again.

Chapter Three

For "A" Company, the end of the war came on the last day of April, when they were taken off the line and sent to spend several meaningless days in foxholes in the rain. Then they were taken in trucks to an undamaged town and billeted in dry, windproof, excellent houses; and it was while they were there that the news of the German surrender broke over Europe. There were several nights of drunken celebration and consorting with German girls in open defiance of the regulation against "fraternizing," and then they were removed to an even better place – a small, sunny town called Kierspe-Bahnhof, where all they had to do was stand guard over a thousand newly liberated Russian D.P.'s. The Allied Military Government had moved the Russians into what must have been the best residential section of the town, a colony of neat two-story houses on a hill well away from the partially bombed-out plastics factory that had been the town's only industry. One squad at a time, in shifts around the clock, the men of the Second Platoon would stroll up and down the pleasant streets to be greeted by happy smiles and waves from all the houses, to be surrounded at times by handshaking men and affectionate women, to be pressed into accepting glasses of home-made vodka, and to join in singing Russian songs to the accompaniment of harmonicas. And each night, if they dared to slip away from their rounds and risk being found absent by sergeants in patrolling jeeps, there was every promise of girls to be had for the asking.

Several of the younger divisions in Europe were being processed for shipment halfway around the world to what everyone called the C.B.I., to help finish the war against Japan, but the 57th was not among them: it would remain here. In accordance with the Point System, the older men in the outfit would soon be removed and sent home for discharge; the younger, low-point men could expect to stay in Europe for six months to a year.

In the meantime, everything was nice in Kierspe-Bahnhof. The Company kitchen had been set up in the undamaged part of the plastics factory, and the food became better and more plentiful. Each man received a shot of schnapps before lunch and dinner and a choice of red or white wine with the meal. There were hot showers every day, and to top everything off they were issued fresh uniforms – not new, but clean and sweet-smelling, faded and shrunken from the Quartermaster laundry. Instead of steel helmets they wore only clean helmet-liners now, each emblazoned on one side with the Divisional insignia in enamel paint.

There were irritants in the new life too – "chickenshit" things like Reveille and Retreat formations, like formal inspections and formal five- and ten-mile hikes – but in general the days were slow and rich and lazy.

Everyone seemed happy except Prentice, who felt a nagging sense of unfulfillment. The war had ended too soon. Whatever chance he might have had to atone for Quint's death had been denied him, and there would be no more chances. The purpose had gone out of his life. There was nothing for him to do now but exist from day to day, enjoying the peace and the luxury that he felt he didn't deserve. And he was bored and irritated with the tireless, rambling, gossiping reminiscences that had come to form the Company's major pastime.

". . . 'member the day Underwood and Gardinella got killed? The day we had to cross that field? . . ."

". . . 'member the night we crossed that canal? And the eighty-eights were zeroed right the hell *in* on us? . . ."

The worst time of all, it was generally agreed, was the day their own artillery had fired short rounds – the day Krupka had been killed and Lieutenant Coverly had been evacuated. It was Klein who told, several times, about what had happened to the lieutenant. "He just went to pieces" – a snap of Klein's fingers – "like that. When the first of those shells came in, we all hit the street and kind of got around the side of this house; then the second one comes in, and the third one – only it was a dud. The damnedest thing: we're waiting for this explosion and all we hear is this 'Clunk, a-wunk, wunk, wunk' – like that, and here's this God damn shell bouncing around in the street. It looked so *small*, you know? A one-oh-five's really kind of a small, skinny shell – and it comes rolling down the street to where we're at, and it stops about a foot from Covey. He reaches out and touches it, and he says, 'It's *hot*!' I thought he was laughing. Then he sticks his fingers in his mouth and he says, 'It's *hot*! It's *hot*! It's *hot*!' – and then he went to pieces. Just like that."

Soon a number of Bulge veterans came back to the company, men who'd been hospitalized with wounds or frozen feet. New replacements arrived too – shy boys fresh from the States, or from England – and they made an excellent audience for the reminiscences. But the stories of the Bulge were always so much the best, so much richer and more frightening – " 'member the night the Jerries came at us in *waves*? The night Cap'n Summers was killed?" – that the post-Bulge men found it hard to compete. They tended to fall into the same respectful silence as the new replacements, as if they too had missed the war.

And this seemed to have an especially depressing effect on Walker. He would sit through the discussions with a glum, petulant look, clearly resentful that he hadn't seen enough of the war to talk about and that his performance in it had been inept. That at least was what Prentice saw in his face, and it was so much like the way he felt himself that several times he had to turn away from Walker's eyes in embarrassment.

Then, before the first week in the new town was over, Walker did something that made him a laughing stock. The company clerk broke the news, and within an hour it had become general knowledge, setting off little bursts of incredulous laughter wherever it was told.

"You're kidding!"

"No! I swear to God! That's what he did!"

Walker had gone to Captain Agate and made a formal request that he be allowed to volunteer for service in the C.B.I. The rest of the story was that the captain hadn't taken him seriously – "Old Agate just looks at him, says, 'What's *your* problem, soldier?'" – and that the interview had collapsed in the derisive laughter of everyone in the C.P., from which Walker had stolen away with a crimson face.

Prentice laughed with the others when he heard about it, but he knew he was laughing in relief that it had been Walker, instead of himself, who had made such a foolish mistake.

If he'd taken little part in the storytelling before, Walker stayed away from it altogether in the day or two following his disgrace. And it wasn't more than two days later, just before noon, when the conversation took an unexpected, pleasurable turn for Prentice. The talk, for once, was about the Ruhr:

"'member the day they turned the anti-aircraft gun on us? On the railroad tracks, where old Drake caught it in the leg?"

Finn and Rand and Mueller and Bernstein were all there, and Prentice felt his stomach tighten in fear that the account of that day might soon lead to his own disastrous performance that night – a fear that was intensified when Sam Rand took up the story.

"Jesus, I remember old Prentice that time," he began, already starting to laugh through his words so that the listening faces smiled in readiness. "We was about halfway acrost the tracks when the gun opened up, remember? And we each of us had to get behind one of them brick pillars? Damn things weren't but about an inch wider than your shoulders? I remember old Prentice standin' there like this—" and getting to his feet, Sam stood stiffly at attention, holding an invisible rifle at order arms. "He's standin' there like this with the damn anti-aircraft shells comin' in, and Cap'n Agate yells out, 'Hey *Prentice!* Par-rade – *rest!*'"

A thunderclap of laughter broke around him – even Finn was laughing; even Bernstein – and it seemed to Prentice that never in his life had he heard a sweeter sound. It wasn't much, but it was something, and the pleasure of it carried him out of the house and down to the factory mess hall with a buoyancy he hadn't known in a long time. He lingered over his schnapps, which sent a fine warmth through his veins, and then he moved along into the savory smells of the serving counter. They were having fried chicken, a special meal, and he carried his heaped and steaming mess kit over to a place at one of the tables beside Owens, the little headquarters man he'd known last winter, and with whom he'd been evacuated that day in Horbourg.

"Hi. How you doing, Prentice?"

"Pretty good. This place free?"

"Sure. Sit down."

He'd had only a few very brief talks with Owens since coming back to the company, but now, in the liquor- and wine-flavored leisure of this excellent lunch, they sat chatting as amiably as buddies. They even stayed to talk over coffee and cigarettes, after they'd finished eating, and they took their time about getting up, slinging their rifles, and strolling over to join the line of men waiting to wash their mess kits.

"I'll tell you one thing, though," Owens was saying, "I'm not too happy about all this chickenshit we've been getting lately."

And Prentice agreed. "Matter of fact," he said, "if they keep this up I wouldn't be surprised if there's more than *one* guy volunteering for the C.B.I."

And he would have thought nobody but Owens was listening until, from the corner of his eye, he saw a figure detach itself from the crowd moving past on the right. Even before he could turn and see who it was, the man had taken him roughly by the arm. It was Walker.

"How's that, Prentice?" he said, "What's all this shit about the C.B.I.?"

It was such a surprise that Prentice could only smile like a fool. "Huh?"

"You heard me." Walker was stiff and trembling. "Whadda *you* got to say about the C.B.I.?"

Prentice pulled his arm free, which jogged his mess kit and sent the chicken bones dancing in the greasy pan. He felt a warm flush in his face, and it seemed to his startled ears that all the reverberating noise of the high, wide mess hall had stopped. "Look, Walker. This is none of your business."

The silence around him was no illusion now – everybody *had* stopped talking – and Walker couldn't have asked for a quieter stage on which to enact the passion of his next words: "How come *you* don't volunteer for the C.B.I.? Huh? You know why? Because you're *yella*, that's why!"

"Oh, for Christ's sake, Walk—" But he got no further than that before everything went red and spun around in his vision. Walker had taken his face in one hand and shoved it; with the other hand he had grabbed his arm and swung him around, so that Prentice went reeling across the factory floor and hit the wall in a whirl of flying chicken bones, his rifle flailing at his elbow and his helmet liner bouncing away. It took him only an instant to get free of his rifle sling, to gather himself in a crouch against the wall and spring forward with both fists cocked in what he hoped was an approximation of fighting stance, but before he could take a swing he felt his arms being clamped from behind, and Walker was being pulled back by two other men. Instead of silence now there was pandemonium ringing from the walls:

"Hey!"

"Yeeow!"

"Fight! Fight!"

Owens was holding one of Prentice's arms, saying, "Easy, Prentice, take it *easy*," and Mueller had the other one. For several seconds he and Walker strained at each other, five feet apart, with only their eyes locked in combat. Prentice was greatly relieved to be in bondage but he knew it was important to keep struggling, for the sake of appearances.

"Just what the hell is going *on* here? *Quiet*, everybody." It was Loomis's authoritative voice: he had appeared from nowhere and was looking from Prentice to Walker with righteous eyes. "Where the hell do you kids think you *are*?"

Someone in the crowd said, "Walker started it, Loomis. He just—"

"You're fuckin' A I started it," Walker said, curling back his lips to display his clenched teeth, "and I ain't finished it yet, either."

"All right, *quiet*," Loomis said. "I don't care who started it and I don't care what it's about. You're acting like a couple of babies. Christ's sake, if you want to fight, *fight*, but take it out of the mess hall. Walker, get on outa here and back up to your billet. That's an order. Prentice, you get back in the wash line. Everybody else, as you were."

Somebody handed Prentice his rifle and helmet liner, and somebody else collected his scattered eating utensils. Mueller began to laugh, shaking his head at the absurdity of the whole thing, and others were laughing too. By the time Prentice reached the washing pails the men around him had found other things to talk about. It was as if nothing had happened. But in bending to the ritual of cleaning his mess gear he was tense with fright, and he started to tremble as he walked through the corridor and out into the sunshine of the factory yard. Owens and Mueller were somewhere behind him now, and Loomis was even farther back in the crowd. The view ahead was blocked by the high wall that surrounded the factory. As he approached the gate that opened onto the street he knew Walker would be waiting for him on the other side, so he was able to keep from registering any surprise, let alone any fear, when he passed through the opening and found Walker blocking his path.

Walker had propped his rifle against the wall and laid his mess kit and helmet liner neatly beside it. His feet were set well apart. His thumbs were hooked in his cartridge belt, but he slowly removed them as Prentice came closer. And there was a smiling audience – six or eight men walking backwards up the street, lingering to see what would happen.

Prentice put his own equipment down beside Walker's. Then he squared off and joined Walker in a circling, shuffling, awkward little pugilistic dance. None of the watchers yelled "Fight!" – they didn't want to risk its being broken up again –

so there was silence except for the fighters' breathing and the scuffing of their boots on the street. Walker was upright and bouncing lightly on the balls of his feet, both fists held in close to his neck; Prentice's stance was more classical – crouching, sidling, leading with his left – but that was only because he was so much less confident. He tried what he hoped would be a left jab, but he misjudged the distance and Walker had only to pull in his chin to avoid the weak flick of it; then he stepped in and tried to follow through with a right, but Walker blocked it and caught him with a quick right to the ear that stopped his hearing on that side. He broke away and danced out of range for a second or two, trying to look alert and menacing; then, because he knew the audience would laugh unless he moved in again, he moved in and got clubbed again on the same ear. Where the hell was Loomis? Why didn't somebody break this thing up? He backed clumsily out of range again, and then, in panic, he rushed at Walker with a wild looping right that never had a chance to land because somebody had grabbed his belt from behind and pulled him back – Loomis – and at the same time Walker's arms were caught and held by another man.

"What the hell's the *matter* with you?" Loomis was shouting. "Can't you kids obey orders?"

Prentice was so relieved that he was barely able to listen to Loomis's upbraiding: all he could do was stand there moistening his dry mouth and trying to control his breathing. Loomis's objection this time was that they were fighting in the street. He'd told them to take it out of the mess hall, for Christ's sake, but any idiot ought to know he hadn't meant here, in front of all these German civilians. Only then did Prentice see that there were indeed some civilians watching from across the street: several old men, a young one-legged man on elbow crutches, and a woman who had clutched her apron to her mouth at the spectacle.

"Walker, you go on back to the house, like I told you. Report to my office and wait for me. Prentice, you stay twenty-five yards behind. I want to see you in my office as soon as I'm finished with Walker. All right, get going, Walker."

On the long, slow trip back to the Second Platoon house, keeping his distance of twenty-five yards, Prentice gave all his attention to retaining his dignity. Loomis was walking ahead of him, Owens and Mueller were somewhere behind him, and all the other witnesses of the abortive fight were strung out in twos and threes along the street. He knew his face was red and was afraid it might look, from a distance, as though he were in tears. To dispel that impression he smoked a cigarette.

The sense of being under everyone's amused and curious scrutiny was even worse as he sat in the living room outside Loomis's "office," waiting for the interview with Walker to end. Klein sat nearby, cleaning his fingernails. Mueller was on a sofa across the room, thumbing through a copy of *Yank* magazine that he didn't seem to be reading. In the hallway, just out of sight, were Finn and Sam Rand, who must by now have heard about the fight and were talking quietly together. Once Prentice thought he heard Finn saying "C.B.I."

The office door opened and Walker came out, looking neither to right nor left as he strode past everyone's eyes.

"All right, Prentice," Loomis called.

He was sitting behind the heavy carved table that he had appropriated as his desk, and he looked very solemn and official. "Shut the door," he said. "Now, suppose you tell me your version."

"I was just talking with Owens, and—"

"What? I can't hear you."

"I said I was talking with Owens." His voice sounded high and far away, and this was only partly because of his boxed, ringing ear; it was mostly because of a warm and terrible constriction in his throat. Of all the shameful events of his life so far, surely the worst would be to start crying here, under the stare of Sergeant Loomis. He wanted to say, "And we weren't even *talking* about Walker, that's the ridiculous part. I just happened to say, kind of as a joke—" but he couldn't trust his voice for any lengthy explanation. "And then Walker came over and started fighting," he said. "That's all."

Loomis lowered his eyes. He spread his big hands on the table, palms down, and studied them as if they were the scales of justice. "All right," he said. "Tell me this, Prentice. Don't you think that if a man wants to volunteer for the C.B.I., that's his own business?"

And again the trouble was that Prentice couldn't trust his voice. He took a deep breath and said, "Yes. I do. But when a man calls me yellow, that's my business."

That seemed to please Loomis's theatrical sense. "I see your point," he said, nodding. "I see your point. All right. I'll tell you what I suggested to Walker, and he's agreed to it. If you agree too, that's the end of it."

"The end of it" had a hopeful, peaceful sound – the plan might be to bring Walker back into the office and have them shake hands, man to man; but that wasn't it.

There was, Loomis explained, a small field behind the barn up on the hill, well away from the sight of anyone in town – Americans, Germans, or Russians. Tomorrow morning, before breakfast, Prentice and Walker would proceed to that field – just the two of them – and "have it out." They would be excused from Reveille for the purpose. Would Prentice agree to that?

It wasn't until after he'd said "Yes," left Loomis's gratified eyes, and walked back through the living room, that fear began to crawl in his bowels. From the speculative, quizzical looks he received during the rest of day it was clear that the news of Loomis's arrangement had spread throughout the platoon. But nobody spoke to him about it until late that night, when he was walking his post in the Russian D.P. area with Mueller.

"You really going through with that business in the morning?" Mueller asked him.

"Looks that way."

"How do you feel about it?"

"I don't know."

"You know much about fighting?"

"Not much, no." And that was certainly true. Except for the formless and tearful playground pummelings of childhood he had had only three real fistfights in his life, all of them in his first year of prep school, and he'd lost them all. It troubled him now, looking back, that he hadn't really tried to win them, any more than he had really tried to hurt Walker on the street today while waiting to be rescued. He had gone into each of those fights with the sole purpose of surviving, of proving that he could take it and that he wouldn't quit until some self-appointed referee came in to stop the thing. And tomorrow morning there would be no referee.

"Well," Mueller said, hitching up the sling of his B.A.R. "I know I wouldn't want to be in your shoes. I mean for one thing, he must outweigh you by a good thirty pounds. If I were you I'd be scared shitless."

And if anyone else had said this it might not have mattered much; but this was Mueller, the plump, soft-looking boy who had astonished everyone by riddling an armed German and saving the lives of Finn and Sam Rand, so his words had a considerable effect. For the rest of his rounds that night Prentice walked with a stately tread and bearing. He had resolved now that he would do more than endure the fight: he would do his best to win it.

It seemed very important to be up and ready before Walker in the morning, so he was up and ready before anyone else in the house. He sat alone in the living room, with its stale smell of last night's beer and cigarettes, and to prove that his hands weren't shaking he paged through several of the magazines that lay strewn on the floor.

As one man after another came clumping downstairs for Reveille, he felt he was on display. Whether they looked at him squarely or not he knew he was being examined for signs of panic, and he took pride in making his face wholly expressionless. Then very suddenly he had to go to the bathroom – his bladder seemed about to burst – and when he came back he found Walker waiting for him. Everyone else had gone.

"You ready?" Walker said.

"Any time you are."

The path leading up to the hidden field was steep, and they were both short of breath before they were halfway there. Prentice hoped there would be no talk; he needed silence to maintain his anger and his determination. But, "Tell you what, Prentice," Walker said. "As long as there's just the two of us, we better agree on a couple of rules. Okay?"

"Okay."

"I mean let's keep it fair. If one of us gets knocked down, we break until the man's back on his feet. Right? And then do you want to agree that a certain number of knockdowns wins the fight, or do you want to fight until one of us quits?"

"Fight until one of us quits."

"Okay."

They leaned their rifles against the barn and removed their helmet liners, cartridge belts, and field jackets. They stood facing each other, and at Walker's nod they moved out into the dewy grass in the approximate center of the meadow, where they turned to face each other again.

"Okay, kid," Walker said. "This is it."

And it was the absurdity of that phrase – nobody said "This is it" except in the movies, unless they were phony bastards like Loomis – that roused Prentice to his first real anger of the morning. He wanted to smash and break the head of anyone stupid enough to say a thing like that; he wanted to kill all the posturing fraudulence in the world, and it was all here before him in this big, dumb, bobbing face.

He swung and missed, swung and missed again, and the next thing he knew the sky had spun around and he was lying on the grass. He had been hit on the side of the jaw, but now as he scrambled back upright it was clear that he hadn't really been knocked down: he had simply lost his balance; if he'd been braced right he could have absorbed the punch. It had been an unnecessary fall, an awkward, tangle-assed fall, and it only increased his rage as he rushed at Walker again, crouching and trying to put all his strength behind a blow to the belly that was supposed to double him over, to be followed by an uppercut that was supposed to straighten him out. But the first punch seemed to hurt his own wrist more than Walker – he had hit a rib instead of the soft part of the belly – and the uppercut missed. He tried dancing out of range but his boots were extraordinarily heavy in the wet grass. He couldn't possibly be nimble, and the worst problem now was his breathing. How the hell did prizefighters breathe? Air was rushing in and out of his throat in great gasps that took all the moisture out of his mouth and made it hang open, blubber-lipped. He stepped in again and caught one on the ear – the same ear that had taken all the punishment yesterday – and then without quite knowing how it happened he felt the knuckles of his right hand make a sharp, solid connection with Walker's front teeth. He saw Walker's eyes go blank with pain and surprise, but then, at the very moment when he should have hit him again, Walker took two or three backward steps and said: "Pretty good one, kid." At least he was rattled enough to say it twice, wincing and blinking – "Pretty good one, kid" – but his recovery was so quick that the moment of triumph was over almost before it began. Walker came back and punched him hard on the nose and then even harder on the point of the chin, and this time there was no doubt about his being knocked down.

He rolled over and got to his hands and knees, watching warm drops of blood spill out of his nose into the grass. When he got up he staggered, and Walker said, "Had enough?"

"Hell no, you son of a bitch. *You'll* find out when I've had enough."

He went back, trying again and again for Walker's mouth, but all his swings were wild and Walker was wholly in charge now, taking his time, ponderously landing blows to the belly and the head and the heart.

Prentice lost track of how many times he went down, sometimes only to sink to one knee for a rest, sometimes sprawling helplessly. The important thing was to keep on getting up. Then once, after getting up, he walked head on into the earth as if it were a wall, and he had to curl up and sit holding his head until the world came wheeling back to normal: grass beneath him, sky overhead, barn and trees over there, where they belonged.

He felt Walker's hand closing around his arm and knew with a terrible mixture of outrage and relief that this meant the fight was over, but he pretended not to understand.

"Stick to your own fucking rules, Walker. Take your hands off me until I'm up."

"No, look, listen. I don't want to fight you any more."

Walker was trying to help him to his feet, but he shook him off and made it by himself, swaying.

"You think I'm quitting now you're crazy."

"You're not quitting." Walker backed away and nursed the knuckles of one hand in the palm of the other. "*I'm* quitting. Far as I'm concerned it's finished, that's all. I'm satisfied."

"So. Big deal. You're satisfied. Well, I'm not. Put up your hands."

And then the worst thing happened: Walker's wide, unscarred face broke into a kindly smile. "Aw, come on, Prentice," he said. "Cut it out." He turned and walked away toward the barn where they'd left their equipment.

"Come on *back* here!" Prentice called after him. "You called me yellow, you bastard!"

And Walker turned around with infuriating friendliness. "Okay, then. I shouldn't of said it. I take it back. Hell, you're not yellow. Don't you think you just proved that?"

No. He didn't think he had proved anything. It was turning out like everything else since Quint's death, like the ending of the war itself: no settling of accounts, no resolution, no proof.

"And what the hell did you expect, Prentice?" Quint would have said. "Do you think everything's going to work out the way it does in the movies? Aren't you ever going to learn?"

They were walking back down the hill, and Prentice didn't know which was more humiliating: the way he had to keep wiping blood from his nose and mouth or the weight of Walker's arm around his shoulders. And the worst part, as they came into view of a little cluster of men near the back door of the Second Platoon house, was that he found himself unable to keep from enjoying the picture they made: victor and vanquished, modest winner and plucky loser, a couple of good guys who'd gone up behind the barn and had it out. It was a sight to please Loomis's

Hollywood heart, and there he was, sternly smiling in the middle of the group.

"You fellas can prob'ly still get some breakfast," he said, "if you hurry on down."

In the bathroom, washing up, he examined his face in the mirror and was glad of its distortions: swollen nose, split lips, and the beginning of what promised to be a black eye. There were also two open cuts on the knuckles of his right hand, and he rubbed them hard, trying to worsen the swelling and make them bleed more, hoping someone else would notice them too.

On the center of his bed lay a new letter from his mother.

Dearest Bobby,
This has been the happiest day of my life!!! Last Friday I got your wonderful letter saying you were out of danger, but of course I was still worried, and now today is V.E. DAY!!! They played the Star-Spangled Banner on the radio and I just fell on my knees and cried and cried and offered all my thanks to God. . . .

He seemed to hear her voice in his head as he and Walker made their way out of the house and down to breakfast – a voice whose warm, soft, reassuring rhythms he had heard all his life and would probably never wholly escape. It was oddly similar to Walker's voice as they sat forking down cold pancakes and jelly in the deserted mess hall: "I don't mind telling you, Prentice, that *one* you clipped me with was a damn good shot," and, later: "Listen. If we get passes to Brussels next week, you want to go together? You and me?"

No account ever really needed to be settled; nothing ever really needed to be proved. Everything would always come right in the end as long as a couple of good guys went up behind the barn and had it out, as long as a mother fell on her knees and offered all her thanks to God and they played the Star-Spangled Banner on the radio. That was what these voices had to say; that was their lying, sentimental message, and it all went down as smoothly as the pancakes and jelly.

But it came up again the minute they were out of the mess hall; it came up all over the side of the factory wall while Prentice crouched and shuddered and heaved, hanging onto the wall for support, and while Walker hovered nervously in the background saying "You okay? You okay, fella? . . . Here, wait, I'll get you a drink of water . . . Rinse your mouth out . . ." It all came up, and with it, in the final, painful spasms, came the last acrid bile of his self-hatred.

There was no more talk as they made their way back to the platoon house, and Prentice kept to himself as much as possible in the truck that took them up to the D.P. area.

For the rest of that bright, pleasant day, as he walked his rounds in the sunshine, he felt strangely purged and purified. Every face he passed, the Russians and the men of "A" Company alike, met his gaze with open goodwill, and that was the way he met theirs.

He had proved nothing, he had made no viable gesture of atonement, and he knew now that he probably never would. If he could have talked with Quint's ghost now he could only have said: "I'm sorry; there's nothing more I can do."

And Quint, he knew, would have said: "Right; you're absolutely right about that. And do you know what that is, Prentice? It's tough shit, that's what it is."

How then could he feel so good? What possible right did he have to be at peace with himself?

He didn't know. All he knew that day – and later that night, as he and Walker and Mueller sat half drunk in the upholstered chairs of some German living room, each with a squirming Russian girl in his lap, and later still when he took his own girl by the hand and led her out to the privacy of a dark, fragrant field of grass – all he knew with any clarity was that he was nineteen years old, that the war was over, and that he was alive.

Epilogue: 1946

Alice was dreaming of Riverside. It was a leisurely dream: she and Bobby were walking down a long bright avenue of autumn trees – oak and stately poplar and monumental beech – and Bobby was talking in the high, eager voice he'd had at eleven or twelve.

"And you know what else she said? Miss Osborne? She said my pictures were the best in the whole class."

"Why, that's wonderful, dear." Now they were moving out across the great expanse of lawn near The Big House, with the river and the Palisades in the distance, and the western sky was ablaze with sunset.

"Or not exactly the best," Bobby said, "I guess she didn't say that. She said they were the most imaginative. And she said probably the reason they were so imaginative was because of you being my mother."

"Well! Wasn't that nice."

"And you know what else?"

She looked down into his happy, serious face and wanted to stop and reach out and gather him in a hug, holding him close. Instead she said, "What else, dear?" But the dream evaporated before he could reply.

It was a natural awakening – there was no alarm clock because it was Sunday – and when her eyes came open to the sun she closed them again, turned over, and did her best to recapture the dream. For several seconds it seemed she was almost succeeding – she was able to call back the scene and the sound of Bobby's voice, if not wholly able to hear what he was saying – but then it was gone.

She often dreamed of Riverside, and she guessed – getting up to accept the reality of this ugly bedroom, with its view of bricks and a fire escape – she guessed that this was because Riverside, of all the places she had ever known, was the one place in which she had felt she truly belonged.

Because it was Sunday she could move slowly through the apartment in her bathrobe, starting the water for coffee, taking her time in getting ready for church. Not until tomorrow morning would she again have to pull herself together in a frenzy of haste, rush downstairs and out into the street and down into the bleak, iron-smelling subway, there to be imprisoned in a grim ride that would end only in the nick of time for her to punch the clock at the lens-grinding shop.

This was a day of rest. While sipping her coffee she listened to a man on the radio who was trying to explain atomic energy. There had been any number of radio programs like that, and magazine articles too, since the ending of the war with Japan last fall. She did her best to understand but it was hopelessly confusing: all she knew was that the United States now possessed an explosive powerful enough to obliterate a city with a single bomb.

A picture postcard from Paris was propped on the kitchenette shelf beside the whiskey bottle: it was the last communication of any kind she'd had from Bobby, and it was a month old. It wasn't like him not to write for so long.

And on the table, beside her coffee cup, was the unfinished letter she had written last night.

Dearest Bobby:

I know that when you don't write it just means you're busy, but even so I wish you would write more often. I do feel so out of touch when it's such a long time between letters.

Dear, I've been thinking a lot about what we'll do when you come home. I know you hate my having to work at this horrible job and I know you will want to do something about it. I imagine you plan to take some sort of job yourself, so that I can quit mine.

But I do want you to be free to go to college. This "G.I. Bill of Rights" is a wonderful thing – you can go to any university in the country and the Government pays for everything. You could even go to some place like Harvard or Yale and get a wonderful education.

But here is the trouble. I read an article in The New York Times Magazine that said next year, in the fall of 1946, all the colleges will be swamped with applications because so many boys are getting out of the service. This article said only boys who have already applied to colleges can count on being admitted – an awful lot of boys will have to wait until 1947, and I guess that will include you. That means you will have a year to wait, and in a way that will work to our advantage. If you take a job for that year I will have a whole year of freedom, and in that length of time I *know* I'll get back on my feet. I'll be able to take my sculpture out of storage, and I'll do a lot of new work and it will be no time at all before I am settled, professionally and financially. I already have enough good work for a one-man show, and with a whole year of freedom I'll have enough for two or three shows. There is no telling what good things will come our way. It may be a difficult year for us in some ways, but you and I have come through difficult times before, haven't we. Remember the Caliche Road?

Anyway, that is my plan. I hope you will approve of it, and I hope

That was as far as the letter went, and now, thinking back, she couldn't remember why she hadn't finished it last night. All she had to do was end that sentence: "and I hope you will answer this letter soon." She found her pen and wrote those words, and she concluded it with "All my love, Mother."

She mailed it on her way to church. The long crosstown walk to St. Thomas Episcopal Church was one of the few pleasures of her week – it meant leaving the squalor of the West Side and heading eastward until she came to Fifth Avenue – and it was especially invigorating on this fine May morning. The flags, the soaring pigeons, the Gothic beauty of St. Thomas itself, and the lofty music of its tower chimes – these had come to represent a renewal of peace and hope each Sunday. It didn't even matter that her black rayon dress was stained in several places and far from new, for she was wearing a neat, expensive-looking feathered hat, picked up as a bargain at Klein's last week, and it gave her a sense of looking like a woman of substance, a distinguished person. She enjoyed mingling with the other worshippers at the front steps: all of them were plainly residents of the Upper East Side.

It was a Communion Sunday. She chose a shadowy pew toward the rear, as she usually did, and sat there with her head bowed in meditation as the organ filled the church with solemn preliminary chords in counterpoint to the high, distant pealing of the tower bells. She didn't exactly pray – she didn't form words and sentences in her mind with the salutation "Dear God"

– but she willed her mind to rid itself of all but humble, pious thoughts: she made herself ready for God's mercy and God's blessing. Then, inhaling the brown, dry, holy smell of the place, she allowed one deep and insistent plea to take shape in words: Oh God, let him come home soon.

She raised her head when the organ rumbled into the opening strains of the processional: she wanted to see it all. First came the crucifer, a boy only a little older than Bobby had been at Riverside, holding the shaft of the cross high as he led the singing choir. When the girls and women had passed, their soprano and alto voices making gooseflesh break out on her arms, she happily watched the men. And the most important of the men, the one who claimed most of her attention, was the tenor soloist. He was very tall and slim, something like Bobby, and his voice, even in the midst of all the other voices, was strong and clear and independent. It reminded her, always, of George Prentice's voice long ago.

> O God, our help in ages past,
> Our hope for years to come . . .

The minister, a gray little man who was much less inspiring than Dr. Hammond in Riverside, seemed pressed for time as he hurried through the first part of the service, and this was irritating: she wanted him to linger over each of the prayers and psalms and the General Confession, to make the ceremony last as long as possible.

But soon it was time for the offertory, and the choral selection proved to contain a long, splendid solo by the young tenor. It was as if the tenor's voice had found resonance in the chamber of her own swelling throat: she could close her eyes and let the voice become a part of her. It took her back many years to the time when she had first discovered that George Prentice, an attentive, rather staid man she scarcely knew, was a singer of great beauty and power. Time and again, wherever there was a piano to accompany him, he would hold her entranced with "Danny Boy" or "La Donna è Mobile"; but he only laughed when she said he really ought to be a professional. "I've got a good amateur voice," he said, "that's all." There was a piano in the house they rented in New Rochelle, after they were married, and he would sometimes accompany himself as he sang soft love songs to her. His voice made him popular at the parties they attended, too; but when the marriage began to go bad she found that her bitterness was only aggravated by his singing. Certain of his songs, in fact – "Lindy Lou," "Because," "Overhead the Moon Is Rising" – had come to typify her unhappiness; for years she had never been able to hear them on the radio without a keen sense of grievance and old anger.

But now, in church, listening to this other tenor, there were other and far more recent memories that made her weep. When she'd first come back from Texas, chastened and determined to live within her means, when she and Bobby were settled in the modest studio apartment she'd been lucky enough to find not far from Washington Square, she had found to her surprise that she and George were able to talk on the phone without quarreling. And the following spring, the triumphant spring when "A Portrait of the Artist's Son" was accepted for exhibition in the Whitney Annual and chosen to be photographed on the art page of *The New York Times*, George had called her up for no other purpose than to offer his congratulations. "I saw your head of Bobby in the *Times*," he said. "I must say it looks very fine indeed."

"Well; thank you."

"Do you suppose I could get a copy of that photograph? I'd like to have it framed."

"Certainly, I'll send you one. I'm glad you like it."

After that, the only serious argument they ever had was over the question of sending Bobby to prep school, and she managed to settle that one more or less amicably by agreeing to move to a smaller apartment.

Then one afternoon a year or so later, he called her from a telephone booth around the corner. "I happened to be in your neighborhood," he said, "and I wondered if you'd mind my dropping in."

"No; not at all. Please do."

There wasn't time to straighten up the studio; there was barely time to wash her hands and face and fix her hair. It occurred to her, as she busied herself at the mirror, that he must have made the trip downtown especially to see her: surely there was no kind of Amalgamated Tool and Die business that would bring him to the Village.

He surprised her by being so short – for some reason she always thought of him as taller than he really was – and by looking so old.

"I'm afraid the place is a terrible mess," she said. "I wasn't expecting company."

"That's all right."

He was dressed as always in a very conservative business suit and small, narrow black shoes. He looked uncomfortable and wholly out of place as he made his way among the shrouded sculpture, crunching stone chips on the floor.

"Well," he said. "It looks like you've been doing a great deal of work."

"Can I get you a drink?" She led him back through the studio to the alcove she used as a sitting room.

"This is very nice," he said, glancing around as he accepted his whiskey and water.

312

"I'm sorry about the dust," she said. "It gets into everything when I'm working on stone."

"That must be very difficult, carving in stone."

"Well, it is, but I love it. Would you like to see some of my newer things?"

And he followed her respectfully, carrying his drink, as she took him back through the studio. He seemed to approve of everything. "The whole idea of stone is very different from modeling," she explained as he stood nodding at one of her half-finished carvings. "It's purer, I think. It's more truly sculptural."

"My Lord." He had picked up one of her three-pound hammers and was hefting it in his hand. "Is this what you use? Isn't it too heavy for you?"

"I guess I'm used to it," she said. "I've probably developed a lot of strength in my arm. Still, I don't think I'll ever give up modeling. There are some pieces that *have* to be modeled, like the head of Bobby you liked so much."

"Is that here? Can I see it?" And she led him to a pedestal against the wall and removed the muslin cover from the head. "Yes," he said. "That really is fine. It looks even better than in the photograph."

They had another drink or two before he inquired, shyly, if he might take her out for dinner. As they walked together through the Village she was aware of how they must look to passing strangers: a mild, pleasant, middle-aged couple out for an evening stroll. And the restaurant turned out to be a place they had visited long ago, before they were married.

George did most of the talking. Amalgamated Tool and Die, after nearly going under in the Depression, had burgeoned into a new prosperity with wartime, and there was no visible limit to its potential growth. So far, the expansion hadn't had much effect on George's department – not, at least, on its salary

313

structure – but there was every reason to hope for better times ahead. "For one thing," he said, "I think we can stop worrying about putting the boy through college. We certainly ought to have enough for that."

"Wonderful." But she didn't want to hear any more talk about money or business; she was afraid he might begin to bore her, and that would spoil her pleasant mood.

"Have you kept up with your singing, George?" she asked him.

"Oh, good Lord, no; I haven't sung in years. I'm all out of practice."

"That's too bad. You did have a fine voice. I imagine you still would, if you'd keep up with it."

"Well, maybe; I don't know. Would you like a brandy with your coffee?"

"That might be nice."

And it was over the brandy that he took her wholly by surprise: he reached across the table to take both her hands in his and asked her, not quite meeting her eyes, to marry him again.

"Alice," he said, "I'm fifty-six years old. I've already had one heart attack, and I—"

"I didn't know you'd had a heart attack."

"Last spring; just a very mild one. I'll probably live to be ninety. But Alice, the point is I don't want to grow old alone. Do you?"

And it was acutely embarrassing: she hadn't the faintest idea of how to feel or what to say. All she could think was that this was incredible; this couldn't really be happening. But she had to say something.

"I don't think about growing old," she said.

"I know you don't. That's one of the things I admire about

314

you, Alice. You have some kind of boundless faith in the future. You never give up."

"I suppose I'm an optimist."

"You certainly are. Alice, I don't suppose we can settle anything tonight. Anyway, it's getting late. But I want you to think about this. Will you do that? And can we talk again soon?"

"All right."

He walked her back to her doorstep and hesitated there, bashful about whether or not to kiss her goodnight. At last he leaned forward and lightly kissed her cheek, squeezing her arm with his hand.

Then he was gone, and less than a week later he was dead. He had collapsed at his desk in the middle of a business day and died before the ambulance arrived. A tactful personnel executive at Amalgamated Tool and Die broke the news to her; in view of the circumstances, he said, the company would take care of the funeral arrangements.

For three days she couldn't stop crying. Bobby's coming home from school for the funeral, pale and severe and embarrassed by her tears, only made it worse. She wanted to make him understand: she wanted to say, But I *did* love your father; only last week we were planning to . . . But she couldn't find the words. She knew he would never believe it.

And even now, years later, she was helpless with grief whenever she thought about it, or whenever this particular tenor sang a solo in church.

She managed to compose herself for the sermon, but after the minister's first few words she allowed her mind to drift away. She thought of how fine it would be to come to this church with Bobby: they would sing the hymns together and kneel together for the prayers; they would go together to the

315

Communion rail, and afterwards they would walk home and discuss their impressions of the sermon.

"The Lord be with you."

"And with thy spirit."

"Let us pray."

Then it was time for Communion, and she made herself the picture of reverence and humility at the rail.

"Take and eat this in remembrance that Christ died for thee, and feed on Him in thy heart by faith, with thanksgiving. . . . Drink this in remembrance that Christ's blood was shed for thee, and be thankful."

And with the wafer slowly dissolving against her palate she allowed her most urgent prayer to form itself again: Oh God, let him come home soon.

The recessional hymn was one of her favorites: "Glorious Things of Thee Are Spoken." She loved the line that went, "Who can faint when such a river Ever will their thirst assuage?" And it sent thrilling tremors down her spine as the choir came to that line with the young tenor sounding high and clear.

Back in the apartment, she poured a good-sized drink of whiskey, fixed herself a modest lunch, and spent the afternoon drowsing over the Sunday papers. Only very occasionally, as the hours wore on, did she go to the kitchenette for another nip from the whiskey bottle.

And shortly before five o'clock she roused herself and straightened up the apartment with a pleasant sense of expectancy: Natalie Crawford was coming over to go out to dinner with her.

Sometimes she had to remind herself that she didn't really like Natalie Crawford and never really had; it was just that somehow, over the years, they had managed to become each other's closest friend. Except for Maude Larkin, back in Riverside, Natalie was the only person in whom Alice had ever confided the whole story of Sterling Nelson's desertion; and Natalie alone had been told about the last, bittersweet few days before George's death. Since then Natalie had been a dependable, readily available source of comfort, and she was especially welcome on anxious, melancholy Sunday evenings like this one.

"God!" she said, coming weakly into the apartment with one hand clutched to her heart. "Those *stairs*. How do you stand those *stairs* every day?"

"I guess I'm used to it. Let me get you a drink."

"Wonderful."

Alice knew, as she made the drinks in the kitchenette, that she would now have to listen to an exhaustive account of Natalie's week, and that she would have to make appropriately sympathetic comments after each piece of news. Natalie was the private secretary of a robust, hard-drinking advertising executive, and Alice had long ago come to understand that this was the most important fact of her life. The man was married to a socially ambitious woman whom Natalie called Madame Queen; his three children, whom Natalie called the Snots, were enrolled in expensive colleges; and Natalie had been achingly and hopelessly in love with him for fifteen years.

". . . and she said, '*Follow the Girls*? But I told you explicitly I wanted tickets for *On the Town*. I made that perfectly clear.'"

"Well, by this time I'd really had about all I could take. I felt like saying, 'Look, Mrs. Thayer, as far as I'm concerned you can take your tickets and stick them you know *where*.' So I said—" And batting her eyelids, Natalie made her voice a model of patience and conciliation. "I said, I'm afraid there's been a misunderstanding, Mrs. Thayer.' I said, 'Mr. Thayer told me that if I couldn't get tickets for *On the Town* I was to go ahead and get tickets for any other musical. I simply carried out his instructions.' And even *then* she wouldn't let it go. She said, 'But surely you could've done better than *that*.' She said, '*Follow the Girls* is a cheap, vulgar revue. Couldn't you at least have gotten tickets for *Up in Central Park*?' I said, 'I'm sorry, Mrs. Thayer; I did the best I could under the circumstances.' But can you imagine the *gall* of the woman? Honestly, Alice, I don't know how he puts up with it. I don't know how I put up with it."

"It must be very – difficult," Alice said, and she hoped this wouldn't lead to other anecdotes about the Thayers because she knew she would soon stop being able to listen. That often happened: Natalie would go on talking, elaborating on the injustice of her position, and after a while Alice would lose all sense of what she was saying. She would sit watching Natalie's talking mouth and shrugging shoulders and gesturing hands with her mind far away on other things, waiting only for the silence that would mean it was her turn to talk.

". . . and menopause is no *excuse* for that kind of behavior," Natalie was saying. "God knows we've all been through it – you have, I have – but we haven't *indulged* ourselves in it. Isn't that right?"

"Let me get you another drink."

Natalie was still talking when they left the apartment, but she fell into a weary silence as they made their way slowly to Columbus Circle.

"Isn't it funny?" Alice said. "I always used to think Childs restaurants were dreadful, but this really is the only decent place around here – all the others are so horribly expensive – and I think it's kind of nice, don't you?"

And as they settled down over their first round of Manhattans, having ordered chicken croquettes, Natalie ventured to open a new topic. "Have you heard from Bobby?"

"Well, not since he was in Paris; that was several weeks ago. I know it's just because he's busy."

"Wasn't this the month you said he'd be coming home? May?"

"Well, I said I thought he *might* be coming home in May. Maybe it won't be till June or July. It's all based on something called the Point System; I don't really understand it. Anyway, it's bound to be soon, and I can hardly wait. That's all I think about, every day. Every time I feel I can't stand this horrible *job* of mine a day longer, I just close my eyes and think *Soon*."

"You're planning to quit the job then, when he comes home?"

"Well, I know he'll want me to. He hates my having to work there. And he'll have a whole year before he can get into college, you see. And can you imagine what I'll be able to accomplish in a whole year of freedom? I already have enough good work for a one-man show, or at least almost enough. And have I told you about my wonderful new idea?"

"No, I don't think so."

"Oh, it's going to be marvelous. First of all, do you remember my head of Bobby? The one you always liked so much? The one that was photographed in the *Times?*" And taking a deep, satisfying sip of her drink she allowed her mind to dwell for a moment on that lost, happy year – the time she had created and perfected the one piece of sculpture on which she felt her reputation might rest. Nothing had ever been quite as gratifying as the publication of that photograph. People she hadn't heard from in years had called up to praise her and to renew their acquaintance, and there had been that memorable call from George. For just a second she was tempted to tell Natalie about that: And have I ever told you what George did? How he called me up and asked for the picture? I really think that was the first time he ever – we ever—

But she checked her impulse, If she got started on that story now it would lead the talk away in another direction.

"Anyway," she said, "*I've* always thought it was the best thing I've ever done. And what I want to do now is the same thing all over again. I want to make a *new* Portrait of the Artist's Son – a head of Bobby the way he looks now; the way he'll be when he comes home. A man. A beautiful, sensitive, resolute young man. Won't that be wonderful? Can't you picture it? And then you see *that* will become the best thing I've ever done. I'll exhibit them side by side – the boy and the man – and together they'll be my sort of crowning achievement, the justification for my whole career. Oh, I can't *wait* to get started on it." And she severed one of her chicken croquettes with the side of her fork, content to let her voice subside for a while.

"Mm," Natalie said, picking up her own fork. "That sounds fine, Alice. Really fine. It must be wonderful to have a talent like that."

But Alice could tell that Natalie wanted her own turn to talk now, and she gracefully yielded the floor. She concentrated on her food, grateful that there was still a deep two thirds of her second Manhattan in the stemmed glass at her elbow. If she was careful with it, taking tiny, well-spaced sips throughout the rest of the meal, it would tide her over until she got back to the apartment – where, luckily, there was still something more than half a bottle of whiskey for protection against the night.

There was, she reflected, a lot of good nourishment in chicken croquettes if you chewed your bites thoroughly before swallowing; there was nourishment too in hot mashed potatoes, even if these were a little watery, and in hot, sweet green peas. Life was good; God was in his Heaven; Bobby would be coming home soon, and there was still nearly two thirds of a Manhattan beside her plate.

Natalie's mouth was working constantly, her lips and teeth and tongue taking the shapes of gossip, confession, ribaldry, and nostalgia. Alice watched the movement and made her own face a register of smiles, sad looks, and other suitable responses, and she was reasonably sure that Natalie couldn't tell she had stopped listening.

The Manhattan was gone by the time they'd finished their main course, and Alice felt she couldn't face a dish of ice cream. "Let's just skip the dessert, Natalie. I'm really too full, aren't you? I don't think I even want coffee." And all she could think of, as they walked home, was the bottle that stood waiting on the kitchenette shelf.

"You'll come up for a drink, won't you, Natalie?" she said as they reached the doorstep. "Please do. It's much too early to go home."

"Well—" and Natalie hesitated. "I'd love to, dear, but I really think I'd better get back. Thanks anyway."

"Oh, *please.*" It came out sounding more desperate than she'd intended, but even so she had to say it again. "*Please,* Natalie. Just for a minute." And looking anxiously into Natalie's face she felt a terrible dread of being left alone. She couldn't possibly climb the stairs alone and go into that ugly apartment alone; she couldn't possibly sit alone there – or walk alone, pace the floor alone – waiting until it was time to go to bed.

"No, really," Natalie was saying, taking several backward steps on the sidewalk. "Really, Alice, I'd better get back. I'll call you during the week, all right?"

Natalie's face, withdrawing now in the harsh light of the street-lamp, was suddenly a mask of insincerity. How ugly and old she is, Alice thought, and it seemed odd that this had never occurred to her before. She wanted to say, Natalie, I don't really like you at all, and I never have. Instead she said, "All right. Goodnight."

And she was alone. But the whiskey bottle was in the apartment, as faithful as any friend. Still breathing hard from the stairs, she locked the door firmly behind her and poured herself a stiff drink even before she had taken off her hat. Then, taking her time, she went about the business of getting out of her clothes and into an old, torn bathrobe that was almost as comforting as the drink. She was ready for the night.

Early in the next month, June, she received a letter from Bobby enclosing a postal money order for three hundred dollars, which he said he had earned by selling cigarettes on the black market in Paris. He wrote that he had decided to take his discharge overseas and go to live in England, where he would either find a job or enroll in an English university – he hadn't yet decided which.

In July, she received another letter with a London postmark and no return address, enclosing a money order for one hundred dollars, which he explained was half of his mustering-out pay. He said he was out of the Army now, and feeling well, and that he would write again soon. He wished her luck.

Also By Richard Yates

*"Soft-spoken in his prose and terrifyingly accurate in his dia-
logue, Yates renders his characters with such authenticity that
you hardly realize what he's done."* —The Boston Globe

YOUNG HEARTS CRYING

In *Young Hearts Crying*, Yates movingly portrays a man and a
woman from their courtship and marriage in the 1950s to their
divorce in the 70s, chronicling their heartbreaking attempts to
reach their highest ambitions. Michael Davenport dreams of being a
poet after returning home from World War II Europe, and at first he
and his new wife, Lucy, enjoy their life together. But as the decades
pass and the success of others creates an oppressive fear of failure in
both Michael and Lucy, their once-bright future gives way to a life
of adultery and isolation. With empathy and grace, Yates creates a
poignant novel of the desires and disasters of a tragic, hopeful couple.

Fiction/Literature/978-0-307-45596-3

REVOLUTIONARY ROAD

In the hopeful 1950s, Frank and April Wheeler appear to be a model
couple: bright, beautiful, talented, with two young children and a
starter home in the suburbs. Perhaps they married too young and
started a family too early. Maybe Frank's job is dull. And April never
saw herself as a housewife. Yet they have always lived on the
assumption that greatness is only just around the corner. But now
that certainty is about to crumble. With heartbreaking compassion
and remorseless clarity, Richard Yates shows how Frank and April
mortgage their spiritual birthright, betraying not only each other, but
their best selves.

Fiction/Literature/978-0-375-70844-2

VINTAGE CONTEMPORARIES
Available at your local bookstore, or visit
www.randomhouse.com